The Bear's Heart

Guinevere
Book Two

Fil Reid

ARE YOU SIGNED UP FOR DRAGONBLADE'S BLOG?

You'll get the latest news and information on exclusive giveaways, exclusive excerpts, coming releases, sales, free books, cover reveals and more.

Check out our complete list of authors, too!

No spam, no junk. That's a promise!

Sign Up Here

www.dragonbladepublishing.com

Dearest Reader;

Thank you for your support of a small press. At Dragonblade Publishing, we strive to bring you the highest quality Historical Romance from some of the best authors in the business. Without your support, there is no 'us', so we sincerely hope you adore these stories and find some new favorite authors along the way.

Happy Reading!

CEO, Dragonblade Publishing

Additional Dragonblade books by
Author Fil Reid

Guinevere Series
The Dragon Ring (Book 1)
The Bear's Heart (Book 2)

Dedication

To all my friends at Critique Circle.

The Legend of King Arthur

Long ago, after the Roman legions abandoned Britain to defend their city of Rome, a time of turbulence came upon the land, and many men fought for the right to rule. A proud tyrant named Vortigern seized power, making himself High King above all other kings. At first, he ruled well, but when he was old and beleaguered on all sides by his enemies, he retreated into the mountains of Wales. Here he planned to build a great fortress and lock himself safely inside, leaving his people to their fate at the hands of the invading Saxons.

Each morning, the workers found the walls they'd built the day before had fallen down, and they had to start again. After many days, despairing, Vortigern called his wise men to him and sought their counsel. They told him to find a boy born with no mortal father and sacrifice him, and only then would the walls of his fortress stay standing.

Vortigern sent his knights out to search the length and breadth of Britain for a boy who fitted this description. At last, they brought such a boy to him, who, when questioned, answered that he had no mortal father, being supposedly the son of a demon. His name was Merlin Emrys. The wise men were about to sacrifice this boy when he asked why they had need of him. On being told that the walls would not stay standing, he informed Vortigern and his wise men that if they dug down into the hill, they would find a lake. Vortigern ordered this done, and the wise men found a lake beneath the hill.

Merlin then asked the wise men what was in the lake, but they knew not. So he told them that if they had the lake drained, they would find two dragons fighting – one white and one red.

The wise men did so, and sure enough, there were the two dragons, fighting. Some of the time the white one gained the upper hand, and some of the time the red one appeared to be winning.

Merlin asked the wise men if they knew what the two fighting dragons meant, but they knew not. So he told the High King that the white dragon represented the Saxons, and the red the British who would eventually, under a great leader, defeat the Saxons.

Vortigern was able to build his fortress and, needless to say, he didn't have the boy sacrificed. Instead, he named the fortress Dinas Emrys after the boy. And thanks to the High King's patronage, young Merlin Emrys became the king's chief advisor and enchanter.

When Vortigern died, a new High King came to power – Uther Pendragon, who was a brave and successful warrior, and was also, in his turn, advised by Merlin. He ruled for many years from his capital in London, with much strife against the enemies of the British: the Saxons from the eastern seas, the Irish from the western seas and the Picts from beyond the wall.

At Pentecost one year, Uther called together his knights for a tournament in London. Gorlois, Duke of Cornwall, left his home of Tintagel Castle in Cornwall and journeyed to London to take part, bringing his young wife, Ygraine. At the tournament, King Uther fell deeply in love with Ygraine, and seeing this, Gorlois fled with her back to Tintagel.

Uther was angry, and ordered Gorlois to return, but the duke did not. So, taking his army, Uther marched into Cornwall and fought against Gorlois at his castle of Dimilioc. Desperate to have Ygraine for himself, Uther persuaded Merlin, his enchanter, to help him. Merlin said that he would as long as Uther gave him the child who would result from this union to bring up himself. Consumed with lust, Uther readily agreed, and one night, while Gorlois was engaged in battle at Dimilioc, he came to Tintagel disguised as Ygraine's husband. Allowed inside by the unsuspecting guards, he spent the night with Ygraine and his son, Arthur, was conceived.

The following morning news came to the castle that Gorlois

had been killed, and Ygraine realized she had been fooled by Uther. As the victor, he now took her as his wife, but when her child, Arthur, was born, Uther had to fulfill his promise to give the child up to Merlin as the price he paid for the enchanter's help.

Merlin took the baby far away to the home of the knight Sir Ector for the boy to be brought up as his own son, stepbrother to Kay. And there Arthur grew to be a young man of sixteen. Sir Ector was ignorant of who his young ward was.

King Uther, meanwhile, took a wound in battle that was incurable, and eventually he sickened and died without ever seeing his heir. On his death there was dispute as to who should reign after him, and to settle this, Merlin set up a sword embedded in a stone, with the instruction that whosoever could draw the sword from the stone was the true-born king of Britain. Many came and tried their hands, but none could draw the sword.

A tournament was held, to which all the knights in the land were invited. Sir Ector came with his son, Sir Kay, and young Arthur accompanied them as Kay's squire. On the morning of the tournament Sir Kay realized he'd left his sword in their lodgings and sent his squire to fetch it. On the way, Arthur spied the sword in the stone, and thinking to be quicker, drew the sword and brought it back to Sir Kay. The young knight recognized the sword and asked his father if this meant that he was king, but wise Sir Ector realized his stepson was the one who should be king. The boy was taken back to the stone, and the sword returned to it. Before all the knights in the realm, Arthur drew the sword a second time and Merlin proclaimed him king.

Arthur became a great king, ruling wisely for a long time from his capital of Camelot. Many great knights came to his castle – Bedivere, Gawaine, Agrivaine, Tristan and Percival, to name but a few. At length the sword from the stone broke in battle, and riding past a lake Arthur saw a hand rise from the water holding a new sword – Excalibur. Taking a small boat he rowed toward the hand, and took the sword for himself. The hand retreated into the water.

For a wife, Arthur took the beautiful Guinevere, daughter of King Leodegrance, and for a long time they were both very happy. He fought many battles against the Saxons, culminating in his famous Battle of Mount Badon, where he bore the image of the Virgin Mary upon his shield and drove the Saxons back once and for all.

But he had two sisters, born of his father's marriage with Ygraine: Morgana and Morgawse. And unwittingly, before he knew Morgawse was his sister, he lay with her and the boy Mordred was born. Morgawse married King Lot of Lothian and bore other sons, and eventually these sons all came to Camelot to become knights of the Round Table which Merlin had provided for Arthur.

When Arthur took his army to fight in Gaul, he left Mordred as his regent, and Mordred, knowing his parentage and thinking that the kingdom could be his, seduced Guinevere and took her for his own. When Arthur returned, he and Mordred came to the final battle of Camlann, where Mordred was eventually slain, and where Arthur was sorely wounded.

Dying, Arthur called his faithful knight Bedivere to his side and, giving him the sword Excalibur, asked him to take it to the nearby lake and throw it in. Bedivere went to the lake, but he could not bring himself to throw away so beautiful a sword. He returned to Arthur and told him he'd done as he'd asked. Arthur asked him what had happened, and Bedivere could not say, so Arthur knew he had lied. A second time he sent Bedivere to the lake, and a second time that knight could not throw the sword away, and Arthur knew he lied. Finally, on the third time of asking, Bedivere threw the sword as far as he could into the water and a hand emerged to grasp it by the hilt. As he watched, hand and sword disappeared beneath the surface of the lake. When Bedivere told him what had happened, Arthur knew Bedivere had at last done as he was asked.

The dying Arthur was then carried to the edge of the lakes around the Island of Avalon. Here, a boat bearing three queens came to carry him away from the land of the living to be cured of his wounds and put into a deep sleep from which he would only waken when the island of Britain was in dire need of his help. To this day, he sleeps there still, waiting for the moment when he is needed again.

Place Names

Din Cadan South Cadbury Castle in Somerset, refortified Iron Age Hill Fort

Ynys Witrin Glastonbury, which once was an island surrounded by marshes

Viroconium Wroxeter Roman Town (near Shrewsbury)

Caer Baddan Bath (Roman Aquae Sulis)

Caer Ceri Cirencester (Roman Corinium)

Caer Gloui Gloucester (Roman Glevum)

Caer Luit Coyt Wall (Roman Letocetum)

Caer Legeion guar Uisc Caerleon (Roman Isca Silurem) South Wales

Caerwysg Exeter (Roman Isca Dumnoniorum)

Castle Dore Stronghold of King Mark of Cornubia (Cornwall) near Fowey

Tintagel North coast of Cornwall

Caer Pensa Ilchester (Roman Lindinis)

Caer Gwinntguic Winchester (Roman Venta Belgarum) Hampshire

Caer Lundein London

Caer Ebrauc York

Caer Ligualid Carlisle (on Hadrian's Wall)

Caer Lind Colun Lincoln

Linnuis Kingdom centered on Lincoln

Sabrina Sea Estuary of the River Severn (Sabrina)

Metaris Estuary The Wash

Chapter One

O N THE MIST-SHROUDED hilltop of Glastonbury Tor, I stood inside the circle of gaunt standing stones, trapped in limbo between two worlds and two men: Nathan, in the twenty-first century, and Arthur in the fifth.

Fear wrapped me in its icy shroud. Thoughts flashed through my mind in flickering, cinematic images. Of Nathan, left behind when I'd tumbled back in time eight weeks ago. Had he climbed the Tor to search for me when I didn't return? Then stood alone in the ruined church tower on top of the Tor with my abandoned backpack clutched in his hands? Had the wintry wind played with his sandy hair, oblivious to the anguish distorting his tear-streaked face?

Separated by the yawning gulf of fifteen hundred years, was Arthur, king of Dumnonia, my husband of a brief six weeks, waiting for me beyond the mist? Or did he think I'd returned to my old world, leaving him for another man?

Like the first lightning strike of a storm, came the realization that my own indecision had led me here, to the point where losing both of them was a real possibility.

I wanted Arthur, not Nathan.

"Arthur!" My eyes frantically searched the smothering mist as I called his name, my voice small and feeble, and full of desperate longing.

Only now it might be too late.

I tried to run toward where I thought he was, disoriented by the mist that grasped my feet like strands of seaweed. A high, musical note throbbed in my head to the rhythm of my pounding heart, as all around me the magic swelled and grew. The ragged hole in the mist, my unwanted doorway back to the twenty-first century, ate its way ever closer, pulling me back to where I no longer belonged. Through the hole, the stone walls of the old church tower, and the slate grey sky on the Tor were fading, like a half-forgotten dream.

I called again – "Arthur!" – as I struggled against the super-natural forces dragging me back to my old life. A life no longer important to me.

More images flashed with startling speed. My little semi-detached house in the nondescript town outside Nottingham, and the library where I worked, with Glynis behind the front desk talking to an old lady about a book she'd ordered. Nathan again, his smart blue fleece and chinos showing his rugby player's physique as he stood in front of our empty house, bereft. My treacherous mind was forcing on me all the reasons why I had to return.

I'd loved Nathan once, and thought I'd loved him still. How-ever, two months in the fifth century had changed me forever. It was Arthur I wanted now. Arthur, with his hard, warrior's body and his hilltop fortress, and the promise of a world filled with excitement and danger. A world where men died in battle, not in their beds, and a threatened doom hung over our future like a black cloud.

My true identity came upon me like a thunderclap. I wasn't just ordinary Gwen Fry, librarian. I was, and always had been, the real Queen Guinevere. Merlin had been right. Only one person could have married King Arthur. Me. It was my destiny. In his wisdom, my father had named me after myself, and my whole life had been leading to this.

"Arthur!" In desperation, I cried his name again, and the mist thinned in response. About my feet the snaring tendrils loosened.

I staggered like a drunkard as I groped for the standing stones, the only tangible link between present and past. The air swirled, thick and hard to breathe, so moisture-laden it felt as though I were under water. My heart pounded and my breath came in little gasps. My hands and legs trembled. Arthur must be somewhere out there. He must. I couldn't lose him.

Beneath my feet, the ground shook, and in fear, I twisted to look over my shoulder. The sides of the hole slid together, sparks flashing about the ragged join as the door to the modern world closed with a clap of frightening finality. The damp mist swirled, shrouding the scar it left, leaving me alone and lost in its dense grey veil. Tears sprang to my eyes; this was the final straw. I stretched out my arms and wailed.

"I didn't mean it! Take me back to Arthur!"

Out of the mist, a strong, warm hand grabbed my cold one in an iron grip.

I hung on tight.

For what felt like an eternity, I gripped that hand, feeling the rough calluses, welcoming the touch I knew so well. It wasn't too late. He was here to save me. Hot relief coursed through my body. Then his other hand grabbed my forearm and wrenched me, blinking and dazed, out of the mist and into the raw light of a fifth century winter's day.

I fell forward, limp as a stringless puppet, into Arthur's arms, and together we tumbled to the damp ground, rolling over in a tangle of limbs.

We came to a halt, him holding me tight, his body trembling as much as mine, hot tears on my skin. They were his.

Putting my arms around him, I held him close. My nostrils filled with the scent of horses, leather and sweat, mixed with the faint aroma of the lavender his clothes were stored in.

"I couldn't leave you." My voice grated roughly in my throat. "I couldn't." Dry sobs racked my body. "It's you I love, not him. You I want to be with."

He lifted my chin and kissed me on the lips, a salty, wet kiss that I wished would last forever.

I clung on. The thought I could have lost him, terrifying.

My cheeks were wet. I, too, was crying.

"I love you," I said when he released my mouth, louder this time, because I wanted to hear the words. "I love you, Arthur Pendragon."

He kissed me again, and I pulled him closer, as though I could meld our bodies into one being. When our lips parted, I nestled in close against the warmth of his chest, the feeling of belonging overwhelming.

"I love you too," he whispered against my hair.

The foreknowledge of the doom of Camlann that lay in wait for him lay heavy on my heart. The final battle where Medraut would bring about the fall of Arthur. Perhaps, with this fore-knowledge, I could avert that doom. Maybe Merlin was right. Maybe I was supposed to help Arthur fulfill his destiny and become the king that everyone in my time remembered. Maybe Arthur needed me as much as I needed him.

I sagged against him, exhausted.

Eventually he spoke. "What did you see?"

Did he really want to know? This was magic, after all, the domain of men like Merlin, and women like Arthur's sister, Morgana. Did he think it my domain, as well? He cupped my chin in one hand. "Was there a doorway?"

I nodded, shifting my weight. "Something," I said, then paused to gather my thoughts. "Something magic...I think...opened a door like the entrance to a cave, and I saw my old world through it." My voice quavered. "But I couldn't leave you." I swallowed the lump in my throat as a sob threatened to rise. "I thought I'd lost you and it was all my fault. Then you took my hand, and I knew it wasn't too late."

He gently kissed my wet eyelids. "Welcome home, Queen Guinevere. Your king is glad you've chosen him."

Turning my face into his chest, I nestled closer still. Nathan was pushed into the back of my mind, a mind that refused to acknowledge the tiny doubt gnawing at my insides. The worry that I might not be able to do anything to change Arthur's future. I'd think about that later.

We rose to our feet and, hand-in-hand, walked back down the hill to find Nial, the man from the Lake Village, who'd brought us here in his boat.

NIAL SAT ON the jetty, a dozen silvery eels lying on the dark boards between the ribs of his flat-bottomed boat. When he heard us coming, he scrambled to his feet to make a hasty bow. A small, middle-aged man, his face was as lined by his outdoor life as an ancient apple.

"Did Milady like what she saw of the Holy Island?"

I was at a loss.

Arthur answered for me. "Well enough, but time moves on and we need to be back at Din Cadan before nightfall. There's rain in the air."

Nial took a deep sniff with his not inconsiderable nose. "Aye, ye're right there. I can smell it on the wind. Comin' from the west."

Arthur handed me into the boat, and I took my place on the plank bench as the two men untied the little craft fore and aft. How much difference a few hours can make. I'd thought never to lay eyes on Nial and his ramshackle boat again, and now here we were, preparing for the hazardous journey back down the flooded River Brue to the Lake Village where we'd left our horses.

Nial pushed us off and took up his position in the stern with his long pole. The boat nosed out into midstream as we rode with the current, guided only by the gentlest steering. Arthur took my hand in his and held it tight, while the dragon ring that had brought me to his world glinted on my finger. Did he think I might change my mind and run back up the hill to the circle of standing stones if he didn't keep a hold on me?

His touch was comforting; his hand, so warm in mine, anchored me with him, and I clung onto it like a lifeline as we sat side-by-side in companionable silence.

Often in my life, when I'd had to make a big decision, I'd made it, and then felt my choice might have been wrong. Was this the right university course? That new car, was it the right one? The new job, did I really like my new colleagues? And that was how I felt now. I'd committed myself to living in the Dark Ages. I'd committed myself to a life of danger, of warfare, of lawlessness, of hardships. Could I really handle it? Or was I deluding myself, in love, not just with Arthur, but with a romantic dream kindled from my knowledge of the legends about him?

The Lake Village came into view. It crouched low over the dark water on spindly wooden stilts, its center resting on a wide heap of rocks and earth, a single narrow wooden causeway connecting it to the shore. Houses jostled for space on the decrepit platform, and smoke rose from their rooftops to mingle with the mist. Nial brought our boat into the same sloping jetty we'd left from and quickly tied her fore and aft. With a deep-felt sigh of relief that we were back safely, I took Arthur's proffered hand and stepped out.

In the tiny central square, the women still squatted, mending their husbands' nets, their dirty children playing about their feet as though nothing of any great consequence had happened that day.

A fine mist of rain fell, and the wind had whipped up waves on the surface of the lake. It was good to feel my feet on dry land again, even though it meant braving the rickety walkway from the village to the shore. Once there, we waved away offers of food and drink with polite thanks, and said goodbye to Nial. Mounting our well-rested horses, we set off back the way we'd come only a few hours before.

We rode in silence along the gloomy forest track. I had much to think about. I was considering afresh just what I'd given up to stay here in the fifth century with Arthur, and still wondering if I'd done the right thing. Arthur gave no hint of his own thoughts.

It was he who eventually broke the silence.

"Tell me about the world you're from."

That wasn't the question I'd been expecting. Had he, like me, been brooding on what I'd given up for him? What was there to tell him that wouldn't profoundly shock him? The truth would be too much. Only Merlin knew the truth, and even he had no real idea of my world and how different it was.

"Our worlds are very different." That was an understatement. "Putting it into words is really hard. I *will* tell you about it, I promise. I just don't want to think about it right now."

He seemed to accept that.

"Will you miss it?" His horse moved closer to mine, and our knees brushed. His face was solemn, brows furrowed, jaw set. He wasn't yet convinced I was his to keep. I wasn't convinced, either.

"Yes." There was no denying I'd miss it badly.

He went quiet for a while. I concentrated on the track ahead, stretching away between the tall, bare trees, here and there patched with stones in the worst mud holes.

He broke the silence. "What will you miss the most?"

I chewed my lower lip. That was a tough question. There was so much. Most of which I couldn't tell him. Artie's face sprang into my head.

"My brother," I said, hitting on the one thing he might understand. Artie was the only member of my family left.

He thought about that for a moment. "Is he like you?"

I shrugged, thinking of Artie, my careless, carefree brother, named by my father for the man by my side. "Not really. We're twins. He went off round the world and left me to look after our father. He didn't come back when Dad was dying. I wanted him to, but he didn't. I guess we're only as alike as brothers and sisters usually are."

"My brothers and sisters aren't alike."

That was true. Morgana, who possessed the Sight, had a clever, sly face matching her tough personality. By contrast, Morgawse, the youngest in the family, whose baby son, Medraut, I'd helped deliver, seemed fragile and delicate. And as for Arthur's aggressive, envious half-brother, Cadwy, very little about him resembled Arthur.

We rode on in quiet companionship, the light rain falling steadily, beading in our hair and on our woolen cloaks. A certain complacency clung to Arthur, as though my not mentioning I'd miss Nathan had been significant. Which it had been. When he'd asked what I'd miss most, Artie's face had sprung to mind, not Nathan's.

Chapter Two

A S WE EMERGED from the forest onto the plain, a damp early-evening mist was already rising over the farmlands. Our horses were nearly as tired as we were, and the familiar bulk of the hillfort, with smoke rising from its unseen rooftops, was a welcome sight.

Through the evening gloom, a score of heavily armed warriors led by Merlin and Cei rode into view, an unwelcome interruption to our intimate ride back.

"Where in God's name have you been?" Cei almost shouted as he rode up to us, his big face suffused with anxiety. "We didn't even know which direction you'd taken." He glanced over his shoulder at Merlin, who sat his horse with a resigned expression on his thin, ageless face. Had he guessed where we'd gone? After all, he did possess the Sight and, using it, had stolen me from my own time to bring me here to marry Arthur. He'd surely have known, as soon as our absence was noticed, that we'd headed to the Tor.

Arthur might have been tired, but the events at the Tor had buoyed him up. "We rode to the Lake Village," he called out, urging his horse up to Cei's.

Merlin's gaze fell on me, his dark eyes full of speculation. I schooled my face into indifference. By bringing me here from my world, he'd made me a queen, and now he would have to live with the consequences.

Arthur clasped Cei's hand. "I'm sorry we worried you. We took a boat to the Holy Isle…a longer trip than I expected."

Cei's serious face softened into a grin. "Did you meet our boyhood shades there, fishing for fat trout from Nial's boat?"

Arthur laughed. "No, but it was Nial who took us across to the island. In the same boat, I'd wager. Not so watertight as it used to be, I fear."

Their carefree laughter at these shared childhood memories rose to the evening sky, and for a moment I felt excluded. I didn't mind. The ride back from the Lake Village had been one of deep, mostly unspoken intimacy between Arthur and me, and nothing had the power to dispel that. My decision to remain in the fifth century when I could have returned home had cemented us firmly together.

Cei's search party wheeled their horses. "I'd have sent out parties east and west as well, but Merlin felt sure you'd come this way."

"His instincts were right," Arthur said, as he fell in beside his half-brother.

Behind them, Merlin brought his horse in next to mine. He rode close enough for our knees to knock together, his long legs hanging loose by his horse's sides. Unlike mine, which were supported by the stirrups Goff the smith had made to my design, an innovation to fifth-century Britain. "Did you climb the Tor?" he asked in an undertone, curiosity in his voice.

With my eyes fixed on the road ahead, I nodded, unable to keep the smile off my face. Inside, despite my reservations, I glowed with the intoxicating thought that I loved Arthur and he loved me, so much that he'd been prepared to let me go because he thought it was what I wanted.

"And did the doorway open?" Merlin asked.

Our horses' hooves clattered as we reached the cobbled road that ran between the farmsteads below the hillfort. Smoke rose from their thatched roofs, pigs rooted in muddy pens, and on a rooftop a cockerel with no sense of time crowed loudly to the setting sun.

I nodded again, giving Merlin a quick sidelong glance and trying unsuccessfully to remove the smile from my lips. I'd just done something he'd been actively trying to prevent during all my time in the fifth century. Would he be angry?

He smiled, a glow of triumph in his eyes. "You didn't step through it." He paused, looking at Arthur's straight back ahead of us. "You chose to stay."

"Yes."

"I knew you would."

Damn him.

A thought struck me. Had he *let* Arthur and me ride out by ourselves, so Arthur could take me to the Tor? Maybe he'd recognized my need to choose before I could commit to a life here as Arthur's queen. Had he known what my choice would be? He didn't appear in the least bit worried, merely curious. Perhaps he'd also known we'd be quite safe out together with no guards. He did possess the Sight, after all.

Turning in my saddle, I looked at him properly. "I chose to stay," I said. "Not because you wanted me to stay, or because a prophecy said I should. But because I love Arthur." A frown flitted across his face. "And also because I know the future and believe I can change things." I paused. "As you do, too."

But what lay in the future? Not the events of Mallory's *Morte D'Arthur* or stories about Sir Gawaine and the Green Knight and Lancelot du Lac, that was for sure. Yet most of the legendary players seemed to litter this world, with a few extras thrown in for good measure. Morgana, with her possible magical powers, held the post of advisor to Arthur's jealous half-brother, Cadwy. Their younger sister Morgawse, wife to Arthur's friend and ally, Theodoric, had not long ago given birth to Medraut who, in the future that was no longer my present, would be known as Mordred, a man perhaps destined to betray his uncle. Merlin, with his magic and mystery, had ranged himself on Arthur's team beside the legendary names of Cei and Bedwyr and Gwalchmei.

Merlin's gaze flicked to Arthur, deep in conversation with Cei a couple of horse's lengths ahead of us. The rest of the warriors were the same distance behind our horses. "You don't understand my gifts," he said, the frown returning. "Because neither do I. They come and go, and I'm rarely privy to a clear view of what's to come." He paused. "Although *you* could tell me."

I'd already thought of that. "I can't," I said, without any tinge of regret, because even if it were possible, it couldn't happen. "I don't know myself what's true and what isn't. I told you about the sword in the stone and you made it happen. Together we made a story into real history. Who knows what we've changed. That can't happen again."

Standing in the old Roman forum in far-off Viroconium, Arthur's half-brother Cadwy's capital city, was an enormous rock with a sword sticking out of it – a sword that almost everyone, bar Arthur himself, had tried to wrench out. Unsuccessfully. The writing on the stone proclaimed that the sword could be drawn only when it was needed. Merlin had set it there, and now that old myth from the future had become present-day fact.

Merlin's brow furrowed. "Why don't you know what's true?"

Our horses were nearing the pathway up the side of the hill. The scent of wood smoke and middens hung in the cold air, a scent that had come to mean home to me. "Because my time is fifteen hundred years into the future," I said. "By then, we know almost nothing about your time – about now. The only things we have are a few bits written long after you're all dead, hundreds of years from now. No one even knows if Arthur was a real person. Or you. To us, you're just stories from a time when history wasn't written down. Because we know so little, we call this time the Dark Ages."

"But it is written down. At the abbey they keep records of everything – of births and deaths, of battles fought, of crops and trade and judgements made. They have lists of the warriors from other kingdoms who've come to fight for Arthur now he's Dux Britanniarum. The monks keep good records."

I sighed. "Well, by my time, all their records have disappeared. Most likely, they were lost or destroyed somehow in the century or so after they were made. Nothing exists in my time." Wouldn't professors of medieval history tear their hair to think of those lost documents.

Might the invading Saxons have destroyed them in the chaos after the loss of Arthur at fateful Camlann? I couldn't tell Merlin that, or share the looming tragedy of that final battle. I didn't even know how many years into the future Camlann lay, although if Medraut were to fight there, he'd have to be a man grown. As he was just a baby now, that should give us many years of safety.

Our horses began the climb up the hill, as in the west the sun dipped beneath the horizon, and darkness crept over the land. I'd come home. For the first time ever, the fortress felt like just that. At the stables, servants came to attend to our horses, and Arthur and I managed to break away from Merlin and Cei and escape to the great hall and our private chamber.

As soon as the door closed behind us, Arthur turned to me, and I stepped into his arms. I'd been wanting to do this ever since we'd left Nial at the Lake Village.

He held me close, his mouth against my hair, his breath hot on my scalp. I breathed in the smell of horses on his clothes, of musky maleness, of wintry air and wood smoke, taking deep lungfuls in, as though wanting to steep myself in him. Earlier today I'd thought I'd never stand like this again, inhaling his primitive, masculine smell, as different to my modern boyfriend Nathan's aroma of aftershave and shower gel as the smell of a wild horse to a domesticated one.

"I love you." His words were muffled by my hair, his arms holding me pressed tight against him. It seemed that having once given voice to his feelings, it was easy for him to repeat them.

I lifted my head to look up into his deep brown eyes, their flecks of gold shimmering in the torchlight. "And I love you." Now that I'd put it into words, I wanted to keep on saying it.

Linking my hands around his neck, I pulled him down to kiss me, my fingers in his long dark hair, my eyes closed. For a long moment we lost ourselves in the oneness of our being, as though we'd never kissed before. The Tor had made new people of us.

Cottia, Arthur's maidservant and childhood nurse, came bustling in through one of the other doors.

She had no compunction about breaking us up.

"I've brought 'ot water," she said matter-of-factly, setting two still-steaming buckets down on the flagstoned floor near the brazier. "Though cold might've bin better. And come to 'elp the queen with 'er dress." She gave Arthur, who'd released my mouth but not my body, a firm look that clearly said that sort of thing should wait for later.

Like a naughty child caught in the act of mischief, he released me and went obediently to his chest of clean clothes, unbuckling his belt. With Cottia present, we would have to wait.

THE GREAT HALL thronged with men whose faces were slowly becoming familiar to me. Some were easy to recognize, like Drustans, the rebellious son of King March of Caer Dore. He'd stood up at the Council of Kings and defied his father to enlist in Arthur's army – the army of the newly elected Dux Britanniarum drawn from the many kingdoms of Britain. A handsome boy, with red-brown curls that reached his shoulders and a faint fuzz on his upper lip and chin, he was young yet, but big and strong, and a good swordsman.

Girls sat on either side of him, giggling in appreciation at what he said. I recognized Abria, the pretty oldest daughter of one of Arthur's warriors, and Eirin, a plump and cheery teenager no older than Drustans himself, grand-daughter of Cottia. Drustans had already acquired a bit of a reputation with the girls, and I could see Abria's father watching him from the next table, a frown etched on his face. Eirin's father was dead, but Cottia and the girl's mother were also eyeballing Drustans with mistrust.

By custom, we ate in the great hall almost every evening. It wasn't always full, but now it felt crowded and hot, with all the extra warriors who'd come to us after the Council of Kings, and who laid out their bedrolls in the hall after the meal had been cleared away. Arthur and I presided over an extended High Table on a little dais at the top of the Hall, close to the doorway into our private chambers. Cei, Theodoric, Merlin, and Cei's wife, Coventina, whom I was slowly getting to know, shared it with us.

Coventina was an exceptionally tall, dark-haired woman hardly any older than I was, who'd produced Rhiwallon for Cei several years before he'd married her. But married they now were, and to her surprise, she'd gained the title of Lady of Din Tagel by the act, although she'd told me she'd been born only a humble farmer's daughter. I liked her. She always thought carefully before she gave her opinion and said what she thought. I'd found her a good source of advice as to how a queen should behave.

Behind the high table stood the two guards Merlin had insisted should always be posted on the door to Arthur's chambers. You couldn't be too careful when there were so many foreign warriors sleeping in your hall, he'd advised. Although Arthur retorted somewhat over-confidently that as they were *his* warriors now, they'd vowed their allegiance to him alone and not to the kings of the lands they'd come from. I didn't feel so sure myself, not after my experiences at the Council of Kings, when Arthur's brother Cadwy had tried to poison us both. I was glad of the human barrier between us and the warriors in the hall when we slept.

Tonight, the Hall had been decked in greenery because, according to Arthur, this evening marked the start of the Christmas celebrations. During the day, the women had brought in evergreen branches, bunches of berried holly, and sprigs of mistletoe, and these festooned the rafters and pillars in opulent abandon, daring the guttering torches to set them alight.

My historian father had told me the Romans had celebrated both the Saturnalia and the Festival of Sol Invictus, the birthday of the unconquered sun, at about the same time as we celebrated the Christian Christmas. It didn't surprise me to find a queer mixture of all three celebrations going on, still echoing down from the days of the Roman occupation only eighty years earlier.

Beer, mead and wine flowed freely, and in no time everyone became very merry. Beside me, Arthur, who usually partook with caution, had just had his goblet filled for the third time. I hurried to put my hand over my own half-full goblet as the servant leaned over me with his jug.

Arthur took a long draught of his wine and turned to me with a smile. Beneath the table, his hand rested on my thigh, his touch hot and full of promise. Not for the first time, I reflected on his animal attraction. Long, dark hair reached his shoulders, swept back from a high forehead to reveal solemn black brows over brown eyes. A haze of dark stubble shadowed his firm chin. Even the pale scar on his cheek added to his looks. I couldn't help but smile back.

He covered my hand with his, fingers lacing themselves between mine, and my breath caught in my throat at the look of desire in his eyes.

Thrown together from the start by Merlin's machinations, it had taken all this time for us to acknowledge how we'd come to feel about one another. Although, perhaps it had been Merlin's interfering that had made me so determined from the start not to accept Arthur or anything he could offer.

One of the serving women was going round the tables with a large sprig of mistletoe and holding it over the heads of the women regardless of their marital status. Coventina good-naturedly had to kiss both her husband and Theodoric. The serving woman herself kissed Merlin. Now she came to the high table and brandished it over my head. Arthur needed no other encouragement to lean toward me and plant a kiss on my lips. A cheer of approval went up from the body of the Hall, and heat rushed to my cheeks. Unabashed, he raised his goblet to his people in salute.

Bedtime came all too slowly, but at last we could reasonably retire from the Hall and into the privacy of our chamber.

The servants had cleared the tables, and the warriors were already moving them aside so beds could be rolled out, as Arthur and I finally retreated into our chamber. Closing the door behind us, which shut out most of the hubbub of noise, Arthur pulled me roughly into his arms.

I went more than willingly. I'd been waiting for this moment since we'd walked back down the Tor together that afternoon, and the interruption earlier by Cottia had only served to heat my desire. My hands were on his belt, tugging the buckle undone. The heavy bronze clasp clattered to the flagstones and my hands slid up under his tunic to the soft linen of his undershirt and the hard, well-toned muscles beneath.

His mouth came down on mine and his hands tugged at my dress. Nothing gave. It was firmly laced down the back. Releasing my mouth, he swung me around, and with unsteady fingers began to fumble with the laces.

Cottia, or Maia, my maid, could have done it in minutes, but whether because of his impatience or the amount of wine he'd drunk, he made heavy weather of it, swearing under his breath.

"Jupiter, what do you women fasten yourselves up like this for?"

This made me giggle, and in turn that made him laugh, too.

"I prefer you in your boys' clothes – they're easier to get you out of. Let me put my knife to these laces."

The dress loosened on my shoulders a little and suddenly fell away, the laces all cut through. I turned back to him in just my undershirt, my whole body on fire. Dropping the knife, he lifted me off my feet and carried me to the bed in a few long strides. Masterful felt good.

In the hall beyond the dividing wall, someone began to sing a lilting song, the words softly rising to the arching roof, and the murmured voices of the warriors joined in with the lullaby refrain. To the sound of what might have been a very early Christmas carol, I put my arms around my husband and pulled him down on top of me.

Chapter Three

THE CHRISTMAS FESTIVITIES rushed by in a whirl of torch-lit feasts in a smoky hall hung with greenery. Endless cider and wine flowed, beef and pork roasted whole over a blazing fire, and jugglers, singers, and storytellers amused the hot and overcrowded revelers. To honor the New Year, a bonfire was lit in the courtyard. Everything about those days between Christmas and New Year so blossomed with enjoyment that I didn't have a moment to think of what I'd turned my back on.

Just after New Year, heavy snow blanketed the fortress and the plain below in a shroud of white. Icicles formed on the thatch, and water troughs froze overnight and had to be hacked free of ice with axes. Llacheu, Arthur's seven-year-old son, rushed out to make grubby snowmen and have snowball fights with his friends. Children here found the same pleasure in snow as they did in my old world.

The snow clung on with determination, eventually turning to filthy slush within the fortress walls and making life difficult for everyone. Even the children at last grew fed up.

It was already fifteen days into January when Arthur declared it was time for the ritual first hunt of the New Year. Over the festive period we'd been feasting on farm animals culled for the winter, and it was time to supplement this with some game.

"Do I get to come?" I asked as we pulled on our warm boots in the comfort of our bedchamber that morning. "I've never been hunting." What I didn't tell him was that in my previous life, in my student days, I'd actually been a keen member of the anti-hunting lobby. However, this was different – this was hunting for food, not sport. When we killed an animal, it was going to feed the people who depended on us. Its death would have a purpose, and if I were going to eat it, I should be prepared to hunt for it, as well.

"Of course. If you want to." Arthur finished fastening his broad leather belt and tucked a long dagger into the ornate scabbard that sat on his hip. It was the knife he'd shown me the first day I met him – the one he'd taken from the Saxon he killed near Caer Durnac. How far we'd come since then. He smiled. "Not many women do, but my mother always used to ride out with the hunt. Morgana as well. I daresay she still does. No reason why you shouldn't."

We were both dressed in close-fitting woolen braccae. On top of our thick linen undershirts we had warm tunics topped off with jackets made by sandwiching a layer of raw wool between two pieces of cloth and then quilting it. The wool stayed pretty waterproof because it still contained most of the natural lanolin and was an excellent insulator, even if it did smell strongly of sheep. I didn't miss my waterproof twenty-first-century jacket at all.

Beneath my braccae, I wore the new underwear Cottia's older daughter, a seamstress, had stitched for me. Lacking elastic, I'd resorted to a tie-string waist, but the silk knickers she'd produced were not unlike boxer shorts and very comfortable. Silk, she informed me with pride, which had been brought to Din Tagel by ships from the Middle Sea. That name made my ears prick – modern Tintagel was where legend said Arthur was born, and where Arthur's mother now ruled in his half-brother Cei's stead. It was a place, and she a woman, I would very much like to see.

The underwear fascinated Arthur. Cottia's daughter was now working on knickers for some of the other women. Coventina, for one, was most satisfied with her pairs. Luckily, my bra was still soldiering on, although I was busy with a design to recreate one.

Having breakfasted on thick porridge sweetened with honey, Arthur and I went into the great hall. Merlin, in his outside clothes, was sitting on one of the trestle tables near the hearth fire, chatting with Cei. Morgawse's husband, Theodoric the Goth, who usually made up their number, had departed to join his ships at Caer Legeion several days ago, as soon as the snow melted enough for him to travel.

The hunting party consisted of a couple of warriors from each of the many British kingdoms who'd so far provided men for Arthur's Dux Britanniarum army, as well as half as many again of his original Dumnonians. So it was a numerous and mixed bunch that clattered out of the fortress gates and down toward the plain that morning.

I rode the chestnut mare, Alezan, that Arthur had gifted me at Christmas. She was an altogether flightier animal than the sturdy bay who'd carried me to Viroconium and back, and today she was bouncing with excitement after her enforced inactivity due to the snow. Slung from her saddle was a short stabbing spear, and a dagger hung from my belt beneath my traveling cloak. Both Llacheu and Arthur had been giving me lessons in how to use the spear so I didn't feel completely out of my depth. Although I had no intention of getting near enough to any prey to use it.

It was good to be out in the fresh air after the stuffy, smoke-filled confines of the hall. I was as much in need of exercise as Alezan.

Descending the curving track, Arthur headed the hunting party, talking volubly to Cei and young Drustans, pointing toward the dark shadow of forest that lay to the west. Bowyn the huntsman, accompanied by three lanky teenage boys in his employ, had gone out first with the pack of slavering, brindled hounds. Their eager barks and howls already echoed up from the plain below. Behind us rumbled the carts that would bring home whatever game we killed. The cheerful voices of men who'd just been released after being housebound for weeks rose into the crisp winter air.

Merlin fell in beside me, his horse's already hot flanks rubbing against my leg. Alezan side-stepped and tossed her head, sending foam spraying. Merlin reined back as his own excited horse tried to get ahead. Our mounts were all a bit of a handful today.

I'd been avoiding him over the holiday period by making sure I was always with someone else whenever he approached. I didn't want him asking me any more awkward questions about the future. Now, on the narrow path down the side of the hill, there was no escape.

"Are you glad you chose to stay?" he asked, when he had his horse back under control.

I weighed up whether to be truthful or not. "Most of the time."

He smiled, and I reflected not for the first time that it was hard to put a finger on his age. Certainly, when he smiled he looked only a few years older than Arthur and me, but sometimes, when he was pensive, I looked into his eyes and saw an old man looking back. By his own admission he'd lived through the reigns of three High Kings. That alone made him the oldest man I'd met so far, even if he didn't look it.

"Do they hunt in your time?" he asked, as we reached the foot of the hill and took the cobbled road westwards between the farmsteads and small fields.

I shook my head. "Not like this. We did have fox hunting, but that was outlawed. And I think some people do something called deer stalking in the highlands. Rich people like the Queen."

His eyes lit up with interest. "Your Queen hunts – what about the king?"

"We don't have a king...our queen's father only had daughters so the oldest became queen when he died. She's really old now – in her nineties, I think."

His eyebrows rose. "And she hunts still, at so great an age?"

He was obviously impressed with her physical prowess.

This made me laugh. However, we were getting into the realms of the ridiculous. Besides which, I didn't want to talk to Merlin about where I was from. I didn't want him to know anything about it. Even though I'd made the decision to stay here with Arthur, I was still annoyed that Merlin had engineered it without even asking me. "Yes, she does," I snapped. "People in my time can live to be a hundred, easily."

He didn't look surprised by this revelation; maybe he was heading in that direction himself. Beneath me, Alezan curvetted with annoyance at my suddenly harsh hand on her reins, refusing to walk properly and insisting on a bouncy jog-trot. I relaxed my hold and ran my hand over her already sweaty neck trying to calm her, but it made no difference.

In the small stubble fields, enclosed by earth banks and straggly thorn bushes, the hounds milled about, with Bowyn cracking his whip at them and having great difficulty keeping them under control. We riders spread out from the cobbled road, all the horses full of the joys of being out after three weeks confined in the stables. My mare gave an excited buck, kicking out her back legs and pinging me forward onto her neck. I righted myself and shortened my reins so she couldn't get her head again. It wouldn't do to show myself up by landing in the mud.

With Cei's help, Arthur organized who was to ride in which party. I found myself with him, along with Cei, Merlin and Drustans, and a number of others. The rest split off from us, each party taking one of Bowyn's youthful helpers and a batch of overexcited hounds. We were left with Bowyn himself, the most experienced huntsman.

Bowyn's hounds leapt and bounded and had to be driven back from running after the chickens who'd been scratching on the midden of a nearby farm. We followed the hounds at a trot westwards toward the dark line of the forest edge, scattering a small flock of sheep across the open ground in front of us. Bowyn had his work cut out preventing the hounds from pursuing them, as well. The teenage boy who'd been in charge of the sheep watched us pass with a hard-done-by expression on his grubby face, or it might only have been the cold that had pinched his features.

Underfoot, the ground remained half frozen. Snow clung on in icy drifts up against the walls of houses and the palisade fences around the farms. Overhead, the sky was a promising blue, but the cold wind bit our noses and fingers.

We rode across the bleak plain for some time behind the questing hounds, leaving the farms behind us. A few clouds scudded across the sky, chased by the wind, and I wished I had a hat to keep my ears warm.

Arthur brought his big, grey mare, Llamrei, in beside Alezan. Although well-schooled, even she was on her toes in the cold morning air. Alezan turned her head toward Llamrei and the two sniffed in greeting, then laid their ears back, squealed and sprang apart.

Arthur tightened his reins. "Steady, Llamrei."

I brought Alezan back under control with some difficulty, her ears flat back in bad-temper at his grey. "I don't think they like each other overmuch."

Arthur laughed. "Women." Then he changed the subject. "We're going to draw the forest with the hounds and see what they put up. Could be deer, could be a wild boar. Bowyn knows these woods like the back of his hand. If there's game, which there should be, he'll find it."

I looked ahead at Bowyn, astride his small garron, expertly driving the hounds forward as they rushed about, noses to the ground and tails waving in the air. With their brindled, wiry coats and long legs, they didn't look anything like modern foxhounds.

"What do I do?" I asked, more than a little nervous, although that was mixed with the excitement of the hunt.

"Stay with Merlin and just do what he tells you." Arthur gave me a grin and urged his horse forward as the hounds lifted their heads and suddenly set off at a run, baying as they went, with

Bowyn in hot pursuit.

Alezan needed no encouragement. As the body of the hunt charged after the pack of hounds, she snatched at her bit and broke into a gallop, fighting to get her head. I somehow managed to keep her behind Arthur and Cei as we plunged into the forest, hard on the heels of the hounds.

A cart track stretched in front of us, just wide enough for three horses to gallop abreast. As I ducked beneath overhanging branches at breakneck speed, I became aware of Merlin and Drustans galloping beside me. The thunder of hooves behind us made me fervently hope that Alezan would do nothing to unseat me. If she did, I'd be trampled underfoot.

Leaning forward over her neck to avoid the branches didn't encourage her to slow down, though the gallop was exhilarating. If anything, she increased her speed as up ahead the hounds leapt into the denser forest to the left of the track. Bowyn was on their tails, his smaller pony surefooted and agile.

"Forward," Arthur shouted to his men, pointing down the track ahead of us. "Head them off."

The mass of riders reacted as one – one being, with one mind. We took a left fork, clods of mud flying from our horses' hooves. The thrill of the chase zinged through my blood. It must be there lurking in all of us, a remnant from primeval times – the lust for the kill, the thirst for blood.

The path twisted through the trees like a roller-coaster. Unseen to our left the hounds raised a howl of triumph. Fifty yards ahead, a huge stag with a magnificent set of antlers burst out of the undergrowth. Hounds bayed right behind him. For a fraction of a second, the stag turned his head toward us. In that second, I took in his soft brown winter coat, his wide, dark eyes, his frantic breath making clouds in the cold air.

I hauled on my reins with all my strength.

Arthur swung back his arm and launched his spear. His aim was good; the spear struck the beast in the chest. The animal staggered to the edge of the track, his legs crumpled, and the heavy body fell. Blood pulsed from the wound to the rhythm of his dying heartbeat. The creature's hooves kicked a few times in the mud and his head twitched. He couldn't still be alive. Not with a spear in his heart.

I fought Alezan to an untidy halt in the track amongst my fellow huntsmen. Steam rose in a cloud from our horses' hot flanks, and their breathing rasped in the cold air. I, too, was panting hard.

Bowyn emerged from the wood behind his hounds, who circled the dead stag with interest, occasionally lapping at the blood still oozing from the wound, while he cracked his long whip to get them to stand off the carcass. Arthur jumped down from his horse, his long dagger flashing in his hand.

Alezan's flanks heaved. My hands rested on her wet neck as I stared down at the ruin of the stag. He lay as though sleeping, the weight of his antlers tipping his noble head slightly to one side. His slender legs had folded under him, the spear protruding from his beautiful body. His dark eyes stared blankly. All the life had gone out of him, flown away in an instant. All the beauty of his movement, all his wild spirit.

A lump rose in my throat. Tears sprang into my eyes. He'd had to die. He'd feed so many of us tomorrow or the next day in the great hall. Yet somehow, the reality of this death was too much. I gave a great gulp and turned Alezan away, pushing through the other riders toward the rear of the hunt. I couldn't bear to see what happened next.

Merlin noticed, of course. He shouldered his horse through the crowd of riders to stand next to me, to watch in silence as I finally allowed the tears to spill. I flushed hotly, conscious of the curious gaze of the nearest riders.

"First time?" he asked, as I wiped my snotty nose on the sleeve of my jacket.

I nodded dumbly, and gave an inelegant snort to clear my nostrils. What wouldn't I give for a hankie. I'd seen fighting, been amongst it, seen a boy die in front of my eyes, and yet the death of this animal seemed unaccountably worse. Maybe because warriors chose that life, whereas this stag had played no part in choosing his fate. This morning he'd been browsing quietly in the forest, unaware of his impending death until Bowyn's hounds had surprised him and driven him into our path.

"You'll get used to it."

I shook my head. "I won't."

He didn't reply. He was probably thinking he was right, and I was wrong. At least he seemed to have some inkling of how I felt right now, which was more than Arthur.

Alezan pawed the churned up muddy path with her front hoof and gave a snort of fellow feeling – I imagined. One of the men rode past us, on his way to guide the meat wagon in to collect the stag.

"I don't think I can do this," I said to Merlin, in a low voice so the nearest warriors, who seemed inordinately interested in me, wouldn't hear. "I've never seen an animal killed like that before." I stopped short of saying it was barbaric, but that was what I was thinking. My head told me this was something they had to do in order to supplement the meat they had from their farm stock, that there was no other way to do this. My sentimental heart was crying out at how wrong it was to deprive such a beautiful wild animal of his life. To say I was conflicted was an understatement. I might be living in the fifth century, but most of my outlook was still resolutely twenty-first.

"Do you want to go back to Din Cadan?" Merlin asked, with a tinge of understanding in his voice. He must have some idea of how out of place I felt.

I nodded. "I understand," I said, hoping to explain, "but that doesn't mean I like it. I...I think it's going to take a long while for me to really feel at home here – with hunting, at least. Perhaps I shouldn't have come."

He gave a shrug. "I'll tell Arthur, and get a couple of the men to escort you home."

Relieved, I nodded. I didn't want to witness another death

like this one.

Alezan fidgeted under me, and I tightened my reins as Merlin pushed his way back to the front to tell Arthur I was going home. In a few minutes, Arthur brought his horse back to mine, followed by Drustans, like a faithful puppy. Spots of dark blood stained Arthur's sleeve.

"You want to go back?" He sounded surprised. "Are you tired?"

Not wanting to go into my sensibilities, which he wouldn't understand, I nodded. "I've had enough. I'm sorry. Will that be all right?"

His expression gave his feelings away. Concern for me mingled with his own longing to keep on doing something he enjoyed after idling inside Din Cadan for weeks, thanks to the snow.

I put my hand on his arm and managed a smile. "I can ride home on my own."

Arthur shook his head. "No, you can't."

"I can take her," Drustans spoke up, and Arthur turned to look at him. The boy colored hotly. "It's not far. I know the way."

I did, too. Arthur and I had ridden through this forest together many times since we'd returned from Viroconium.

"Not on your own," Arthur said, his love for the hunt winning over his concern for me. We weren't far from Din Cadan, after all, and it would be an easy ride. He glanced at the nearest warriors, whose faces I recognized but whose names I didn't know. "Kelwyn, Gorsedd, you can accompany Drustans and the Queen." He paused. "Return as soon as you've done so, and try to find us, of course. You, too, Drustans. Once you've seen the Queen safely to Din Cadan."

Kelwyn and Gorsedd bowed their heads in acquiescence, and Arthur moved close enough to plant a fleeting kiss on my lips. "Ride safely." Then he turned away, moving back through the group of hunters toward the front again.

"Come on then, Milady," Kelwyn said on a sigh. "We'd best

get started. The sooner we get you home, the sooner we can be back here on the hunt." He and Gorsedd exchanged glances, and I had the momentary impression something had gone unsaid.

Drustans fell in at my side, his youthful face alight with interest. "It certainly is tiring to ride at a gallop through the forest," he gabbled, sounding self-conscious and young. "The first time my father took me with him, I fell asleep on my pony on the ride home and fell off in the mud. How my father laughed!"

Having met King March of Caer Dore, laughing was the last thing I could imagine him doing. He'd seemed a man devoid of mirth, but maybe his son had experienced a different side.

We set off, heading in the direction of the fortress but keeping our horses, who were still steaming, at a walk. Drustans rode beside me while Kelwyn and Gorsedd followed behind, talking quietly to one another. After a while, we encountered the meat wagon, creaking and bumping along behind a sturdy pair of oxen, escorted by the rider Arthur had sent to find it. We had to retreat into the trees at the side of the path to let it pass. The wagon rumbled off up the path behind us and was soon lost to sight around a bend.

I gave Alezan a long rein so she could stretch her neck, and Drustans followed suit, chattering away to me about his home in Cornubia, full of boyish charm. I liked him a lot – he was an engaging lad, and he clearly liked me.

A pheasant flew up out of the undergrowth at the side of the path just in front of us, carking loudly, and Alezan threw her head up in alarm.

Kelwyn brought his horse up on my left and Gorsedd on Drustans' right, pressing in far too close because there was very little room for four.

I was startled. "What're you doing?" I asked, turning toward Kelwyn as he put his hand out and grabbed Alezan's reins near her bit. At the same time, Gorsedd raise his spear butt and swung it at Drustans. The butt connected with the side of the boy's head with a loud thwack. For a moment, shock held me rigid. Then realization that this was not something my escort should be doing kicked in. I snatched up my reins as Drustans toppled backward off his horse onto the muddy track.

Drustans' horse was between me and Gorsedd, but Kelwyn had firm hold of Alezan near her bit. I did the only thing I could think of – I threw myself off Alezan onto Drustans' empty horse, swinging my leg over the saddle and managing to kick Gorsedd hard in the side as I did so. Kelwyn gave an angry shout and let Alezan go. She shied away, turning into the track, and headed back along the way we'd come in a trot, reins hanging loose.

I grabbed for the reins of Drustans' horse, driving my heels hard into his side. He sprang forward between Kelwyn and Gorsedd. However, Gorsedd still had the spear in his hands. The shaft hit me across the stomach, knocking me backward off the horse. I landed on my back in the mud just feet from Drustans' inert body, and all the air shot out of my lungs. For a moment I saw stars. Then horses' legs came into view perilously close to my head. I coughed and spluttered, gasping for breath that didn't want to come.

"Ye shouldn't have done that," said Kelwyn's voice, disembodied and far away. "We're s'posed to fetch 'er without 'urting 'er."

"She was going to get away," Gorsedd's voice retorted.

A pair of booted legs landed close by me and strong arms dragged me to my feet.

I was spitting. "What d'you think you're doing?" I gasped as soon as there was breath in my lungs. "Get your hands off me. I'm your Queen."

Kelwyn, who had tight hold of my upper arm, didn't let go. For the first time today, I paid him proper attention. Several inches taller than me and probably no older than I was, he had dirty brown hair, a crooked nose and hazel eyes. He didn't possess the sort of face I'd have expected a kidnapper to have, but then, neither did Merlin, and he'd kidnapped me from my own world.

"No use struggling, Milady," Kelwyn said with a hint of apology. "Our orders is to take you to our lord. We won't 'urt ye, but it'll be best if ye come quietly, else we'll 'ave to bind your 'ands at the least."

I looked from Kelwyn to Gorsedd in fury – and in trepidation. "My husband is your lord," I said with as much dignity as I could muster. "You owe allegiance to none but him."

"Not so," Gorsedd butted in. With his villainous countenance he looked well suited to his new role as kidnapper. "Our first allegiance is to the lord of Dinas Brent, where we come from."

"Dinas Brent?" I'd assumed they had something to do with Cadwy, Arthur's brother, who'd already unsuccessfully tried to prise me away from Arthur.

"Shut up, Gorsedd," Kelwyn snapped, tightening his hold on me as I twisted to get away. Alezan disappeared around the bend in the track, in the same direction as the meat wagon. Surely the wagon and its drivers couldn't be that far ahead of her and would see her and come to my rescue?

"You're Melwas's men?" Now I knew where they were from, their lord's face came back to me. I'd seen him in Viroconium at the Council of Kings that had elected Arthur as Dux Britanniarum. I remembered his narrow, sly face, his aquiline nose and calculating eyes, and his straight black hair flecked with grey. What could he want me for? What did any man want a woman for in the fifth century? Not conversation, that was for sure.

Gorsedd brought the horses.

"Get up on this one and don't try anything, Milady," Kelwyn said, releasing my arm and offering his hand to give me a leg up. My stirrups had departed with Alezan. "And 'urry up. We've a long way to ride."

I couldn't think what to do. I couldn't run away because they'd catch me, and then they'd tie me up and I'd have to go anyway. Pretending to faint would most likely see me unceremoniously dumped across the saddle. Maybe I could keep them talking. I looked across at Drustans lying sprawled on the cold ground, an angry red mark on the side of his pale forehead. "At least let me check if he's all right," I said, wanting not just to take a look at the boy, but also to play for time.

Kelwyn shook his head. "Leave 'im. There's no time. Up you go."

With great reluctance I put my foot in his hand and he hoisted me up into the saddle. Settling down, I grabbed for the reins, but Gorsedd flicked them over the horse's head and hung onto them.

For the second time in the fifth century, I was a prisoner.

Chapter Four

I T WAS THIRTY miles to Dinas Brent – the Isle of Frogs – through wintry forest that eventually thinned out to become marshy wetlands. A narrow, hardly visible causeway wound between stunted trees and open pools of brackish water where shreds of mist hung damply about the thorn bushes like snagged silk.

Drustans' horse kept up well with those of Kelwyn and Gor-sedd, but I kept glancing over my shoulder, hoping for signs of pursuit. Surely Alezan had caught up with the meat wagon. Surely they'd come across Drustans, left for dead in the mud. Surely I'd been missed by now, and Arthur would be hot on my heels.

No help came.

Thoughts jostled through my head. What did Melwas, King of the Summer Country, want with me? Why had he risked offending Arthur, his overlord, by stealing his queen? The questions rattled round in my head as Dinas Brent drew ever closer, the huge hill rising out of the flat wetlands like a brooding threat.

"You won't get away with this," I said to my captors, with a false show of bravado. "My husband will come after you. You're dead men."

They ignored me.

"He's Dux Britanniarum, not just your king. Every kingdom in Britain will be after you."

Kelwyn glanced at me, his homely face unmoved by my threats.

I tried a different tack. "Why've you taken me? What does Melwas want with me?"

Still no response.

Infuriated, I kicked my horse up closer to theirs. "Is he doing this for Cadwy? Is he being paid?"

But Kelwyn and Gorsedd just looked away from me toward our ever-nearing destination, their surly faces as unmoved by my protests as if I'd been a buzzing fly. Ignored, I gave up and settled into silence as well, acutely aware that where they were taking me was not about to turn out to be a nice place. Fear pricked at my skin whenever I thought about what lay ahead. Being a captive woman in the Dark Ages was not something I was likely to enjoy.

Farms clustered cheek by jowl at the foot of the isolated hill that was Dinas Brent, crowded onto the slopes of the encircling dry land. A narrow, rutted roadway climbed upwards to the summit. My horse, still being led by Gorsedd, picked its way through the potholes and mud to wooden gates set in a palisade wall that was a pale shadow of the immense fortifications at Din Cadan. These gates swung open in answer to a shout from Kelwyn, and we rode through them into the inner circle of the fortress just as night began to fall.

Dinas Brent was considerably smaller than Din Cadan. The houses were distinguishable from the barns and storage huts only by the smoke that rose from the dark thatch of their rooftops and the chinks of light glimmering through the cracks in their warped wooden doors. Miserable looking cattle huddled close together in a pen, the mist of their breath rising into the darkening sky, and the bleating of sheep carried from a dilapidated barn. Middens were heaped everywhere, steaming warmly, one giving a bed to half a dozen brindled hounds.

In the center, on the highest ground, loomed a smaller, shab-bier version of the great hall at Din Cadan. Close behind it, the square shape of a half-ruined Romano-Celtic temple rose out of the gloom, the plaster flaking away from its crumbling walls. In places, a few terracotta tiles still adorned the skeleton of the roof.

Gorsedd and Kelwyn halted in front of the hall and dismounted. I stayed sitting on Drustans' horse, the thought that I might outsmart them yet, even in the lion's den, still at the forefront of my mind. But Gorsedd looped my reins around a post, and there was nothing I could do.

"Down you get then, Milady," Kelwyn said, with some rather-too-late respect.

Giving him my hardest and angriest glare, I slid from the saddle and smoothed my tunic. The ride had been long, and it was good to have my feet back on the ground – just not this ground.

"Inside." Kelwyn gestured toward the unguarded door into the hall, and Gorsedd threw it open in front of me.

Stiffening both my backbone and my resolve, I followed Gorsedd into the hall. The dim light of smoldering torches set in iron brackets illuminated the interior. Long trestle tables ran down the center, cluttered with dirty plates and overturned goblets. Beyond the tables, a lackluster hearth fire burned in a shallow pit, filling the air with enough acrid smoke to make my eyes sting and tear up. On the far side of the fire pit stood a single table and at that table, poring over a map, sat Melwas.

He glanced up as we entered, his narrow lips curving into a satisfied smile as his hooded black eyes took me in from head to toe. He reminded me of a snake waiting to strike, and a shiver ran down my spine.

"You got her!" He rose to his feet, letting the map roll itself back up again. "At last. Bring her here."

Kelwyn took my elbow and propelled me down the hall, my feet scuffing in the dirty reeds underfoot. A damp musty smell, reminiscent of wet dog, rose to my nostrils, and a couple of scrawny hounds slunk further beneath the tables as we passed.

I stopped two paces from Melwas, who had come round the

table to stand in front of me. He was taller than I remembered, and more powerfully built, but then, I'd not gone anywhere near him in Viroconium. His dark, lascivious eyes looked me up and down hungrily. "Yes, this is she. You've done well." He took my hand in his and stared down at the dragon ring on my finger. "So, this is the dragon ring we've all heard so much about." He twisted it around to examine every side. "As promised in that prophecy, the ring that bestows power on the man who holds the hand that wears it."

I snatched my hand back, feeling soiled by his touch, afraid of the lust in his eyes.

What could I do or say to deflect his intention? Desperation inspired me. "My Lord Melwas," I said, as haughtily as possible, drawing on all Cottia's advice about how a queen should behave. If only I were wearing an elegant gown and my gold circlet crown instead of grubby braccae and tunic. "Kindly have me escorted back to my husband's fortress. And have these men thrown into prison. They struck my loyal guard and dragged me here against my will. If you return me now, my husband, your king, will be most grateful and reward you for your kindness." It was worth a try. Maybe Melwas could be brought to see that this was all a big mistake and that he ought to pretend it wasn't his idea and send me straight home.

He shook his head, the hint of a smile at the corner of his thin-lipped mouth. I hadn't really expected it would work.

"You cannot be returned," he said smoothly. "You will remain here with me for the time being. You are to consider yourself my guest."

I decided to keep going as the affronted Queen. "This is intolerable." My own twenty-first-century queen would have been impressed by my hauteur, not that she'd ever had to face being kidnapped. "You must return me at once to my husband or face his wrath." Inspiration flowed; the words just popped into my head.

Melwas's smile widened, giving me a glimpse of his yellowed

wolfish teeth, but the smile didn't reach his cold pebble eyes. "I have no intention of returning you to that usurper."

Icy fury rose in me. This was an insult not just to me but to Arthur, as well. I kept my voice steady. "My husband is your rightful king and overlord. And when he rescues me, you will suffer for your actions this day."

"Your husband," Melwas said, scorn etched into his voice, "is bastard born. The only trueborn son of King Uthyr is Cadwy, son of Queen Aelfled."

"Untrue." I lifted my chin. "Arthur's mother was Queen to Uthyr, and you know it. You can say what you like, but you won't make Arthur a bastard any more than you can make yourself an honest man."

He showed his teeth again in a travesty of a grin. Not only were they yellow, but they were also crooked. He could have done with the attentions of an orthodontist as a child.

"I have no pretensions to being an honest man. Why would I? How many honest men rise to the heights I have?" He laughed, a hollow, false sound that rose to the smoke-veiled rafters above our heads. Then he took a step forward, bringing him close enough to bend his head and hiss his words into my ear. He smelled strongly of exotic perfume and stale sweat. "I'm king here because my brothers are dead," he whispered. "My older brothers. Do you think they died natural deaths to pave my way to kingship? They did not. I killed the first when I was ten years old and he just thirteen. And I'm proud to own to it."

I stared at him in horror, longing to step back but afraid to show weakness. He was so much worse than I'd imagined. I hadn't liked the look of him when I'd first set eyes on him at the Council of Kings. He'd made me uneasy with his cold gaze and his narrow, sly face, but I'd considered him nothing more than an unpleasant man, the only one apart from Cadwy who'd not voted for Arthur to become Dux Britanniarum. Now, my skin crawled with revulsion.

My fingers tightened on my cloak, instinctively drawing it

closer as though it might protect me. "What do you want with me?" I fought to keep the rising panic out of my voice. He was so close, the smell of his rank breath filled my nostrils.

He licked his thin, bloodless lips. "King Cadwy wants you for himself," he said slowly. "It was his idea to place trustworthy warriors within that fool's army who could wait until the perfect moment arose to snatch you." He gestured at Kelwyn and Gorsedd who'd seated themselves on the trestle table near the fire. "But I've a mind to keep you for myself now I've seen you up close." He picked up my heavy plait and fondled it with his long fingers. His nails were filthy. "Why should Cadwy get the joint benefits of the power you bring and a woman like you in his bed? I can have all that for myself." Lust smoldered in his black eyes, and his tongue darted out to lick his lips.

My shiver of disgust was impossible to suppress. The only upside to being handed over to Cadwy was that it would take time – time in which Arthur might come to my rescue.

I had to do something to stave him off. "So you are a believer in that prophecy," I said, with as much steely scorn as I could muster, my heart hammering in my chest. It was an enormous effort to keep the shaking out of my voice. "A believer in magic and fate – someone who thinks the future can be written, long before it happens."

His black brows came together in a heavy scowl.

Before he could reply, I went on. "If you believe that, then know that Arthur is the chosen one – the Pendragon who will save the kingdoms of this island from the Saxon menace. Not you. Nowhere in that prophecy is the tin-pot king of the Isle of Frogs ever mentioned. Just by seizing me you cannot change words that have already been spoken." I took a deep breath to steady myself. "If you believe in that prophecy, and that it is I who hold the secret to Arthur's power, then taking me yourself will not give you that power. It won't be you that leads the armies of the Dux against the Saxons. It will be you lying dead at my husband's feet, your kingdom of the Summer Country forever a part of Dumnonia once again."

I held his gaze, unwavering, my hands clenched at my sides to stop them shaking. Every cell in my body screamed out in fear as I balanced on a knife edge.

Further inspiration came to me, and I drew myself up taller, lowering my voice for impact. "I am the priestess of Ynys Afallon, sent to this world by Gwynn ap Nudd, Lord of the Otherworld." I groped for words that would sound authentic enough to make him believe me and fear to touch me. "The power of Afallon resides in me and can only be used to help the Pendragon protect the lands of his people." Confidence crept back into me as I recognized uncertainty in his eyes. He might be a king, but he was evidently as superstitious as the ordinary people of Britain. "You are a nobody. Power cannot pass to you."

A shiver that he transformed into a shrug ran through his body. "Kelwyn, Gorsedd," he snapped, and they hurried forward. "Take the Lady Guinevere to the place of safety we have prepared, and lock her in." He glared, fury bubbling near the surface.

I schooled the triumph out of the gaze I returned, locking it away inside. The power of my words had saved me today from the proverbial fate worse than death, and that filled me with confidence and scorn for this man.

"I need to think," he said angrily, and turned away.

THE PRISON WAS a small and windowless thatched house beside the hall, with a door that opened outwards, which they could bar with a solid oak beam set in iron brackets. Kelwyn seemed apologetic as he ushered me inside, but Gorsedd's rough face was set in stony dislike. The door closed behind me, and the bar thumped into place as they locked me in. I was alone.

The fire burning in the small hearth made the interior smoky and unpleasant, but at least it was warm. A single torch smoldering on a wall post only added to the smokiness of the air, making me wonder about the likelihood of developing breathing problems if I were left in here too long. The atmosphere made that of the hall appear positively beneficial.

The guttering torch light revealed a single bed in one corner and at the opposite end of the room, a table with a rough stool. In a corner sat the latrine bucket. As prisons went, it appeared to be quite well equipped. I sat down on the bed, which felt lumpy, and put my head in my hands.

I'd managed to put off the awful prospect of being raped by Melwas, which I was sure had been his intention, but what would he decide to do now? It was too late to release me. By now, Arthur would have been made aware of my kidnapping and would be scouring the countryside for me. Hopefully Drustans didn't have a fractured skull from that blow, and Arthur could be relied upon to find where I'd been taken. But would he arrive in time to save me from whatever fate Melwas had planned?

I finally gave in to the fear that had been threatening to overwhelm me for most of the day. As I allowed my tears to fall, I kept my sobs as quiet as possible in case anyone was listening outside the door.

Chapter Five

AFTER THE FIRST morning, I was allowed out of the prison during the day. They provided me with a gown to wear instead of my tunic and braccae, and I was put into the care of an elderly woman. She came to my prison on the day following my capture, with a servant bearing the gown, some porridge and a flagon of weak ale. I sat at the table eyeing her with suspicion as she watched me eat. Something about her thin face felt familiar, but what it was escaped me.

White hair stained dirty yellow by smoke hung in a wispy plait to her waist. A face scored by deep wrinkles held faded blue eyes filled with a palpable sadness. Her own dress hung loosely, as though once she'd been a bigger woman, and her back was rounded in a knobbly hump. That, along with the wrinkles and the hair, betrayed what must be her great age, but when I asked her later she told me she was not yet sixty.

After twenty-four hours without food, I ate the porridge in a hurry, scraping the bowl clean. They'd not bothered to feed me the night before, whether out of spite or just out of simple forgetfulness, I had no idea.

"Thank you," I said, getting to my feet and then pausing. The old woman was half a head shorter than me, and the servant had left. Overpowering her would be easy, but then what? I'd still be inside Dinas Brent, and the servant and a guard were probably right outside the door. So instead, I held out my hand to her. "My name's Gwen."

She looked at me, a furtive expression on her face, before timidly setting her scrawny hand in mine. "Olwyn."

I smiled, determined to make her my friend. I was going to have need of any I could recruit.

"Do you know what Melwas intends for me?"

Her eyes widened in fear. She shook her head hurriedly and snatched her hand back as though I'd bitten her.

Compassion rose in my heart, and I used the tone I'd have tried on a child. "It's all right. You can tell me. I won't tell anyone what you say. I don't mean you any harm." She must be some old retainer of Melwas's, maybe a slave, although surely her grubby dress was made of too fine a wool for that.

She took a step closer, glancing toward the firmly closed door. "You need to do as he says," she whispered, each word crystal clear in the quiet of my prison. "Don't cross him or make him angry. He…he has a temper." She was very well spoken. Not a slave then, nor even an old retainer. Possibly the wife or widow of one of his older warriors?

"I'm your queen," I whispered back, assuming she was right in thinking someone might be eavesdropping. "It is he who must obey me, and he who should be fearful of my anger." I drew a deep breath and stood up taller. "And right now I'm very angry."

Olwyn laid her hand on my arm. "I know what you are," she whispered. "But here that doesn't count. This is Melwas's kingdom…and Melwas's stronghold. You're a long way from your husband now, and far from safety. Be warned by one who knows – do not test his temper. He may not kill you, but there are ways to punish a woman who crosses him." She drew up the loose sleeve of her gown revealing her forearm, its skin puckered like crinkled paper. It was the scar from a terrible burn.

"He did that to you?" The question came on a hiss of breath.

She nodded mutely, and pulled the sleeve down to cover the scar.

"Why?"

Her lips clamped together in a thin line of bitterness. For a moment, I didn't think she was going to tell me, then she leaned forward and put her mouth to my ear, as though this was a secret so dark she couldn't risk the air between us catching it. "I mourned my son."

Realization began to dawn. "Who *are* you?" We were very close now and my voice made hardly any sound. No one could have overheard us from the other side of the door or even from inside the prison if they were more than a few feet away.

Her mouth worked soundlessly, as though getting out the words was the hardest thing in the world. Her throat convulsed with the effort, her eyes darted toward the door, and her bony hands balled up the loose material in the front of her gown. She opened her mouth to speak. "I am his mother."

"You're Melwas's mother?" I repeated, shocked to the bone that she was so downtrodden and timid, that he or one of his followers had inflicted that burn on her arm, that she was the mother of the boy he'd boasted about killing.

She nodded.

No wonder she seemed familiar. Now that I knew I was looking at Melwas's mother, I was no longer puzzled. She had a strong facial resemblance to him, with narrow features and a hooked nose; one day, when he was old, he would look much like her, except his eyes were black whereas hers were faded blue.

I licked suddenly dry lips. "Your son who you mourned. Did Melwas kill him? He told me he killed his brother when he was only ten years old, but I wasn't sure whether to believe him or not."

She nodded again, seeming to shrink in on herself as her memories flooded back. Tears sparkled unshed in the corners of her rheumy eyes.

This was something I needed to know, and maybe it was something she needed to say. Maybe there'd been no one here she could ever confide in, no one who cared. Maybe it would help her to tell me. "What happened?" I asked gently, taking her arm and steering her to the bed where the servant had left my gown spread over one end. We sat down side by side, and I put my arm around her bony, hunched shoulders.

The touch of my arm seemed to soften the tension in her body. She relaxed against me, so with my other hand I covered hers where they lay clasped in her lap. They felt like a bird's fleshless feet, dry and scaly and bony. "Tell me your story," I whispered.

She licked her lips, avoiding my gaze and looking down at our hands. "My husband was Vortimer, oldest son of Guorthegirn, who was king of Powys and High King of all Britain." Somehow, telling this story in a whisper seemed to add weight to it. "After his father was killed and Ambrosius became High King, my husband was given Dinas Brent to rule. They'd been friends – brothers in arms – and Ambrosius didn't want to punish him for his father's sins. We had four strong sons. Melwas was the youngest."

I held her close and she nestled into my body, like a kitten to its mother, her tongue loosened by the contact.

"My husband was a good man – a strong warrior, a wise king. Our oldest son was killed in a riding accident. He was out hunting with his father when the girth on his saddle snapped at a gallop, and he fell and hit his head. It took him three days to die. He was just thirteen."

Was this the boy Melwas had boasted of killing when he was just ten years old himself? Could a child have interfered with the girth? Not a guaranteed death, but one that had worked well for him. Just two older brothers left between him and kingship.

"Our second son drowned while fishing with Melwas the following year. I began to have my suspicions, but he was only eleven. How could a child be evil enough to kill another child?" She heaved a deep sigh. "My child could. But I watched him after that."

A noise outside the door made us both start, but the door remained firmly closed, and no one came in. Olwyn's hands beneath mine clenched and unclenched convulsively.

"Go on," I whispered. Had she ever spoken to anyone about these things before? Was I the first she could confide in?

"Five years passed. Melwas's only remaining brother grew toward manhood. He was like his father – tall and strong and handsome, with my blue eyes. A son to be proud of." A smile flitted across her face as she called back his shade, and I sensed he stood before her, forever a boy in her memory, preserved in the aspic of his youth.

And Melwas, the youngest, had grown long and sly with eyes as dark as coal, and a lust for the throne of his father that would one day be his brother's by right of primogeniture. I didn't need her to tell me.

"My husband grew old. He'd taken many wounds fighting for his father and Ambrosius, and he was tired and worn out. One day at dinner in our hall he got to his feet clutching his chest and fell dead onto the table in front of us."

A heart attack perhaps. Would they even know what that was? Probably not.

"My third son was seventeen when he became king, and seventeen when he died in his bed, writhing in agony, just twelve days after his father." She paused, her gaze faraway, and I guessed she saw her golden son once more, lying on his deathbed. "And Melwas became king."

I swallowed. It seemed he'd killed his way to his kingdom with impunity. "And he did this to you," I touched her arm, "when you mourned your son?"

She nodded. "I no longer had my husband to keep me safe. He said I could not mourn my son. I had to celebrate his own kingship." She gave a little shudder. "When I said I could not, he took my arm and set my sleeve on fire with a burning torch. It was only the help of my faithful old manservant, Henwas, that saved my life. He rolled me in a rug to smother the flames. My son had his head lopped off and set on a spike outside the hall as warning to all those who might think to go against him. Melwas

was just a boy of sixteen himself, but already the traits of his tyrant grandfather, Guorthegirn, were strong in him."

I couldn't think of anything to say to this, but I was wishing she hadn't told me, wishing I didn't know the lengths to which Melwas was prepared to go. When I hadn't known, bravery had been easy because I'd never met a man as ruthless as he was, and had never suspected the depths to which he might sink. Now, with the knowledge of what he'd done to his brothers and his own mother, fear coiled about me like a snake, making my heart beat faster and sweat spring out on my skin.

Tightening my arm about Olwyn's shoulders, I swallowed my fear. "My husband will come for me," I whispered into her ear. "And when he does, Melwas will be made to pay for all his wickedness."

THREE DAYS PASSED, which I spent in Olwyn's company, learning as much as possible about Melwas and his fortress. This wasn't much, as we were only allowed to walk between the prison hut and the hall, or watch Melwas as he practiced sword fighting with his men, which he did daily. He was an expert swordsman.

In all that time, he didn't touch me, although in the early evenings he forced me to sit beside him in his hall to eat my evening meal, while Olwyn sat at a lowly table with his men and their womenfolk. I had no appetite, for fear was my constant companion, and I was repelled by the proximity of my captor with his lank black hair, his wolfish yellow teeth and his air of self-satisfaction that he had me in his power. Every day I scanned the horizon from the rise where the hall stood, for any sign of Cadwy arriving to take me to Viroconium, or Arthur coming to demand my return.

But no one came.

On the morning of the fourth day, Olwyn and I were standing

in front of the hall, both of us wrapped in thick cloaks against the biting wind. To the west, the Sabrina Sea lay silvery in the pale sunlight, the hills of South Wales a dim grey haze beyond. To the east, the distant hump of Glastonbury Tor rose just visible out of the flat plain.

The fortress gates, which had been kept firmly shut since my arrival, swung open, and three riders entered on hairy little garrons. I'd have known the first one's tall frame and tonsured head anywhere – Jerome, Abbot of Glastonbury. My spirits, which had been down in my boots, rose, and I tightened my grip on Olwyn's hand. As no guards stood near enough to eavesdrop, I leaned toward her and whispered a hurried question. "Does Abbot Jerome come here often?"

Without looking at me, Olwyn gave a tiny shake of her head. "I've never seen him here before."

The three riders picked their way up the slope toward the hall, warriors and womenfolk gathering about them like an escort party, and someone disappeared into the hall to fetch Melwas. With no one to force us away, Olwyn and I stood our ground and waited for Abbot Jerome to reach us. His two fellows appeared to be laymen. With a start, I recognized Corwyn, the man who'd first escorted me, my hands bound as a prisoner, from Glastonbury to Din Cadan just over two months ago. Neither Abbot Jerome nor Corwyn seemed in the least bit surprised to see me.

Melwas emerged from the hall, and Olwyn and I moved away from him, her grip on my hand tightening as though for support.

Jerome brought his garron to a halt and swung down from the saddle. I was pleased to see that as an exceptionally tall man, he topped Melwas by half a head. Melwas's people shambled to a halt behind the horses in a ragged semi-circle.

"My Lord Melwas," Jerome said firmly, his head inclining in the smallest of bows. Not having seen him bow to any other kings, I couldn't be sure, but this curt bow could have been seen as a measure of the lack of respect he felt toward this particular king.

Melwas returned a similarly slight bow. His heavy brows knit together in barely suppressed anger, and the muscles of his jaw kept tightening as though he were repeatedly clenching his teeth. "Father Abbot." The words squeezed between his teeth with marked reluctance.

Jerome glanced at where Olwyn and I now stood, as far from Melwas as we could get. "I come from King Arthur in search of his wife," he said calmly. "He waits with his considerable army beyond the marshes, ready to cross them and take Dinas Brent if necessary."

Melwas's black eyes blackened further, if that were possible, and those thick brows lowered in a scowl that would have quelled lesser men than Jerome. "Do you think that scares me?" he asked with measured scorn. "Another army advances even as you stand here. Three days ago I sent riders to Viroconium. King Cadwy will soon be here to claim his prize. He'll see off that insolent pup who thinks he rules Dumnonia."

Jerome shook his head slowly, his calm serenity never changing. "I fear you are wrong." His voice never rose. "The Dux Britanniarum has had his men in the forest surrounding Dinas Brent all of that time, and your men were apprehended before they headed north. The message they were carrying is in King Arthur's hands, not those of his brother. King Cadwy does not even know you have the queen."

Relief poured over me. Here I'd been, thinking Arthur couldn't know where I was, when all that time he'd had us surrounded, biding his time. Indignation that he'd left me here so long rose to the surface. I bit my tongue to stop myself from crying out to Jerome.

Melwas glanced at me and Olwyn, his narrow face suffused with fury. My heart, which had been soaring, skipped a beat in fear. This was a man who now found himself trapped, an animal at bay, surrounded by his enemies. And I was still his prisoner. I could see him weighing the possibilities that lay in front of him.

Silence stretched between the two men. Anger, shock, disappointment and cunning flitted across Melwas's face in quick succession. His plans had been thwarted. Cadwy wasn't coming to his rescue. He'd kidnapped the wife of his overlord, and his fortress was surrounded. If he had any sense he'd be working out how best to turn this situation to his advantage.

"And what is it you offer me in return for the Queen?" he asked.

Jerome regarded him without speaking for a moment, then sucked his lips thoughtfully and straightened his back, bringing him taller still than Melwas. "The safety of your people," he replied.

Melwas gave a snort of derision. "You think I care for that? Give me something better, or I'll have you kicked down the hill by my womenfolk. No prating priest tells me what to do." He hadn't lost any of his monumental ego.

Jerome stood silent. There was an impasse between the two of them.

"Let me tell you what I want," Melwas said. "I want you to tell that imposter king to take his army and leave, or I'll send his wife back to him in pieces, starting with her pretty little nose."

My heart, which had already been pounding, now leapt into my throat. After the things Olwyn had told me over the last few days, I had no reason to doubt Melwas would do exactly what he said.

Jerome stood his ground stoically. "If a hair on her head is touched," he said, never taking his eyes from Melwas, "I'm to tell you that King Arthur will raze not just your fortress but the whole of this Isle of Frogs to the ground with not a single person or animal left living. But no man will kill you, for he will reserve a special punishment for you. Your death will be a long one."

Behind Jerome, Corwyn licked his lips, a grin spreading across his broad face.

Melwas looked beyond the riders toward his warriors. What was he thinking? His men shifted uneasily, glancing at one another or their feet. None met his gaze. An awkward moment passed. Their support for him hung in the balance.

"I have my own conditions," he said finally. "Do not forget the queen is my prisoner, and now I also have you…" His voice trailed away, edged with menace.

Jerome regarded him with equanimity, not a trace of worry touching his somber face. I remembered how much I'd liked him the first time we'd met, how I'd felt he was a man I could trust. If anyone could get me out of here, he could. Perhaps that was why Arthur had sent him.

"You would do well not to threaten a man of God," Jerome said. It was a good thing men of God in the fifth century were nothing like the priests and vicars of the twenty-first, who mostly had to deal with nothing worse than Bible study classes and village fete organization. But this was the Dark Ages, when people still believed God's wrath could come down in thunderbolts. Even Melwas, conceited as he was, must feel that fear…

Melwas strode over to me and, seizing me by the upper arm, dragged me to face Jerome. Olwyn's hand was pulled from my grip as she shrank away from him, like a beaten dog. Melwas's hard fingers dug into my flesh like pincers. I was going to have bruises.

"Do not forget she is my prisoner," he snarled, lips curling back from his yellowed teeth. "I can do what I like with her, and neither you, nor your posturing lord, can stop me."

I bit my lip, partly to stop myself from crying out at the pain from his grip, partly to school my face to hide my fear.

"If I let you take her." Melwas's voice oozed menace. "Then I want a guarantee from you – from the man of God you claim to be – that I will be left unharmed. That Arthur will march away from here with his army and leave Dinas Brent and my Summer Country untouched." He gave me an angry shake. "Or I'll send just a few parts of her back with you right now." From the sheath on his hip, he pulled out a dagger, a long, evil blade that caught the glow of feeble light from the winter sun. He set the point against the side of my nose. "And we'll start now, with this."

The point pricked my skin and warm blood ran down my cheek, salty on my lips, the smell of iron strong in my nostrils. My treacherous stomach began to heave.

"I repeat my warning," Jerome said, apparently unmoved by my imminent danger. "If you harm a hair on her head, and that includes her nose, then Arthur will hunt you down like the dog you are." He might have been discussing the weather with an old acquaintance. I had to admire his sangfroid, but acknowledge that I didn't share it. I couldn't stop shaking with fear as the point of that lethal dagger dug into my nose.

"You're a man of God," Melwas spat, gobs of spittle striking my cheek. "If you give your word, then I expect you to keep it – and make sure he does the same." His angry glare looked impotent now. "Do I have your word?"

Jerome pursed his lips in thought.

What was there to think about? The man was about to slice off my nose. Tears mingled with the blood now, even though I'd been trying hard not to cry. Out of the corner of my eye, I spied Olwyn wringing her hands in terror. It wasn't her nose in peril. Did she fear his recriminations if he had to let me go?

The silence was absolute as every man's gaze rested on Jerome.

"You have my word as a man of God," the Abbot said.

The dagger dropped from my face and he released my bruised arm. My hand went up to my nose automatically and came away wet with blood. I stepped away from Melwas.

"Come here, child," Jerome said, holding out his hand to me.

Glancing sideways at Melwas, I stepped up to the Abbot, and he set his hand gently on my shoulder. "Get up behind Corwyn on his horse. Be quick about it." He never even looked at me, but held Melwas's furious black eyes with his own, as though he feared that if he were to look away, Melwas might change his mind.

Corwyn stretched a hand down to me, and I took it. The garron wasn't large, but she looked sturdy. My legs were still shaking. When Corwyn gave me a pull there was little I could do to help him, but his brute strength got me up onto his horse behind his saddle. The skirts of my gown rode up to my knees as I sat astride, revealing my tall, soft leather riding boots. Locking my arms firmly around Corwyn's waist, I held on tight, my cheek against the comforting rough cloth of his cloak. I didn't care that he was only a lowly layman who'd been quite mean to me when I'd been his prisoner. Now he was one of my saviors, and I couldn't hold on tightly enough.

Jerome held out his hand to Melwas. "Thank you," he said, as Melwas grudgingly took it. "You have my word, my Lord Melwas." A murmur of something that might have been agreement echoed through the watching warriors.

Melwas's eyes flicked sideways and I followed his gaze to Olwyn, who was trying to make herself as small as possible. He licked his lips in what could only have been anticipation.

I lifted my head. "Wait!" I said imperiously, fighting to keep the tremor out of my voice and regain the gravitas of a real queen. "I need a servant, and this woman has served me well these three days." I pointed at Olwyn. "I want to take her with me to serve me at Din Cadan."

I'd deliberately used the word servant. I was counting on the fact that Melwas might think making his mother my servitor would be a suitable punishment for her, rather than wanting to torture her himself. She didn't glance up, but her narrow shoulders hunched a little more. She couldn't have looked more like a potential servant if she'd tried.

There was a long silence. Only the wind coming in across the salt flats from the sea whispered in the eaves of the hall behind us.

Melwas's mouth curved into a caricature of a smile. "Take her," he said. "Do with her as you will. What do I care?"

Jerome held out his hand to her. "Come, Mother, sit up behind Calum." He led her to the second layman and helped her up to sit behind the man, her thin arms around his sturdy waist.

Without another glance toward Melwas, Jerome sprang with

surprising agility into his own saddle, his bare calves and heavy ankle boots exposed as his habit rode up. He turned his horse sharply downhill toward the gates. Corwyn, and Calum, the second layman, followed behind him.

Chapter Six

"**Y**OU DID WHAT?" Arthur shouted, his face suffused with rage.

Jerome stood in front of him in the forest clearing, his expression calm as ever, hands neatly folded into the opposite sleeves of his habit. He didn't answer. Arthur knew exactly what he'd done.

Standing to one side of Arthur, I held Olwyn close in the circle of my arms as she shook with fear. "It's all right," I whispered. "Arthur's not like Melwas. He's just angry about the conditions Jerome's agreed to."

We'd ridden down the hill and taken the narrow causeway through the marshes to the forest edge, where the track widened considerably. None of it was recognizable. On my way to Dinas Brent, which had now retreated to a distant hill in the grey of the afternoon, I'd been too frightened to take anything in.

At the forest edge, guards Arthur had posted signaled our arrival on ahead and we came upon Arthur's camp about two hundred yards inside the forest.

As we rode into the wide clearing where they'd made camp, in overgrown fields around the clustered, ramshackle buildings of a long deserted farm, Arthur came striding to meet me, closely followed by Merlin. Slipping from Corwyn's horse, I ran into Arthur's arms, tears of relief streaming down my face. As he held me close, his face buried in my hair, I clung to him, breathing in the scent of sweat and horses and campfires that I'd feared never to smell again.

"It was my fault," he said. "I should never have entrusted you to those three. I should have paid more attention to who I was sending to escort you."

"You couldn't have known." My voice was muffled against his cloak. I was willing to forgive his oversight now that I was safely back in his embrace. He bent his head and lifting my chin, kissed me on the lips. I reached up to touch his cheek, hungry for comfort.

But then Jerome told him what he'd agreed to in order to get me away from Melwas, and Arthur was not pleased.

"That dog deserves to die." He released me, and I stepped back to stand with Olwyn. "He planted agents within my army with only one thing in mind – treachery." He turned to his waiting warriors. "Fetch his other four men here at once."

The four men who had come from Dinas Brent with Kelwyn and Gorsedd to join the army of the Dux Britanniarum were dragged forward by Cei and a crowd of other warriors. They'd been stripped of their armor and stood shivering in their undershirts and braccae. Their arms were bound behind them, and their ankles had been hobbled with ropes to stop them from running. Every one of them was bruised and battered, lips split and eyes blackened.

Arthur looked them up and down with disdain. "You are Melwas's men. Your fellows swore allegiance to me when they arrived at Din Cadan, just as you four did. Yet they lied. Their intent was always to steal away the Ring Maiden, so Melwas might present her to my brother Cadwy. What do you have to say to the charge that you, too, were complicit in this plan?"

They were young men, scarcely more than boys, and not much older than Drustans, whom I'd seen with a bandage around his head. A murmur of anger rippled through the watching warriors, and those behind the four shoved them forward roughly. In their hobbles they staggered and nearly fell.

The tallest spoke up. "My Lord Arthur, we didn't know.

Kelwyn and Gorsedd are older warriors, and we weren't privy to their plans. They were among Melwas's most trusted men." His voice was nasal, as though he had a cold, thanks to a crooked broken nose he'd probably not had three days earlier.

The second, a ginger-headed youth, added his pennyworth. "We didn't even go on the hunt. They made us stay behind at Din Cadan, training. We had no part in this." A hiss of disbelief rose from the crowd of watching warriors toward the chill winter sky.

The other two stood silent, still shivering in the biting cold, heads hanging.

Arthur fingered the hilt of his sword. "If you knew Kelwyn and Gorsedd were in his inner circle," he said with care, narrowing his eyes, "did you not think it strange that he should let them come to me, with you four who are no more than striplings? Did you not ask yourselves whether there might be an ulterior motive?"

Easy to be wise with hindsight. Had he not noticed this himself? Had Merlin not? Did some of the blame for this lie at his own door? I didn't want to blame him for what had happened to me, but a small part of me questioned his security levels at Din Cadan.

All four of the young men shook their heads vigorously.

From the warriors crowding close behind them came muttered suggestions of what to do with them, none of them reassuring.

Merlin moved up to stand beside Arthur. He pointed at the youngest of the four with a long, gloved finger. "Him. Question him. He knows something."

A look of terror flashed across the boy's acne-ridden face as Cei dragged him to stand in front of Arthur. Someone had taken his boots. His bare feet were scratched and bleeding and filthy with mud.

Silence fell amongst the watching warriors. "What is it you know?" Arthur asked, a hint of menace in his quiet voice.

The youth shook his head. "Nothing, Milord, nothing." He

swallowed. "I swear."

"It's in his head," Merlin said coldly. "Waiting to be dragged out."

"Think hard, boy." Arthur had his sword half-drawn from its scabbard. "Your life depends on it."

The boy gulped down a sob of fear. "I-I overheard them speaking. I didn't know. I swear." His eyes slid from Arthur's angry face to Merlin's implacable one, but studiously avoided his friends.

Merlin stood straighter. "What did you hear?"

The boy glanced from left to right as though searching for an escape, but there was none. "I wanted to go on the hunt. Kelwyn said it wasn't possible. He was talking with Gorsedd. They said if they were lucky, the day had come – the day they'd been waiting for."

"And you didn't think to tell your king?" Cei reached over and grabbed him by the front of his dirty, blood-stained under-shirt with a great fist. "It was your *duty* to tell your king if you heard anything like that. Why didn't you?"

"I-I didn't think," the boy stammered. "I th-thought he m-meant a day to get out of the f-fortress after the snow had g-gone. I s-s-swear." He was very fond of swearing things, but that didn't make what he was saying true.

Merlin put a restraining hand on Cei's arm. "He's not lying. Let him go. He was not party to this."

Cei released the boy and took a step back, both he and Merlin looking at Arthur for a decision.

Arthur's face hardened. "These four will have their goods returned to them," he said. "Their horses, too. They may have had no hand in the deeds of their countrymen, but I cannot have them within the army of the Dux."

A rumble of angry disagreement buzzed through his warriors as though they wanted vengeance for my kidnapping, and would wreak it on these young men if they could.

Arthur frowned at them. "I must have absolute loyalty. These sorry apologies for warriors have proved this is not possible from the men of the Isle of Frogs. They have no place within our ranks. Escort them to the causeway and send them to their lord."

The prisoners stared at him, round eyed. Perhaps they'd feared he'd exact his revenge on them and have them killed as the only men of Dinas Brent he could get his hands on. But they didn't look as relieved as I would have expected. Maybe returning to whatever fate a furious Melwas might have in store for them was worse than remaining here with Arthur's men, who looked as though they were only waiting for the word to tear them limb from limb.

Beside me, Olwyn stirred and pointed a wavering finger at the battered young men. "If they go back," she intoned, her voice low, yet carrying clearly, "he'll make an example of them. Join the Dux and this is what will happen to you. It is his way. They're dead men walking."

"And so they should be!" came a rough voice from the crowd. Others around him murmured in agreement.

Turning to look at Arthur, Broken Nose's voice rose an octave in desperation. "Please don't send us back." He dropped to his knees in the half-frozen mud. "We were your men from the moment we swore allegiance and made a solemn vow to follow you into battle. A vow that meant a great deal to us. Your enemies are our enemies, and that makes Melwas our enemy as much as yours."

Arthur's face didn't soften. His brows came together in a frown.

Something had to be said to save them. I stepped away from Olwyn to my husband's side. "Listen to them, Arthur," I pleaded. "They're afraid to go back. Olwyn says her son will kill them. He keeps his men, and all his people, in line through fear. I've seen it. Please don't send them back."

"Her son?" That had certainly distracted him. "She's Melwas's mother? You've brought that monster's mother into our midst?" Incredulity brought him up sharply.

All eyes swung to look at Olwyn. She hung her head and hunched her shoulders in what looked like an effort to make herself look insignificant.

I returned to her and taking her arm, pulled her to stand in front of Arthur. Before she could protest, I rolled back her sleeve. "Look what he did to her. Because she mourned his older brothers – his own brothers, her sons, who he killed to make himself king. Yes, he's a monster. I should know. But she is not. Look at her. She's terrified. I had to bring her with me because he was going to take out his frustrations on her, and she's too old for that."

My breath came hard and fast as though I'd run a marathon, and my face flushed with the injustice of blaming the actions of others on these four youths.

Arthur, whose eyes had been fixed on me during my impassioned speech, slid his gaze sideways and down, to stare at the puckered, melted flesh on Olwyn's skinny forearm.

I kept going, but now my voice was so low only he could have heard me. "And maybe you should stop to think whose fault it was that the men who kidnapped me had the opportunity to do so. You accepted them into your army. You chose them to escort me home. Without you, they'd never have been able to snatch me."

He stared back at me, and along with the flash of anger that flared at my words, I spied guilt in his eyes as they sank in. I hammered it home. "So please don't tell me I can't offer Olwyn a home."

There was an awful moment of suspense as he stood still, and then the anger visibly seeped out of him and his jaw relaxed. Turning to Olwyn, he put a gentle hand under her chin, raising her head to look into her eyes. "He did this to you?"

She nodded, licking her cracked lips, and whispered, "And he'll do the same, or worse, to these boys if you send them back."

Arthur looked over her head at Cei. "Very well. We'll give them a chance. But see each is paired with one of our own warriors. I'll not have sedition spreading. Untie them and give them back their armor and horses. We ride for home."

I WAS NEVER so glad to see Din Cadan as that night. We rode up the cobbled roadway to its gates under a clear sky and a full moon, frost already sparkling on every blade of stunted grass. Before us, the double gates opened wide, and the massed forces of Arthur rode through them into the fortress's wide interior.

Exhaustion overwhelmed me, so Arthur had to lift me down from the saddle and carry me into the great hall whilst others attended to our horses. Once inside our chamber, he tenderly undressed me and, having found a clean undershirt, tucked me into our bed with hot stones all around me.

Blissfully happy to be back, I lay there, letting the warm glow of the brazier and torches lull me to sleep, the sound of voices from beyond the door into the hall barely noticeable. I was back where I belonged. I was home.

The next morning, the persistent pawing of the tabby cat who frequented our bedchamber woke me – the same one who'd kept me company my first night there, alone in Arthur's big bed. She was kneading at me as cats do, snagging her claws on the finely-spun blankets. I turned my head, but the Arthur-shaped space beside me was empty and cold.

Sitting up, I pushed the cat aside. My body clock told me it was much later than normal, but as I had the excuse of exhaustion, not having slept well in Melwas's clutches, I took my time dressing. Today was not a day for braccae, as I had no intention of riding anywhere unless heavily guarded. My choice was an ankle-length undertunic followed by a shorter overtunic gathered with a wide woven belt.

I found Arthur on the training fields beyond the horse pens with his young warriors, all of them sweating hard in their armor.

They were using real swords for their training session today, their wooden swords discarded in a pile. The frost of the day before had vanished, and the fighters slid all over the place in the slippery and treacherous top half-inch of ground.

To the right, close below the outer wall, Merlin and Gwalchmei, the musician, were supervising a dozen small boys, all armed with practice swords and round, white painted shields. Wandering over to watch, I spotted the dark curly head of Arthur's son, Llacheu, going at it like a dervish with a boy several inches taller than he was. A lucky blow sent the older boy's sword spinning into the mud, and Llacheu let out a shriek of triumph.

Arthur, who'd been fighting against one of the young warriors from Dinas Brent – Ginger – was momentarily distracted, and the younger man's sword caught him hard across the ribs. He staggered under the blow but then returned it twice as hard, hammering at the young warrior with as much gusto as his son. Ginger fell back under a rain of blows, his shield split down the center. He dropped his sword as a stinging blow across the back of his hand with the flat of Arthur's sword knocked it from his grip. He tripped over his own feet and fell backward onto the muddy ground.

I had to wonder if Arthur had chosen this young man as an opponent for a reason.

Leaving the young man lying in the mud, Arthur strode over to join me, his dark hair sticking damply to his brow despite the cold, his breathing hard after the exertion.

"Gwen!" He put an arm around my waist, drawing me nearer, and bestowed a kiss on my lips. "I thought you'd never wake and come out. I've finished here, so let's walk." His eyes were troubled.

We climbed the steps to the walkway that ran around the perimeter of the fortress. It was manned at intervals, and on a strict rota, by Arthur's warriors who were neither resting nor involved in training.

He took my hand in his, pulling it through the crook of his

arm, and we set off slowly in the direction of the main gates. For a while we walked in silence.

That something had been brewing in his head had been obvious from the moment he'd almost lost control as he'd attacked Ginger. That, and his suddenly solemn countenance, worried me.

At last he pulled me to a halt overlooking the village at the foot of the hill, the tiny wattle and daub church spire rising out of the bare treetops. He looked me in the eyes. "Did he – did he touch you?"

Of course. I'd been ostensibly alone with Melwas for over three days. I would have thought the same things.

"No, he didn't," I said, trying to keep my voice level and calm. I didn't want to think of those days of captivity, of the terror that had stalked my every waking moment, of those last minutes when I'd thought Melwas was about to slice off my nose.

He slid his hand up my left arm, making me wince as he touched my bruises. "And these? How did you get these? I noticed them when I undressed you last night." There was a tiny hint of accusation in his voice. Did he think I was lying?

"He grabbed me when he was talking to Abbot Jerome." I was aware this sounded like an excuse. "When he threatened me with his dagger, before Jerome persuaded him to let me go." I wasn't sure if Jerome had told him how Melwas had threatened to return me piece by piece, starting with my nose.

Arthur ran his hand up and down my arm. "And that was all? He left you alone apart from that? He made no... no suggestions to you?"

This made me bristle with annoyance. Maybe it was the fact that Melwas had held me prisoner for so many days, and that now I was home I wanted to forget the whole incident. Obviously, Arthur couldn't. "Why don't you just come out and say it?" I snapped, more harshly than I'd intended. "You want to know if he raped me, don't you?"

He looked taken aback at my bluntness, but he didn't shy away from it. His hand stopped moving and he looked me directly in the eyes. "Did he?"

I shook my head. "I thought he was going to." It was painful having to think about those moments again. I didn't want to, and he was forcing me to do it. "But I told him I was a priestess from Ynys Afallon, sent by Gwynn ap Nudd. He believed me, I think. I told him my power was only for you, not him, that he was nothing, no one."

He let out a sigh of inheld breath, and relief showed in his face. "My brave girl, facing down that monster on your own." I ignored this rather patronizing remark. It was a good thing I loved him. I let him take my hand in his.

This time he held onto it. "But why did you feel the need to bring his mother with you?"

"I couldn't leave her with him," I said, after a brief pause. "At Dinas Brent, she was the only person I could talk to. I couldn't leave her to her son's revenge, not after she'd shown me what he'd done to her." I paused again. "What will you do? Will you stick to Jerome's agreement?"

I badly wanted to see Melwas punished for what he'd done to me and for all his past evil: for the murders of his brothers, for his cruelty to his mother.

Arthur bit his lip in thought a moment or two before he answered. "Until he makes his next wrong move. Then I'll strike. I won't forget what he tried to do with you."

Chapter Seven

T WO WEEKS LATER, the non-arrival of my period brought me to the disconcerting conclusion that I was pregnant. For the last couple of years with Nathan, my modern-day boyfriend who was now my ex, I'd had the three-monthly contraceptive injection as it was considered safer than the pill and, of course, less fiddly than condoms.

I'd been due for a top up injection shortly before Christmas, but I'd been here in Din Cadan where injections didn't exist. When I'd made my decision to stay with Arthur and not return through the time portal on top of Glastonbury Tor, the question of contraception hadn't been at the forefront of my mind. If the thought had crossed my mind at all, I'd just have hoped the lasting effects from my two years of injections would keep me safe for at least twelve months – which was what advice on the Internet said. So, missing my period after not quite three months in the Dark Ages was a bit disturbing.

My first thought was that I'd miscounted the days. But the next day, with no sign of my period, I began to get nervous. On the third day, with still no sign, it started to dawn on me that maybe there was a reason for this, and it might have something to do with our vigorous love life.

Maia, my young maidservant, came across me that morning sitting on the edge of the bed with my head in my hands, wearing only my undershirt. She'd brought me breakfast on a tray –

porridge with honey, and weak beer. She set it down on the table and approached me.

"Milady?" Her voice was tentative. When she got no response, she tried again. "Be ye all right?"

Heaving a sigh, I raised my head, sighed again and gave what I fancied was an eloquent shrug.

Her homely face creased in consternation. "Be ye ill? Should I find the king? Or Cottia?" Her default mode every time was to appeal to a higher authority.

"No." My voice was emphatic. I didn't want either of them to know of my suspicions, at least not until I'd come to terms with them myself.

"Then what can I do?" She sounded anxious now, overburdened with something she didn't want to shoulder. She was, after all, a servant, used to being told what to do by others. Responsibility was not hers.

I gave another shrug. What could she do? It was too late for anything now. In my own world, I could probably have gone for an early termination, taken a few pills, and it would have been over. Here, in the fifth century, there was no such thing available. Or was there?

She stood in front of me, now nervously wringing her hands. They were reddened and rough with work. I looked up into her face, fixing her with a steady gaze. "I need your help."

Her eyes widened, partly in surprise, and partly, I suspected, in fear of what I might be about to ask of her. "O' course, Milady. I be yours. I'll do whatever ye say." She didn't sound all that convinced.

I wetted my lips with the tip of my tongue, as nervous as she was. "Have you ever – have you ever been…pregnant?"

Her face reddened to match her hands. She looked down at them and wrung them some more. It appeared as though the answer might be yes. She was very young, but people in the fifth century seemed to mature every bit as early as they did in the twenty-first.

I pressed my advantage home. "What did you do?"

She kept her eyes down, two bright red spots burning on her soft cheeks. They made her seem even younger. "I – I went to Mother Nara." The words came out in a whisper.

"Mother Nara? Who's she?" I put a hand on Maia's sleeve. She was trembling. "Where do I find her?"

Maia raised her eyes to mine. They were wide with fear. "But ye be the queen," she whispered. With her fingertips she touched my belly. "This be the king's child, not a common servant's. Why'd ye not want it?" In this world, where a woman's primary function was childbearing, she evidently couldn't comprehend of a married woman, a queen at that, who wouldn't want to have a child.

The enormity of my intention was reflected in her gaze. I swallowed. How to explain. How to make her understand? "I'm afraid." My voice was scarcely above a whisper. "I'm afraid of dying if I have a baby."

The silence stretched between us. Maia didn't try refuting my fears. She must have known as well as I did how dangerous a pregnancy and birth could be in the Dark Ages. I didn't know the percentages, but I could take a good guess at them.

"Mother Nara be the midwife," she said at last.

Of course. She would be, wouldn't she? The woman who not only attended to the deliveries but who also had medicines for those who didn't want their babies. She must know of plants that would terminate a pregnancy before it was too far along.

I swallowed. "I can't go and see her myself." My voice was conspiratorially low even though I knew no one could overhear us. "You'll have to go and see her for me. You'll have to tell her it's for you."

Now Maia looked terrified. "But it's the king's child," she repeated, the words hissing out on a breath of disapproval.

I shook my head in determination. "No, it's *my* child. It's in my belly, not his. And it's not even a child yet. It's a clump of cells." My fingers closed on her arm as she looked at me in confusion. "A clump of cells which is only going to grow if I leave it. And it might end up killing me." I paused. "Like Birte." She was the wife of one of Arthur's warriors, who'd not long ago died a horrible death in childbirth, her baby as well. I stared into Maia's frightened eyes. "I don't want to end up like Birte. You have to get me something to end this."

Maia hesitated, biting her bottom lip and shifting from one foot to the other.

"D'you want me to die?" I asked.

She gave a little furtive shake of her head. "No, Milady." She'd balled up the front of her tunic with her fists. "I – I'll go and see 'er when I can."

I'd won. Yet I felt curiously flat at the victory, filled with guilt at what I was proposing to do, and the involvement I'd forced Maia into.

The day stretched out interminably, a day in which I was convinced everyone who looked at me would know my secret. I felt sure my stomach had bloated out already, and my breasts were straining against my clothing in the most tell-tale manner. I was on the verge of a nervous breakdown by the time the evening came around, and Maia returned, one hand tightly clenched around a small leather pouch.

Like a guilty conspirator, she came creeping into my chamber. It would have been laughable if I hadn't been as terrified as she looked.

"I have it," she whispered, unfolding her fingers to reveal the tiny drawstring bag. "Ye have to drink some in 'ot water before ye go to bed for three nights. Ye'll get cramps and then – then it should come away. But Mother Nara told me it don't always work."

"But it did for you?"

She nodded, her brow furrowing with worry. I didn't blame her. After all, she was procuring medication, which might be construed as poison, for the queen. "But..." she shifted from one foot to the other. "I do 'ear say it were what caused Corann's wife, Ardena, to die. Mother Nara did say so, too."

"What?" I looked down to the innocuous-seeming bag lying in her outstretched palm and then back up at her. "Now you tell me." My hand, which had been about to take the bag, dropped to my side.

"Mother Nara said as 'ow I should know the risks," she whispered. "This did 'appen since I took it myself. She did say as it were rare fer a woman t'die of it."

Rarer than in childbirth? I had no idea which held the highest risk and no way of finding out. I could hardly go and ask Mother Nara myself.

Voices sounded in the Hall. I recognized Arthur's, and the other was Merlin's. Maia did, too, because she stuffed the little pouch into my hands and ran, the side door banging shut behind her.

For a moment I stood irresolute, looking down at what lay in my palm. Then I ran to the bed and, pulling out my old walking boots from under it, slipped the pouch into the toe of one of them. I was straightening up when Arthur and Merlin came into the room.

They were laughing together about something that had happened down at the practice field, but when Arthur saw me, he strode over and took me in his arms for a kiss. My nerves stiffened me, and he must have sensed it because he released me quickly and stood gazing at me in surprise.

"Is anything wrong?"

Behind him, Merlin, too, eyed me askance. The fact that he had the Sight had quite slipped my mind, as he so infrequently used it. Guilt blossomed again, deep in my heart – guilt at the thoughts of what I was about to do, guilt at my wish to kill this baby, guilt at my deception of my husband.

Merlin raised a quizzical eyebrow, and my cheeks flushed hot.

"Nothing," I said as lightly as possible. "I was just wondering when you'd be ready to eat. I'm hungry, is all."

Arthur seemed satisfied. While he bent over the basin of tepid water I'd used for my ablutions, I glanced back at Merlin, who was waiting near the door, and was unnerved to discover him watching me.

The smile I managed to raise felt so false I could have screamed.

His eyes narrowed. Did he know what I was thinking? Did he know about the baby? Of all the people here at Din Cadan, he was the one most likely to guess my secret.

Arthur threw water over his face noisily, then used a rough cloth, which served as a towel, to dry himself. He straightened, and I turned to him with a fixed smile that was feeling like a rictus grin by now, my whole being fixated on the tiny parcel beneath the bed, fighting the impulse to look straight at it.

Arthur smiled. "Our food awaits us, and I'm starving." Taking my hand, he led me into the great hall.

I DIDN'T TAKE the powders that night. No opportunity arose, as I was never alone for a moment, and could hardly have sneaked out of bed in the middle of the night to seek hot water. The hall would have been full of snoring warriors who might have woken, not to mention the two guards on our door who should have been wide awake. So I spent a fitful night worrying through the situation.

I was pregnant – that much was painfully obvious. I'd never been late or missed a period; they were like clockwork every twenty-eight days. No variation, not even with the injections, and now I was nearly four days overdue.

Hidden underneath the bed lay a concoction of who knew what, that might or might not get rid of this baby while it was the cluster of cells I'd described to Maia. Or on the other hand, it might do to me what it had done to Ardena, whose death had scarcely touched me until this moment. Corann, her husband, was a much older man, she his second wife. He already had grown sons with families of their own. I had no idea why she'd wanted to terminate her pregnancy – maybe from the same fears I harbored, or maybe Corann hadn't wanted the baby. But evidently she had got rid of it, with disastrous consequences. Officially, she'd died from blood loss after a miscarriage, but now I knew that for a lie.

However, the powders from Mother Nara had worked for Maia. She'd taken them in three draughts, and she'd got rid of the baby she hadn't wanted. Or had that been going to happen anyway? Had she just believed it was the powders that had done it? I had a vague idea a fair number of pregnancies did end in early miscarriage. My friend Sian, from university, had suffered at least one before she'd had her baby. And my own mother had miscarried after she'd had my brother and me. It must be common.

So, I could risk my life and take these powders, or risk my life and carry on with a pregnancy which might end prematurely anyway. And if I did try to end it, and it worked, what was there to stop me getting pregnant again? Nothing. No contraception here. A sobering thought.

But then again, supposing I did nothing, and went ahead with this pregnancy, and the baby was born healthy, with me unharmed? What then? I'd have a baby, a little, dependent, mewling baby. All mine. I remembered going to see Sian in hospital and peering at the tiny pink thing lying sleeping in the glass-sided cot by her bed. I remembered thinking it was too much responsibility. Taking on the care of a new life in the safe twenty-first century had seemed a daunting task, but here, in the depths of the darkest period in Britain's history, it felt insurmountable.

But was I just over-dramatizing? Was I looking on the black side of everything? Restless, I turned in bed and looked at Arthur. The glow of the brazier faintly illuminated his face, relaxed in sleep, his tousled dark hair falling across his eyes. A baby who would look like him, who might grow to resemble Llacheu, of whom I was very fond. Wouldn't that be rather nice? Wouldn't I like to have a baby with the man I loved?

I slid my hand to my stomach, but it was still washboard flat. It wouldn't stay like that for long. Before I knew it, I'd have a belly like Morgawse's had been before she'd given birth to Medraut. And look what that had done to Theodoric, her husband. He'd gone running off to brothels.

No. Strictly speaking that wasn't what Theodoric had done in response to his wife's pregnancy. He'd probably been doing that for a long time before she fell pregnant, before he even married her. I didn't like Theodoric all that much and cared nothing for his attitude toward his wife. But was Arthur the same? I didn't know.

There was a lot I didn't know about Arthur, even after nearly three months in the fifth century, three quarters of that time married to him. I knew he'd kept a mistress here in Din Cadan, a beautiful mistress who was the mother of his only son, a child he'd fathered when he'd been little more than a boy himself. Tangwyn was still here, living in her own house not far from the great hall where I lived with Arthur, often eating in the Hall in the evening, watching him out of her slanting cat's eyes, her expression saying clearly that it was only a matter of time before he was hers again. He'd kept away from her since we'd arrived back from Viroconium, but his son was everywhere, in and out of the Hall, at the practice grounds, in the classes Merlin taught to the younger boys. A constant reminder of his lovely mother.

A small part of me feared Arthur might be as fickle as his brother-in-law. A wife resembling a whale might well drive him back into Tangwyn's slender arms, which was the last thing I wanted. He was mine now, and I intended to keep it that way. I wasn't about to let Tangwyn into his life again.

Pushing thoughts of the little bag of powders under the bed into the back of my mind, I snuggled up close to him. He stirred a little and put his arm around me, drawing me nearer. I put my cheek against his chest, the hairs tickling my nose, and closed my eyes. But sleep was a long time coming.

THE NEXT MORNING, after sleeping in late, I woke to the renewed disappointment that my period still hadn't arrived, something I'd been hoping would take away the necessity for those powders. I felt hungover and heavy lidded from my restless night, and my head throbbed painfully. Breakfast of congealed porridge stood cold on the table, so I downed the flagon of small beer but felt no better. If anything, I felt worse. Going without sleep for most of the night was not to be recommended when you were newly pregnant.

I lay back down on the bed for a while, and the cat came and sat on my chest, cleaning its paws in a companionable manner. But at last, I had to get up. I couldn't lie in bed feeling depressed all morning. What I wanted was a ride, so the fresh air could blow the cobwebs away and with them my headache.

The great hall was empty, so, dressed in tunic and braccae, I stepped out into the cold winter daylight.

Arthur was busy with his men down on the practice field, so engrossed, he didn't see me watching. The smaller boys had congregated in a corner with Cei and Gwalchmei, practicing with their stubby wooden swords. Which meant they weren't being taught theory by Merlin today.

I set off in search of Merlin.

He was sitting on a log in Goff's forge, watching the burly smith as he hammered away at a glowing piece of iron. When he saw me, he got to his feet and emerged into the daylight. Behind him, the ringing tones of the hammer on iron beat out an almost musical rhythm.

He made me a little bow in greeting.

I went straight to the point. "Could we go out riding? Arthur's busy, and I'm longing for a gallop." I managed a smile. "I've got a headache, and the fresh air would do me good."

Tilting his head to one side, he narrowed his eyes as though trying to read my mind. Deliberately, I thought hard about Alezan and how nice it would be to take her for a gallop. Just in case. Whether or not he could read minds, he certainly had good intuition.

"Not on our own," he said. "I'll go and find us an escort."

HALF AN HOUR later, we rode down the cobbled road toward the plain, followed by half a dozen heavily armed warriors. Alezan, always lively, skipped and sidled beneath me, and for the first time ever, I felt a pang of nerves. Supposing I were to fall off? What would happen to the baby? It puzzled me that I should care about this when all I wanted was to be rid of it. An odd sensation.

We skirted the foot of the hill, following the road that threaded its way between the farmsteads. Washing fluttered on a line, chickens ran squawking to get out of our way, small, grubby children played in front of houses, and men sat on log stools beside their doors, sharpening swords or mending tools. Further out, on the open pasture lands, sheep browsed, watched over by the older boys and their brindled dogs. Where the land was wetter, shaggy cattle grazed knee-deep in the marshes.

We rode east. The cobbled road vanished, and we were soon on open rolling grasslands where the figures of a distant herd of grazing horses looked like toys.

Alezan wanted to have her head. She knew this was where we galloped and was eager to be off. I touched my legs to her side, and she sprang forward from an impatient jog trot straight into a gallop, the bit between her teeth. Crouching forward over the saddle horns, I urged her on. She was arrow fast, and I wasn't heavy. Her thundering hooves ate up the ground as though she were a thoroughbred racehorse. A glance over my shoulder showed me Merlin trailing some way back on his bay. Further behind him, the half dozen warriors of our escort struggled to keep up.

The wind whipped at my hair, snatching at my short riding cloak, and I drummed my booted heels against Alezan's side, pushing her to even more speed. Beneath her hooves, the ground rushed past in a blur, the distant dark line of the forest ahead of us drawing ever closer. Her breath came in rhythmic snorts, and beneath me she eventually began to flag. For want of a stick, I whipped my reins from side to side across her neck, and she found another burst of speed. But now she was no longer pulling, and I could feel the weakness of exhaustion in my own legs and arms. I let her slow to a canter, then a trot, and she almost fell into a walk. I gave her a long rein, and she stretched her head and neck down toward the ground, clouds of steam rising from her heaving flanks.

It was a minute or two before Merlin brought his own sweat-drenched horse to a walk beside us. "What was that for?" Anger tinged his voice. "Look behind you. We've no guards because they couldn't keep up. These horses are trained for short bursts of speed in battle, not long-distance gallops."

I glanced over my shoulder. Nearly half a mile behind us, our guards had slowed their tired horses to a walk.

He reached out and grabbed Alezan's left rein and gave it a tug. "We need to walk back to meet them. Now."

Wrenching on the rein myself, I turned Alezan away from him. "I don't want to."

His hand had been out ready to grab my rein again, but now he stopped. "Why?" he asked. "What's wrong?"

Annoyance rose to the surface. "Don't you know? Haven't you seen it with your Sight?"

He drew rein, and his horse halted. Alezan, exhausted after her gallop, stopped of her own accord. He eyed me up and down. "I realized something was wrong yesterday. Did you bring me out here to tell me about it?"

Had I? After all, in a way this was all his fault. He'd brought me to this world. If he hadn't, I'd be safely home with Nathan, working in the library, and definitely not pregnant.

"I needed some fresh air." I gave Alezan a small kick, and she started walking again, but this time in a large curve as Merlin's horse gradually pushed us around so that we'd soon be heading back the way we'd come. There wasn't much time.

The words came tumbling out. "I don't know what to do. I don't have anyone to talk to about...about something." The wind blew strands of my hair, loosened in my gallop, into my eyes, making me toss my head to be rid of them.

He rubbed his stubbly chin. "Well, I can't give you advice if you don't tell me the problem."

Putting my reins into one hand, I laid the other protectively on my belly. His eyes followed the movement.

"Did your prophecy – the one about me – did it...did it mention anything about an heir to Arthur?"

His gaze sharpened. "Not directly," he said, still looking at the hand on my flat belly. "But it didn't specify there wouldn't be one." He paused. "What about what you know of Arthur from your own time? Is there an heir in the stories you know?"

I shrugged. "I don't know everything that's been written. And even if there was an heir, the stories might not have come down to us. They're all a terrible jumble, and nothing contemporary survives."

He was still looking at my hand. "Why do you want to know about an heir?"

I swallowed. "You said once that you saw the future, and that mine was tied up with Arthur's...that I was essential to what he was to become." My turn to pause. We were now heading back toward our guards, who'd come to a halt in the distance, waiting for us. A brace of partridge flew up out of the grass in front of our horses, startling them. "In that future, was I always there...I mean, to the very end?"

Merlin halted his horse again, and Alezan followed suit. The headlong gallop had taken it out of her. "Yes," he said firmly. "I saw you with him to the end. If there is one."

If there is one. What an odd thing to say. There always had to be an end, surely. In the end we all die. But maybe not. The legends said that Arthur didn't die, that he was whisked away to Avalon by three queens, where he would lie in sleep until Britain's hour of need. Was that what Merlin meant? Was Arthur really never going to die? I gave myself a little shake. Impossible.

"So you didn't see my death?" I'd reached the nub of the matter. The words were difficult to say.

He shook his head. "No. You were with him to...the end."

Relief washed over me. Three months ago the reassurance by someone with the Sight that I wasn't about to die in childbirth wouldn't have left me feeling anything other than amused and skeptical. But this world had changed me. I'd got here by magic and seen a sword that no one could pull out protruding from an enormous stone that had appeared in the forum of Viroconium overnight. And I'd met a woman who'd sent Saxon foederati out to snatch me because she'd seen my arrival inside her head. So I believed him when he said I'd be with Arthur to the end. Whatever end that was.

I rubbed my stomach gently with my hand, almost caressingly. If he was right, this meant I wasn't going to die in childbirth, or from taking those powders Mother Nara had given Maia. Maybe I was going to have this baby and give Arthur the son who would be his heir– an heir who history would forget for some reason. Maybe this baby was meant to be.

"You're with child, aren't you?" Merlin said.

I looked at him for a long moment before nodding. I didn't need to say a word. He might well have been able to read my mind.

"And you're afraid of dying in childbed."

I nodded again. Somehow it was easy to tell Merlin all this. He alone knew where I'd come from and had a vague idea of how different our worlds were. Arthur might be my lover, but what I needed now was a friend.

He sighed. "I can't promise you it won't be difficult. A woman's lot in life is hard. In pain and suffering she brings forth sons for her husband, only to see them sicken and die as babes, or grow to manhood and be killed on the battlefield. I cannot say that your baby will even be born living, or that you won't suffer pain in his birth. I cannot say that he won't die of illness before he's weaned, or fall from his horse and die while just a boy. I cannot say he won't be killed fighting by his father's side." He paused. "But I do know that *you* won't die. I've seen you by Arthur's side, throughout his reign. You are a fixed point about which this world revolves."

That was something, I supposed.

"Maia brought you powders from Mother Nara, didn't she?" His voice was all of a sudden gentle. "You've thought about being rid of this baby."

I nodded. "I'm frightened. I saw Morgawse give birth. I've read books. I know what can go wrong." I didn't mention all the *Call the Midwife* episodes I'd seen.

He reached over and put his hand on my arm. "Don't worry. Many women feel fear as you're doing. And for most, the fear is groundless. Morgawse had her baby, didn't she? The baby's alive and well, and so is she. And so shall you be."

I thought of the powders under the bed again. I'd throw them away. They weren't worth the risk. I was a queen, and this child was going to be a prince.

Chapter Eight

W HEN WE RETURNED to Din Cadan, I took the little leather pouch out from the toe of my walking boot and threw it on the brazier before I could change my mind. Afterwards I regretted it and sat for a while on the edge of our bed, considering the frightening future.

Merlin had promised not to tell anyone about our conversation, especially not Arthur, so this meant it was possible to keep my condition to myself for a while longer. In fact, in the end I didn't have to tell Arthur because he guessed. For the third morning on wakening I was unable to eat my breakfast and threw up in the bowl Maia had placed at the side of the bed.

Arthur, already in his braccae and calf-high leather boots, with his undershirt hanging untucked, came and patted me sympathetically on the back. "You're with child, aren't you?" His voice was gentle. Too gentle. I wanted some other kind of reaction, although I didn't know what. He smiled. "I suspected you might be the first time you were sick, but now I'm certain."

Feeling very sorry for myself, I looked up at him, having just spat what looked like diced carrots into the bowl. I nodded. No use denying it now, not if puking was going to be my lot for the next month or so.

His smile widened into a grin of what I considered inappropriate delight. "I'm going to be a father again. That feels good. When will our child be born?"

I glared at him. How could he be so cheerful about it? Typical man, thinking only of himself. It was all right for him. He'd done his bit, the fun part. It was me stuck with the grind of pregnancy and birth…and puking.

"In the autumn." A pretty vague answer, but then, no one here seemed to follow an actual calendar. Not for the first time it occurred to me that it might be a good idea to get some sort of paper – vellum perhaps – so I could write myself a calendar. I'd been here for over three months now, but the only reason I knew that was because I'd been counting the days between my periods. I had a strong inner need for order, and to know the date, and I wanted to mark off the time in a physical way.

Arthur dropped to his knees in front of me, putting the bowl of sick to one side. He took my hands in his lean tanned ones. "This is wonderful news." His dark eyes shone up at me, and my heart did the little flip it did every time he looked at me like that. I couldn't be annoyed at him for long.

"I'm frightened," I said in a small voice. "Childbirth is dangerous. And pregnancy is no walk in the park."

He raised curious eyebrows, so I rephrased that sentence. "Being with child isn't all that easy."

He nodded. "Especially not at your age."

What? Was he after a thick ear? My face resumed its previous glare. "You'd better mind what you say," I retorted. "In my world, women often don't start having babies until well over thirty."

"Over thirty?" He sounded shocked. "They're grandmothers here by that age."

I sighed, managing a faint smile at the thought of all my as-yet childless modern-day female friends in their thirties who'd be horrified to discover they were thought of as over-the-hill grannies by men of Arthur's time.

Seeing my smile, he smiled back, probably mistaking it for my pleasure at his pleasure. Leaning forward, he planted a kiss on my cheek. "I'm sorry, but it's true. The younger you have your first baby, the easier it is. My own mother gave birth to my brother Cei when she was sixteen. Morgawse, at seventeen, was getting old for a first baby."

Thank goodness Merlin hadn't tried to snatch me when I was a teenager. That was one thing to be thankful for. At least now, at twenty-four, I felt strong enough to deal with what life here threw at me – from being abducted while spreading my father's ashes to discovering my pregnancy in a world where childbearing was one of the most dangerous things a woman could do.

"Get up," he said. "You need a hug."

I got to my feet, and he took me in his arms, pressing me close, his hand in my hair on the back of my head. "You don't need to be afraid. I'm here to take care of you. This baby will be a healthy, strong boy, a prince to follow in my footsteps. He can't be anything but, with parents such as we."

He lifted my chin and, bending, kissed me on the forehead.

Burying my face in his neck, a thought came to me. Maybe this prince would be a princess.

APART FROM THE fact that I threw up as regularly as clockwork every morning, and my breasts started to grow alarmingly and get very tender, my pregnancy seemed to be passing uneventfully. Mother Nara came to see me, on Arthur's insistence, although I'd have rather not met her at all. At least she didn't know who those powders had been for. Or so I thought.

"So, ye decided ter keep yer babby, did ye?" she said, as soon as she was alone with me in my bedchamber. She had a face as wrinkled as an old apple and skin the color of a nut, not only from exposure to the weather. Into the room with her came the unmistakable aroma of the unwashed. I was pretty used to smelly people by now, but, oddly, I rather fancied that a health worker should be clean.

My mouth fell open in shock.

"Don't catch flies like that," she scolded. "Close yer mouth an' tell Mother Nara when ye had yer last moontime. The start o' it, not the finish."

I told her.

"An autumn babby," she opined, only saying what I already knew. "Let's feel yer belly then."

I lay down flat on the bed, and she slid her bony hands over my abdomen, prodding at me with surprisingly strong fingers for one so old and skinny. I had to hold my breath when she bent over me because of the smell.

"Aye," she concluded, "ye're right."

Well, of course I was. I wasn't an idiot, and I'd learned all about the reproductive system in biology at school, and the workings of the human body. I probably possessed a lot more knowledge about this than she did. And I really didn't want someone as dirty as she was around me when the time came for me to give birth. Historically, what most women died of as a complication of childbirth was infection – and this grubby old woman harbored a walking laboratory of bacteria.

When she'd gone, and Arthur came back in, I jumped to my feet and flew into the attack.

"She's not coming anywhere near me when I'm in labor," I said, with all the firmness I could muster.

Arthur's eyes widened in surprise.

I kept going. "Have you stood next to her? She stinks. I could hardly breathe when she was bending over me. For a start, I won't be able to hold my breath the whole time I'm in labor. And for a second point, did you see her hands? Her nails were black and her hands were blotchy brown with dirt." I shuddered at the memory.

He raised his brows.

I went in for the kill. "Anyone delivering a baby should be clean. That's what kills mothers – dirt brought in by their midwives."

He frowned in disbelief.

"I'm right," I said. "And I know I am."

His brows creased still further. "How do you know? This is your first baby." He paused and I saw a thought strike him. "Isn't it?"

Annoyance rose to the surface. "Of course it is. I know because where I come from, doctors have discovered how infection is spread. I learned about it in school. Everyone learns about it."

The frown deepened. "You keep telling me things they do where you come from." He sounded puzzled. "Yet you don't tell me where that is – ever. Don't you think I deserve to be told?"

I'd walked into this one. Swallowing, I sucked in my lips in consternation. He was right – he did deserve to be told. Husbands and wives shouldn't have secrets from one another. Perhaps I owed it to him to tell the truth, especially now our relationship was about to mature into parenthood.

We were face to face. Putting out a hand, I took one of his. "You probably wouldn't believe me."

"You said that once before. You might be surprised."

I hesitated. How to put it so he wouldn't think he was married to a nutter, for a start. "I told you I come from a different place – that Merlin brought me here through that portal on top of the Tor. That the stone circle somehow held a door back to my world."

He nodded. His belief that Glastonbury was the possible entrance to the Celtic Otherworld had helped when I'd told him I needed to go home through that portal. His belief in magic made him more open than someone from my own world would have been. At least, I hoped so.

I'd known that one day he'd have to hear this, but it had never felt like the right moment. Was it now? I swallowed again.

"The world I come from," I began, choosing my words with care, "isn't somewhere else in your world. It's not another kingdom we can get to by traveling."

He regarded me through narrowed eyes. Was he thinking of

Annwfn again, the magical realm of Gwynn ap Nudd? He'd asked me once if that was where I was from, half convinced he had himself a fairy bride.

I ploughed on, determined to get it out this time. "I came from exactly the same spot in my world, tumbling into yours. Merlin brought me here with his magic because he thought he needed me to fulfill that prophecy. He first saw me as a little girl. He watched me grow up, and then one day when I climbed the Tor in my world to scatter my father's ashes, he left the dragon ring inside the tower, and I picked it up. And before I knew it, I found myself here in your world. Same Tor, same spot, just in a different time."

He stayed silent for a minute, looking at me as if seeing me for the first time. Then he spoke. "You're from the past?"

Not the question I'd been expecting. But of course, why would he jump to the conclusion that I was from the future when the past was probably what he best comprehended?

I shook my head and held his hand all the tighter. "No, I'm not from the past. I'm from the future."

"The future?" he echoed, emotions flitting across his face at speed: shock, surprise, curiosity, and then a flash of anger. "Merlin knew this? All this time Merlin's known you're from the future?"

"Yes." Merlin needed dropping in it.

The frown returned. "Why didn't you tell me before?" He paused. "How far into the future? Fifty years? Not...a hundred?"

It was now or never. I took a deep breath. "Fifteen hundred. And I didn't tell you before because I was afraid of how you'd react."

There was only shock on his face now, deep, unmistakable shock. The seconds ticked past before he found the words to speak.

"But...that's forever." It was a plea of desperation, him begging me to say that it couldn't be true. Fifteen hundred years was too far into the future for him to comprehend. Was telling him a big mistake?

"I know. It feels like forever to me as well. Everything that made up my world for the first twenty-four years of my life is so far away it's like it never existed. I left behind a boyfriend, my twin brother, all my friends, a job, a house…my whole life. When I chose to stay here with you that day on the Tor, I left behind the world I knew, a world of good things, and of bad things too."

He seemed to realize I still had his hand in mine, and raised it, clasping his other hand around it as well and cradling it to his chest. "And your world is one where midwives have clean hands, and women have their babies when they're over thirty?" He put his lips to my fingers. "What else can you tell me of your world? Am I – do they know of me?"

I was at a loss what to say. I had a very strong instinct not to tell him anything, for fear that my butterfly wings of knowledge, scant as they were, might change the course of history. I chose my words carefully. "You're not in our history books. There are stories – legends – about you, but scholars think you're just that…simply a story. Not a real person. The truth has been lost down the years. They call the time you live in – no, the time *we* live in, the Dark Ages, because so little is known about it."

"And what do the stories say?"

What to tell him? Platitudes would have to do. "That you were a great king who once fought the Saxons and drove them back to the sea." That was pretty much what the prophecy said, so it couldn't harm to tell him that.

His eyes crinkled as a tiny smile curved his mouth. "And my queen? Does history name her?"

I smiled back in relief. It was in my power to tell him that. "It does indeed. Her name was Guinevere."

He rubbed his stubbly chin. "What about your brother? You told me once his name was Arthur. The two of you were named Arthur and Guinevere – why?"

I'd thought before how quick on the uptake he was, and now was no exception. It had been long ago that I'd told him my brother was named Arthur, like him, but he'd not forgotten. "We were named after you and your queen by our father. He was an Arthurian scholar."

"Arthurian." He rolled the word off his tongue, deep in thought. "There are men in your world – scholars – who study *me*?"

I hadn't meant for him to jump to that conclusion. I was getting in too deep. I needed to watch my words more closely. "A few," I said, feeling awkward.

A smile flashed across his face. "And your father was one of them. I like that."

I kept my face serious. "But there's one thing you have to understand. I can't tell you anything about the future – nothing that can affect what you do here. Because I might inadvertently change history, and the future would be different because of something you or I did here. It's bad enough me knowing things, without you knowing too."

"I don't understand." His brows knit in a frown. "Surely it would be a good thing for you to use your knowledge and help us defeat the Saxons."

I shook my head, my heart heavy. "That's just it. If I tell you about the Saxons, if things happen...I mean, if I make things happen here, then we might just change things too much. Things that are meant to happen might never occur. People who are meant to die might live. People who are meant to live might die. I might even cause the death of my own ancestors, and then I might not exist. And if I didn't exist what would happen then? Would I still be here helping you?" It was so hard to explain when I didn't really understand it myself. "And Merlin says I have to be here. He says I'm essential to your success."

He ran his hand through his hair in what looked like exasperation. "It's a paradox."

I nodded, seizing on his conclusion. "You're right. A paradox no one can begin to understand, because as far as I know no one else has done what I'm doing. I think you have to believe me when I say I can't tell you anything that might change the future...change what's history in my old world. We just don't know what harm we might do."

With reluctance, he nodded. "I think I understand. It would be the same as if I were to go back to when the Roman legions first came to our shores to tell the tribes who met them what was going to happen. That the legions were going to invade and be here for four centuries, oppressing the British tribes, and then leave us in the lurch and ignore our pleas for help. Nothing might change, and yet there is a possibility it could – that when I returned here, to my time, it would be to a changed world. A world which the Romans never came to. We'd not be speaking Latin as we are now." He paused. "I might not even exist."

It never ceased to surprise me that we were speaking a language that was so foreign to me, because my words, and everyone else's, always sounded just like English to my own ears. The discovery that I'd been speaking and understanding these languages with Abbot Jerome had been the first thing that had alerted me to the part magic had played in my arrival here.

I drew his hands toward me and kissed them in relief. I hadn't expected him to be so easy to win around. "There isn't much to tell you, anyway. I only know a few legends that probably aren't even true. Like I said – this is the Dark Ages."

He sat down on the bed, pulling me down beside him, his face alight with curiosity. "I understand that you can't tell me anything that might change things, but could you tell me some things about your world that don't matter? Is it very different from here?"

I thought hard. I didn't want to shock him too much, but on the other hand I had an overwhelming inclination to have a bit of a boast and not just tell him about everyday life. "Men have walked on the moon," I said.

His eyes opened very wide at that. "On the moon? How? It hangs in the sky and lights us at night, like a great lantern. You can't reach and touch it, still less walk on it. And it's very small.

Sometimes just a sliver."

"Well, some people did," I said, glad I'd picked something so strange it would fascinate him. "It's a long way away and much bigger than it looks. Men went up in a rocket – a sort of flying machine – and they landed right up there on the moon, which is like here, only there's just rocks and no air to breathe. And they brought bits of it back with them."

"A flying machine? A machine? What's that?"

"A machine is something that works without you having to pull it or push it. A bit like how the mill down in the village does the work women used to do with a quern. We have machines for lots of things. Some can carry us about without horses, and there are machines that can fly, and boats that don't need sails or oars."

He looked overwhelmed and slightly disbelieving, but he fastened on something that hadn't occurred to me. "Yet you chose to be here, instead of there. You prefer it here." His eyes narrowed again. "Tell me the bad things about your world."

An easy task. "There are too many people. Everywhere's too crowded. The machines have to run on hard surfaces so there are roads everywhere – all over the country. Everyone has to go to work to earn money to pay for their houses. Not like here where you can just build one where you like. Everything revolves around money. I worked in a library, a place full of books, every day from morning until evening. I was saving up to buy a house of my own. If you don't earn money, you can't buy food or pay for your house. Mostly only farmers grow food. And there's lots of pollution."

"I know what a library is." He sounded affronted. "But I don't know this word pollution."

The relief at having at last been honest with him loosened my tongue. I explained at length about pollution, which led me into the realms of science that I knew very little about. However, as Arthur knew even less, I reasoned that a few mistakes on my part wouldn't matter. We ended up back on healthcare eventually.

"So you see why I don't want Mother Nara putting her dirty

hands anywhere near me when I go into labor," I said. "In your time – no, in our time, lots of women die because they catch infections from dirty hands during the delivery. I want someone clean, someone who knows what she's doing, someone who knows a bit about a woman's insides."

He put his arm around me. "We'll go to my town of Caer Pensa. I've a house there, not so big as Cadwy's palace, but it's a house with a hypocaust and baths and servants. Different from here. We'll take a part of the army so we're well defended and leave the rest here with Cei. I want you to have all the care you'd be having if you were back in your own time."

I rested my head on his shoulder. "I don't need mollycoddling, but in this cold some underfloor heating would be nice. And a house with baths would be wonderful."

So the next day we rode to Caer Pensa.

Chapter Nine

C AER PENSA WAS only about eight miles from Din Cadan along muddy cart tracks that eventually led to the paved Roman Fosse Way. High, well-built stone walls surrounded a sizeable settlement of some twenty acres. Within these walls, townhouses constructed over a century ago decayed gently alongside more recent wattle and daub buildings. Between the houses, cabbage patches and root vegetables grew, and pens of pigs and chickens squeezed into whatever space was left. Outside the walls clustered more houses, running out along the road in both directions, and interspersed with industry. The air hung heavy with the smells of the tanneries and the smoke from forges and kilns.

Arthur's house, the Domus Regis, was a large townhouse whose doors opened onto one side of the old forum. The flaking, plaster-covered walls and terracotta roofs betrayed its Roman origins. Alongside it, a stable block of later construction squatted low and thatched, like an old British woman beside an ascetic Roman. Here was where Arthur's men and their horses were accommodated.

I liked the house straight away. Especially the hypocaust, which kept every room pleasantly warm even in this, the drear end of winter. Unlike the Imperial Palace at Viroconium, the house possessed an atmosphere of cozy intimacy, with most of its rooms opening off the garden courtyard or the atrium. I settled in with no trouble and made the most of the small suite of still-usable baths.

I rode the eight miles there on Alezan, and kept up my riding when the weather permitted, exploring the countryside that surrounded the town and farmlands with Arthur, or, more often, Merlin. Marshes abounded, so we always took a local man familiar with the safer paths. Higher ground snaked between the wetlands, with stunted thorn trees and willows dotting the landscape. Sheep and cattle grazed these rough pastures during daylight hours, but were brought in every night to the safety of their pens.

Now that my condition was known, Merlin refused to let me gallop as I'd done the day he'd guessed my secret. Instead, I had to be content with keeping to a steady pace as we explored the surrounding countryside while spring's warm fingers crept across the land.

The days were lengthening nicely, and spring flowers had begun to show their delicate faces on the grassy field banks and in the meadows, when Cei came riding down the road from Din Cadan. I was on my hands and knees in the courtyard garden of the King's House planting primroses, which some of the younger warriors had dug up for me in the woods. At the sound of footsteps, I looked up to see him striding toward me along the stone-flagged pathway.

"Milady." He executed a generous bow as I got to my feet. "I trust all is well with you and –" He paused and vaguely indicated my still nearly flat belly, "—the babe."

I smiled a welcome to him. Of all Arthur's men, his brother, Cei, the huge ginger-headed warrior, was my favorite. On first meeting him I'd thought him as tough as he looked. However, now that I knew him better, I'd discovered that beneath his gruff exterior lurked a bit of a softie. He was very attached to his own son, Rhiwallon, a lanky ten-year-old who saw himself as a budding warrior, and was equally fond of his nephew, Llacheu. I often spotted him off with the boys practicing archery or sword fighting, or simply playing games, and I liked him very much for that.

I put my hand on my belly. "The sickness has gone at last, so I'm feeling much better and able to eat my breakfast every day. How is Coventina?" I'd been sad to bid farewell to his wife, whom I'd made friends with at Din Cadan. Cei tried hard to conceal his love for her, but it was impossible. Everyone knew they were a couple the gods had smiled on. His only disappointment was that ever since she'd had a miscarriage when Rhiwallon was two, there'd been no further pregnancies. Because of this, and his love for his younger brother, I assumed, he was interested in my progress in his own shy way.

"That's good." He gave me a bashful smile as we were discussing women's things. "Coventina's well. She told me to tell you she was sick all the way through with our son, but that usually it passes after a few months."

Sitting down on the wall of the fountain in the center of the garden, I stretched out my legs which had grown cramped with kneeling to plant flowers. "Sit beside me." I patted the stone coping.

He sat, a little stiffly. "I'm looking for Arthur, really, but it's good to see you...to find that you're doing well here. A military fortress like Din Cadan is no place for a queen. Especially not a queen who's, er...in your condition."

"Is there anything wrong at Din Cadan?" I was suddenly worried, perhaps because of Cei's awkwardness. However, if there had been a serious problem, Cei's open, honest face couldn't have hidden it.

He shook his head emphatically. "No, nothing. Spring ploughing is just starting, lambing is underway already, and we've had a few calves out in the grazing lands. The houses for the new warriors are coming on quickly now we've the weather for building. The boys are growing fast. I'm sure they grow quicker in the spring. Rhiwallon's had his braccae lengthened for the second time since autumn. Llacheu's learned to jump up on his pony without a mounting block."

I laughed. These were the things that mattered to Cei: that the agricultural year should be proceeding unhindered and the boys he loved should be doing the same.

"So, what brings you here?"

He frowned. "I've had…" he began and then stopped and bit his lip. I stayed silent, waiting for him to continue. "*We've* had a visitation."

His reticence puzzled me. "What sort of a visitation?"

His Adam's apple bobbed up and down as he swallowed. On his lap, his hands bunched into fists and he deliberately relaxed them. "A messenger from our mother."

"Oh." I knew next to nothing about Eigr, the mother of Cei and Arthur, bar what the legends in my old world had told me. She'd been married to Gorlois, Lord of Din Tagel, when Uthyr Pendragon, then king of Dumnonia, took a fancy to her. Gorlois ended up dead, Uthyr got the woman he wanted, and Arthur was born. Cei had been three years old when his father, Gorlois, died.

One cold night in Caer Baddan, on our way to Viroconium, Merlin had told me that Arthur hadn't seen his mother since he was seven or eight. She and his father, Uthyr, had fought ferociously over his future, and Eigr had taken herself off to Din Tagel in a huff, along with her youngest child, baby Morgawse. The old slave woman, Breanna, brought him up, until his father banished him from Viroconium to Din Cadan as a rebellious teenager. But, as far as I knew, his mother had made no effort to get in touch with him since he was a child.

"She wants to see Arthur." Cei kept his eyes on his fingers, which were now digging into the flesh of his thighs through his thick braccae.

I was surprised. "Will he want to see *her*? Do you want to see her?"

He looked up. He had startlingly blue eyes. I wondered if his mother might have the same blue eyes. He was nothing like his younger half-brother. His thick, rusty-colored hair, high-cheekboned face, wide, strong shoulders, and big-boned, muscular frame contrasted strongly with Arthur's narrower horseman's build, and his dark eyes and hair. He shrugged. "I saw her two years ago. She rules my lands, but I visit every so often to keep an eye on her. She's a good steward."

"Has Arthur never been with you?"

He shook his head. "He's always had an excuse. I don't think he's ever forgiven her for abandoning him to Cadwy's cruelty."

"But she abandoned you, also."

"I was older, nearly a man grown."

I raised my eyebrows. *Ten or eleven*. Still a child, in my opinion.

He went on. "Arthur needed her more than I did. He needed her to protect him from Cadwy. I didn't. Cadwy had nothing against me. I hadn't usurped his place in their father's affections. But whether it was against her will or not, she left Arthur with Uthyr and at the mercy of his half-brother. It was me that heard him crying tears of anger and frustration into his pillow at night, after Cadwy had given him a beating, and when he thought no one was listening."

I tried to remember what Merlin had told me about this. A long time had passed since our talk and much had happened in the meantime.

"Why did she do it?"

"Hah!" He uttered a bark of rough laughter. "She and Uthyr fought over what Arthur was to become. He was a second son and she wanted him to go into the church. Uthyr thought otherwise. She told him that if he didn't, Arthur would indeed become the king Uthyr wanted him to be." He paused. "But he would be betrayed by his own kin, and his kingdom would fall in rivers of blood. She'd seen it in her scrying glass. She has the Sight – or claims she has. Uthyr didn't believe her. They fought. I was there. I saw them and so did Arthur. The whole of Viroconium must have heard their shouts. He won, of course. He was the king. He took Arthur, and she locked him out of her bedchamber.

And that was the beginning of the end."

I shifted uneasily, and he kept going. "She packed her things and left Viroconium. She wanted to take all her children, but Uthyr would only let her take Morgawse, who still needed her mother. She left Arthur, Morgana and me behind. She turned her back on us all, but it was Arthur who was most affected. He thought it was his fault she'd gone. Not once did she ask for us to visit, not once did she come back to Viroconium. She's stayed in Din Tagel all this time. She never talks of Arthur when I visit. They've been dead to one another for sixteen years."

"Yet you visit her."

His lips came together in a thin line. "She rules my lands for me. When I became a warrior, Uthyr couldn't stop me from going. I found she ruled well. I was still half a boy myself, but I recognized that I could leave her in charge, because where I wanted to be was serving the High King, and near my brother. Someone had to stand between him and Cadwy."

I'd never before realized how Cei saw himself as Arthur's protector. It made me see their relationship in quite a different light.

"And do you still think he needs protecting?" I asked.

Cei's mouth widened into a rueful grin. "Sometimes." His eyes met mine.

"From his mother?"

"Perhaps."

I guessed there was more to tell, but at that moment Arthur came hurrying into the courtyard garden from the public rooms at the front of the house where he did his daily business with the magistrate of the town. He was wearing his customary dark tunic and braccae and carried the simple gold circlet he wore as a crown in one hand.

Cei got to his feet. "Brother." The two of them embraced.

"I came as soon as I heard you were here." Arthur's eyes were alight with pleasure. "But the magistrate here goes on and on, and it's hard to shut him up politely."

"The perils of being a king," Cei said, laughing, and clapped his brother on the back so hard Arthur staggered.

"What brings you here?" Arthur asked.

Cei sobered on the instant. "We have a summons. A messenger came to Din Cadan from Din Tagel. Our mother requests our presence."

The sparkle went out of Arthur's eyes, and his dark brows came together in a heavy frown. "She requests our presence?" His voice rose in a mix of astonishment and anger. "A summons? After all these years of nothing?"

Cei had the look of a man who'd been expecting this reaction – resigned and sympathetic. He laid a hand on Arthur's arm. "She says she's asking to see you because now your father is dead, and you're a king, there's no one to stop you coming." He glanced at me. "And she wants to meet your queen."

Arthur's eyes flashed with anger. "So after all this time she thinks she can click her fingers, and I'll dance to her tune?"

Cei shifted uncomfortably. "I don't think she means it to seem like that." It felt as though he were making excuses for her. He probably was.

Arthur shook off his brother's hand. "Not a word. Not a single word – ever. She might have been dead. And now she's curious about my wife, she thinks she'll send a message, and I'll be at her beck and call." He walked away from us, halted abruptly, then spun on his heel and returned, fists balled at his sides. "After everything she did and said – after how she manipulated me as a child – after leaving you and me to our fate – she thinks a simple summons will wipe all that away?"

Cei remained silent. Probably he couldn't think of anything to say in reply to this tirade. I sat motionless on the fountain's edge and watched them both.

Arthur walked away again, this time nearly to the bathhouse before he turned back toward us. "Why now?" His eyes narrowed in anger. "Why choose now to show an interest? What makes now so different from then?"

Cei's eyes slid toward me. "The Ring Maiden." He kept his voice low. "She knows you have the Ring Maiden as your queen."

Chapter Ten

T HE NEXT MORNING, we took the westbound Fosse Way out of Caer Pensa on our way to Din Tagel. Ahead of us lay Caerwysg, the Roman town which would one day become modern Exeter.

Dressed in the tunic and braccae in which I was most comfortable, I rode Alezan at the front of the heavily armed line of warriors strung out along the old Roman road. Arthur sent scouts up ahead of us and kept a few men further back as a rear guard. Every man was on the alert for sudden attack. We were entering, Arthur told me, the time of year when Saxon raids were more likely to happen. The seas were calmer, the weather more conducive to sailing, and men everywhere were hungry as winter dragged tardy feet toward its close.

Against my will, I'd been kitted out with my own mail shirt. This must have weighed a good twenty pounds, and made me hot and sweaty in the mild spring weather. A squall of rain that drenched us for twenty minutes brought a welcome relief, the rain plastering my hair to my head and trickling down my neck.

The paved Roman road led south-west past villages encircled by sturdy palisade fences, where excited children came running out to gaze open-mouthed upon the splendor of their king and his army. Between the villages lay farms whose inhabitants watched us with suspicion from behind their meager fortification of banks and ditches. From time to time we passed the ruins of abandoned settlements, some just charred footings, their acrid stink pursuing us along the road. Had they burnt down by accident or had raiders set them alight? No one remained to tell us.

In late afternoon, we forded a river beside the collapsed ruins of a bridge. The supports still stood, but the wood between them had long since rotted away. Posts on either bank marked where to cross. The water was so deep it would have made my feet wet had I not kicked them out of my stirrups and hooked my legs up high like a modern jockey. After that, the land rose steadily as we headed toward the south coast, and as evening fell, we reached the still inhabited remains of a small town beside the overgrown ruins of a Roman military fortress.

At least Arthur and I got a room with a proper bed in the ramshackle inn, unlike most of our men, who ended up bedded down in the stables and the barn beside it, or on the taproom floor. From the way they were holding their heads the next morning, I suspected the ones in the taproom had partaken too heavily of the barrels of cider belonging to the indignant innkeeper. But when Cei paid him generously, it put a smile back on his face.

For our second day of riding, we had drier weather and covered the twenty-eight miles from the nameless little town to Caerwysg in just under six hours. My knowledge of modern day Exeter's importance had led me to expect it to resemble Viroconium's decayed and crumbling version of a Roman city. What we found had more in common with the tumbledown town we'd left that morning.

As we rode down toward its once-imposing gate towers, Arthur must have seen the disappointment written on my face. The town, encircled by a much robbed-out stone wall, sat on the high ground above the eastern bank of the modern river Exe, which Arthur pronounced as Oosg. Entering by the unguarded east gate, we rode along the main street of the town toward the central forum, the tumbledown walls echoing the clatter of our horses' hooves back at us. Not a soul was to be seen. We'd come upon a ghost town.

I looked a question across at Arthur.

"Fled inland," he said. "The river here gives too easy access to Saxon pirates. Bringing their ships right up to the old wharves is easy for them. It's long since anyone lived here."

Scarcely a building had a roof on it, and the spring growth of new weeds was already pushing up between the cracked paving stones. Brambles and ivy shrouded the buildings, and the walls of many houses, attacked by the weather, had collapsed. A few stray cats and dogs slunk away from the sight and sound of us, and we heard distant running feet down side alleys. The only people who might be living here now would be the homeless and destitute.

In the forum, we halted. Here had once stood the basilica, but now that was long gone. Instead, broken columns pointed at the late afternoon sky like bony fingers, and the marble facing from the buildings lay in scattered chunks on the uneven weed-strewn paving stones. At some point, someone had constructed a small, wattle-and-daub church right in the center. The blackened thatch of its roof was much in need of repair, and clustered close around its mossy walls were the unmistakable humps of old graves.

"We'll make camp here," Arthur said, as his advance guard came trotting to join us from the street opposite, gesturing that all was clear.

Once we'd unsaddled our horses and fed them the crushed oats we carried in our packs, the men looted what wood still remained in the nearest ruined buildings and started a blazing fire outside the church. Arthur and I found ourselves in the center of the camp, his men spread out around us. Sitting on chunks of broken masonry, we ate a cold supper of bread, salted pork and onions, washed down with cider, warm from being carried next to the hot bodies of our horses.

With the fall of evening came the cold, a reminder winter wasn't far behind us. After Cei had organized the guard rota, we wrapped ourselves in our thick cloaks, preparing to sleep on the hard ground. Bone weary after two long days of riding, I snuggled up to Arthur.

When I awoke, it was still dark, but a pale line in the east suggested dawn was on its way. For a moment, I lay wondering where I was, before the hard ground and the cold reminded me. Arthur had rolled away from me in his sleep, one arm thrown over his head. Wide awake now, and cold, I heard again the noise that must have woken me, and turned my head in its direction. A faint scraping, as if a door were being pushed open.

Arthur stirred as if he too heard it in his sleep, but he didn't waken.

The abandoned church stood only yards away from us, and as I peered into the darkness, something seemed to move near the broken door. What was it? Darker than the darkness, a small shadow shifted, creeping toward the embers of our fire and closer to me.

A child. A little girl with long, ratty hair and a thin, hungry face. As she approached the fire, the soft glow of the still hot embers reflected faintly on her skin. She was looking at the remains of our evening meal: a few wooden plates and the bags the food had been carried in. Kneeling beside one of the saddle-bags, with well-practiced stealth, she rummaged inside.

I watched.

Finding some bread, she broke off a chunk and stuffed it into her mouth, but the rest she set on a piece of rag laid out on the ground beside her. Diving into the bag again, she came out with a lump of hard sausage and then a couple of small onions. These joined the bread on her rag and, seemingly satisfied, she dragged the corners together to make a bag and scrambled to her feet.

"Don't go," I whispered.

Her head turned toward me, eyes wide with terror, frozen like a rabbit in a car's headlights.

"I'm a friend," I said quickly. "I mean you no harm."

Beside me, Arthur stirred again and rolled toward me, his arm reaching and not finding me.

The little girl, who couldn't have been more than eight or

nine, got over her shock in an instant and sprang to her feet, but as she did so she tripped over the straps of the saddle bag and went sprawling over the nearest sleeping warrior. He woke with a start, and before the girl could pick herself up, seized her by both arms and held her fast.

Letting out a single terrified cry, she struggled like a trapped wildcat. The man had to fight to hang onto her.

Arthur came awake at the commotion. "What's going on?" The drawn sword in his hand shimmered in the firelight. "Is there an intruder?"

All over our camp the men started to stir.

The warrior who had grasped the little girl stood up, dragging her to her feet. He kept a tight grip, holding her at arm's length as she tried to kick out at him with her bare feet. "Yes, milord." The warrior gave a grunt as her foot collided with his shins. "And I 'ave 'er 'ere."

There were a few minutes of hectic activity as the now wide-awake warriors checked for more intruders and threw wood on the fire, making flames leap toward the inky sky. Then Arthur turned his attention to the child, who'd dropped her stolen goods in her efforts to escape.

He looked her up and down, and she glared back at him through a tangle of dirty hair, her lower lip jutting in defiance.

"Well," he said in an amused voice, "you seem to have caused quite an uproar, sneaking about in the middle of the night. Didn't your parents ever tell you to steer well clear of mounted men? Not all soldiers are as kind to little girls as mine."

The child spat a gob of phlegm at him. It hit his left boot.

Arthur shook his head. "That's no way to behave when you're a prisoner of a superior force. If I were you, I'd be on my best behavior." He still didn't sound angry with the child.

I spoke up. "Look at her. Look at how thin she is. She came here looking for food."

One of Arthur's men picked up the tumbled rag and its contents. "She did, that. And 'ere it is. She were stealing from us."

"From me!" called the owner of the saddle bag who'd found it open by now. "I'll teach 'er not to go stealin' from the warriors what keeps 'er safe. Little varmint. Give 'er 'ere."

"She's starving," I interjected in anger. "Look at her, why don't you?"

The sky was fast lightening in the east, now a paler shade than when I'd woken. Dawn wasn't far off.

Arthur looked back at the girl, who gave another convulsive wriggle. "If I ask him to release your arms, you have to promise me you won't try to run." His tone, though gentle, held a veiled threat. "Because if you try that, you'll be caught again straight away and my men won't be as gentle with you a second time."

The girl's eyes flicked back and forth over the men who surrounded her. She gave a quick nod, and Arthur indicated to her captor to release her. In relief, the man let her go, and took half a step back. Like a cornered animal, the girl stood there, her narrow chest, scarcely concealed by her ragged tunic, rising and falling much too rapidly.

I came to stand beside Arthur, hoping she wouldn't spit on me, too. "What's your name?" I used my gentlest tone in an effort to reassure her she'd come to no harm if she cooperated. "Mine's Gwen."

She licked her lips. She really was the dirtiest child I'd ever seen. "Nola." Her voice was low and harsh, matching the way she looked.

"Where do you live, Nola?"

Now I was closer to her I could see the emaciation of her body, her arms and legs like sticks.

"'Ere." Her small hand encompassed the forum and surrounding buildings.

"Where are your parents?"

"Ent got none." The harshness in her voice lessened a little.

"You must have had parents once," Arthur interrupted. "Where do you come from? No one lives here in Caerwysg now – nor have they for generations."

She eyed him with scorn. "Us do."

"Are there more of you?" I asked. Surely this little orphan couldn't be on her own – there must be others here or a child her age would never have survived.

She shifted uneasily, aware she'd dropped herself in it. "Dunno."

I thought of the poor children I'd seen begging on the streets of Caer Baddan. I'd vowed that if I stayed with Arthur and became his queen, I'd help their plight. And I'd done nothing. Events had overtaken me, but that was really just an excuse. Those children would be in as bad a way as Nola after months of winter's cold. They might even be dead.

But right now, I could do something for the children here.

I turned to Arthur. "We have to feed them." I put my hand on his arm. "We have to help these children. They've got no one. If we don't help them, they'll die."

There was a long silence. All the men were watching and listening.

"Please," I held his gaze. "For me."

There were no gains to be made with helping orphan children. No lands to win, no riches. Could I persuade him toward altruism in a time when it might never have existed? I held my breath.

Arthur gave a shrug. "The Queen is softened in her heart by her present condition, and wishes to help this child and any others that might be hiding here. Children with no parents and no one to look after them. I will grant her wish, and we will feed these children."

There was a general murmur amongst his men, but it was hard to tell if it was in agreement or dissent. Charity, I'd discovered, was not a common trait in the fifth century. The child looked round at them from under her unkempt, and without doubt verminous, thatch of hair, the whites of her eyes showing bright in her grimy face. Had she even understood?

I smiled at her. "Where are your friends? If you have friends, you need to call them because we're going to feed you. They can come, and we'll feed them, as well."

Her lips came together in a thin line of defiance.

I bent down to her level. "Do you understand, Nola? We're going to feed you all."

She shook her head. "I dursn't trust 'ee." Her voice emerged in a whisper. "I seen soldiers 'ere afore. Them yeller 'airs took me big sister an' kilt some of us. Thass wot these soldiers're goin' ter do ter me."

"We're not Yellow Hairs." I kept my voice gentle and un-threatening. "This is the king. Your king. His soldiers are not like the Yellow Hairs. They don't kill children."

Seemingly determined not to believe me, she just shook her head again.

I turned to Arthur. "We need to show her we're different. We must feed her."

I put out a hand. "Here, come with me, and I'll show you we mean you no harm."

She looked at my hand for a long moment, then with great diffidence, put her own filthy little paw into it. I led her to the fire where some of the smaller lumps of masonry made seats, and we sat down together.

Merlin brought us food, and I gave the little girl a hunk of bread. She set about it like the starving waif she was. Merlin cut her some cold meat and she stuffed that down, too, then took the wineskin of cider I passed her and swallowed a big gulp. Perhaps she'd decided that even if we intended to kill her or kidnap her for a slave, she might as well take advantage of the offered food before fate overtook her.

Arthur came and sat down at the fire, keeping his distance, because she really smelled bad and was probably crawling with lice. He watched her eat. All around us, the camp was springing back into life as the men breakfasted and brushed off their horses, ready to leave. Above the ruins of the city, the rising sun had chased the night away.

Everything we put in front of the girl she ate, until she couldn't possibly have any room left. And then she ate some more. Beneath her tiny ribcage, her stomach bulged. At last, she wiped her mouth with the back of her hand and belched in loud appreciation.

I laughed, and she jerked her head up sharply, as though laughter was a sound she'd never heard before. "Better?" I asked. "Do you want to deny your friends the same luxury you've had? Go and get them, Nola, and we'll feed them all."

She looked across at Arthur, eyes wary, instinctively knowing he was the leader and the one with the final say. He was just finishing his own breakfast, and gave her a friendly nod. "Go on, there's food enough for all of you. You can come and go as you wish. No one will stop you. But I do suggest you come back. My wife has a mind to help you."

Nola got to her feet and stood looking at me and Arthur, as though in two minds what to do. No one made a move to hold her. She took a few steps away from us, as if wary that when she moved someone would grab her. The warriors kept on doing their morning chores, most of them ignoring her. She walked through them, stepping with delicate care over their belongings. At the edge of our camp, she broke into a run and disappeared down a dark alley between the remains of the nearest buildings.

"She won't come back," Arthur said, getting to his feet. "She's had a meal and she doesn't trust us. We won't see her again. We'd better get our horses saddled."

I looked around at the ruined city. What sort of place was this for children to live? How could they scratch a living here? And what had brought them to such a fate? I wiped a tear away from the corner of my eye and went to saddle my horse.

But Arthur was wrong. Just as we were preparing to mount up, with dirt kicked over our fire to put it out, Nola returned. And with her came four more scrawny children. The oldest couldn't have been more than twelve and the youngest barely five. They emerged from behind the columns of the basilica, thin and wan, like dirty little ghosts.

Leaving Alezan, I approached them slowly, aware that any sudden move might make them all turn and run. And if they did that, death could only be around the corner.

"Nola." I smiled at her in what I hoped was friendly reassurance. "You brought your friends. I'm so glad. We've food for all of you. Come." Turning away from her, I walked back to the dying fire without looking to see if they followed. They did. We found them bread and cold meat and more cider and each one of them ate ravenously, standing near the still hot embers, their pinched little faces beginning to glow from the heat.

It was fully light by the time they'd all finished, and the warriors were growing impatient to be off.

Arthur came to my side and put a hand on my shoulder. "We have to go."

I looked at the five children, who were holding their thin hands out to the fire to warm them. "We can't just leave them."

He sighed. "What else can we do? We're soldiers. They're children. The two don't go well together."

My hand went to my belly, thinking of our own child growing there. "If we leave them here, they'll die. Maybe not tomorrow, now we've fed them. But look how thin they are. They can't have eaten anything decent in days, weeks even. If we leave them, I'm sure of one thing – they'll die before very long."

He sighed again. "So what do you want to do? Take them with us? With an army? Five children?"

I nodded.

He put his hands on his hips. I held his gaze. The silence between us drew out. I won. With a bark of wry laughter, he turned and called to some of his men to come over. "We're taking these children with us. Each one of you is to take one up behind you on your horse. Quickly now."

The children were somewhat more difficult to persuade than the warriors. For a start, they thought we were going to kidnap them into slavery – or eat them. I overheard the smallest child, a boy, whisper this question to Nola, who though not the oldest, appeared to be the leader.

I called them to me, and to my surprise, they all came. "We're going to help you," I said. "The king is my husband, and what he says, goes. None of these soldiers will hurt you. I promise. We're going to take you somewhere safe and warm where you'll have food and clean clothes – and a bath. But you can't walk there. You need to ride, like us. A soldier will take each one of you and you'll be quite safe. We can't leave you here. There's no food for you and you're starving. Please let us help you."

Eventually, we got the children up behind the soldiers who'd been set to take them. Arthur had deliberately picked those men who had children of their own, and I noticed that the littlest boy was not behind his soldier but cradled in front of the man, where if he fell asleep he wouldn't fall off.

Satisfied at last that I was going to make a difference in Arthur's world, however small, I mounted Alezan, and, at Arthur's side, rode out of the ruins of Caerwysg on the road to Din Tagel and the looming meeting with Eigr.

Chapter Eleven

W E LEFT THE town by its northern gates, or rather, through the gap in the walls where the gates had once stood. Time had reduced the towers to broken walls and piles of rubble, and the wooden gates were long gone. Glancing back along the river, I spotted in the distance the ancient wooden bridge that still spanned the wide expanse of the tidal River Exe to the west of the town. The tide was out, and the exposed mudflats glistened in the sunlight.

Merlin brought his horse up beside mine. "Impressive, isn't it?"

I nodded. "Is it Roman? How on earth did they build it?"

He grinned. "See those timbers? They took tree trunks and drove them into the river bed. No one knows how they did it. But the angle they're at was to counteract the effect of the current." He twisted in his saddle to point. "The timbers of the roadway had to be strong enough to support wagons coming into the market, or an army going out to fight."

Even from this distance, I could make out gaps in the timbers. And the barriers at the sides of the bridge looked flimsy in the few places where they still remained. Presumably they'd been washed away by high tides and flood waters. The bridge didn't look as if it had been used for many years, possibly not since the Romans left.

"Thank goodness we don't have to go that way."

He laughed. "That road heads too far south, otherwise no

doubt we'd have tried it."

Turning my back on the bridge's scary possibilities, I looked up the road we'd taken, which headed inland, roughly north-westwards. The Devon countryside in my time is beautiful, but here, unspoiled by centuries of development, it rolled away before us in all its wild primordial glory. We rode through thick forest, bursting into fresh green life, on a road that hugged the high ground above the Exe, until at last we came to a spot shallow enough for our horses to ford. To my surprise, someone had lined the crossing with flat, square-cut slabs, raising it a little above the level of the rest of the riverbed. The water was only knee deep on our horses this time.

Cei, who'd come to ride beside Arthur and me, spoke up. "When there's been heavy rain, you can't cross here at all. This river runs in spate all too often and can be deadly."

I guessed he knew this route well, as he'd been so often to visit his mother.

Arthur, who was becoming more and more silent as the day wore on, didn't bother to answer.

On the western banks of the Exe, the land began to climb steadily, and the forest thickened. As well as a substantial advance guard, we had a reinforced rear guard, and everyone was even more on the alert than before. Forest, Arthur told me, was ideal for foot soldiers to stage an ambush and not the best place for cavalry to fight to their advantage.

To my great relief, the graveled Roman road emerged at last onto rough grazing and moorland dotted with sheep, where small farms clustered on the open ground. Surely, if there were this many settlements, then we must be in safer territory. To our southwest rose the great hump of land that was Dartmoor in my time, only now its rolling slopes of heather and gorse seemed to stretch a lot further than I was used to, stretching over most of the land we could see. Amongst the scrub and bracken, green oases nestled in hollows and deep river valleys, where the farmers had cleared the moorland for grazing and crops.

About evening, with all the children now carried in front of the warriors, their heads lolling in exhaustion, we came to a faded villa surrounded by a sprawling and lively village. Our vanguard had warned the inhabitants and the villa owner of our imminent arrival, and they all came out to welcome us. The waiting hands of several burly peasants lifted the sleepy children down and handed them over to the villa servants.

The villa owner introduced himself as Cahal and found accommodation for all our horses and men, and then invited Arthur, Cei, Merlin and me into his house. I was exhausted, but, after a bath and some food, began to feel much better and was alert enough to listen as Arthur negotiated the future of our five new members. For a small sum, Cahal would keep them for us, wash them, delouse and deflea them, and give them clean clothes, and on our return from Din Tagel we would collect them again and take them back with us to Caer Pensa.

Two days later, with Arthur having begrudgingly agreed to also do something to help the poor children I'd seen at Caer Baddan on our return, we rode down the steep rocky valley that led to the fortress of Din Tagel.

DIN TAGEL IS a high, rocky promontory sticking out into the Atlantic Ocean on the North Cornish coast, reached from the village in my time down a tarmacked path through a steep-sided valley. Straddling what was once a land-bridge are the two halves of a medieval castle that has nothing to do with the legends of King Arthur. To reach the inner ward of the castle, the modern visitor has to cross the sort of foot-bridge Indiana Jones would be used to, because the land that linked them has long since fallen into the sea.

Fifteen hundred years before I was to first see it for myself in my own past, the narrow land-bridge still existed, and the medieval castle had not yet been built. Instead, a ditch and bank surmounted by a high palisade wall blocked our way. Beyond, on the steep-sided promontory itself, the fortress buildings that made up Cei's stronghold clustered against the inhospitable rocky backdrop of the island. Somewhere, beyond that wall, I would finally meet Eigr. Nervous tension knotted my stomach.

Again, our vanguard had reached there before us, and the guards on the gates threw them open as soon as they saw us approaching to allow us to pass inside unhindered. I gazed around. Dark Age Din Tagel didn't seem too different from Din Cadan, except that the only side needing defending was the landward side – the steep cliffs and the sea provided enough defenses on all the other sides. The sound of the waves crashing on the rocks in the cove below was a constant reminder of this.

We dismounted, and men came to take our horses to the long low stable buildings that stood on this side of the land-bridge. For a moment, Arthur stood looking uncertain as they led away his horse, and I realized with a jolt that this place was stranger to him than it was to me. This must be the first time he'd been here. Legend had Din Tagel down as the place he was born, but I had no idea if this were true. Perhaps I'd ask him later.

Cei came up behind him and slapped him encouragingly on the back. "Come, brother, best to get this over with straightaway."

Arthur turned to me, his dark eyes somber and brooding. "It's you she wants to see, not me." Was that a faint hint of resentment in his voice? Could his apparent reluctance to come here hide quite different feelings?

I doubted very much that she wanted to see me more than him. What mother would not want to see her long estranged son once the controlling father who'd prevented this had died? Had it never occurred to Arthur that it was his father who'd kept her from him? Along the journey I'd been thinking about this summons. All those years when Uthyr Pendragon had been living, Arthur's mother had supposedly made no effort to see her younger son. Yet now, with Uthyr barely cold in his grave, and Arthur elevated to kingship, she'd sent a message as soon as the spring weather set in. I was more than curious about her motivations, and about meeting a woman I'd read so much about in legends.

We passed between the houses, barns and middens of the fortress, heading toward the looming bulk of the hall. Blowing hard from the west, the sea wind snatched away the smoke rising from the rooftops and tugged at our cloaks.

Eigr was standing alone on the wooden platform just outside her hall, holding her cloak tight around herself. A tall, white-haired woman, upright as a pillar, she held her chin high, and an air of cold unapproachability clung to her like a second skin.

Arthur halted several paces short, and I stopped beside him. Disregarding her icy front, Cei strode up and seized her in his strong arms to hug her close. "Mother, you look well. Winter's not treated you so badly." He planted a kiss on her pale cheek.

Over his shoulder, her pale blue eyes, like Cei's in color but not in warmth, regarded me stonily. Arthur reached out and took my hand, his fingers interlacing with mine in a gesture of solidarity I felt grateful for. I determined to be strong, glad of this physical support. Or maybe it was me supporting him. I couldn't be sure.

Cei released his mother and stood to one side, giving her a clear view of Arthur and me. I made a little bow. After all, she was my husband's mother, and had once been a queen, like me. Arthur inclined his head infinitesimally, but from what I could see of his profile, he appeared to be scowling. As for her, hunger filled her eyes, gnawing hunger, perhaps for a son she'd been driven apart from so long ago.

"Arthur." Just one word that cut through the chill spring air. Overhead, a bevy of gulls rose shrieking from the cliffs and were caught on the sea wind to be sent somersaulting away.

"Mother." He answered her with a matching single word. I was reminded sharply of the way he'd greeted Cadwy at his father's deathbed.

She held his gaze for a good minute, before shifting her eyes to me. "So, this is your queen. The long awaited Lady of the Ring." She didn't sound that pleased to see me.

His hand tightened around mine. "It is."

Another silence ensued.

"Shall we go inside?" Cei put in, his voice edged with discomfort. He liked people to get along. "It's blowing a gale out here."

Eigr seemed to remember herself with a start. She'd been staring at me as though seeing something quite different, looking through me into the far distance, reading my inner thoughts, perhaps. After all, people said she possessed the Sight. I tried hard to think nice things about her, just in case.

"Of course. I'm remiss. Come inside. Your queen must be fatigued after so long a journey." She looked straight at my flat belly. "Her being with child."

My free hand went to my belly in a telltale protective movement.

I'd have sworn nobody could have got a message to her over the winter to tell her I was pregnant. Could she tell by just looking, or was it the Sight? Common sense inclined me not to believe that anyone could foresee the future or read minds, but then again, I'd got here by magic, so who was I to quibble?

We followed her inside the hall – a smaller version of the one at Din Cadan, aisled, with pillars down either side supporting a thatched roof, and divided widthways by a wall two thirds of the way down. A fire burnt in the central firepit, and the pile of wiry-coated hounds who slept beside it stirred to get up and lazily sniff us newcomers.

Although there were no windows, the hall was well lit by torches burning in brackets on the pillars, and now I found time to take a better look at Eigr by their light. She was a beautiful woman, even at her age, which, despite her white hair, couldn't have been much above her early forties. Still slender, despite her many pregnancies, she wore a gold-filigreed belt over her fine, green wool dress that minimized the slight thickening of her waist. Now that we were out of the wind, she shrugged the fur-lined cloak from her slender shoulders and tossed it onto a table.

"You came." She was looking at Arthur. "You came to me at last." A hint of triumph edged her voice, and a quaver. Could she be close to tears? I had a sudden vivid picture of her arguing with Uthyr Pendragon over the possession of their children. She would have been a formidable opponent.

Arthur didn't reply; he was still wearing his cloak despite the warmth inside the hall, almost as if he were prepared to make a hurried departure if things went wrong.

Her face softened, or seemed to, but it might only have been the effect of the golden torchlight on her skin. She half raised her hand to him. "I have missed you."

Arthur still didn't answer. His eyes remained as stony as hers. She let her hand drop to her side.

It seemed she wasn't prepared to take no for an answer, however. "I know you're angry." Her voice carried through the empty hall. "I know you hate me for what I did. The reason I've asked you to come here and visit me is because I want to explain to you why. We need to start again." She paused. "You are my son." She was almost pleading.

He stayed silent – a technique I'd used many times. Usually the recipient begins to gabble.

"Food!" Cei said, the one forced to gabble in this instance. "We need food and drink before the Queen faints from starvation. I'll send for food." He marched to a low door at the side of the hall and flung it open. "Hoy!" I heard him shout. "Your lord is here and so is your king. We need refreshments. Now! Get about it, you idlers, or I'll have you chucked over the cliffs."

I doubted Cei, with his inner core of soft putty, would do anything of the sort, but as a threat, it worked. Straightaway several servants came running into the hall bearing trays of cold meat, baskets of bread, bowls of olives, a wheel of cheese and some pitchers of wine.

Cei looked pleased. He was a man fond of his stomach, there being a lot of him to sustain. "Sit down, sit down," he said as though no face-off were going on. "Help yourselves." He sat down at the nearest table and began to tuck into the provided food with gusto. I looked from Eigr to Arthur and down at the laden table, then took a seat opposite Cei and helped myself to some of the meat. I was as hungry as he was. After a moment, Merlin, too, sat down and sliced himself a chunk of the cheese with his dagger.

"Please eat, Arthur," Eigr said, gesturing to the benches with a curiously formal wave of her hand. After a pause, in which I had the distinct impression he might refuse, Arthur sat down, his back as ramrod straight as hers, but didn't take anything to eat. Eigr took a place opposite him, while I kept on eating. I was coming to realize where the phrase "eating for two" came from now I was no longer being sick.

"It's good to see how you've grown into a man," Eigr said, a woman forced into making small talk with her prodigal son. "I see you resemble your father somewhat."

He picked up a piece of bread and began shredding it into small pieces on the table, his long fingers tearing at it fitfully. "What do you care about my father?"

Cei poured some wine into goblets and passed one to Arthur. "Drink, brother, you're tired and thirsty."

Arthur ignored the goblet.

Eigr's back stiffened with what looked like resolve, and she drew herself up taller. "I cared very much for your father." She glanced across at Cei. "For both your fathers."

"You hid it well," Arthur said, picking up the goblet and draining it in one gulp. "I didn't see you coming back to fulfill your wifely duties in a hurry."

She bristled. "He wouldn't have me back."

Arthur banged the empty goblet down on the table. "I know. I was there. I saw and heard every moment of your fight. So did Cei."

She nodded. Was that a hint of what might have been regret in her frosty blue eyes?

"He banished me here." She was unable to keep the bitterness from her voice. "He wouldn't let me take my children. I fought him for you. He only let me take Morgawse because she was just a baby. And then when she was twelve he even took her. I was left with nothing…no one."

"And us?" Arthur said. "What about us? What were we left with? Cadwy, that's what." He picked up the flagon of wine and slopped more into his goblet. He really needed to eat something or he was going to get drunk. "He was a man grown, and dangerous, and you left me to his mercy. He would have found a way to kill me in the end if I hadn't been sent to Din Cadan when I was sixteen."

"You had your father and Merlin to take care of you, and your brother Cei."

Arthur laughed, a short bark. "Cei was a child himself. Cadwy made my life a misery whenever he was in Viroconium, and there was nothing Cei could do to stop him other than help me hide. You left me to a miserable childhood without a backward glance."

"Be fair," Cei put in, his mouth full of food. "Cadwy wasn't there that much and when he was, he was taken up with being your father's battle leader. He didn't have that much time for going after you."

Arthur glared at his brother. "You don't know. You were training to be a warrior with the other older boys. Only Breanna and Merlin stood between him and me, and Merlin was often busy with my father."

Eigr's gaze slid to me. "But you survived. And now you're a man grown yourself, a king, a husband, and soon to be a father." Her eyes hardened. "And your wife is the Lady of the Ring."

Merlin, who had been silent throughout this discussion, held up his hand. "But we are here now," he said, his voice calm and quiet. "And you have seen the Lady of the Ring."

The pause that followed stretched into eternity. Outside the hall the cries of gulls rose above the noise of the wind. Inside, the flames of the hearth fire crackled loud in the silence.

"Yes. I have seen the Lady of the Ring." Eigr's eyes narrowed and her voice hissed in the quiet of the Hall. "I have seen her many times in my scrying glass and always in a sea of blood." She fixed me with her stare. "She carries death with her, death and destruction." She looked at Arthur. "You should have gone into the church as I wanted. Your father should have listened to me. Instead, you've taken the path to fame, bloody betrayal and death."

A finger of fear traced its way up my spine, and every hair stood on end. I'd thought I was the only one who knew what might happen here, with my modern knowledge of the legends. How could Eigr have any intimation of what was to come? Unless she truly had the Sight. Maybe she did. After all, her daughter, Morgana, appeared to have it – she'd seen me coming to Viroconium and sent her brother's foederati after me.

Arthur was unmoved. "You think I'm going to believe your mad predictions any more than my father did? You think your words can sway me even now? Gwen might be the Lady of the Ring, and I might be the king of Dumnonia, but nothing you see in your scrying glass will make me believe she brings death." He paused. "Death lies ahead for all of us. I am a warrior and a king. If there was no blood in my future, I would be worried. And as for you, you haven't changed one bit. You're still as melodramatic as ever. No wonder my father was glad to see you go."

This reunion wasn't going well.

Eigr turned her attention to Merlin. "You brought her here. You've put in motion the bloody end that is to come. I see it now; she's veiled in blood. She carries death in her hand and in her heart."

I was affronted. She didn't even know me and was casting doom and gloom over my so far very short marriage to her son. Was I going to sit here and let her? I thought I knew what lay ahead for the Arthur and Guinevere of legend, but that might not apply to the real Arthur and me. And surely if I were forewarned like this, I could avert it?

"Arthur is right." All their heads turned toward me as though taken aback that I might have a voice of my own. "Death lies ahead for all of us. Battles will be fought, men will die, but I have a prediction of my own to make." I had their attention now, but it was Eigr's I wanted to hold. I stared into her eyes. "King Arthur, with me by his side as his queen, will become the most famous king of all time. Fifteen hundred years from now, people will still speak of him with awe all over the world, and his battles will have gone down in history. Whatever you see in your scrying glass, nothing will change this. It is his destiny."

Well, if anyone could make a prophecy like this it should have been me. My eyes met Merlin's, and he gave me the smallest wink.

Arthur stared at me coldly, most likely wondering why I hadn't told him this before.

From the opposite side of the table, Eigr fixed me with an even colder stare, possibly indignant that someone would dare to steal her thunder. What might be the extent of her supposed powers? Could she tell how angry I was feeling?

Cei got to his feet. "I think we all need to go to our bedchambers. We can cool off a bit and resume this conversation later."

Wise move. He was something of a diplomat.

Arthur got to his feet as well, pulling me up beside him. "The Queen and I will take the royal chambers." He pulled me close. "I don't care where the rest of you go. We need to be alone." And with that he marched me through the door at the end of the hall and into the chamber that no doubt belonged to his mother.

"She doesn't know what she's talking about." Arthur slammed the door behind us and pulled me forcefully into his arms, holding me against his mail shirt. "Don't listen to her."

So easy for him to say, but far more difficult for me to do. Without my knowledge of the legends, I might have been able to dismiss what she'd said, but around my heart a fear was creeping inexorably to encircle it. A fear that she might indeed have the Sight and have seen Arthur's future.

I put my arms around him, uncertain what to do or say. We stood like that for a few minutes before he gently pushed me away, holding my arms and looking down into my face. "But what you told her...is that true? That I'll be remembered as the most famous king of all time?"

I'd done it now. I nodded. "Where I come from, everyone knows about you." In for a penny. "But no one really knows who you were. You're a name, a cipher from a time long ago, an enigma...a mystery." I put my hand up and stroked his stubbly cheek. "And it's because of the mystery that surrounds you that you're known world-wide. So many legends cling to your name – so many have been added over the years, it's impossible to know what's history and what's fanciful fairy tale."

"That's enough for me." His face was serious. "Don't tell me anything else. I don't want to know if your legends hold anything of what my mother predicts. I don't believe in prophecies. A man carves his own fate with his deeds. I refuse to let her carve mine for me with her mewling fortune telling. It's a trick, a way to control me, to win me back. Well, it won't work. You're my wife, and I refuse to listen to her lies about you."

Taking my hand, he led me to the bed. "Come, lie down and rest. We've had a long four days of riding and you've been sleeping on less than comfortable beds."

I lay down on Eigr's bed and let Arthur pull my boots off. He was right. I was exhausted. He sat on the edge of the bed and gently stroked my hair. "Nothing will ever come between us," he said. "I won't let it."

I closed my eyes and tried to push away the images that kept jostling for space in my head, of his rebellious nephew Medraut and of the far off battle of Camlann.

Chapter Twelve

W E SPENT FIVE long days at Din Tagel. Cei had business that needed attending to with his warriors, and on three of those days, he and Arthur rode inland, to visit some of Cei's villages. While he was there, Arthur kept me close to him, almost as though he suspected his mother planned to do me harm. When he was absent, Merlin, like a watchful guard dog, kept me by his side.

Arthur and his mother had agreed to an uneasy truce. They exchanged small talk when we ate together, but the atmosphere between them remained icy and neither of them appeared able to thaw it. He plainly didn't want to, and she didn't know how. If I hadn't felt so awkward around her, I might have tried myself to foster some sort of accord between them, but what with my constant bodyguard, I didn't get the chance.

It didn't surprise me that there was no love lost between Merlin and Eigr. According to the story I knew, Merlin had been the one who'd transformed Uthyr's appearance so that he resembled her husband, Gorlois, and could gain entry to Din Tagel to have his way with Eigr and conceive Arthur. Although I doubted this version of events was true, I had no doubts that Merlin had played his part in somehow bringing about Arthur's conception.

On the fourth day, a trading ship arrived from the Mediterranean. Arthur and I walked with Cei over the headland and down the precipitous path to the rocky landing stage on the leeward side of the island. I was curious to see a ship of this era and what sort of goods they'd brought. We'd wrapped up well, although the day was bright. A stiff westerly wind sent small clouds scudding across a blue sky that had changed the sea from the grey of our arrival to a deep green, fringed with the white caps of the waves. Gulls called overhead, and the salt smell of sea spray was in the air.

The ship was much smaller than I'd expected, with only one mast and a single sail, now furled. Tied fore and aft to metal rings hammered into the stone, she bobbed against the rocky wall of the jetty, her painted sides protected by ropework fenders. A large party of men from the fortress was already at work, laboring to unload a cargo of tall amphorae.

"Wine from Gaul, olive oil and olives from Hispania, and if we're lucky, some garum from Byzantium," Cei explained when he saw me looking at them.

I frowned, puzzled by the last item.

"Fish sauce." His honest face broke into a grin. "Made with fish guts. Stinks to buggery but tastes like heaven when it's used in cooking. We don't often get any."

There were also crates, which Cei told me contained fine tableware, and smaller pots of exotic spices and perfumes, along with some well-wrapped bolts of cloth. The camphorous smell of the cedar chests the cloth had been packed in was strong. At the same time, another group of men hauled what looked like ingots of metal, partly wrapped in rough cloth and bound with rope-handles, back onto the ship.

"Tin from our mines," Cei said. "And copper, too. We do a good trade every summer when the ships come. Thanks to the fine weather, this one's quite early. They vie to be the first, and this one's had the jump on the rest."

The captain of the ship approached us. A small, hennaed beard covered his chin, and gold earrings decorated both ears in abundance. He wore curious baggy trousers, gathered at the ankle, and a brightly colored tunic covered by a leather jacket studded with shiny copper buttons. A red bandana round his head gave him a piratical appearance.

"Milord Cei." They clasped each other's hands. "You 'ave a good amount of the tin thees time. Good it ees that the weather 'as given to me the advantage over my rivals."

Despite his accent, he spoke our language well. Latin, I presumed, as it was unlikely a trader from the Mediterranean would be familiar with the Celtic tongue.

Cei grinned. "Lucky for you, Xander, and for us." He gestured at the wares piling up on the dockside. "But first I must present you to my king." He turned. "Arthur of Dumnonia, and his Queen, the Lady Guinevere, this is Captain Xander of the *Blue Siren*."

Captain Xander swept us a deep bow and came up with a roguish smile, his black eyes looking me up and down. "Milord Arthur, Milady Guinevere."

I liked the way our names rolled off his tongue and the irrepressible look in his bright eyes. It was impossible not to smile back.

"It ees a lucky man you are, milord Arthur," he said. "To be 'aving a queen of such beauty ees a rare and unexpected gift." He laughed. "Few men are so blessed. I myself 'ave to me four wives – each in a different port, but none 'ave the grace and elegance of yours."

Arthur gave him a friendly nod. "Thank you, Captain Xander. I can only think that four wives would be a burden to a man such as yourself."

The captain let out a guffaw of laughter. "That they would be, if ever any got wind of the others!"

All three men laughed together, united by their common masculinity and the marriage arrangements of an old sea dog. Then Arthur questioned the captain about the news from the Mediterranean, talk of people and places I didn't know, so instead of listening, I watched the captain's men working alongside Cei's.

They were all as dark or darker than their captain, and one or two looked as though they came from Africa. Although the captain spoke our tongue, these men conversed with one another in a language I didn't recognize.

Despite us being on the leeward side of the island, a stiff wind still blew, and the *Blue Siren* bobbed up and down, scraping against the side of the stone jetty, making it difficult for the men to load and unload her. But at last, they had all the goods from the ship stacked on the jetty, and almost all the tin was in the ship's hold.

"Are you staying long?" I asked the captain, as we stood to one side while the last of the tin disappeared into his hold.

He shook his head. "I would be most honored to spend time with you, Milady the beautiful Queen, but the tide will not allow it. Soon it will begin to ebb and my ship will 'ave to be on 'er way. We can never dawdle 'ere, much to my sorrow. Especially now that I see there ees a lady so beautiful with whom to speak." He certainly knew how to flatter a woman.

He was right about the tide. Already it was falling, and the *Blue Siren* was sitting lower in the water as her load of tin increased. Much longer, and it would be impossible to board her.

Captain Xander bowed to Cei and Arthur with a flamboyance that matched his personality. "Until the next time, my lords. The captain, 'e return now to the Middle Sea and will sell on your tin at great profit so that 'e may buy more goods and bring them 'ere to your leetle fog-wrapped island. But next time, I will bring jewels for your queen and gifts that will please 'er. Maybe an educated bird that speaks like a Roman consul, or a monkey to make 'er laugh. And I will tell all I meet of the beautiful queen 'idden in the far west, so that 'er beauty will be known throughout the world. And I will tell that she ees the queen of the great King Arthur of Dumnonia."

My cheeks flushed at the compliment.

The smile on Arthur's face was genuine. He held out his hand. "And I look forward to meeting you again one day, Captain

Xander."

They shook hands, and with the agility of a mountain goat, Xander took hold of a shroud and vaulted down onto his deck, just as his men released the fore and aft ropes holding the *Blue Siren* to the wharf. They pushed her off with long poles and in a moment, she swung away from the rocks out into the ocean swell. The men on board hauled up her sail, chanting as they did so.

As the wind filled the sail, the ship pulled away, and the last I saw of Captain Xander was his red bandana as he took it off and waved it at us.

ON THE LAST day of our visit to Din Tagel, I finally found myself alone with Eigr. Arthur and Cei had ridden out to inspect the fishing village up the coast first thing that morning. I was tired after the previous day spent at the landing stage, so Arthur left me in bed, dozing. As a consequence, Merlin must have grown bored with waiting in the Hall and wandered away to climb to the peak of the promontory, taking advantage of the clearness of the day. So it was into an almost empty Hall that I emerged, halfway through the morning.

Eigr was seated at the high table, where we'd eaten every evening with her warriors, no, with Cei's warriors. Hard to think of them as his when he was never there. Realizing Eigr was alone, I hesitated on the threshold, unsure whether I wanted to encounter her by myself. Her fanaticism and conviction that I had blood on my hands frightened me to my very core. I might be a twenty-first-century girl, but the longer I stayed in the fifth century, the more its superstitions seemed believable. However, since our first meeting, there'd been no more talk of prophecies of impending doom flowing with blood. Any time we'd spent with her, the talk had remained about the surrounding lands over which she ruled in Cei's stead. So after the briefest hesitation, I continued into the Hall.

Today, I'd chosen a flowing, dark blue gown, conscious of the fact that the color suited me well. My chestnut hair was bound in two long plaits that reached to the small of my back.

Eigr must have sensed my presence, because she looked up from what she was doing and her cold blue eyes took me in from head to foot.

Scattered about her were some thin tablets of wood, about the size of the average paperback book, and a brass inkwell with a wooden pen lying beside it. This piqued my interest. So far, I'd seen very little sign of literacy in the fifth century, apart from Uthyr Pendragon's last testament, a brief document actually written by Merlin on Arthur's instruction before we'd even left Din Cadan.

Determined not to let her psych me out, I gave her a pleasant smile and dropped a sweeping curtsey, something she'd never have seen before as the curtsey originated in the sixteenth century. She looked surprised, but I was sure I looked elegant performing it.

"My lady Guinevere," she said, frostily, as I rose from the curtsey.

I could be just as frosty. "My lady Eigr."

"I trust you slept well." She reached out to gather the tablets of wood. "Cei tells me your day at the wharf tired you out."

"I did, thank you," I said sweetly. "And yes, I was tired after yesterday. But the bed is very comfortable." Too late, I remembered it was her bed. I pressed my lips together and vowed to think before I spoke again.

There wasn't much else to say on the subject, so she remained silent. We continued to regard one another, like two dogs eyeing each other up for a fight. The seconds stretched out, before she remembered what she was doing and started stacking the wooden tablets. When they were finally arranged to her liking, she pointed to the seat beside hers. "Why don't you sit down and tell me about yourself."

As an invitation, it could have done with a bit more welcome in her tone.

Nevertheless, I came around the table and, pulling out the seat, sat down beside her. She smelled of a rich perfume that no doubt Captain Xander or one of his fellow traders had brought from the Mediterranean. Running my eyes over the table top, I noticed that the top wooden tablet had lines of small spidery writing, but it was too far away to read. Eigr picked up the pen and slipped it into a leather pouch, but not before I saw it was made of a piece of doweling with a thin length of metal coiled around one end, finishing in a shaped point for writing.

"Could I have a look at your pen?" I asked, unable to think of anything else to say that might break the ice between us.

With reluctance, she drew the pen out again and put it into my hands. Turning it over, I saw how cleverly it had been constructed and yet so simply. You could dip the pen into your ink and, when you were writing, the spiral of closely wound metal would act like a tiny ink cartridge and funnel the ink down to the tip. I turned it over in my hands before handing it back to her with a plastered-on smile.

"Very interesting. Thank you."

"Are you an educated woman?" she asked.

Telling her about my university degree seemed pointless. "I can read and write," I said. "And do some mathematics."

For the first time, her face held something other than hostility to me. "You can reckon?"

I guessed she meant arithmetic, so I nodded, thinking of the grade A Maths GCSE I had. Although I couldn't imagine any problem she could put to me would involve a calculation more complicated than Year Six maths.

She picked up the top tablet and pushed it over to give me a better look. The writing was hard to read because she hadn't made her letters the way I was used to seeing them. However, I could make out that it was a list, and after struggling to read the first few lines, I realized it consisted of the goods Captain Xander had delivered the day before. It was an inventory of what she had for trading further inland. Beside each item was a number in Roman numerals – not renowned for their capacity to make arithmetic easy.

"What is it you're doing?" I asked.

For a moment, her hostility seemed as though it would hold her silent, and then what must have been desperation took over. "Reckon up how much of each item we have without having to go and count them again. My steward's had the goods moved to our store rooms, but he counts badly, and now I've got thirteen amphorae of olive oil here." She pointed with a long, somewhat inky finger. "And eleven more here. There's spices mentioned here and here and here. It's all in a muddle, and I've always found reckoning a tedious task."

I had an easy solution for this. "Can I have a blank writing tablet, please?"

She paused as if to think about it, as though anything I might have to offer would be tainted by the blood she saw hanging over me. Then, still with marked reluctance, she handed me a blank tablet. I picked up the pen and dipped it in the ink. It wasn't as easy to use as I'd expected and the first thing I did was get inky fingers and make a big blot on the tablet. I tapped the pen to lessen its load of ink and carefully wrote the numbers 1 to 10 on the tablet with a fair few more blots and smudges. Not my best work.

I let myself chuckle as I finished. "It's really hard to use this pen but I think I'll get better at it."

"What have you written?" She was clearly puzzled. I pointed to my numbers and said their names aloud, which must have been the names of the Roman numbers as she didn't quibble. "It's called the Arabic numbering system. They come from the Middle Sea." I almost said the Mediterranean and just managed to stop myself in time. "It's much easier than the system you're using. Having a single symbol for each number makes reckoning so much simpler." I pointed to the three amphorae and the other two, written so far apart, and wrote 3 + 2 on her tablet. "On this list," I went on, putting my finger on the 3, "move the two further down and the answer is 5. See?"

And that was how I won Eigr over to my side – by giving her a maths lesson.

She was highly intelligent, and very soon picked up the new notation, so I showed her how to add two figure numbers and the basics of the Arabic decimal numbering system and explained the concept of zero. Within an hour, she was adding numbers in their hundreds with ease, and very pleased with herself. And without actually lying, I'd managed to imply that I'd come from a country so far away we'd produced all this useful mathematics without having to share it with the rest of the known world.

Flushed at her own success, she looked up at me with an excited sparkle in her normally cold blue eyes. "For sharing with me your number magic," she said, as though she were bestowing a great honor on me, "I will take you to look in my scrying glass. The future is fluid, and there's always the chance you will observe something I might have missed."

I swallowed. Part of me wanted to see this scrying glass, the part that was adjusting itself to life in the fifth century, but the still dominant twenty-first-century part of me was thinking that whatever she showed me would all be hokum. And yet, I'd gone to the fortune teller at the County Agricultural Show last summer. Although in all her wisdom, she'd neglected to tell me I'd be marrying a tall, dark, handsome stranger who happened to be a king. How remiss of her.

She put her thin hand on my arm. "Come with me, and together we'll look into the glass."

Mesmerized, almost, I got up and went with her.

She led me to a small thatched and stone-walled building reminiscent of an old Iron Age roundhouse. Inside, with the door closed behind us, it would have been very dark had she not lit a single candle.

"Sit." She indicated a wooden bench before a low table upon which stood a block of wood.

I sat.

She stood the candle on the table and turned away. After a moment, she turned back, and from a dark cloth brought out a round mirror the size of a tea plate, made of black obsidian. She set it on the table just behind the candle, propped up against the block of wood. The candle flame reflected in it, guttering in a slight draught.

Eigr took her place beside me, laying her hands on the table, her fingers spread. "Look at the mirror," she said. Gone was her previous friendliness, and in its place her voice was commanding and cold.

I looked at the glass. The candlelight flickered across its inky surface.

The silence in the little round house was complete. It pressed in around me, and I couldn't take my eyes away from the circle of blackness. The woman beside me was forgotten. I blinked, and the candlelight shimmered across the obsidian. My face, reflected as a pale oval, looked back at me. Opening my mouth, I was about to say I could see nothing, when the surface of the mirror rippled as though a stone had been dropped into a black pool.

No longer was I looking at the dim reflection of my candle-lit face. Instead, a blood-stained battlefield littered with broken banners lay before me, with the humps of dead horses and a river running red beneath a sky where the setting sun had stained even the clouds red. I blinked again and the battlefield vanished. In its place, the circle of standing stones on the Tor stood gaunt against a leaden sky, and at my feet, through a mist of red, I saw Arthur lying on the grass. His eyes were closed, his face a mask of blood, his breathing shallow. He was dying. I blinked again, and the stones shimmered in the air like an image in water, and the ruined tower of St Michael's church rose up before me, solid and real, with a little girl in a red coat standing, arms outstretched and eyes closed.

A noise by the door disturbed us, and light spilled in. My eyes darted sideways. Merlin stood on the threshold staring at us with his eyes wide and mouth half open. The spell was broken.

"What are you doing?" His voice brimmed with accusation.

Eigr's cold face suffused with annoyance at his interruption. "My new daughter is learning my skills, as I have learned hers." Her imperiousness would have matched her son's.

I got to my feet in a hurry, like a child caught out doing something illicit and forbidden, my heart hammering, frightened by Merlin's disapproval. "I taught the Lady Eigr how to use the Arabic numbering system," I said, rather too quickly, in an effort to defuse what could have been a tricky situation.

Eigr got to her feet as well and smiled at Merlin, her cold face bright with the excitement of her intellectual achievement. "Your magic can't contend with this," she declared in triumph. "Gwen has shown me the magic of numbers."

I forced myself to beam at him, although all the while I was thinking of what I'd seen in the black mirror.

"I can show you as well, if you like." I felt I ought to offer.

He looked us up and down, then shook his head. "It's not for me."

Now we'd been disturbed, there was no point in staying inside the round hut with the blank scrying glass. Eigr and I followed Merlin out into the spring sunshine, and he walked away from us back toward the Hall.

When he'd gone, we exchanged conspiratorial smiles, and Eigr put her hand on my shoulder. "Perhaps I was wrong. You are a woman of many talents. This skill of yours is most useful and should be shared. Perhaps you're even clever enough to avoid what the fates have in store for you." She paused. "I think you saw something that can help you."

I turned to look out over the white-capped waves. Beneath the cliffs, the sound of them crashing on the shingle beach thundered, and I could taste the salt in the air. "I don't believe in fate," I said with deliberation. "Like my husband, I believe a person makes their own future."

Eigr shook her head, her eyes shifting from excited to sad in an instant. "My scrying glass never lies, but the future can be interpreted in different ways." She sighed, clasping her hands together as though she were wringing them. "When Arthur was just a boy, I looked into the glass and was shown what lay ahead if he were to follow the path his father wished to carve for him." She looked me in the eye. "I saw you too, a little girl in a blood red coat running toward a windswept stone tower on a grey winter's day." She put both hands on my arm. "The world that gave you birth is far away, but you will see it again, one day."

Goosepimples prickled my skin. How could she know where I'd come from, and that I'd been wearing a red coat the first time I'd met Merlin, back in my world? Did she know what I'd just seen myself? And was she right when she said I'd go back?

Curiosity held me. The part of me that was on its way to becoming a believer wanted to know what this woman had foreseen, although another part, buried deeper than ever, cried out that this was nonsense. I couldn't help myself. "What else have you seen?" I asked.

A faint smile curved her mouth. She thought she had me now. "That there were two paths possible for my son." Her voice was low and melodious, as though her words were a mere story. "He could enter the church as many second sons do, and forge for himself a life of devotion to God, a long and worthy life, ending at a great age, in his own bed." She paused, and her eyes glittered with suppressed anger. "Or he could follow the path his father intended, the one Merlin swore he was born to follow." She said Merlin's name with contempt. "If he chose the second path, he would meet you." Strands of her long white hair whipped across her face. "A woman veiled in blood. Choosing this road would bring him, in his prime, to an end on a far-off, blood-soaked battlefield. My scrying glass was drenched in the blood that will flow."

Her blue eyes challenged me to deny this. How could I,

though, when I'd seen that same battlefield in the glass just now. Had she seen it with me?

I was at a loss for what to say. How could I placate her when the stories I knew about my husband corroborated what she was predicting, and I had seen? But I was a free agent. I wasn't the Guinevere of legend going unwittingly to my fate, taking a lover and betraying her king to bring the whole of Britain to war. I was Guinevere Fry, librarian, well-read, clever, and above all, possessor of all the foreknowledge the legends could give me.

I put my hand on hers. "I won't let that happen. If I know it's coming, I can avert it. Nothing's written in stone. The future can be rewritten. Even a prophecy may not come to be."

But was I right? I'd seen it in her glass just as she had. Could the future be rewritten when it was really the past?

Chapter Thirteen

W E RODE AWAY from Din Tagel on a bright spring morning. Below the fortress waves crashed onto the shingle beach, and above our heads gulls bent their backs against the never ending wind, to dive shrieking to their cliff-side roosts. I was glad to leave the fortress behind, despite the common ground I'd eventually found with Eigr. However much she'd considered me useful, maybe even come to like me, she would never change her mind about what she'd seen in her scrying glass. For her, I was the woman who would bring doom upon her beloved son.

At the villa where we'd left the orphan children of Caerwysg, we found that baths and over a week of good food had wrought huge changes. All five of them had gained color in their filled-out cheeks, and the haunted look had left them. They were still thin, but their hair, which someone had cut short to help rid them of their lice, was clean. Nola turned out to be a dark strawberry blonde. It made me wonder if she might have been the offspring of a raiding Saxon.

At some expense, Arthur commandeered a wagon for the children, which slowed our journey somewhat, but the weather held, and we had time on our side. On the pleasant return journey, the children, now alert enough to enjoy the sights, began to behave like real children and not terrified beggars. For part of the time I rode in the wagon with them, Alezan tied on behind, so that I could talk to the children, in particular Nola, who'd taken a shine to me. I kept them amused by retelling the timeless fairy stories my mother had told me as a child – Little Red Riding Hood, Hansel and Gretel, Cinderella, Rapunzel. Nola made me repeat Goldilocks and the Three Bears endlessly.

At Caer Pensa we took the children to the King's House, where Arthur, good-humoredly and at my urging, had decreed they should stay and be educated in a trade. Arthur called the master craftsmen before us and asked each to take responsibility for a child and introduce them slowly to their new tasks. Even the smallest boy was given the job of sweeping the workshop of his new master.

"They're not slaves," I told the masters. "And you're not to treat them as such. They're your apprentices, and you should be teaching them your trade. We shall come back this way later this summer to check the children are being treated well. And the steward of the King's House will report to me if it comes to his ears that you're treating them as anything other than apprentices."

Round-eyed, the children looked on as we decided their future, but at least now their eyes were no longer sunken in half-starved faces.

I took Nola to one side. "I wish I could take you with me, but it would be selfish of me. You belong with your friends. They're your family. But I will come back to see you. I promise."

She regarded me in solemn silence.

Bending down, I put my arms around her, a lump rising in my throat. It was a wrench to have to say goodbye, but a military fortress was no place for her after all she'd suffered. For a moment her little body stiffly resisted my embrace, then she softened, and her thin arms went around my neck and hugged me back.

Leaving Caer Pensa behind us, we returned to Din Cadan for the summer. My short period of experiencing Roman comforts was at an end.

In every farm we passed, thanks to the continued fine weather, the farmers were ploughing their small square fields with pairs of oxen. When compared with deep modern ploughing, the shallow furrows their primitive ploughs made seemed like mere scratches on the land. It was the same in the farms below Din Cadan, where out in the grazing lands, lambs skipped jauntily after their mothers, calves followed the cows, and the wandering horse herds had foals at foot already. The forest had gained a thick blush of green, transforming its shadowy darkness, and everywhere buds were bursting forth on branches, as if the land were springing into life in one great overnight leap.

We arrived at Din Cadan to find the whole fortress preparing for a spring celebration. Men brought wagons of greenery and May blossom from the farms and forest below and festooned not just the inside of the great hall but the outside too. Every man, woman and child took part in the construction of two huge bonfires in the clear space in front of the Hall.

"Beltane," Merlin explained. "A traditional festival even the Christian God can't wipe out." Not for the first time I wondered about his religious beliefs. From the way he spoke, I had the impression he was a dispassionate observer of their customs.

He gestured at the houses inside the fortress. "This was a community of farmers before it was ever a community of warriors. Before these farmers began paying lip service to Christianity, they worshipped the old gods who gave their lands and animals – and their women – fertility. The Christian God isn't the god of farmers. He's the god of monks and priests in monasteries and abbeys. These people still believe the old gods bring life back to their world after the living death of winter. It's little wonder they cling to their ancestors' traditions. They say their prayers once a week in their little church in the village, but daily they venerate the old gods in their homes. And at the feast of Beltane they'll drive some of their cattle symbolically between these bonfires at nightfall."

This surprised me. "I'd always imagined everyone here was Christian. Arthur did tell me they still believed the Tor was the entrance to Annwfn, though. And I've seen the odd thing that's made me think some of them still keep their old beliefs. But you make this sound as though they all do."

He smiled wryly. "There's a fine veneer of Christianity, but they hedge their bets. Every one of them will be at the Beltane fires, fearing that if they're not, there'll be no fertility bestowed on them this year."

"And you?" I said. "What do you believe?"

He was a clever man, a man who'd seen the future, however briefly. A man who might question any beliefs that had no proof.

He gave a shrug. "I believe in me."

BUT WITH THE spring came more than Beltane – with the spring came the Saxons.

Not to us, safe in the south-west, but to others who were less lucky.

With my knowledge of Arthurian Britain, gleaned from a life in the shadow of a father who'd been obsessed with all its aspects, I knew the Saxons were most troublesome along Britain's East coast, Rome's old Saxon Shore. The Saxons had been raiding there since before the legions sailed back to Gaul in AD 410, leaving the British to fend for themselves. So when the news came that Linnuis, a kingdom with a shore on the vulnerable North Sea coast, was in dire need of help, it was no surprise.

Arthur, after a winter spent training his warriors, couldn't hide his excitement. It hadn't taken me long to discover he was a man for whom the love of a woman wasn't enough. He needed more than me. Not other women – no, he'd been faithful to me despite the ever-present temptation of Tangwyn. But he needed war, as was evidenced by his fanatical devotion to his men's training. Nothing fired him up the way war did.

I saw it in his face when the rider from Linnuis arrived, weary and travel-stained, bearing the message from King Manogan asking for the help of the Dux Britanniarum. He came hard on the heels of the feast of Beltane, riding through the gates in the gathering darkness of evening. He urged his tired horse up the cobbled road toward where the twin Beltane fires still burnt, after the cattle had done their dash between them. Some of the people were already departing with lit torches to relight their own previously extinguished hearth fires from the sacred flame.

Outside the great hall, Arthur and I still sat in the two ornate thrones from where we'd presided over the celebrations. Dampness hung in the air, but it wasn't cold, and the day had been a great success. The fortress had filled to bursting with people from the farms, who'd climbed the steep road from the hill's foot to join us in our celebrations. Tables clustered all around the great hall, and in freshly dug fire pits servants had roasted the last of the year's overwintered beef. Bakers had spent the day before laboring red-faced at their ovens, and Arthur had ordered barrels of home-brewed beer broken out, and cider from last autumn's delivery from the Ynys Witrin monks. Beer and cider for the people, and amphorae of Mediterranean wine for his warriors.

Through all of this the gaunt rider on his exhausted horse, as welcome a sight to me as Banquo's ghost at Macbeth's feast, threaded his way with purpose toward Dumnonia's young king.

Arthur got to his feet, his food and wine forgotten. I sensed the tension quiver through his body as though he knew without being told what this solitary rider foreshadowed.

The man dismounted amongst the crowded tables and let his horse's reins drop. The beast hung its head almost to the ground as the rider approached us on unsteady feet.

"My lord king." He dropped to one knee, his head bowed, whether from respect or from his own exhaustion, I couldn't tell.

Arthur stepped forward. "Rise."

As though every bone in his body ached, the man rose to his feet. He was young, but the fatigue etched on his drawn face added years and made his long nose jut from between his angled cheekbones. He was as tall as Arthur, auburn-haired and bearded, with dark shadows beneath his hazel eyes.

"I come from my father, King Manogan. I am Beli, now his eldest born."

Arthur inclined his head. It was obvious the arrival of Prince Beli with such urgency had lit in my husband a hunger. His face betrayed his feelings as clearly as if they'd been written on the pages of a book. At one of the nearby tables, Merlin turned his head to watch, his dark eyes alight with curiosity.

"What is it I can do for King Manogan's son?" Arthur's voice was quiet in the hubbub but it carried through the cool evening air. Silence fell about him, rippling out in concentric circles like a stone thrown into a pond.

Beli drew himself up straighter with an effort.

"My father was at the Council of Kings," he began, with dignity. "He was there with my late brother. He voted for your election as Dux Britanniarum. We have six young men training in our city of Caer Lind Colun, near ready to join you this spring – my younger brother, Anwas, amongst them." He paused for breath, and a tremor passed through his body. "But now we have need of your help, before ever our young men have joined you. My father sent me south after the Saxons defeated our army in battle not ten miles from our city." He faltered, his heavy brows furrowing with emotion. "We were three brothers – sons of our father, the king. Now we are but two, for my brother Farrell fell against the Saxon horde, defending the Roman road from the south."

It had come. The first request from one of the many kingdoms that made up Britain in the fifth century. The request I'd been dreading. The request that would take Arthur away from me and into terrible danger. He had to go. I knew his destiny better than any, even Merlin. And yet, inside I couldn't help the irrational fear that my presence here, a living chronoclasm, might have already changed things irrevocably and be the thing that would lead to his premature death.

I had the list of Arthur's battles off by heart. Nennius, a monk of the early ninth century, had passed them down from antiquity, and since I'd married Arthur, I'd gone over the list so many times the names were graven on my soul. Right at the start sat the battles of the River Glein and River Dubglas – in Linnuis. To anyone else that would have been meaningless, but with my knowledge, combined with Merlin's lessons on contemporary politics and history, I knew Linnuis was modern Lincolnshire and Caer Lind Colun, its capital, was Lincoln.

The cogs of fate were whirring, and at their end lay the one battle I dreaded above all – Camlann. The battle in which Arthur would fall. The knowledge of it lying ahead of us weighed heavy in my heart, as certain as any piece of information I possessed about the fifth century. Reinforced by the fact that I now believed Eigr had seen it in her scrying glass. It lurked in the shadows, an ever present threat that could be coming in one year or five or twenty, but coming it undoubtedly was, and this first envoy asking for his help heralded its inexorable approach.

Arthur nodded. "Help will come to you," he said, raising his voice so that more heads turned. "Your brother will not have died in vain. Your father will sleep easy in his bed once more. I swore at the Council, before all the kings, that I would ride to the help of any who called upon me. You have the honor of being the first." With a flourish of his hand, he encompassed his watching warriors seated at the trestle tables. "Tomorrow we ride north to Linnuis."

Beli bowed his head as a murmur of approval ran through the listening people. Warriors thumped the tables in enthusiasm, clapping one another on the shoulders excitedly. They too had spent a winter of frustration, itching for the good weather to come so they had an excuse to get out their swords for a real fight instead of their interminable practicing. I'd felt their restlessness rising to a boil as the days had lengthened and Beltane approached. Now, it seemed that restlessness had been released, a coiled spring unbound.

Cold fear wrapped my entrails in bands of steel.

Despite the prospect of marching north with his army in the morning, Arthur was late to bed that night. I lay awake, sleep eluding me, until I heard him come through the door from the great hall into the gloom that was our bedchamber.

I lay silent while he undressed, just a silhouette against the faint light of a single clay oil lamp and the dim glow of the brazier which stood in the center of the room. The bed creaked as his weight came onto it, and he lifted the heavy covers and slid in beside me, naked.

I waited a moment, but he didn't turn toward me as he usually did, wrapping his long limbs about my body and holding me close. His breathing was quick and light in the quiet of the night. I waited a moment longer but nothing happened. So instead, I rolled onto my side and put my arm across his flat belly.

He turned his head. "You're awake." He sounded surprised. Did he think I could have slept with the thought of his departure in the morning in my head? Did he know me so little?

The cold of the spring night had chilled his body. I slid my feet down to his cold ones. "I couldn't sleep."

He pressed his lips to my hair. "You should try. We have far to ride in the morning."

What? Had I heard him right?

"Why?" My heart was in my mouth.

"Because I'm not leaving you here."

My breath caught. Was this what I wanted to hear? That I was to accompany the army and be where I could see he was safe? Or watch him die. Fear clutched at my heart. Would it be better than sitting here alone at Din Cadan waiting for his return – possibly over many months with no news of his safety?

"You're not?" was all I could think of to say.

He put a finger under my chin, raising my face to his. "I couldn't leave you, could I? You're the Luck of Arthur. All my people think so. It's because of you I'm king – or so they say."

Was there just the smallest hint of resentment in his voice?

I swallowed. I'd heard them say this, that I'd brought luck with me when I'd come from Ynys Witrin. A heavy responsibility to bear.

"And you?" My voice was small and hollow. "Do you think that's true?"

He bent his head and kissed me on the lips. "Of course not. It was me that made me king, not some prophecy. But my people think it, and that's what matters. I wouldn't disillusion them even if I could. Their belief reinforces their trust and ties them tighter to me. With you at my side as we ride north, they're already confident we'll triumph."

He put his arm around my shoulders, and I nestled in against his still cold body, but sleep wouldn't come. I lay awake a long time, listening to the steady rhythm of his beating heart.

Chapter Fourteen

THE FLOCK OF rooks rose in a cloud of dirty washing, black wings beating the heavy air, their harsh cries plaintive in the silence of the battlefield. Only it wasn't silence, was it? There's never silence in the aftermath of a battle.

There are groans. Because the dead are not all dead. They're wounded, grievously, mortally, fatally, and they're a long time in dying. A sword bites through flesh and blood vessels, sinew and tendons. It punctures intestines and lungs and stomachs, but it doesn't always kill.

And the stench. I'd read about battles in books, seen them dramatized in films, in TV dramas, in documentaries, but never had anyone mentioned the smell. You had to be there, in it, amongst the dead and the dying, to know what that smell was like. It was blood and sweat, and above all, it was shit. Because dying men vacate their bowels at the point of death as all the muscles finally relax.

But I wasn't in the fray. I was just an outsider – an observer. Stationed with my guard in the tree line above the river, I'd watched it all unfold before me as the early morning mist cleared and the sun came creeping up over the far horizon, gilding the forest's treetops with its warm glow. A deceptive warmth. For there was no warmth in what lay before me now. The sun had turned its face away to hide behind a veil of cloud, as though disowning what lay before it, brutal and raw upon the banks of the river.

Smoke rose from the burning boats drawn up on the foreshore, and the camp the Saxon raiders had made lay broken and twisted, unrecognizable in the dirt.

Like them.

Shock held me mesmerized. Shock and fear, although it wasn't a fear for my husband, whose white horse singled him out amongst the riders now clustering near the ruin of the boats. He was safe. He was alive. He had won. Blood streaked his horse's shoulders – the blood of the enemy, and I could see him giving orders as his dismounted men sorted through the stolen booty won back from the Saxons.

If I turned my head, I'd see Merlin, stationed like a guard dog to my left. On my right, Bran sat his restless horse, the animal a window to his own feelings. He was the young warrior whose arm I'd stitched all those months ago, on the day I'd first set eyes on Arthur. He'd missed the battle and all that entailed, and here he was sitting nursemaid on the Queen while all the others got first pickings over the stolen booty.

All I could feel was shock. It seemed such a small span of time since we'd come to the edge of the forest and looked down at the sleeping Saxon camp through the pre-dawn gloom. I'd certainly been shocked when I'd seen its size. Five ships were drawn up on the shore, burnt skeletons now, embers still glowing, the oily black smoke from their tarry sides rising skywards.

"Two hundred warriors," Merlin had informed me in the lowest of low voices. "Forty to a ship."

Thinking Manogan's army had retreated to lick its wounds in his stronghold at Caer Lind Colun, the Saxons had posted few lookouts. Arthur's scouts had dealt with them, making the edge of the forest ours, with its view down toward the dark, peaty snake of the River Glein and the low-lying marshes beyond.

Faced with the reality of two hundred enemy warriors in the camp, fear had seized my entrails in its icy hand. Even the curt order from my husband – for Merlin and Bran to take me to a place of safety on a little rise just inside the treeline – hadn't steadied my anxious heart.

I could make no pretense to having had any understanding of the battle. How could I have? I was used to keeping books in order in a library, and the most fighting I'd needed to do was in the January Sales. Yes, I'd seen action in the skirmish on the road to Viroconium with the Saxon foederati belonging to Arthur's brother, Cadwy. I'd even stabbed a man in an effort to save myself, but that had been nothing like a full-blown battle.

So when it began, I watched with a horrible fascination as though it were far away and nothing could possibly touch me. I'd felt like this before – detached from a reality I couldn't understand or accept. Those weren't the men I knew, galloping their horses down the muddy slope toward the river, shooting fire arrows into the furled sails of the boats, shrieking war cries at the tops of their voices.

"Dumnonia!"

"For Arthur the Bear!"

"Linnuis!"

"Pendragon!"

That wasn't my husband at their head, the first rays of the cold sun catching the glinting light of his mail shirt, his white horse a beacon and far too clear a target. I wouldn't believe it. If I refused to believe, then he couldn't die. It wasn't real.

But it was. The Saxons, deprived of their lookouts by stealth such a short time before, were sleeping – lightly, but sleeping still. Of course, they heard the thundering hooves and the blood curdling war cries; of course, they slept with their great axes by their sides, wearing their chainmail, ready for any attack.

But they had no time to group themselves to face their enemy. The horses thundered through them, the British warriors sweeping a swathe of sharp iron, like the blades of a scythe, through their ranks. They stood in their new stirrups, swinging their swords wide and low, hamstringing some, gutting others. Heads flew, severed from thick Saxon necks, and great gouts of blood pumped like fountains as hearts beat on for seconds after their owners died.

The shouts of men, the screams of horses and the clash of metal on metal broke the peaceful quiet of the dawn. From the trees behind my horse, a flight of rooks, disturbed by the noise, took to the air with shrieks as coarse and raucous as those of the dying men. Three of the ships caught fire. Flames shot skywards, sails billowed out in the updraft caused by the heat and then collapsed in upon themselves in clouds of ash.

Was that tall warrior with the bright helmet rallying the Saxons? Was he their leader? Around him, his men formed ranks, some with shields but many without. The initial impetus of the cavalry charge was dissipated now, and our warriors fell to hand-to-hand fighting. I glimpsed Arthur's white horse, the only one amongst his army, but then the battle closed around him again. I couldn't pick out his helmeted head above the crowd, nor his white shield with its dark bear emblem rearing across it.

To me, watching, heart hammering with fear, the battle seemed to last forever, and yet in a trice it was over. How could something feel at the same time long and yet so short? But time has no meaning in a battle, and the sun had risen well above the horizon in the east and was rushing headlong toward those glowering clouds when at last the fighting ceased.

The taste of blood was in my mouth. I must have bitten my tongue. The familiar feel of retching came over me as the stench of blood and dying men came to us on the still morning air, and I hawked and spat.

Merlin looked at me, his face as sharp and knowing as ever.

I shook my head. "It's the stink of blood. I can't stand it."

He looked away.

A group of prisoners stood gathered on the riverbank. Not many. Maybe twenty at most. The rest lay scattered across the battlefield, dead already or soon to be so. Their cries rose like the bleating of sheep, plaintive and mournful.

Men. These were men lying there dying. Real men. This

wasn't television or a film; this was reality. These were men for whom life had come to an abrupt end, men whose graves, if they ever got any, would be lost forever, their names forgotten with the passing of this day.

Down on the battlefield Arthur raised an arm and waved at Merlin and Bran.

"We can go down there now," Merlin said. "It's safe."

Alezan picked her way through the fallen men. Here and there the hump of a horse rose out of the mud, one or two of them still alive. I looked away, sickened by the sight. The cries lessened. If I turned my head, I'd see Arthur's men walking amongst the dead and dying, finishing them off with their quick knives. The wounded horses, too.

I didn't want to see. Maybe I was like the man in the Bible, who, when he saw the wounded fellow, passed by on the other side of the road. I certainly couldn't have been the good Samaritan.

Not that I didn't want to help. I did. But I knew it would be futile. Or that was what I told myself. They were doomed men, just as Arthur and his men would have been, had the battle gone the other way. I could do nothing to save them. Best to let our Dumnonian warriors finish them off quickly. Death would come one way or another, and I was impotent to save them.

But the carnage drew my eyes. No matter how hard I tried to look away, to avoid the stench that rose like a miasma from the dead and dying, my gaze kept creeping back. The desolation held a fatal fascination. I'd had a friend at school who'd been obsessive about pictures of accidents. I'd stayed the night with her once and she'd whipped out a textbook of her older brother's, who'd been training to be a doctor. She'd shown me dreadful photos of people – run over by trains, injured by machinery, disfigured in crashes. It had revolted me, yet I hadn't been able to drag my eyes away. I felt the same now.

Men lay higgledy-piggledy everywhere, arms and legs grotesquely akimbo in the dance of death. Guts spilled out like slimy grey sausages draped about their owners' torsos. Blood and more blood and still more blood lay in a veil over everything, even the mud where my horse trod.

I leaned over Alezan's shoulder and threw up onto the ground.

Merlin's hand touched my back in comfort or sympathy, or maybe just to make sure I wasn't going to fall off into this muck of death. I straightened up, spat and wiped my mouth on my sleeve. I was a queen. I had to behave like one. That much I'd learned in the bare six months since I'd made the decision to stay.

My mount had seen all this before. With no urging from me, Alezan stepped carefully over the bodies, picking her way toward Arthur, who sat, still mounted, thirty paces from the burning boats.

He had his helmet tucked beneath his right arm, and had hooked his shield onto one of the horns on his saddle. The shield showed fresh gouges like gaping mouths, but it had withstood the battle well. Sweat plastered his dark hair, freshly cut for the campaign, to his head in short wet curls. His face was flushed and dirty, flecked with blood and bits of grey matter whose origins I didn't want to know. Putting up a hand, he smeared the bits across his skin and a wave of sickness rose up in me again. I had to make a great effort to keep it down.

Smoke billowed our way, acrid and bitter. I coughed, but in a moment the breeze whipped the fumes round in another direction entirely, eddying like the currents of the river.

"Well fought." Merlin slammed his hand against Arthur's in the fifth century version of a high five. They grinned at one another like schoolboys after a rugby match.

How could they? Amidst all this death and desecration, they were happy. The differences between them and me could never have been any wider than at that moment.

My gaze traveled to the other riders. They were as dirty as Arthur, disheveled, bloody, most still with swords in hand, the blades darkened by blood. They were difficult to recognize like this because they all looked the same. Like feral dogs. White teeth flashed in filthy faces, dark hair lay slick about their heads; gore speckled their horses' flanks.

"Well, what did you think?" Gwalchmei, the musician, spoke up, his curly brown hair matted with blood.

I couldn't think of anything to say. My mouth tasted of dry cardboard and vomit.

Merlin came to my rescue. "A great victory." He must have sensed my feelings. Apart from Arthur, he alone knew this wasn't what I'd been brought up to.

Gwalchmei nodded and turned toward Cei, who was swinging himself down from the saddle, sword in hand. He stepped toward the huddle of all that remained of the Saxon raiding party, apart from the dead and those who'd fled on foot into the forest.

Arthur pushed his horse forward. The man I'd glimpsed leading the Saxons was not amongst the prisoners. Had he escaped, or did he lie unrecognized amid the faceless dead? The Saxons gazed in surly defiance at their captors. Deprived now of their swords and axes, they looked smaller than they had on the field of battle, their yellow hair dirty, lank and matted with blood, nothing like the golden color I'd pictured.

This was the first time I'd properly laid eyes on the ancestors of my people – the English. When they'd attacked our camp on the way to Viroconium it had been dark, and I'd seen them only by the light of the campfire.

At home, in Din Cadan, Arthur's son, Llacheu, had painted a picture of them as monsters. Of course, he was just a seven-year-old whose mother had probably fed him those stories to frighten him into obedience. *If you don't behave, the Yellow Hairs will get you.* I'd taken what he'd told me with a pinch of salt.

Now I looked at them in fascination. Was I like them? Could I see myself in them?

The answer was no. These men had nothing of the twenty-first-century Englishman about them. Big-boned and muscular, with not an ounce of spare flesh on their bodies, their angry eyes ranged from the blue of the summer sky to grey like the winter seas they'd sailed.

I went no closer.

They were surrounded, with nowhere to go, and every British warrior had a sword in his hand. So why didn't I feel safe? Why did I feel as if I were at the zoo looking at the tigers who were looking back at me hungrily from behind the flimsiest of barriers?

It would have done them no good to try to make a run for it, though. There was nowhere to go. Behind them the smoke from their burning ships rose into the dull grey morning air. Their fellows who'd fled would have a long trek to the east coast and the safety of Saxon-occupied territory.

Arthur halted his blood-spattered horse ten paces from them, wisely not getting close enough for any of them possessed of a death wish to make a lunge for him. Theodoric the Goth, who'd joined us from his fleet at Caer Uisc, brought his own big bay cob up beside him.

"Men of the East," Arthur began, pausing for a second for Theodoric to translate. "You have fought well against my warriors." His gaze roamed from face to surly face, gathering them to him as he would have done his own men. "But we are the victors here. And you are our prisoners." Theodoric translated this and the Saxons exchanged wary glances.

"My warships have need of oarsmen, the mines have need of labor and you are strong. You will go west to the mines, or to join the British Fleet, or," he paused, "you will die today. That is your choice."

Visions of the film *Ben Hur* came charging into my head. Did he mean to chain them to the oars of Theodoric's fleet as Ben Hur had been chained in the Roman galley? Or worse, in a quarry like Spartacus? Theodoric had brought his Goth ships to Britain after Gaul had fallen to the Franks. What sort of ships might these might be, and could it be slaves that powered them? The existence of slaves working in mines in the fifth century was a discovery, even though I'd seen the ingots of tin at Din Tagel.

A silence fell amongst the prisoners. They looked at one another as though seeking for someone to take the lead, rudderless without their captain. The British warriors shifted uneasily, and weak sunlight glinted off their swords as they moved. Metal clinked on metal and their mail shirts rattled.

What sort of a choice did these prisoners have? Slavery or death? It went against everything I'd ever held dear until the moment I'd fallen back through time. Yet understanding, hard-won over the months I'd spent in Din Cadan as Arthur's Queen, held me silent. I had to think of these men as the enemy – an enemy who would do the same, or worse, to us.

One of the Saxons stepped out of their ranks. A forest of swords pointed at his chest.

His words came haltingly in our tongue.

"We sailors." His voice was deep and heavily accented, guttural in the way a modern German accent is. "Ships our home. Choose ships. Not die."

Arthur turned his horse away. "Bind them and send them west to Caer Uisc to join the fleet. They'd be wasted in the mines."

He saw me and flashed a smile, his teeth white against the dirt. He almost looked like the Arthur I'd come to know, but not quite.

"The wounded need you." He twisted in his saddle toward the young warrior approaching us across the battlefield. "Bedwyr, take the Queen to the wounded so she may treat them with you." And then to me. "He has a pack horse with bandages and spirits and anything else you may need."

I went with Bedwyr. Arthur didn't need me. He was deep within a world in which I could only ever be an observer on the sidelines and never the partner I wanted to be. Nor was it a world I felt ready to be a part of, now I'd seen the reality of battle.

The wounded lay on a bank above the river where the ground was drier and less churned by the hundreds of feet that had been fighting there. Most had sword cuts to arms and legs that I could disinfect with the strong spirit Bedwyr passed me, then stitch and bandage. It was bloody work, but not too many men had been wounded. The Saxons had been caught by surprise, not expecting a new army to appear in Linnuis out of the blue, and the battle had never swayed in their direction. They'd fought well and fiercely but had been unable to claw any advantage.

Near the burning ships the British warriors constructed a pyre and laid our own dead on it with punctilious respect. While I worked on the living, Arthur took a torch and thrust it into the kindling stuffed into the base of the pyre. The flames caught, and smoke rose toward the lowering sky, soon accompanied by a stench of roasting meat that made my stomach roil.

I was just bandaging the last man's arm when the order came to march.

Merlin brought Alezan. We helped the wounded onto their horses and I took Alezan's reins, and, setting my foot in my stirrup, swung myself up into the saddle. Left behind us lay the still-burning funeral pyre, the scattered bodies of the enemy dead, the mud, the blood, the smoking hulks of the ships and a battle site that would be remembered forever, thanks to an obscure ninth-century monk called Nennius, as the battle of the River Glein.

Chapter Fifteen

THE ROMAN CITY of Caer Lind Colun, that would one day become modern Lincoln, sat on the rising ground beside the River Witham. Its walls stretched down to stone wharves where long ago hundreds of ships from across the Roman Empire must have docked to unload their wares; small, single-masted trading ships like that of Captain Xander. That charming polygamist was no doubt safely through the Bay of Biscay by now, on his way back toward the Straits of Gibraltar carrying our tin and his tales of far-off Britain. Now, however, the wharves lay empty of all but a few scruffy boats that looked no more than river craft.

Riding between Arthur and me, still flushed with his own success in battle, Prince Beli of Linnuis pointed to the river curling away south-eastwards from the city. "Our river – the Witham. Beyond lies the Metaris estuary and beyond that the German Ocean, filled with more Saxon pirates every year." He grimaced. "And each year, to north and south of my father's kingdom, their settlements spread toward us like a canker."

The frown on Arthur's face deepened as he surveyed the city lying before us, but he remained silent. I had to wonder how safe this place was.

Two days had passed since the battle of the River Glein, and now, escorted by Prince Beli, we finally reached the city to find the lower east gates flung open to let us in. High, well-maintained walls towered over us, dotted with guards, their crenellations still in remarkably good condition. But when we passed inside, something quite different lay before us. Just as in many of the old Roman towns I'd visited, across the old geometric street plan new lanes twisted, narrow and muddy. Over great swathes of the city the Roman houses had been refurbished, or completely replaced with wattle and daub wooden buildings sporting roofs of tatty thatch.

In the once majestic Roman forum in the upper part of the city, the buildings which had housed the bureaucrats had long since been knocked down or bastardized. As in Caerwysg, and every other Roman town or city I'd seen, broken pillars like jagged teeth were all that marked where the state offices had stood. At some point, someone had ordered the construction of a wattle and daub church. It was bigger and more impressive than most I'd seen, with cloisters huddled by its side and a lone bell tower beside the clergy's lodgings.

"Our cathedral." Prince Beli's voice was tinged with bitterness. "Where our bishop celebrates mass every day." He turned his head away, as though he couldn't bear to look at it, his upper lip curling. "Where my father spends most of his time, on his knees praying for salvation to a God who isn't listening."

A market selling all manner of useful things occupied the remainder of the forum. Stalls, some up against the very walls of the cathedral, sold wooden kitchenware, livestock ranging from baskets of young chicks through goats and sheep to horses, metal farm implements, sweetmeats, bolts of cloth, shoes, strings of misshapen cured sausages, and hot food, the rich scent of it enticing. The thronging people trampled piles of animal droppings and food remnants without seeming to notice, and the noise of their voices rose toward the overcast sky. The whole place bustled with lively vigor, and over it hung the miasma of stale urine, dirty stables and unwashed mankind I'd begun to accept as par for the course in fifth-century Britain.

Our horses' hooves clattering on the paving, we rode past the cathedral, where beggars of all ages, from ragged, skinny children to old crones leaning on crutches, sat on the wooden steps, holding out their hands in supplication. Beyond the cathedral and behind the market stalls lay a series of haphazard, animal-filled pens and barns, with manure heaps steaming in the early evening chill. A cockerel strutted his stuff on top of a midden and, lifting his head toward the sky, benefited us with a chorus that would have woken the dead.

"Shut up, you stupid bird," shouted a man dragging a sheep away by its curly horns. "'Tis nearing time to sleep, not rise."

A ripple of laughter spread through the ranks of warriors as we passed him.

King Manogan's palace was another example of the curious cobbling together of Roman and British architecture I'd seen in other towns. A thatched hall, like the one at Din Cadan, had been stitched onto the side of a decaying Roman townhouse which possessed a pillared portico and impressive marble steps manned by heavily armed guards.

Beside the palace stood the customary stables and accommodation for our men and beasts. It wasn't until we'd settled and cared for our horses, and Arthur had assured himself our weary warriors were being received with enough hospitality, that he allowed us to follow Beli into the hall.

King Manogan sat on an elaborately carved throne which occupied a raised dais at the top of the hall. Long red robes reached to his bony ankles, where his dirty feet, with yellowed nails like a bird's talons, showed in open-toed leather sandals. A full head of silvery grey hair fell to well below his shoulders like a mane, and a beard, which should have been white but was stained yellow and brown with dirt, reached nearly to his ornately buckled leather belt. Bushy white eyebrows jutted over shadowed, red-rimmed eyes, and a great beak of a nose overhung a hard, thin-lipped mouth.

The men of his court lined the hall to either side, hastily summoned once our advance guard had warned him of our imminent arrival, I presumed. They were a mixed bunch, some as old as he was, several leaning on sticks for support. Amongst them mingled his warriors, some younger men more of an age with Prince Beli, a few with greying hair who perhaps had been young when Manogan had first become king. Many bore signs of the recent battle Beli had told us about in which his older brother had fallen: bandaged limbs or the odd severed stump, blackened eyes, fresh scars. Perhaps many men were missing for the same reason.

Manogan's warriors had not joined us as reinforcements. Only Beli and the two messengers who'd met us on the Roman Fosse Way, bearing news of further Saxon raids, had taken part in the battle. And surveying them now, I felt glad. They looked a sorry, beaten lot, their faces barely hiding the resentment they must be feeling toward a rescuing army from another kingdom. Not a man amongst them had a smile on his face. Annoyance rose in me for Arthur and our men, but at the same time, I could understand why they might not be feeling too grateful.

We walked up the center aisle of the hall between the rows of watchful men. Arthur, his helmet tucked under his arm, halted at the foot of the steps to the throne, ahead of Merlin, Cei and me. He made a small bow to the older man, a mere inclining of the head. When king met king, it seemed, no one had precedence.

Manogan rose slowly to his feet, leaning one hand on the arm of his throne for support as though his bones pained him, and returned a similar bow. In the twenty-first century, I'd have guessed his age at over eighty, but here, with notoriously shorter life spans, he might well be a little over fifty.

"I bid the Dux Britanniarum welcome." His voice rasped, deep and husky. "And thank him for his services in battle." He gestured with his free hand, and half a dozen young men, scarcely older than Drustans, stepped forward out of the shadows behind the throne. "And I present you with our conscripts for your *combrogi*. Linnuis gives to you her young men, that you may make them warriors in your army."

The six young men, all clad in mail shirts and leather braccae, and carrying red painted shields, went down on their knees in front of Arthur, bare heads bent.

"My lord Arthur," began the tallest, a lad with jet black hair and a fuzz of patchy beard on his pimply chin. "We vow to serve in your army until the end of our days, whenever that may be. We vow allegiance to you and your causes, and loyalty to your royal house." He sounded as though he'd learned his speech off by heart. His fellows mumbled the same words in a self-conscious chorus after him.

Arthur bade them rise with a single gesture. "I thank King Manogan for these new recruits. After losing too many of our own men, fighting against the Saxons beside the Glein, they are a welcome addition to the army of the Dux."

His gaze returned to the youngsters. "You will go immediately to join my army in the stables and barracks, and introduce yourselves to my general, Theodoric."

The young men bowed in unison and hurried on their way, perhaps eager to join the victorious army, or maybe just to please their previous king. From now on, though, they would answer to no one other than Arthur.

Manogan lowered himself back onto his throne with the air of a man for whom this was a painful operation. Arthritis, in all probability, inflaming his joints and making movement difficult. What wouldn't modern anti-inflammatories have done for this man.

He gestured to his waiting servants. "Bring seats for my honored guests."

Servants dragged forward four ornate seats, and we sat in a semi-circle before the king. His courtiers remained standing, but shifted restlessly to ease their positions. Prince Beli moved behind and to the left of the throne, beside a much younger, auburn-haired boy, who, by his looks, must surely have been his brother, Anwas. But hadn't Beli told us this brother was training to be a recruit in our army? Why wasn't he amongst the six young men we'd just received?

"Tell me about the battle," Manogan barked, his tone that of a man used to being obeyed. "How many ships? How many of the enemy are no more?"

Arthur didn't seem to mind his host's bad manners. With good grace, he recounted the story of the battle in detail. I didn't need to hear it, and instead, my attention wandered to the other people in the hall.

Standing ramrod straight behind his father's throne, Prince Anwas drew my attention first. He was still beardless, with an unformed boyishness about his rather androgynous face. He wore his auburn hair cut short about his ears, and his face had flushed pink with what might have been anger. Had his exclusion from the six recruits been recent, perhaps stemming from the death of his older brother? He saw me looking, and the flush spread to his ears, his eyes falling to study his boots. He didn't look up again.

Prince Beli, standing beside his younger brother, listened intently to Arthur's version of the battle, occasionally adding a word or two of his own when questioned by his father. However, when it came at last to the fate of the Saxon prisoners, whom we'd sent off to Caer Legeion gwar Uisc in chains and under heavy guard, his father's face darkened with anger.

He banged his age-spotted fist on the arm of his throne. "A single living Saxon raider is an anathema to me." Spittle flew. "You should have slain the lot of them and hunted down the ones that fled. I'll not see a Saxon live who engaged in the slaughter that took my son and heir from me."

Beli glanced at him, his expression pained. He was the son and heir now, and after him came young Anwas, so although war had deprived Manogan of his oldest son, he did at least still have an heir. His father's thoughtless words, apparently forgetful that he had two other sons, must have hurt Beli, and probably young Anwas too.

Arthur's face remained impassive. He wasn't going to rise to any bait Manogan might throw at him. "We have a fleet of warships based at Caer Legeion. They're always in need of men to man the oars. I couldn't deprive my general of twenty brawny sailors. The Saxon prisoners will be kept in irons for the rest of their useful lives. Probably they'll die chained to their oars. They'll never again raise a weapon against a British kingdom."

Manogan's rheumy eyes flashed angrily. "I want your word that if you take prisoners again, you'll give them to me." He pointed at his two sons. "I've but the two boys left. I want my revenge for my firstborn, and I'll have it." He paused. "God has promised it to me."

I very much doubted God had done anything of the sort, but it looked as though Manogan was convinced of it. I began to see why Beli regarded his father's time spent praying inside the cathedral as time wasted.

Arthur shook his head. "I'll make you no false promises. If we take prisoners, they'll go to our fleet or to the tin mines in Cornubia, or the iron mines in Gwent where my cousin Caninus has need of strong arms."

Manogan bristled with rage, his bloodless lips drawn together in a bitter line. "What plan does the Dux Britanniarum have to offer, then?" He was a proud old man, and having to ask another king for help obviously came hard to him. His face mirrored the thoughts that must be flashing through his head.

Arthur leaned forward. "I'll need detailed reports of where the attacks have come, a map of your kingdom, and Prince Beli and your best warriors added to my force. I'll need scouts who know the land, who I can send out to find the Saxon raiders with no risk of capture." He paused. "And accommodation suited to the status of my queen. She's tired after many days' riding. And a bath for her."

I was a tiny bit miffed my comforts had come last in his list of requirements, even though I was getting used to that by now, with a better understanding of his priorities.

Manogan's bushy white brows jutted further in a frown, as though Arthur were asking for his own weight in gold. However, he barked a sharp order to his older son, and the prince disappeared, to return a minute later with a young woman in an ankle-length russet tunic, her long auburn hair bound in a single plait.

"My only daughter, Princess Essylt," Manogan said, nodding to Arthur. "She will see your queen well cared for."

For a moment I was distracted. Essylt? Why did that name seem familiar?

I didn't really want to leave Arthur with the irascible king of this strangely hostile northern kingdom, but he was right. I was exhausted. With reluctance, I rose from my uncomfortably hard seat and went with Princess Essylt through a door in the back of the hall and out into the more Romanized part of her father's palace.

She was young, scarcely more than fifteen, I'd have guessed, and very pretty, with large hazel eyes, a generous mouth and a sprinkling of freckles across her well-proportioned nose. "We've prepared the best guest rooms for you and the Dux Britanniarum," she said as we walked down a wide corridor whose unshuttered windows opened onto a shady courtyard garden.

The best guest accommodation consisted of a pair of rooms opening into one another. The outer was an antechamber with seating and a table. Intricately carved double oak doors led into a spacious sleeping chamber furnished with a wide, fur-covered bed. A mosaic of geometric shapes decorated the floors of both rooms, and faded, vaguely pornographic scenes adorned the walls. She didn't seem in the least bit self-conscious about taking a visiting queen into what looked as though it might once have been a brothel.

A pair of servants were waiting in the antechamber. Princess Essylt sent them off with a wave of her hand to fetch a bathtub and hot water, and sat herself down on one of the cushioned benches. Leaving her there, I went into the bedchamber.

Our saddlebags had been brought in from the stables by a servant and lay on the floor beside the bed. I sat down, glad to have my bottom on something soft at last, and then lay back, letting the comfort of the bed wash over my aching limbs. I laid my hands on the still only slight rise of my belly, thinking about the growing child within.

Essylt appeared at the door and stood for a moment looking down at me. "Are you really a queen?"

I didn't sit up. The bed was too comfortable. "Yes, I am."

"You don't look like one. Not that I've ever met one. My mother died when I was young, birthing my sister. And no queen has ever visited us before. Queens usually stay behind when kings go to war."

"Not me. I'm different." She'd have been surprised at how different.

She nodded, leaning against the doorpost. "I know. You're the Ring Maiden."

I wanted to change the subject. "Didn't your father marry again after your mother died?" If I closed my eyes, I would surely be asleep in minutes.

She shook her head. "He never took another wife. God told him not to. My father is famous for his piety, and now for his celibacy, as well." She stepped up to the bed. "Are you with child?"

"I am indeed."

From outside in the antechamber came the sound of the bath arriving.

She put out a hand and touched my saddlebags. "Do you have dresses in here? Or do you always dress as a boy? It'll look funny when you've a nine-month belly."

I pushed myself upright. "I have dresses with me, but it's easier to ride in boys' clothes. Don't you ever ride?" She was young, and she was a princess, so surely she must ride. The nagging feeling that I should know who she was persisted, but I was too tired to concentrate.

"Not by myself." She sounded shocked. "I hunt sometimes, sitting up behind my father's body servant with my hawk. But I've never straddled a horse as you were doing when you arrived." She paused, and then said, by way of explanation, "I was watching, and saw you. It looks a much better way to ride, but I don't think my father would allow it. He'd say it wasn't ladylike."

I stifled a yawn. "Have you never asked him if you could ride properly?"

She shook her head.

I got to my feet and went to the doors into the antechamber. The two servants were pouring jugs of hot water into a wooden bath which looked like a foreshortened but wide-based beer barrel lined with white sheeting. Just what I needed – a hot soak for my aching limbs.

"I'm tired now and need my bath," I said. "Thank you for your hospitality, Essylt, but I think I'd like to take it on my own." The last jug was tipped in. Herb scented steam rose temptingly off the water in the tub.

Essylt came up beside me. "Don't you need any help?"

I shook my head. "No, thank you. I'll be fine alone. But perhaps, if you could arrange it, and your father wouldn't find it rude, I'd like to eat here in my rooms and then go to bed."

Leaving me to my ablutions, the servants and a reluctant Essylt departed, and I pushed the nagging doubt that had set my senses on edge about her to the back of my mind, as though it were of no importance.

Chapter Sixteen

I MUST HAVE slept through Arthur coming to our bed that night because when I awoke the next morning, an indentation on his side showed me he'd been there but was now gone. Rolling over, I pressed my nose to the hollow, breathing in the faintest aroma of his body, wishing I'd woken early enough to have seen him. But I couldn't stay there forever. Curiosity and the need to pee, which had become much more frequent of late, got me out from between the covers and over to the leather bucket in the corner.

Feeling much more comfortable, I looked round for my saddlebags and found someone had unpacked them for me. My clothes lay neatly folded on a large oak chest underneath the shuttered window. Having washed myself, and then brushed my teeth with powdered charcoal and dried mint leaves and spat liberally, I put on a loose, long-sleeved gown and my soft leather boots.

Much refreshed after a good night's sleep, I stepped into the antechamber.

Essylt was sitting at the table eating breakfast. After a moment, I realized it was probably my breakfast.

"Good morning," she said sweetly, polishing off the last of the dried dates.

I came and sat at the table and took a piece of the bread, before it all vanished, and spread it with some thick creamy yellow butter. Delicious.

"Do you make a habit of stealing your guests' breakfasts?" I asked, between mouthfuls. I was starving.

She gave a shrug. "Only the ones I like."

"The breakfasts or the guests?"

She giggled, and I was reminded of how young she was. "The guests."

I smiled. "You've a strange way of showing you like them."

A bowl of soft cheese caught my eye, but tempting as it was, I didn't take any, mindful of the warning to pregnant mothers in my old world to avoid listeria-bearing foods. Yet another nugget of vestigial knowledge that had come in handy – like my maths skills with Eigr.

"Do you know what's happening this morning?" I took a gulp of the small ale that accompanied the meal. "I slept in too long, and my husband's gone."

She wrinkled her pretty nose. "Well, my father is in the Cathedral praying, as he is every morning. He'll be there until midday, and then he'll shut himself in his office and refuse to come out." She broke the bread she was holding into pieces absentmindedly. "My brothers are usually at the training grounds all day long. But today, with the army of the Dux here, I couldn't say where they might be. I think I heard them talking to your husband about scouting parties last night."

I pushed my seat away from the table. "In that case, I'll just have to go and find out for myself."

She jumped to her feet. "I'll come with you."

We found Merlin in the stable courtyard saddling his horse. The buildings and yard were conspicuous by their emptiness, with only a few of our warriors visible, mostly the less seriously wounded. They sat in small groups, cleaning their tack, polishing their helmets, sharpening their weapons or just basking in the sunshine.

"Merlin!" I hitched up my skirts and hurried toward him, Essylt in my wake. His head turned, and a smile lit his thin face. He put down the saddle he'd been about to set on his horse's back and leaned against the animal's side instead. The sun in the yard held real warmth, and he had to squint against its brightness to look at me.

"My lady Guinevere." How formal that sounded when he usually called me Gwen. It would be for Essylt's benefit, of course. A queen commanded the respect of all her husband's people.

"Where are you off to, and where's Arthur?" I gestured round at the empty stable yard, ignoring protocol. "And all the men?"

He had the grace to look a bit awkward and embarrassed. "Ridden north at first light. A messenger came in late last night with news of Saxon ships seen making their way along the coast and raiding parties attacking fishing villages. There's marshes up toward the Humber, but Prince Beli has scouts who know the pathways through them. The Saxons'll most likely sail up the Humber or beach their ships on the sands and come ashore. That's what the King and Prince Beli think they'll do. They want to be waiting for them."

I felt abandoned. "He went without telling me. I thought he wanted me with him." A hollow pit of worry started in my stomach, worry that Arthur was riding into danger and I wasn't there to bring him luck. Even all my twenty-first-century common sense couldn't dissuade me from superstition, however much I denied it. I'd caught it from the people around me like a common cold, only unlike a cold, it was here to stay.

"He left me to take care of you," Merlin said, as though it were the smallest matter. "He told me you were too tired to travel with the army, and it was too dangerous. I'd agree with him on that. You only saw that first skirmish because we went straight there with nowhere safe to leave you."

"I thought I was supposed to be the luck of Arthur," I retorted. "Won't the men protest if I'm not with them?"

Essylt was listening to all this in fascination, her eyes flicking from Merlin to me.

Merlin sighed. "The men will have to content themselves

with you being here in Linnuis. Arthur told me he's not prepared to risk you again. You're to remain here with me."

"And me," Essylt put in. "It'll be a change for me to have a royal lady about. I've only had brothers since my little sister sickened and died."

Her matter-of-fact referral to the death of a child shocked me. "What happened? What did she die of?" The perils that would threaten my child once it was born leapt to the forefront of my mind.

Essylt gave a careless shrug. "A fever. What do children usually die of? She was never strong. That was a few years ago now. She was six." She paused, suddenly thoughtful. "I still miss her. It was nice having a sister."

From instinct, my hand slid to my belly, cradling my baby. This was an age where common childhood illnesses could be fatal – measles, mumps, diphtheria, smallpox, chickenpox, whooping cough…diseases we vaccinated children for in my time. Even just the common cold or bronchitis might be harder for a child to fight off. An involuntary shiver ran through me.

I looked back at Merlin, anxious for a distraction. "Where are you going?"

He ran his hand down his horse's neck affectionately. "He needs exercise. I thought I'd ride out into the hills and take a look around. Not far, just enough to let him stretch his legs."

"Can I come?"

A frown creased his brow. "I don't know about that. I don't think that'd be keeping my promise to the King to keep you safe. D'you want him to be angry with me?"

"I was safe watching the battle by the River Glein in your company. I'll be safe with you now. We can take some of the men he's left behind as extra guards." I eyed the men. "The least badly wounded ones. Please. I'll only be bored here. Please take me with you."

Essylt looked offended. "I wish I could come," she said, with an air of regret. "My father won't let me ride on my own, though."

I ignored her input and put my hand on Merlin's sleeve.

I could feel his hesitation. "Alezan needs exercise as much as your horse does, and we don't need to go far from the city."

He wavered. "Well...perhaps you could come if we don't go far."

On Merlin's insistence, we confined ourselves to riding around the perimeter of the city walls, jogging along the muddy tracks between farmsteads, which hardly satisfied my longing for freedom, but definitely took care of Merlin's obligation to keep me safe. We could very easily have taken Essylt with us, novice that she was, on a quiet horse.

Little did I know, but this was to be the pattern of my days for some time to come. With Arthur and the joint forces of the Dux and Linnuis out on campaign, I was left in limbo at Manogan's court. Each day stretched longer than the last, while we waited for news of the army. Having been present at the battle of the river Glein, it hadn't crossed my mind that the real burden of having a warrior king for a husband would be the waiting. This was perhaps made worse by the fact that, so short a time before, I'd witnessed a battle with my own eyes, and the confused, tumultuous melee that had made it. I couldn't help but imagine the battles Arthur might be involved in now, battles in which he would constantly be putting himself at risk.

What if he died, and I never saw him again? Horrible as that fear was, I had to contemplate what I'd do if that happened. If I'd been in Din Cadan, I'd have persuaded someone to take me to Ynys Witrin and the Tor, and I'd have taken myself and my unborn baby back to the safety of the twenty-first century. But here, miles from home, what would happen if suddenly I was no longer queen? Could I rely on Merlin to get me back there?

Essylt did her best to distract me, as did Merlin, but I could tell, as the days passed with no word, that he was growing as nervous and worried as I was. Manogan spent most of his time in his cathedral, so I hardly saw him, and I made excuses to eat in my own chambers at night so I didn't have to tolerate the noise and heat of the crowded Hall. Essylt, who seemed to have adopted me as a surrogate sister, ate all her meals with me and kept me entertained as best she could with tales of her brothers, and of the court here in Caer Lind Colun. Sometimes Merlin dined with us, but for the most part we were left to ourselves.

On one of those occasions she confided that she was betrothed in marriage. That took me aback somewhat as she seemed far too young to be married off to anyone, but then I remembered that girls were considered ripe at a far younger age in much of the past. At twenty-four, I myself was almost over the hill for marriage and childbirth in the fifth century.

"Who are you betrothed to then?" I asked in curiosity.

We were sitting in the courtyard garden beside the little pond where lilies were just poking their noses up out of the water. Essylt gave a dismissive shake of her head. "Some old king in the south. I forget his name. They betrothed me to him when I was eleven and I have no idea when I'm to marry."

Some old king? Who could she be talking about? "Aren't you worried about marrying someone so much older than you?"

She shrugged. "He's so old he'll probably die before we marry. And my father doesn't really want me to go. He says I remind him of my mother and he likes to have me close."

The fact that he spent his mornings cloistered in the cathedral and his afternoons in his office, then in the evenings Essylt was with me, gave the lie to this. I didn't feel as confident as Essylt that this marriage was never going to happen. She, however, had the distinct air of someone who thought that if she didn't acknowledge or name her prospective husband, then it wouldn't happen. I felt more than a little sorry for her, likely to be dispatched south at any moment to a man she didn't know.

Who could her affianced husband be? At fifteen, every man over twenty-five looks old, so it could be any of the kings I'd seen at the Council in Viroconium. Perhaps strapping young Natanleod of Caer Gwinntguic. He'd make a good choice for a youthful and romantic princess.

However, in my concern for Arthur, for some time I failed to notice something that was going on right under my nose.

The first intimation of it came a few days later, when Essylt arrived to sit with me in the courtyard garden on a stone bench beneath an arbor of rampant greenery. Flushed and breathless, she almost skipped up the path between the overgrown flower-beds. No gardeners here to preserve what the Romans had once laid out, and the new season's weeds were already pushing their way up between the flagstones.

I'd been sitting by myself thinking about Arthur and the baby in my belly, sure that the fluttering I'd felt on and off for the last few days were its movements. Thrilled with the novelty, and half daring to be excited about it, I wished I could take Arthur's hand and lay it on me so that he, too, could feel it. Essylt disturbed my meditations, dropping down beside me, a wide smile on her face.

Dragging myself back from my thoughts, I eyed her in surprise. "You look cheerful." She'd been in a mope the day before because her father had flatly refused to let her wear men's clothes and ride astride. Now her cheeks were flushed pink with excitement and her eyes glowed over-brightly.

"I am," she said on a breath. "How could I not be?"

A feeling of uneasiness began to dawn. After all, I'd been a teenage girl myself not too long ago. "Where've you been?" My voice came out heavy with suspicion.

"The stable courtyard. But don't tell anyone. Father would disapprove. But he can't stop me because he's always praying. He has no idea what I do. You'd think he wouldn't care about me riding properly for once." Even thoughts of her father's disapproval couldn't shake the smile from her eyes.

It was obvious she hadn't been admiring the horses. Only one thing could make a girl glow that much. A boy.

This could only mean trouble. She was a princess betrothed to another king. A boy from the stable courtyard would not be a good match.

"Who is he?" I asked.

Her eyes widened in surprise. "How did you know?" She gulped. "Is it obvious? Will other people know?" For a moment fear flashed across her guileless face.

I let out a sigh and raised my eyebrows. I could do without sorting the love life of an impressionable princess when all I wanted to do was worry about my own husband. But at least it would give me something else to think about. "I'm a woman. Of course I know. It's written all over your face."

She blushed hotly. "You won't tell, will you?"

I let myself smile. "No, I won't. But you have to tell me who it is. You're a princess and you have to mind what you do."

She buried her face in her hands. "I can't tell you. I'm too embarrassed." Her voice was muffled, but full of laughter. If hers hadn't been such a precarious existence, I would have been happy for her. But she was the daughter of a volatile and eccentric old man who was putting far too much trust in an uncertain God I wasn't convinced even existed.

"I won't look at you. Then you can tell me." I turned my head away and looked out at the straggly garden where a few doves strutted between the weeds.

"Drustans," she whispered and gave a giggle.

Drustans. I don't know why, but the penny didn't drop until that very moment. Her name – Essylt. His name – Drustans. The legendary star-crossed lovers, Tristan and Yseult. And swiftly on the heels of that realization came another – the identity of the king she must be betrothed to. Drustans' father – March of Caer Dore. I didn't know an awful lot about the romance of Tristan and Yseult, but I knew Yseult married King Mark, while in love with Tristan, his son or nephew according to which story or legend you chose to believe. A cold hand clamped over my heart, pushing my fears for Arthur out of my head for the moment.

"No," I said, before I thought about it. "You can't."

She bridled, as any teenage girl would on being told that the boy she'd chosen was forbidden. "Why not?" She was bordering on angry. "He's a prince, so there can be no problem with his rank. I'm not silly enough to fall in love with a stable boy!"

I swallowed. "The man you're betrothed to…"

She interrupted. "Oh, pooh to him. He's an old man, and he's far away. I can persuade my father to annul that and let me marry Drustans. He'll be a king one day himself. It's a perfect match. And…" She paused, a faraway look in her eyes. "He's so handsome. And not much older than me. I'm sure my father would rather see me wed to a boy my own age than some old man."

I wasn't so sure about that.

"The man you're betrothed to…" I tried again, putting my finger to her lips when she tried to interrupt, "…is Drustans' father, I think. March of Caer Dore."

She opened her mouth to speak, paused, and then shut it again. The happiness drained out of her eyes.

I soldiered on. "And I doubt very much, having met him, that he'll back out of his betrothal to you in favor of his son. We know what your father is like. He wouldn't let you learn to ride astride; he's never going to let you break off a betrothal."

Tears glistened in the corners of her eyes.

I took her hands in mine and held them tight. "I think you have to give up seeing Drustans. It's his father you're going to have to marry."

I hated myself for saying this to her. She was a teenager in love, a teenager betrothed to an old man she'd never met, and there was nothing either of us could do about it. I wished Arthur were here. Perhaps he could have persuaded Manogan to allow his daughter to marry whom she wanted in payment for his services against the Saxons. But wouldn't the old king see that as unwarranted meddling in his private affairs?

Her lower lip trembled. "I won't." Her voice quavered. "They can't make me. I won't marry him. It's Drustans I love." She raised her eyes to mine, in pleading. "Arthur is the Dux Britanniarum. You can ask him to intervene for me when he returns. Drustans is one of his warriors. Surely he'll want to help him?" She'd had the exact same thoughts as me, but with more hope involved.

I didn't know what to say. Where I came from it would have been an easy matter to sort out, but Arthur was a man of his time who would see the initial betrothal as binding. I really didn't think he would want to help a princess against her father. If he ever got back, that was.

Chapter Seventeen

T WO DAYS LATER, word came of a battle far to the north of Linnuis, toward the River Humber. A single messenger arrived with the briefest of summaries of how the battle had been won beside a tributary called the Dubglas. Of course. Arthur's next battles after the River Glein had been on the River Dubglas – or Blackwater. It seemed as though that obscure monk Nennius, who no one was certain had even existed, had been right all along about at least some of the battles.

The message didn't bring news of any major casualties, so I could nurse the hope that Arthur was still in good health when the messenger had left the army. But there was no sign of any of them returning yet.

Through a storm of angry tears, Essylt had confirmed to me that her betrothed was indeed March of Caer Dore, and I'd given her a shoulder to cry on. But my worries for Arthur and my daily rides around the city with Merlin distracted me, and I foolishly allowed my concern for her to drop from the forefront of my mind.

Four days after the arrival of the messenger came the realization that she hadn't given up on Drustans at all. Not having seen her all day, even at breakfast, my suspicions were aroused, and I went searching for her. I made my way to her bedchamber in the late afternoon, as a thin drizzle fell from a cloudy sky.

A closed door faced me, which surprised me since she was a

girl who never shut any door she went through. I reached to knock, and paused, a warning going off inside my head. Instead, I put my hand on the door and pushed it open.

The closed shutters had rendered the room dark, so after the comparative brightness of the day outside, I couldn't see much for a moment. Then I saw them, just as they saw me…in the bed. Essylt gave a shriek of horror, and snatched the bedcovers up to cover her nakedness, as Drustans, equally naked, leapt to his feet and reached for his sword on the wooden chest beside her bed.

By his physical state, which was rapidly subsiding due to the shock he'd had, it looked like my arrival might have been just in time to prevent something pretty momentous from happening.

"Gwen!" Essylt's eyes widened with fear.

"My lady the Queen." Drustans snatched up his undershirt from the floor and held it in front of his nakedness. With his red-brown curls and long lean body, Drustans possessed a beauty reminiscent of Michelangelo's David. I could see why any teenage girl, princess or not, would easily fall for his charms, as a fair few at Din Cadan already had over the winter.

For a moment, words deserted me. Then common sense took over.

"What on earth do you think you're doing?" I asked, putting as much disapproval into my voice as possible. "Put your clothes on right now, both of you. And you, Drustans, get back to the stable courtyard and don't come out again. I'll decide what punishment you'll receive later."

Drustans pulled on his shirt as fast as he could, followed by his braccae and tunic. If I hadn't stopped him, he would have run out of Essylt's bedchamber looking like he'd just tumbled out of her bed, which, of course, he had.

"Fasten your belt, straighten your clothes, put on your boots, and take a moment to calm yourself. We don't want anyone else realizing what you've been doing." He did as he was told, breath slowing, and after a minute or two, I let him go.

The door closed behind him, and I turned back to Essylt, who was still sitting up in bed with the covers drawn up over her breasts. "You foolish little girl," I said, but the hopelessness of her situation prevented me from staying cross with her for long. She was only doing what countless teenage girls have always done, especially in my old world.

She burst into tears, ever the retreat of a child surprised in misconduct and scolded.

I went and sat on the bed next to her and amended my reprimanding tone to one of commiseration. "Come on, put your clothes on and we can have a talk about this. We'll get your bed straightened and no one need ever know what nearly happened here. You were lucky I arrived when I did."

She hung her head.

Uh-oh. I waited a moment but she didn't look up, nor did she make a move to grab her clothes.

A sigh escaped me. "This wasn't the first time, was it?"

She shook her head.

So much for being in time to prevent something ill-advised from happening.

"Oh, Essylt." I felt suddenly drained. "There's nothing you can do about this. You have to marry his father. You can never marry Drustans." Apart from any other reason, there was the fact that in all the stories that was what happened. It looked as though it might be unavoidable.

Tears fell onto the bedclothes. She gave a little nod. "I know. I asked my father and he was awful." Her words came out in a frightened gabble. "He said of course I had to marry my betrothed, and I should be glad to marry a king, not a stripling boy. I didn't tell him who it was. He asked me, but I refused to say and that made him angry." She shivered. "I was afraid he'd do something awful to Drustans, so I kept silent. And then he said that because I'd asked him to break off the betrothal, and wouldn't tell him the name of the boy I was mooning over, he was going to send me south to Cornubia so I could be married right away. He's sending me under escort with my brother,

Anwas, and a party of warriors in three days' time." She gave a little sob. "What am I going to do? It's Drustans I love, not his father."

"So you thought you'd force the matter by sleeping with the son?"

She nodded, looking up at me out of red-rimmed eyes.

I shook my head in exasperation. "That won't help you. All it will do is make everyone more determined to see you married off. Drustans could be executed for this. You're his father's property even before the wedding. The betrothal is binding." I'd gently probed Merlin's knowledge of betrothals a few days ago, wondering if it would be possible to influence Arthur in her favor. Merlin had been clear about the consequences to someone who infringed the strict rules of betrothal. An engagement was as good as marriage, so sleeping with someone else was adultery, even before the wedding. And the penalty for adultery was death. For a woman and her lover, that was. No such law for an unfaithful husband, who could take his pleasure wherever he fancied.

She wiped her eyes on the bedclothes and sniffed loudly. "But we love each other."

I thought about my love for Arthur and how hard it had been to choose him above Nathan and my old world. The pain in my heart had been immense. Even though this was adolescent love, it didn't mean Essylt's pain was any less. From what I remembered of teenage love, she'd be convinced Drustans was the one and only boy for her.

"If you've had sex with Drustans, then it could already be too late," I said, with the aim of frightening her into good behavior. "You might already be pregnant. You need to marry March as quickly as possible, so if you are, you can pass it off as his child. If you wait too long, you won't be able to." I paused, not wanting to frighten her too much, but the truth was what she needed to hear. "If March suspects you of infidelity he can have you executed, and the baby as well." I paused. "And Drustans, of course. After he's been castrated, that is."

The tears fell fast and thick. I patted her hand. "Come on, let's get you dressed and make the bed. You'll need to splash some cold water on your face. But then you can come back to my chambers with me, and we'll think of a plan."

WHATEVER I'D SAID to her, there wasn't really much of a plan we could make. Arthur didn't arrive back before Essylt was due to leave with her brother for Cornubia, and the only thing I could think to do was to keep Drustans away from her, lest he gave her away with his moonstruck face. I took Merlin into my confidence, which shocked him immeasurably.

"She's done what?" he almost shouted, necessitating my hand over his mouth and an audible, "Ssshh!" from me.

"Don't broadcast it," I hissed, glancing over my shoulder to check no one had overheard us.

He leaned toward me. "If anyone else finds out about this…"

I nodded with vigor. "I know. It doesn't bear thinking about."

"Her father will probably send her to a house of God."

I frowned. "No one can tell him." I put my hand on his arm. "*You* can't tell him is what I mean." There was a distinct air of the tattle-tale about Merlin just at that moment.

His mouth came together in a hard line of defiance. "She's broken the law of the land. The law of her father's kingdom. She's committed adultery. He deserves to know."

Who'd have thought Merlin was such a prude? But then, though he'd visited the twenty-first century, he'd never lived there and would have had no idea of what he'd see as the lax morals. Part of me was taken aback by his reaction, but a larger part couldn't help but approve that morals were expected to be upheld in this era. Although the fact that it was mostly the morals of women being upheld seemed decidedly unfair.

I gave him my hardest stare. "You can't tell anyone. She's just a child who wants a husband nearer her own age. It's not her fault."

His brows lowered in a heavy frown. "She's a royal princess and should know her duty."

I gave his arm a shake. "She's a child first and foremost. If you tell her father, then she'll be punished and God knows what they'll do to Drustans. You can't. I won't let you. And I'm going to need your help to keep them apart."

With a great show of reluctance, he finally agreed. I was relieved; I needed him to keep Drustans occupied so he had no chance to sniff around Essylt.

Every day when I went for my ride with Merlin, Drustans, looking long-faced and miserable, was one of our party, steadfastly bringing up the rear and refusing all efforts to engage him in conversation. And when we were in the palace, I contrived to keep Essylt close to me, insisting I was lonely, and she should sleep in my bed at night for the three days before her journey south.

I'd managed to make her see sense to a degree. "It's best if you don't see him at all," I told her, with all the wisdom my extra ten years had given me. "It's safer for him. Do you want him to end up castrated and possibly dead?" It was difficult, but I knew I had to be cruel to be kind. If I'd turned a blind eye, someone would have been bound to find out about them. Going to bed together in an unlocked room in the middle of the day was not rational behavior. Essylt had the good grace not to sulk with me the way Drustans was.

On the day she was to leave, she and I met for the last time in the stable courtyard. Merlin had arranged to send Drustans out with some of the other warriors to scout northwards up Ermine Street, looking for any sign of the returning army, so she didn't get the opportunity to say goodbye to him. I felt mean, but having kept them apart for three days, I didn't want her to throw herself into his arms for a tearful farewell in front of a yard full of people, and especially not her own father.

Her escort party numbered a good twenty, including herself and her brother, Anwas, who was looking inordinately proud to be escorting his sister south to her wedding. Two of the number were servants – a burly man on a substantial cob and Essylt's old nurse, a thin woman with a permanent drip on the end of her nose. The burly man had a saddle pad attached to his saddle, and Essylt was to ride there when she wasn't traveling in the accompanying covered wagon.

King Manogan, looking more than ever like an emaciated dirty white bird, had foregone his usual morning sojourn on his bony knees in the cathedral, and was seated on his throne, which his servants had carried out into the courtyard. As Arthur's queen, I stood beside him, watching the preparations and praying Essylt wouldn't give herself away at the last minute.

She emerged from the hall with a gaggle of women surrounding her, head held high, small chin determined, but her eyes were red from crying. In front of her father, she went down on her knees, head bent for his blessing. For a long moment he didn't move, and, puzzled, she raised her face to look him in the eye. He stretched out a shaking hand and laid it on the top of her head. Her eyes closed and a tear squeezed between the lids to run down her pale cheek.

"May the Lord God bless your marriage, my daughter." Manogan's voice was quavery and uncertain. Was he looking round the watching faces and wondering which boy it was she'd taken such a fancy to? As he withdrew his hand, she rose to her feet, then abruptly turned her back on him and walked toward the mounting block.

She climbed onto it and looked for the last time around the courtyard, desperation in her eyes. I couldn't help but think how lucky I'd been that Arthur had turned out to be the man he was. I could so easily have been forced into marriage with a man I could never have loved. But this was the fifth century, and women's desires were not often considered. They hadn't been with me, and they wouldn't be with Essylt. I knew the legends. Her love for Drustans had always been doomed.

Her servant brought his cob up to the mounting block and Essylt got on behind him, her long dress draped elegantly over the horse's quarters. Not the most secure way of riding, but the only one she knew. I wished for her sake she'd been allowed to don boys' clothes and ride astride. At least it would have made the long journey to the tip of Cornubia a little less onerous.

The wagon rumbled across the uneven paving of the stable courtyard, drawn by a team of four horses, the figure of Essylt's old nurse perched beside the driver. At least the girl wouldn't be the only woman on the journey. Essylt craned her head round, scanning the yard. If she was searching for Drustans, then she was out of luck as he was far away with the scouts, heading in the opposite direction.

As the riders filed out behind the wagon, Essylt's eyes, filled with unshed tears, found mine. Anger boiled up in me, anger at my impotence. I'd wanted to help her but my hands had been tied, and her fate, which was already written, moved inexorably onward. March was her destiny, not his handsome son. A lonely grave near Caer Dore awaited that young man, a grave that never proclaimed him as a king, perhaps foretelling an early death for him; a grave I'd once stood beside with my father at the edge of the busy road into Fowey, only a few miles from his father's stronghold.

My heart filled with sad regrets.

MIDSUMMER HAD ARRIVED before the army returned. Essylt had been gone three weeks and was probably already safely married to March of Caer Dore. Scouts preceded the main body of the army, so we were all gathered on the walls above the north gate waiting to welcome them home when they came riding south down Ermine Street. Arthur's banner depicting a rampant bear flew above their heads, fluttering as the breeze caught the light material and made it dance. Wishing for binoculars, I strained my eyes, trying to pick out the white horse that was Arthur's, and failing. Where was he? Why wasn't he riding at the front, as usual?

My heart beat in the base of my throat, the small hairs on my skin stood up and a cold sweat dampened my brow. I lowered my hands to cradle my now gently rounded belly, comforting the restless child within, praying for his father's safe return.

The column drew nearer, and my eager gaze alighted on the white shield emblazoned with the black bear that Arthur carried. I put my hand up to shade my eyes and strained, but he was too far away to be sure it was him. Beside me, Merlin's knuckles whitened as he gripped the edge of the stone crenellations. Was he as nervous as I was, despite his possession of the Sight?

At last, I recognized Arthur's dark head and familiar features, his hair confined by a bandage, and a thick dark beard covering his chin. If I could have flown to him from the parapet, I would have. Inaction ate at me as the column crept slowly toward us along the road, passing between farms where the people came hurrying out to watch.

As the riders approached the gates, I turned from the parapet and ran down the steps to the road below, where the population of the city waited to greet their returning heroes. I shoved between the hot bodies, using my elbows to fight my way to the front. The first horse came through the gates, Gwalchmei carrying the bear standard, and a great cheer went up. My gaze went past him. Another rider emerged from the shadows of the gateway – Arthur, on a chestnut horse I didn't recognize. Where was his beloved grey mare Llamrei?

"Arthur!" I ran toward him. Behind me, Merlin reached the front of the crowd and called my name, but I ignored him.

Arthur's head turned, and I saw with a shock that dried blood crusted his face and beard. From beneath a dirty bandage his dark eyes found mine and lit up. He was off his horse in a second, and I ran into his arms, tears running down my cheeks.

"Gwen!" He held me close, arms tight around me, as though he never wanted to let me go. I clung to him, breathing in the scent of blood and horses and male sweat that once would have made me turn up my nose, but now was comfortingly familiar.

"Arthur!" I could only repeat his name, so relieved was I to have him back with me. "Arthur."

Merlin stepped up to us and slapped him on the back. "Best keep walking or the rest of the army will never get through the gate."

Arthur jerked back to reality and, releasing me from his embrace, took my hand instead and began to walk along the wide street that led to the forum, leading his horse. Merlin fell in just behind us. I had a hundred questions, but for now I was content to walk quietly by his side, basking in the fact that he was back safely with me at last. In my belly, our child turned a little somersault.

Chapter Eighteen

I N THE PRIVACY of our chambers, I knelt beside the wooden bath, sponging Arthur's back as he leaned forward. His body mapped how the war had gone, bruises of varying shades mottling his skin alongside a multitude of grazes and healed cuts. He winced as I applied a little too much pressure, and I hesitated.

Turning his head, he looked up at me from beneath his damp curls. "Scrub as hard as you need. I'm filthy and stink, and can't wait to get rid of the smell of battle."

I rubbed harder again, trying to lather a soap that didn't want to oblige. The sight of him so damaged ate at my heart. If this was the reality of fifth-century warfare, would I have to see him like this time and again? I could understand why Uthyr Pendragon had seemed aged beyond his years, and why Manogan was as mad as he appeared to be. Maybe turning to God, instead of war, was a better alternative. As his mother had wanted.

The cut on his head which the bandage had covered was in his hairline, and relatively new. When I washed his hair, the cut began to bleed afresh. Bright blood trickled down the side of his face to his freshly shaven chin. Rinsing my cloth in a bowl of now bloodstained salty water, I re-applied it to the cut. "How did you get this?"

He gave a shrug. "I've no idea. I only noticed it when the blood got in my eyes."

As well ask a modern car mechanic how he'd got so dirty.

I finished his back, and he reclined in the bath, the dirty, cooling water slopping. Despite the state he was in, he had a smile on his face that I recognized, as he raised a wet hand and touched my cheek. "I thought of you every moment of every day I was away." His thumb caressed my skin, and my heart gave a little leap as I closed my eyes in pleasure. After all these weeks, I'd almost forgotten the way his touch could send shivers through my body.

My breath caught in my throat. "I could think of nothing else but you."

He pushed aside the washing cloth, and I let it drop into the water unheeded. Standing up in the bathtub, he drew me to my feet and pulled me into his wet embrace. I clung to his naked body as if I'd thought I'd never do so again – which, in fact, in moments of doubt, I had. He stepped out of the bath and scooped me up in his arms to carry me to our bed. With infinite care, he laid me down on it, then crawled across me until his face hovered over mine, careful not to put any weight on my still only scarcely rounded stomach.

I reached up to touch his damaged face. The bleeding had all but stopped, and his skin felt smooth and bristle free. "I prefer you without a beard." My fingers traced the contours of his chin. "I like being able to see what you look like." A nasty bruise darkened his cheekbone, and a scab clung where the skin had been broken.

He laughed. "And do I please you?"

My heart thundered in my chest. "You do indeed." My voice had grown husky with desire, and an ache for him was pounding through my body so that I was nearly squirming with anticipation. "Although you'd please me better if you weren't so battered."

Ignoring my rebuke, he bent his head and kissed me, his loose wet curls brushing my skin as his mouth came down on mine. My lips parted, our tongues met, and I reached my other hand to pull him down onto me.

Eventually, we both came up for air, panting. He grinned mischievously, and his hand ran down my body, hitching at my skirts. "You've far too many clothes on."

My breathing came fast and shallow. "I'll remedy that. Get up a minute, and I'll take them off."

With laughter playing on his lips, he rolled off me to lie on his back, watching in open appreciation as I stripped off, letting my clothes puddle about my feet. In a moment, I was back on the bed, straddling him. That he was pleased to see me was more than evident, but I wasn't going to hurry.

Still smiling, he reached up and pulled my heavy plait round to lie between my breasts. With slightly shaking fingers, he undid the tie that bound it, then ran his fingers through the braid until my hair fell loose around me in a shining chestnut veil. "I do believe your hair has changed color since I left."

"Yes. Sunlight does it." I leaned forward, brushing his curls out of his eyes, my own hair cascading over his body. "And missing you." I bent my head and kissed him with all the pent-up emotion I'd been gathering since he'd ridden away without telling me he was going.

Much later, we lay back together on the bed, our bodies slick with sweat. In the midsummer warmth, we had no need of clothes.

After a bit, he rolled onto his side, and I became aware of him studying me with his gold-flecked brown eyes. Conscious of his intent scrutiny, I turned my head and smiled, a sensation of languorous satisfaction perfusing my body. The movement of the baby flittered through me as though aware of its father's gaze.

I took Arthur's hand in mine and laid it on the soft rise of my belly, palm flat against the skin. After a moment of absorbed concentration, a look of wonder suffused his face, and he raised surprised eyes to mine. The baby moved again, slithering beneath my skin, as indefinable as trapped wind, and Arthur laughed, a sound of pure joy, in stark contrast to the seriousness of his normal demeanor. Suddenly, he was my Arthur again, not the

Dux Britanniarum, or the king of Dumnonia.

"That was him?" he asked. "That was our son?"

I smiled back. "Or maybe our daughter."

He shook his head. "No, I know this baby is a boy. Merlin told me so."

I was a little taken aback that he'd had that sort of conversation with Merlin and neither of them had thought to tell me. "Well, we'll see," I said, my tone a little frosty.

He didn't seem to have noticed my momentary irritation though, because he held up his arm for me to nestle against him and, after a split second's annoyed hesitation, I did so. It was so good to be close to him again after all those weeks of worrying. I could forgive him anything, even discussing the gender of our unborn baby with his friend, and having left me without saying goodbye, so long as he was back safe in my arms.

THE VERY NEXT morning, we rode away from Caer Lind Colun, leaving behind Prince Beli and his brave warriors, and King Manogan and his prayers. In his campaign, Arthur and his men had harried the Saxons right across the north of Linnuis, brought them to battle on more than one occasion, and eventually driven them back to the coast where their longships awaited them. Lives had been lost on both sides, but victory had been with the Dux Britanniarum. The Saxons had fled by sea back toward their holdings in the south-east, their tails between their legs and with fewer ships than before.

Our route led us down the Fosse Way to Caer Lerion, a tumbledown road junction occupied by the remains of a once splendid Roman town. We'd stayed there on our way up to Linnuis, and I'd not liked it much then. Now, after Caer Lind Colun, it seemed worse. The majority of the city walls remained standing, but here and there they'd long ago fallen or been knocked down. Had the local population done it deliberately in rebellion against their departed Roman overlords? Or was this damage inflicted by raiding Saxons? As people still lived within the walls, albeit in parody of the previous inhabitants, it seemed more likely to be the former reason.

We spent only one night in the seedy confines of the magistrate's house, and I was glad to put it behind us. From there, we headed west, to join what I would have called Watling Street but Arthur referred to as the Viroconium Road, taking our journey in easy stages. For once, we weren't pressed for time. I rode Alezan all the way. We now had a couple of wagons carrying the wounded who were too weak to ride, and both Arthur and Merlin pressed me to ride in the wagons from time to time, but I resisted with determination. I still had hardly any bump to speak of, and riding was much more comfortable than being bounced around in an unsprung wagon.

Theodoric, and with him the prisoners Arthur had taken, prepared to break away from us and march south, heading to Caer Legeion, where his fleet was based. So too did the wagons carrying the wounded, which were heading directly back to Din Cadan.

"I've had my fill of fighting on land," Theodoric said as he parted from Arthur. "My feet itch for the feel of trusty planks beneath them and my ears for the sound of wind in *The Mermaid's* sails, and the beat of the rowers' drum. My nose misses the salt tang, and my eyes the distant horizon."

Arthur embraced his friend. "Take your patrols around the south coast and up the east side of Britain. Engage the Saxon pirates before they ever set foot on our lands, and you'll be helping the cause far more than if you stayed with my army. We'll deliver Morgawse and your son to Caer Legeion, safe under King Caninus's guard, now the baby's of an age to travel and the weather warm enough. Have no fear of that."

Having parted from Theodoric, Arthur and Cei led the remaining army into Powys, heading for the country villa of

Euddolen, the late Uthyr Pendragon's seneschal. His villa estate lay ten miles south-east of Viroconium, Cadwy's capital. Not quite far enough away for comfort, in my opinion. However, after the dispute before the Council of Kings at the end of last year, Cadwy had pledged not to take revenge on those men who'd sided with Arthur. Back then, it had appeared to be the best place to leave Theodoric's wife, Morgawse, Arthur's youngest sister, with her newborn baby. Better than dragging her miles across wintry Britain.

I wasn't looking forward to seeing Morgawse. When I'd last been at Viroconium nearly eight months ago, I'd helped deliver her baby while Arthur and Cadwy had been scrapping over their inheritance – if that was what you could have called the fight between their two rival factions. While we were barricaded inside the palace kitchen, the baby had been born. A red-faced, screeching boy, clinging to life with a determination that would have been admirable.

Were it not for his name.

For Morgawse had named the child Medraut – the Mordred of the legends I knew, in which he was said to have led a rebellious force against Arthur at Camlann, where Mordred died, and Arthur was fatally wounded. My horror as Morgawse welcomed her son by name had heralded the guilty wish that the baby had died at birth. I was still ashamed of myself for harboring such thoughts.

And now we would be seeing this child again.

We arrived at Euddolen's villa on a balmy summer's evening. The farm, for that was what it was, nestled in a shady wooded valley near a sacred well. Between sweet-smelling meadows of freshly cut hay, a river flowed down the valley to join the distant River Sabrina. Wheat, slowly ripening to gold, stood tall in the small square fields that filled the lower slopes of the valley. And a well-worn track ran away through riverside orchards and willow stands, toward the distant thatched rooftops of the estate village.

Birds sang in the hedgerows as our horses splashed through

the ford and wound their way between the grassy paddocks. It was an idyllic welcome. But the gates on every paddock stood open, and not an animal was to be seen. This was strange, because all the way across the heartland of Britain we'd seen livestock, some in their home paddocks and some grazing out on the hills. Zealous herdsmen had wisely hurried their stock away from our path as soon as they caught sight of so many mounted warriors to watch us in suspicion from a distance.

We were a large party, even minus the wounded heading back to Din Cadan in the wagons. The cloud of dust which rose behind our column should have alerted the villa inhabitants of our arrival. Yet, oddly, no one came into the outer courtyard of the villa to welcome us. Our vanguard had ridden on ahead and as we clattered into the farmyard, they emerged on foot from the stables where they'd tied their horses, as confused as we were.

Arthur didn't dismount but leaned on his pommel and looked down at them, his furrowed brow betraying how puzzled he was. "Where is everyone?"

"We don't know," replied Ban of Benoic, the leader of the vanguard. He was one of the oldest of Arthur's warriors but still not a day over thirty, with short brown hair and a crooked nose he liked to tell people he'd broken in a fight with a giant, but which Merlin told me had actually been broken by a whore. "There's no one here. We've been all through the farm buildings and there's not a soul to be seen. Nor any livestock, save a few hens and a mangy cat."

Merlin looked over their heads toward the half-open gates that led into the inner courtyard. "Have you tried the house?"

Ban shook his head. "We saw you coming and thought we'd best wait for reinforcements. This don't feel right to me."

There was a long silence while everyone, me included, stared round at the apparently deserted farmyard. The few hens Ban had mentioned scratched about in the dirt as though nothing was wrong, and on the red-tiled rooftops, doves cooed peacefully to one another. The place had the atmosphere of a land-bound *Marie*

Celeste.

Arthur dismounted and tossed his reins to Merlin. "I'm going to look in the house. There must be someone here – the fields are all in good order."

"Is that wise?" Cei also dismounted. "I'll come with you. We'll take a guard. It could be a trap."

Nobody needed to say who might be setting this trap. We all had a pretty good idea.

At an order from Cei, half a dozen warriors dismounted and donned their helmets. Swords drawn, they followed him and Arthur through the gates to disappear into the inner courtyard. The rest of us sat on our horses in uncomfortable silence. Unnerved, I glanced around at the quiet farm buildings that now seemed threatening. A shiver of apprehension trickled down my spine. Was Ban sure the barns and stables were empty? Or were we about to be attacked?

We waited for what felt a long time, our horses shifting restlessly. Flies buzzed round their heads and settled on our sweaty faces. I was just beginning to feel very nervous indeed when the gates swung open again, and Arthur and Cei emerged with grim expressions. Between them, they marched Cutha, Euddolen's old midwife who'd attended Morgawse after she'd given birth. Dried blood matted her lank grey hair and the front of her tunic, and her eyes were saucers of terror.

My stomach roiled in sympathetic fear and the baby did a somersault.

Their six guards joined them at a run. "Nothing." The first spread his hands in an eloquent gesture. "Not a person. A lot of blood though."

"How much and how old?" Arthur asked, his voice edged with fury.

I was near enough to see the vein pulsing in his neck. He released his hold on the old woman, who shrank away like a beaten dog.

"Patches of it, congealed and drying," the warrior answered.

"No more than a few days old. Whatever went on here, it wasn't long ago."

Arthur turned back to the old lady. "What happened? Where are your master and mistress? And my sister?"

Thank goodness Cei still had her by the arm. She looked as though without his support she'd have collapsed in a heap. She shook her head, wordlessly.

"Speak." Cei shook her, and she flopped in his arms like a rag doll.

"Don't hurt her," I pleaded. "She's old and frightened." I slid down from Alezan and approached. "It's me. Gwen. You remember. You met me when we came to the Domus Albus last year, when the lady Morgawse had just had her baby."

She stared up at me out of red-rimmed, grey eyes, with a hint of comprehension. However, when I put my hand on her scrawny, bare arm, she recoiled as though I'd struck her.

"We won't hurt you." I made an effort to keep my voice low and gentle, willing her to trust me. "You don't need to fear these soldiers. They're on your side. My husband means to find out what happened here and help you. Please tell us what you know."

For a long moment she gazed at me, tears forming in the corners of her eyes and silently running down her blood-stained cheeks. Then she opened her mouth wide to show me a bloody throat devoid of all but the scabby stub of a tongue.

I must have fainted, because the next I knew I was lying in the shade of one of the buildings on a pile of cloaks, with Arthur kneeling beside me, pressing a cold wet cloth to my forehead.

He looked relieved to see me awake.

When I tried to sit up, he pushed me back with a firm but gentle hand. "You had a shock. Lie still."

The memory of that tongueless throat came rushing back and a wave of nausea washed over me. Fighting it down, I closed my eyes as tears squeezed out between my lids. "That poor old woman."

Arthur covered my hand with his. "They did it out of spite. Left her alive on purpose, maimed, so she couldn't tell us who'd done it." His voice held bitterness.

I opened my eyes. "There must be others here who saw." Ever the optimist, I was full of hope. "You didn't find any bodies, did you?"

He shook his head. "The workers must have fled and haven't had the nerve to return yet. If they saw us coming, that would have scared them even more, thinking they were being attacked again. I've sent my men to scour the village down by the river and see what they can discover."

When I tried to get up, he stopped me. "No, lie still a while. You mustn't forget you're with child."

I lay back. "That's just it. I'm pregnant, not ill. I only fainted because I don't like blood, and that was an awful sight. Can Bedwyr do anything for her?"

Even now, the very thought of what I'd seen inside her mouth made my stomach heave.

He shook his head. "The bleeding had stopped. But apart from that, all she can do is wait for it to heal. I know it looks awful, but people do live after that's been done to them." He felt my shiver and tightened his hold on my hand. "Don't think about it."

"How can I not? I know her. She's someone I met, talked to, liked. A kind old woman who'd committed no crime, and yet someone did that to her. It's not the same as a stranger. That sounds wrong, I know, but it's true. It's worse because I know her."

He was silent. What else could he say?

A horrible thought dawned. "If no one's here, have Cadwy's men taken all of them?"

His jaw stiffened as he gave a shrug. "Perhaps they have. But from the blood we found, I fear some or all of them must be dead."

I closed my eyes and thought of little Medraut, eight months old now, maybe crawling. Might he be dead? Would Cadwy kill his own sister's child because its father had turned against him?

Would that be a good thing? Probably.

Chapter Nineteen

THE MEN ARTHUR had sent to the village returned to the farmyard with the headman, Cocidius, a short, balding fellow with a lazy eye and a large bulbous nose. He approached with reluctance, under guard, and stood wringing his hands in front of Arthur and staring at his own dirty, sandaled feet.

Arthur had allowed me up by then, and I stood beside Merlin, watching this interview in trepidation.

"Tell us what went on here," Arthur said curtly. "Who did this?"

Cocidius trembled with fear. As well he might; Arthur was a tall man clad in armor with a fearsome sword at his side, surrounded by a host of other large warriors. "I-I didn't see," he began, in a voice small with terror.

"Nonsense." Arthur kept his own voice level with difficulty. "We know you are the steward here for Euddolen and his wife. You were here when the soldiers came. Weren't you?" It wasn't a question – rather, an accusation.

Cocidius looked about furtively as though he might find help somewhere, or a place to hide. Finding nothing, he gave the smallest of nods.

"So, tell me." Arthur's hands balled into fists by his sides. "What did you see?"

Cocidius licked dry lips. "We-we was out in the fields." He glanced around, as though fearing he would be struck. "We saw the soldiers come."

"Which soldiers?"

He trembled. "The-the king's. His foederati."

That wasn't news. Even I'd guessed this must be the work of Cadwy. But for him to have sent his Saxon mercenaries and not his own British-born soldiers seemed somehow even worse.

Arthur's dark brows came together in a heavy frown, momentarily giving him a look of his hated older brother. "What happened?"

Cocidius cringed. "We-we 'eard screaming and we 'id." The words hung in the still air.

For a brief moment, I boiled with rage at how Euddolen's people had hidden when danger threatened their master and his family. And then realization swept over me – there was nothing these peasants could have done other than lose their lives or end up like Cutha. Given these circumstances, I, too, would have hidden to save my own skin.

Arthur's jaw twitched, the vein pulsing in his neck. "And did you see what happened to your master?" He was angry, maybe not given to putting himself in the place of others. No wonder Cocidius was so afraid.

The headman nodded almost imperceptibly. "We-we watched. In case there were something we could do." He paused, his eyes faraway and pained, perhaps reliving what he'd seen and how impotent he'd felt. "There weren't. They loaded up all the servants and slaves into wagons. Some was wounded, I think. There were blood on 'em."

The story came in dribs and drabs, jerky and unsettlingly raw.

"They carried the master into the farmyard. Covered in blood, 'e were, like 'e were dead. I didn't see 'is girls. I couldn't watch. I 'ad to turn away." He licked his lips again. "They took 'em all, and all the livestock, too. Two days gone. We been 'iding in the village ever since, afeard they'd be back." He raised his eyes to Arthur's in supplication. "There weren't nothing we could do. We've little'uns of our own, that no one would care for if we got ourselves killed. We couldn't 'elp the master."

Arthur was silent. By his sides, his fists clenched and un-clenched. He turned away from Cocidius. "Send him back to his family." He spoke through gritted teeth.

Cocidius needed no urging. He ran, scuttling between the ranks of soldiers and out of the courtyard, probably glad to have escaped without any retribution.

Arthur turned to Cei and Merlin, his brows still creased in a heavy frown. "I should never have left them here so close to Viroconium, or believed Cadwy's assurances of their safety. I know him. He's ever been a liar and a bully. I should have guessed what he'd do. Promises mean nothing to him."

The sun beat down on the back of my neck, and sweat trick-led between my shoulder blades, thanks to my mail shirt. I thought of Euddolen's two lively teenage daughters, Albina and Cloelia, taken prisoner by a horde of Saxon savages. Of Morgawse and her little son. And Ummidia, who'd been swept up by her husband's support for Arthur in his bid for the throne of Dumnonia. All of these people were innocent and yet embroiled in this. And who knew what had befallen them in the last two days?

"We can't attack Cadwy," Merlin said in a low voice. "He's safe within the walls of Viroconium. And if we did, I'd not give a pig's ear for the chance of any of his prisoners staying alive."

Arthur nodded. "I know. But we can't leave them. Euddolen might well be dead, but his family are innocent. We came to take Morgawse south to Caer Legeion to join Theodoric, and I refuse to leave without her."

I batted the irritating flies, that were everywhere in the farm-yard, away with my hand.

"It's odd this only happened two days ago," Cei remarked. "Almost as though Cadwy knew we were coming this way. It's past midsummer – he's had a long time to take revenge on them and not made a move. Why now?"

Merlin shook his head. "To provoke Arthur. Morgana will

have warned him. She must have seen us coming."

They fell silent.

I watched their faces. From somewhere close by, a grasshopper chirped – the sound of summer.

Arthur broke the silence first. "We have to go to Viroconium and get them back by means other than warfare. That's the only thing we can do. Merlin's quite right when he says we can't attack. I suspect Cadwy wants us to, and that's why he's done this. But we'll call his bluff and ride into Viroconium as allies. Then we'll see what he does. If his aim is to discredit the role of the Dux Britanniarum, then we won't give him the chance."

I didn't like the sound of that one bit. When Arthur had faced Cadwy down before, the city had been filled with kings from all over Britain, witnesses to anything Cadwy might try. And even then, Cadwy had tried to poison Arthur and me. None of us would be safe riding into the lion's den.

I wasn't the only one of this opinion.

"You can't do that," Cei said. "If he's killed Euddolen and taken his family after promising their safety, you'd be giving yourself up to him. D'you think he'd blink at doing the same to you? His reasons are obvious. He thinks he might goad you into attacking Viroconium, which would give him a good excuse to fight back and destroy you. Or he hopes you might be foolish enough to enter his city under minimal guard. In which case you'll have a handy accident, for sure."

I thought again of the poisoned wine, and Breanna's last agonizing breaths.

"He's right," Merlin put in. "That's exactly what Cadwy and Morgana think you'll do – want you to do, even. If you ride into his city, you'll never ride out again."

Arthur scowled, but he couldn't argue with Merlin's words. Thank goodness they were there to calm his impetuosity.

Cei's was the voice of reason. "She's my sister, too. Let me go with just two other men. He's got far less of a problem with me. I don't think he'll lock me up...or kill me. Let me go and bargain for her release."

Merlin frowned. "He'll claim Morgawse is there of her own free will if he's got any sense."

"Then I'll ask to speak with her."

Arthur didn't look convinced. "You think he'll allow you to? It's Cadwy we're talking about here. Cadwy and Morgana. If he thinks you want Morgawse, he'll keep her well out of your way."

"And Ummidia and her daughters?" I interrupted. "What about them? They're more innocent than Morgawse because they're not even related to Arthur. We have to save them, too." I couldn't stand by in silence when the only person they seemed to be thinking of was Morgawse.

"If it's not already too late." Cei's words jarred the hot summer air and jangled in my ears.

Arthur turned to Cei. "If I let you go, then you'll take five warriors with you, not two. If he tries to have you killed, take as many of his men with you as you can. Particularly him." He paused, then added as an afterthought. "No, not him. Leave him for me."

"He won't have Cei and his men killed." Merlin sounded as though he were certain. "Whatever this is, Cadwy intends it as a trap for you, not Cei. He'll bargain, of that I'm sure. But we'll need to be suspicious of whatever he concedes. He's slippery as an eel, and by taking Euddolen and his family, to whom he'd offered immunity, he's taken a step down the road to further evil."

Arthur turned to look at his gathered men, dismounted now, but too many in number for all to be within the walls of the farmyard. "Take five volunteers from our new recruits, not the men of Dumnonia. Choose them well. From five different kingdoms. They'll be your witnesses. You'll go representing the Dux Britanniarum and not the King of Dumnonia. Let him make his revolt against the Dux, and not against me personally."

Five men were swiftly found and, the daylight being long, they left the villa immediately to ride the ten miles to Viroconium, leaving us all kicking our heels in the makeshift camp.

The wait stretched out. Early evening became late evening. We all knew Cei and his escort should have covered the ten miles and arrived some time ago at Viroconium. Every one of us, down to the lowliest warrior, must have been imagining what was going on within those city walls, probably within the Imperial Palace itself, and worrying about Cei and the men he'd taken with him.

The sun finally disappeared below the western horizon, but Arthur refused to come to the bed we'd found in the house. His men were either as concerned as he was or sensed his disquiet, and they too hung around the campfire in the middle of the stable courtyard, unwilling to unroll their blankets and sleep when their lord was wakeful.

I sat by the fire, on a low milking stool fetched from the barn, wrapped in my blanket against the chill of the evening, watching the flames leap toward the blue black of the night sky. In front of the fire, Arthur paced, restless as a wild beast in a cage. By midnight, I'd begun to nod, and Merlin escorted me to my bed. I went with reluctance, wanting to stay with Arthur while this mood was on him, but in the end my tiredness was too much, and I gave in.

I woke to full daylight streaming in through the open shutters of the bedroom Albina and Cloelia might have shared – and straightaway felt guilty for thinking of them in the past tense. Pushing that thought to the back of my mind, I lay in bed luxuriating in the comfort, and then more guilt took hold. Thinking about where they might be sleeping now, I got up and pulled on my clothes. With no further ado, I hurried out of the bedroom and across the garden to the gates into the lower courtyard.

The chill of early morning had long passed, and wisps of smoke rose from the remains of the campfire. The men were busy attending to their horses or cleaning their weapons. A few stood around with skins of wine, passing them to one another with an air of subdued expectancy.

Merlin appeared out of the stables, and, approaching, offered me a wineskin which I took, downing a thirst-quenching gulp. "Where's the king?" I asked, my eyes roving over the faces of the men and finding them looking back at me as though expecting me to be able to do something. The burden of being thought their lucky charm weighed heavy on me that morning.

"He's walked down toward the village," Merlin said. "You need to eat, Gwen, for the baby, if not for yourself."

Shaking my head, I took a second long gulp of the watery wine. "I'm not hungry." I turned away. "I'm going to find Arthur."

He didn't try to stop me.

Arthur hadn't gone as far as the village. I found him down by the little river that ran below the villa, staring into the gently babbling water. Someone had constructed the roughest of bridges out of a fallen tree. Hearing me coming down the path, he looked over his shoulder and his face broke into a tired smile. Dark circles ringed his eyes.

I came up beside him and, without speaking, slipped my arm through his.

We stood in silence like this for a long time, half mesmerized by the flowing water as it chattered over the pebbles and ran away toward the village.

I spoke first. "He won't harm Cei."

Arthur turned his head and looked down at me. "We don't know that." He paused. "I should never have let him go. Cadwy is as untrustworthy as a Saxon. Cei's my brother. I should never have risked him. It's my responsibility to rescue those women, not his."

I squeezed his arm. "If you'd gone, then you'd most likely be dead by now." I put my hand on my belly. "And our son would grow up without a father. If he got to grow up at all with Cadwy all-powerful. He'd have killed you as easy as stamping on a spider, and he'd have taken Dumnonia. Where would be safe for me then, carrying your heir?"

"Walk with me," he said, turning me upstream away from the village. "I needed your common sense."

We followed the twisting riverbank as the sun rose higher in the sky and beat down hot on our backs, the silence between us companionable and comforting. Birds sang in the willows, and in the distance a pair of deer emerged from a small copse, watchful and wary as they sniffed the air. Everywhere was peaceful, an enclave of quiet that should never have been invaded so violently. There was no need for either of us to speak.

"My Lord!" Shouts broke through our contemplations, bringing us round in surprise to look toward the voice. Bedwyr loped toward us, excitement plastered over his homely face. "My Lord, your brother has returned."

We raced back.

Cei waited in the lower courtyard with his five warriors, his face a grim mask. Seeing Arthur, he hastened toward us, closely followed by Merlin.

"What happened?" Arthur asked, relief at the safe return of his older brother strong in his voice. "Did you see him?"

Cei clapped him on the shoulder. "I did." His eyes shifted to me, and taking Arthur by the arm, he steered him away. What didn't he want me to hear?

I followed them. If he was telling Arthur and Merlin, then he could tell me, too.

"I saw him yesterday evening, as soon as I arrived. He seemed disappointed I was not you." Cei's mouth formed a wry grin.

Arthur gave a bitter laugh. "And Morgawse? Did you see her?"

Cei shook his head. "No. I asked, but he didn't let me. He says she came of her own free will, as we thought he would. A likely story."

Arthur banged one fist into the palm of his other hand. "He can say anything he likes and we have to accept it, because he holds the winning pieces. Or thinks he does." He halted. "And Euddolen? Did you find out what happened to him?"

Cei shifted in evident discomfort. "I did. Bad news, I'm afraid. I had my warriors asking around whilst I had audience with your brother. Cadwy took Euddolen on a trumped up charge of embezzling money from the throne – he couldn't call it treason because of the vow he'd made you in front of the other kings, not that it means overmuch to him. According to them, Euddolen 'resisted' arrest. The soldiers sent to take him had to use brute force. He's dead. I'm sorry."

"And his excuse for taking Euddolen's women?"

"For their own safety."

The two brothers faced one another, Cei, huge and thickset, his red head bright in the morning sunshine, Arthur, with his long limbed rider's build and his dark hair in complete contrast. Two brothers less alike it would have been hard to find.

Arthur's hand went to the hilt of his sword. "What conclusion did you reach?"

"He says he will meet you, at a place of his own choosing. To discuss his sister."

Silence stretched out between them.

Merlin broke it. "Don't trust him – it'll be a trap."

Arthur ran his hand through his hair and let out a long breath. "Of course it's a trap. But it's a chance we'll have to take if we're to get Morgawse and her son back safe."

As I listened, a cold hand of fear closed about my heart, and my only instinct was to keep the father of my baby safe. "You can't," I burst out. "If he gets you in his grasp he'll kill you as soon as look at you. Morgawse is safe – he won't hurt her. She's *his* sister, too."

They all three turned and looked at me in surprise.

I plunged on. "If you do go, then take me with you. I won't be left behind again. You said I'm your luck, and it'll be luck you'll need if you meet with Cadwy."

Arthur frowned and shook his head, but instead of answering

me, he addressed Cei and Merlin. "I won't take Gwen to any meeting with my brother. It's too dangerous to risk her and the child she carries. She'll need to stay here, safe under guard, while we go."

I might as well not have spoken. I bristled in silence, knowing argument here would be pointless.

Arthur went on. "Where does Cadwy want to meet?"

"North-west of the city there's an ancient ringfort. It's low-lying and difficult to access. It's called Din Bassas. You'll know it from when we were boys here."

Bassas. The sixth battle on Nennius's list. Without any further evidence, I knew for certain that Cadwy planned treachery at Din Bassas, and this would not be a battle against the enemies of the kingdoms of Britain like the others had been, but closer to a civil war.

I put my hand on Merlin's sleeve, drawing him closer. "You're right." I kept my voice low. "It's a trap, for sure. There'll be a battle. Don't ask me how I know. I just do. You have to go prepared. Cadwy intends to kill you all."

He raised his brows at me. "I thought I was the one supposed to have the Sight?"

Chapter Twenty

"TAKE ME WITH you." In the warm darkness of the summer night, I lay naked in bed with Arthur, neither of us able to sleep.

Beside me, his body stiffened. "I've already told you. It's too dangerous. It's likely a trap, and I can't afford to spare the men to take care of you."

I lay silent for a while, regrouping. "You said I bring you luck...which you'll need tomorrow."

He grunted. "We'll need more than luck. We'll need cunning. We have to outsmart the old fox – play him at his own game."

He hadn't said a definite *no* this time. I clung to that. "What will you do?"

He tightened his arm around my shoulders, drawing me closer. "I know the ring-fort Cei spoke of as well as he does. I've been there many times as a boy. I don't think anyone's lived there since before the legions came. Wetlands surround it. There's but one way in and out. An ancient causeway through the marshes."

I rested my cheek against his chest, the hairs tickling my nose, breathing in his masculine scent. "Wouldn't that make it hard to stage an ambush? Surely he couldn't take in enough men to fight you?"

His lips brushed the top of my head, his breath warm. "They don't all have to go in. Cei said the arrangement is for us to each bring thirty men, including ourselves. But Cadwy didn't say he wouldn't keep his major force outside the marshes. In waiting."

It was clear why Arthur didn't want to give up a single one of those thirty fighting men for me.

I tightened my arm across his chest, nestling closer. "But you can keep your own army waiting there too, can't you?"

He nodded. "I will. And he'll expect me to. The trick will be to catch him before he carries out any other treachery. Outside the marshes, I can match him man for man almost, but within, we don't know what he'll have planned."

"What about his Saxon foederati? He may have more men than you think."

He nodded again, and his mouth moved against my hair. "Very true. He has no more qualms than Guorthegirn the Usurper had about paying the Yellow Hairs to do his bidding."

"And that doesn't worry you?"

His chest rose as he sighed. "Not much. I'd be lying if I said not at all. But they're all foot soldiers, and I have cavalry. The odds will still be in our favor if we can avoid all his trickery."

"It doesn't look as though he thinks so."

He grunted again. "He can think what he likes – my men can best his any day. Whatever he throws at us."

My thoughts shifted to the casualties inflicted on Arthur's army in Linnuis. They were down in numbers due to the men who'd died and the wounded he'd sent back to Din Cadan. Was he right? Did we really have enough men to defeat Cadwy and his Saxons?

A little shudder shook my body as though someone had walked over my grave. "All the same, I don't like not being with you. The waiting is worse than the battle, because at least then, at the river Glein, I could see for myself you were still safe. I didn't have to wait days for news. Those five weeks I spent in Caer Lind Colun were horrendous. I don't want to go through that again. Ever."

He didn't answer. What could he have said? He was probably thinking that whatever I wanted would have no effect on what I received. This was an era where we women waited for our menfolk while they rode off to war. As far as he was concerned, I'd have to shut up and put up with him laying down the law.

For a long time after that, we lay silent, still unable to sleep. At last, he turned on his side, putting his arms around me and holding me as close as he could. He took up the conversation where we'd left off. "I'm sorry. I can't help it. I'm a king, and I'm Dux Britanniarum. You're a queen, my queen, and you're with child. Even if you weren't with child, I couldn't take you into danger. We both know Cadwy wants you for himself. Look at how he's tried to snatch you in the past."

I said what he wanted to hear. "I know."

But inside, I was hatching a plan as I clung onto him, his body cool to the touch now night was well on. I found myself wondering how it would feel if he was dead. Cooler than this? Lifeless? Would I find out if he went to Din Bassas to meet the slippery Cadwy? I had no way of knowing if this was something which had already been written and that he would be safe, or if my being here had changed history, and tomorrow he might be riding to his death.

THE MEETING HAD been set for noon the next day. My sleep was so light that Arthur's getting out of bed woke me, just before sunrise. I reached to touch his naked back as he bent to draw on his braccae. He tensed, and after a moment, turned around. "Go back to sleep. There's no need for you to get up. We need to be off early to lay our own ambush."

I sat up, the covers falling back, and pressed myself into his arms. "How can I sleep knowing you're riding into danger?"

He held me close, his breath warm on my neck. "I'm not going to die." His words were hot against my skin. "How can I? I'm going to be the most famous king who ever lived. You said so yourself. And I've not done nearly enough to merit that yet. If people from your time know of me, there's no chance Cadwy will overcome me now. Have confidence in what you know. I have. I'll be back by nightfall with Morgawse and the baby." He kissed me on the lips and got to his feet to pull on his undershirt and tunic.

I watched him dress, and when at last he was ready he came to my side of the bed and, sitting down on it, pulled me up into his arms again. "Don't worry. If this comes to blows, remember I'll have the advantage. I've better warriors than his, for a start." He kissed me again, harder this time, then got up to leave. I lay back down like a good little wife and pulled the covers up to my chin.

As soon as he'd gone, I rolled off the bed and pulled on my undershirt, braccae, tunic, and boots. With fumbling fingers, I fastened my belt, then, yanking my mail shirt on over my head, hurried in his wake. His men had dumped the stores in one of the barns opening off the stable courtyard. I had to sneak carefully, but as it wasn't yet fully light, and the men were all busy preparing their horses for the march, I managed to arrive undetected.

The spare armor retrieved from their fallen comrades and the enemy had been piled up in here. I put on a helmet and chose a shield, then added a few good smears of dirt around my chin to look like stubble. A thick sword belt and the smallest sword I could find finished the ensemble, then I went in search of a spare horse. I couldn't risk taking Alezan as she was too noticeable.

Finding a nondescript bay gelding no one seemed to have laid claim to, I set about saddling him up. Then, keeping my head down, I swung myself up into the saddle and mingled with the mass of now mounted warriors. I stayed well back from Arthur, Cei and Merlin, and anyone else who might recognize me.

Arthur didn't even look my way as he prepared to leave the stableyard astride the chestnut he'd been riding since Llamrei had been wounded in Linnuis. Turning to the half-dozen men who remained, he barked a curt order. "When the Queen awakens, make sure she eats. Then ride due south with her to the next villa. It belongs to Caswallan, a good friend of mine. He'll keep her safe until I return." And with that last, somewhat vague instruction for my care, he kicked his horse into a trot, and we all clattered out of the courtyard after him.

A good twenty-five miles stretched between Euddolen's villa and the ringfort of Din Bassas. The wide berth we gave Viroconium took us upstream to a ford on the Sabrina River. Here, where a small village crouched close to the water's edge, we crossed the wide waterway to the northern bank, watched by a crowd of wary villagers. Leaving them behind, we struck north through farmland and forest, following the valley of one of the Sabrina's many tributaries along narrow dirt tracks.

I kept my head down and stayed silent toward the back of the column, but I couldn't hope to stay undetected forever. After we'd forded the Sabrina, I caught the unwelcome attention of Drustans. He brought his horse alongside mine and turned to me with a comradely grin that died on his lips.

"Milady!"

My eyes widened in shocked annoyance that he'd seen through my disguise so easily, and I put a hasty finger to my lips. "Keep quiet."

His mouth, which had fallen open, shut with a clack of teeth. "What are you doing here?"

"My husband wouldn't bring me. After five weeks waiting for news in Linnuis, I couldn't stand another day like that. I had to come." I reached across and put my hand on his sleeve. "Don't tell him yet. Please." I had to keep my voice low lest one of the men riding in front and behind us overheard my words.

"But we're going to war." His voice rose in protest, making the heads of the riders in front turn in curiosity. I glared, and he lowered it to an angry hiss. "This is no place for a woman. Still less one who's...who's like you are." He finished with an awkward flush to his cheeks as if he didn't want to say the words "with child." They were simply too embarrassing. He glared. "I have to tell the king."

"No, you don't," I hissed back at him. "Because if you do, I'll have to tell him how I caught you in bed with the Princess Essylt. How you were there before her betrothed husband. How if she bears a child, it could well be yours and not your father's."

Shock spread over his boyish face. "You wouldn't." The men in front turned to look at us again, and I ducked my head to hide my face, wishing he'd stop talking so loudly.

"Try me," I said meanly. "You can tell him later, but not until we're too far from the villa to send me back. I intend to be near enough to know what's happening when he meets Cadwy. I refuse to put up with waiting back at the villa again."

He fell silent. I'd won, but at the cost of destroying the trust of the boy beside me. Of course I wouldn't have told on him, but I'd made him believe I would. Guilt at his glum expression ate into my heart. Was he wondering what else he'd be required to do for me to keep his secret?

The forest thickened, and the land began to rise out of the river valley as the track veered away from the water. Beside me, Drustans rode in stony silence, and I kept my eyes on the forest around us, wondering where Cadwy and his army were. The air hung hot and still, and sweat trickled down my back under my heavy mail shirt. It felt as though this were going to turn into the hottest day we'd had this year. My mouth was dry and papery. If only I'd had the common sense to have brought a bottle of something to drink with me. But as I was also suffering an uncomfortable need to pee, that might not have been such a good idea.

At least the trees afforded us some welcome shade and a brief respite from the buzzing of the interminable flies attracted by our sweating horses. I wiped my sleeve across my damp face for the thousandth time and waved my hand at the swarm of flies circling my head – nearly as many as my horse had. The forest we were riding through hugged the higher ground not far above the wetlands, which probably accounted for the plague of flies.

At last, the column came to a halt. We'd reached the edge of the forest, the trees thinning abruptly as the land sloped down over scrubland toward the marsh. Ahead, rising out of its surrounding, weed-filled lake, lay a low mound which just might have been the remains of a ring fort.

Drustans leaned toward me. "Can I tell him now?"

I nodded, contrite. "I wouldn't have told him about you and Essylt, you know."

He gave me a heavy, sulky frown. "You can say that now, but I don't believe you didn't mean it then. You'd better come with me."

To say Arthur was angry would have been a gross underestimation.

"What in God's name are you doing here?" he almost shouted, only the need for silence keeping him to a more moderate tone. "What part of 'you can't come, it's too dangerous' didn't you understand? You're a woman, and not just an ordinary woman but a queen, and not just an ordinary queen but one who's bloody well with child. Carrying my heir." He turned to Drustans, eyes flashing with fury. "How long have you known she was with us?"

Drustans' eyes widened with fear, and he opened his mouth to drop himself in it.

"He found me just now," I said, in a hurry to forestall him. "He brought me to you straight away." I shifted in my saddle. "And I desperately need a pee."

Arthur put his hand to his head in what looked like exasperation. "When will you learn to do as I bid? By disobeying me you've put yourself and everyone else here in terrible danger. I'll have to leave men to keep you safe, men I need to have fighting by my side. You shouldn't have done this."

I felt like a schoolgirl being upbraided by her head teacher, but that didn't stop my anger with him. My head hung as I regarded my boots, composing words of contrition I didn't feel. "I couldn't sit behind and not know what was going on." My excuse sounded puerile and lame, but I was unrepentant. "Can't I stay here, hidden with your army?" Even to myself this sounded whiney, but I didn't care.

"No, you can't." Arthur kept his coldly furious voice low. "This is no place for a woman."

I bristled, mindful of the number of women who fought in the front line in the twenty-first century. "I don't care. I don't want to fight. I only want to be close by while you're meeting that bastard Cadwy."

A ghost of a smile flashed across his face before his brows came together again in a heavy frown. "That's a woman's lot. You need to remember your place. I won't have you disobeying me."

I was furious in return. Obey him? Only the fact that we were arguing in front of his men kept me silent, but I seethed with righteous anger.

Ignoring me, Arthur nodded to Drustans. "As you're the lucky man who found her, I'm giving you the task of being her guard. Take two others and ride back along the track a way, well back from the forest edge. At least a mile. No, make that two. No, in fact, escort her back to where she's meant to be. And take her for a pee when you're somewhere safe."

Drustans shot me a furious look. He'd been left behind in Linnuis when Arthur's army had ridden north to take on the Saxon raiders, and now, when he had a chance to show what he was made of, he found himself charged with my care. I had the grace to feel sorry for him. Grumpily, he led the way back, calling to two of his friends to follow, and we made our way toward the rear of the column.

As we passed along the line of waiting warriors, one after another of them stretched out a hand to touch my arm or shoulder or leg. Gentle touches, fingertips just brushing my body, and as we reached the end of the line, the last few muttered, "God be with you."

With every touch my anger dissipated a little, and a heavy resignation settled over me. If I had to leave Arthur and his army hidden in the forest edge, preparing to ride out and meet with Cadwy, it was with the knowledge that his men had taken my luck upon themselves. The part of me that was now all fifth century accepted what they'd done as natural and right. The twenty-first century was very far away.

Leaving them behind, the four of us walked our horses back down the track, the three young men grumbling words of disgust amongst themselves, and me feeling as though I just might have helped a bit.

A bend in the path concealed the waiting army from us, and we could as well have been on a pleasure ride for all the indication we had of any impending battle. The trees rang with birdsong, the leaves rustled in a slight breeze that didn't reach us on the hot forest floor, and the sun beat down on our backs.

Time crawled. What might Arthur be doing now? My back itched with sweat, and the flies buzzed incessantly about my head.

It seemed a long time before we came upon a leafy sun-dappled glade and Drustans called a halt, but it had probably not been long at all. There were big bushes aplenty, so I slid down from my saddle and went behind one for my much-needed pee – a great relief after so long on horseback. I was just sorting out my braccae when I heard Drustans' voice in a loud whisper that carried easily to me behind the bush. "Milady, hurry up! I can hear someone coming."

I tucked the last bit of my undershirt in and emerged. The three young men, one of them holding my horse, were all looking toward the far side of the clearing, the horses' heads up, ears pricked. The shout of an angry voice, the creak of a wagon, a baby crying, and the sound of people sobbing carried to us on the hot air.

No wagon had accompanied Arthur's army, so it had to be strangers.

"Could be anyone," Drustans said in a low voice. He looked at the substantial bushes I'd peed behind. "Let's get out of sight."

"This way." I turned back.

The three young horsemen plunged into the bushes, kicking their horses forward and trying to make as little noise as possible. We were lucky. Between them, the people in the wagon were making a lot more noise than we were. I grabbed my horse's reins, and putting my foot in the stirrup, swung myself back into the saddle.

Just in time. A wagon lurched into the clearing. From my position behind the bushes, I saw that apart from the driver, who was shouting a string of abuse in an effort to urge his tired horses on, six people rode in the wagon: Euddolen's widow, Ummidia, his daughters, Albina and Cloelia, and Arthur's two sisters, Morgawse and Morgana. In Morgawse's arms, baby Medraut cried fretfully. Albina and Cloelia, clinging to their mother, were the ones making all the racket with their sobbing. Morgana sat up ramrod straight, a scowl of annoyance on her cold face. Behind the wagon strode four heavily armed Saxon foederati.

Chapter Twenty-One

HIDDEN BY THE dense bushes, my three companions exchanged puzzled glances. Of course, they probably didn't recognize the women. Why would they? Their only sight of them would have been over six months ago on the journey south from Viroconium. The women had ridden all the way to the villa in a covered wagon. None of these young warriors were likely to have more than glimpsed their faces.

I leaned toward Drustans, my voice a whisper. "It's the Princesses Morgana and Morgawse, with Euddolen's wife and daughters."

His eyes opened wide. I could almost hear the cogs turning. There were only four guards escorting the wagon. Huge Saxon foederati, but still, only four of them and on foot, at that. Five if you counted the wagon driver, but he wasn't wearing armor and didn't look as though he were armed.

Drustans nodded to his two friends, who weren't much older than he was, and probably all eager to show off their mettle, even if it was only to me.

"Stay here out of sight," Drustans hissed at me. Before I could protest, all three of them whipped out their swords and sent their horses crashing out of the bushes toward the wagon, letting out blood curdling war whoops of encouragement to one another.

My horse tried to join them, and it was only with a huge effort that I managed to yank him back. He danced under me, snorting with excitement. I'd chosen a proper warhorse.

The Saxon foederati froze with shock for a split second, but were quick to recover. As Drustans and the other two young men bore down on them, the Saxons drew their swords. For the first of them, it was too late. As he was still raising his sword, Drustans reached him, swinging his own weapon in an arc that was carried forward by his horse's charge.

The British boy bent low to his right, helped to balance by his new stirrups, and his sword bit into the Saxon's neck just below his metal helmet. The sword was sharp and the blow true. The Saxon's head, yellow hair flying, went bouncing off toward the wagon where one of the horses gave it a panicked kick. The rest of the body remained upright for a moment, as a gout of arterial blood spouted upwards, spraying rider and mount.

Not giving his dead opponent a second glance, Drustans turned toward the other three foederati. His two companions had charged at them, but weren't as quick as he'd been. This had given the enemy time to draw their swords and stand their ground, thinking they were three against two. But Drustans' rapid dispatch of the fourth man had reduced the odds, and our men were mounted. Swords clashed, sparks flew. The Saxons tried to strike at the legs of the horses but the riders were too quick, parrying the blows.

The driver of the wagon belabored his foam-flecked horses' backs with his whip and shouted panicked encouragement at them. Behind him, Ummidia cast her daughters, now sobbing even more loudly, to one side, and threw herself at the driver, wrapping her arms tight around his neck. Locked together, they toppled from the still-moving wagon, landing close to the severed head. Finding himself on top, the driver raised his fist and hit Ummidia about the head. Blood gushed from her nose.

Helped by the fact that they were on horseback, Drustans and his friends were forcing the remaining Saxons back toward the trees. Only I seemed to have noticed the fight between the driver and Ummidia.

For a moment, I was frozen by indecision. Then I kicked my horse forward into the clearing and slid down from the saddle. The driver's back was to me, exposed and vulnerable.

Awkwardly yanking my sword from its scabbard, I struck before I had time to even think what I was doing. Taking a deep breath and holding it, both hands on the sword hilt, I drove it down into his back. It was more difficult to do than I'd thought. Instinctively, though, I'd turned the sword to slide between his ribs, but the grating of metal on bone almost made me stop. The sight of Ummidia's bloodied face overrode any reluctance I might have had. This was dog eat dog, victory to the strong. The sword slid in deep as I leaned my weight against it.

The driver twisted his body so the sword was wrenched out of my suddenly slack hands.

Still with my sword embedded in his back, he rolled off Ummidia onto his side, the tip protruding from his chest. Blood ran out of his mouth and into his bushy beard, and his surprised eyes stared in disbelief.

Realization of what I'd done washed over me. I bent double and vomited, my empty stomach heaving up only bile. Beside me, Ummidia lay unmoving, eyes closed, her face a mask of blood and her lips split.

But I had no time to allow myself to descend into shock. Wiping my mouth on my sleeve, I straightened up and looked toward the fighting.

A body lay spreadeagled on the ground. All three horsemen were still mounted, so it had to be one of the Saxons. One of the men on foot broke away from the fight and began to run down the path the way they'd come.

"Don't let him get away!" Drustans' voice rose above the noise of battle, and the young man who'd been fighting the Saxon wrenched his mount round and charged after him. The warhorse crashed into the running man, sending him flying. The British youth yanked the beast into a handbrake turn, pulling it into a rear above the prone Saxon, and its hooves came smashing down on his head with a sickening crunch, just as it had been trained to do. Lumps of grey matter and blood sprayed across horse and path alike.

My stomach heaved again, and I had to clasp my hands together in an effort to stop them shaking.

Outnumbered three to one, the remaining Saxon raised his hands in the eternal gesture for surrender, as the three young British warriors surrounded him, swords extended.

"Drop your weapons," Drustans commanded as his two friends dismounted.

With a surly look from beneath heavy blond brows, the Saxon did as he was told, and Drustans, too, slid off his horse.

In the wagon, Morgana clambered, unnoticed by anyone but me, into the driver's seat and gathered up the reins, her eyes narrowing as they searched the surrounding trees, possibly for signs of our reinforcements. Was she deciding what her safest move would be and how to twist this situation to her own advantage?

On the ground by my feet, Ummidia still lay unmoving, covered in her own blood. Turning my back on the dead driver, determined not to think about what I'd just done, I went down on my knees at her side, terrified she, too, might be dead. Her eyes had swollen shut, but when I touched her cheek with a trembling hand, they fluttered open. Fear flashed across her battered face.

Above me, in the wagon, a voice hissed out, serpent-like and vicious. "You!" I'd forgotten Morgana had the Sight and would know me despite my disguise.

Heedless of her, I pulled off my helmet, glad of the air on my sweaty skin, and addressed Ummidia, my voice as shaky as my hand. "It's me. Gwen." Confusion fogged Ummidia's bloodshot eyes. I sought for words of reassurance – for me as well as for her. "You're safe now. All of you are. We...m-my men have killed three of your captors and have the fourth a prisoner." Turning my back on Morgana made the space between my shoulder blades itch as though she were about to plunge a dagger between them, just as I'd done to the driver a moment ago. It took all my self-control not to look over my shoulder, and to keep my trembling jaw steady. Any moment now I was going to burst into tears.

A shadow moved across us, and Ummidia cowered in fear. I glanced up as fearfully as her, but it was Drustans standing over us, looking menacing in his blood spattered armor. "How close is the rest of the army?" he asked, with urgency. "We have to know if more soldiers are coming this way."

Ummidia stared at us dumbly, probably too dazed to respond.

It was Morgawse who answered, from her seat in the back of the wagon, clutching her baby to her chest. "They're setting a trap for Arthur." She shoved the still crying baby into Albina's arms. "Hold him. Properly. And stop blubbing. We're safe now." With a desperate glance at Morgana, who was still sitting on the driver's bench, Morgawse climbed out of the wagon to stand looking down at Ummidia.

This determined young woman didn't sound much like the Morgawse I'd met before.

She turned to Drustans. "Cadwy sent us out of the way of his army...and yours...he thought. They're massed to the south of Din Bassas, waiting for his signal. When it comes, they're going to attack Arthur. Cadwy will let Arthur and his men leave the island first. That way, Cadwy's men will be both behind and in front. A huge force of Cadwy's warriors and foederati is lying in wait."

She looked back at Morgana on the driver's seat. "*She* was to bring us up after the battle." A curious mixture of contempt and sorrow mingled in Morgawse's voice, as though she'd finally realized that her beloved older sister wasn't the heroine she'd always thought.

Morgana drew herself up taller. "He made me," she said haughtily. "He is my king, and I must obey."

Classic. She was only obeying orders. Like that was going to work with us.

Drustans nodded, addressing Morgawse. "The king suspected their treachery, Milady. He's more than prepared and has his own army hiding in the forest. But it's too late to warn him what they plan. He'll be on the island meeting Cadwy even as we speak."

Behind him, Morgana looped the reins around the brake handle on the cart and slid to the ground. I'd forgotten how tall a woman she was, nearly as tall as her brothers. Her normally loose dark hair was confined in a single thick plait and two red spots flared angrily on her cheeks.

"We have to do something," I said, anxiety for Arthur's safety, as well as the shock of having killed a man, overriding anything I might have felt for the women and baby.

Drustans' boyish face, with its fuzz of sparse beard, creased with indecision.

"Where is the body of your army?" Morgawse asked. She was hardly any older than he was, but seemed by far the more capable of decision making. I was happy to let her take command for the moment.

"At least two miles. Through the forest that way." He pointed a long, grubby finger.

Morgawse nodded. "Then send one man on your fastest horse to tell them to move to the south and expect to meet Cadwy's army."

I could see the wisdom in that and nodded with vigor. "Yes. I can do that. Drustans, you and Morgawse can take the wagon to safety." Maybe it was the reaction to having killed someone, but I wasn't afraid anymore. Instead, a curious numbness pervaded my body, as though nothing mattered except that I should be with Arthur.

Morgana was no longer beside the wagon. Somehow, she'd moved closer to Drustans' grazing horse. Yet although I'd seen, the significance of what she was doing didn't seem important, I was so taken up with the idea that I could be the one to ride back to Arthur's army.

Drustans stared at me, aghast. "Milady! I can't let you go. I'm supposed to be keeping you safe. The King would never forgive me. He entrusted you to me. I'm to escort you to Caswallan's villa."

"We need you with us." Morgawse backed him up. "A battle's no place for a woman. And I need help with these girls." She nodded at Albina and Cloelia, who were still to be heard hiccupping their sobs in the back of the wagon in concert with baby Medraut, who sounded hungry.

"But I need to be sure Arthur's safe." It came out as a whine, which wasn't how I'd intended. The fact that I'd killed a man was at the back of my mind, repeating itself incessantly. I tried to ignore it, knowing that if I took notice, it was going to overwhelm me and I would break down. The longer I ignored it, the less real it became. This was not the moment for histrionics.

"Princess Morgawse is right." Drustans drew himself up, looking older than his years. "You can't go. I will. You and the Princess must take charge of the wagon, and get the Lady Ummidia and her daughters to safety. I'll send these two with you." He indicated his companions. "You should be safe enough now we know where Cadwy's army is. You can steer clear of it." He looked for Morgana. "And you can take her –" His voice broke off as he took in for the first time where Morgana was, standing beside his horse, its reins in her hand. But she didn't know what the stirrup was for and, though tall, was hampered from mounting by her gown.

Drustans was across the clearing in a moment, wrestling her to the ground, sending the horse skittering off toward the trees. A brief tussle ensued, but, strong as she was, she was no match for a fit warrior. He climbed off her and dragged her to her feet, her hair full of bits of dead leaves. "We'd better tie our prisoner up."

Morgana gave herself a shake, as though to rid herself of the defiling touch of a common warrior, and lifted her chin defiantly. She'd probably forgotten he was a prince himself. Her eyes slid back to me, dark and brooding.

A little shiver ran down my spine.

Morgawse glared at her sister. "And watch her closely. She's full of tricks."

A rope was found, and one of Drustans' two fellows bound Morgana's hands behind her, none too gently. In the back of the wagon, Albina's and Cloelia's relentless sobbing had ceased, although the baby was still wailing in hunger or in need of the Dark Age equivalent of a nappy change.

Drustans, who must have still been sulking with me, hammered his point home. "We have to get these women to safety. And the baby. You and the Princess Morgawse must get them to Caswallan."

He was going to be as intractable to argue with as Arthur.

An expression of gritty determination on his young face, Drustans looked back at his Saxon prisoner again. "Tie him up, too."

His two friends found more rope from their saddle horns, and in a trice, the Saxon's arms were bound behind him. Looking rebellious and angry, he stood between the two young men.

In the wagon, Albina, who'd been watching this, now shoved the baby into Cloelia's arms. With the agility of a cat, she jumped down to land lightly on her feet in the grass. Her hair was a tangled mess and her dress hung in bloodstained tatters. But she didn't stop there. She marched up to the Saxon, a big man with a drooping moustache like Theodoric's and long dirty blond hair. Before any of us could move, her hand shot out and seized a dagger from the nearest warrior's belt. Without hesitation, she plunged the dagger two handed into the Saxon's belly, right up to the hilt. He didn't see it coming, and staggered, mouth open wide in horror, as she twisted it in the wound, blood pouring out over her hands and filthy gown. With his own hands tied behind his back, there was nothing he could have done to defend himself.

The mouths of the two young warriors who'd been standing on either side of him dropped open in shock. Then they reached for Albina.

"That's for my father," she spat, twisting the knife again. "And for my mother and my sister." She batted the reaching hands away with one hand. "I am your executioner."

The Saxon sank to the ground, taking the dagger with him, his face paper white, blood pumping from the wound so fast it was clear she'd hit an artery.

"Albina!" I exclaimed, coming out of the shock that had frozen me. Fresh in my mind was the feel of my own sword grating against the driver's ribs, and the pressure I'd had to exert to run him through, and bile rose in my throat once more. But somehow this was worse because this was in cold blood. I was nearly as horrified as the dying Saxon.

Albina gave a wild laugh, and bending over, prised the dagger out of the wound. But before she could stab him again, which definitely looked like what she had in mind, Drustans' two friends grabbed her by the arms, yanking her back. On the grass at their feet the Saxon warrior writhed. His feet drummed on the ground, and then he lay still. Blood still pulsed from his wound, sluggishly now, with the last beats of his heart.

"Why did you do that?" I asked, but she didn't answer. Another wild laugh echoed round the clearing, bouncing off the trees.

Turning her head away, Morgawse helped Ummidia to her feet, the older woman cradling her jaw with bloodstained fingers. She'd lost several teeth. Through her broken lips she managed to speak at last. "Don't blame her." Her voice cracked with bitterness. "The king allowed his warriors to have their fun with us, in payment for my husband's supposed embezzlement. I was only raped twice, but the filthy Saxons took a liking to my girls. They kept them all night long." She spat, blood, spittle and mucous landing accurately on the dead man's face. "I'd have stabbed him myself if I'd been able. They're not fit to live."

Cold fear ran through me. I wasn't in Kansas anymore. This was a world where the victors took revenge on the women of their enemies, where battles were fought on an almost daily basis, where there was no higher authority to appeal to if things went wrong. All of a sudden, the forest around us bristled with dangers and a million eyes bored into my unprotected back.

Drustans made a decision. "I'm going back now, to tell the army where Cadwy's men are. We've no time to lose." He looked at his two friends. "You'll have to take the wagon. Hide the bodies in the bushes, take their weapons, and escort the Queen and the Princess, and our prisoner, with the rest of these women to safety. Remember, not Euddolen's villa – Caswallan's, due south of it. No one should find you there. And keep a watch for any stray bands of Cadwy's men. Though I doubt there'll be any."

He bent over the driver's body and wrenched my sword out. As though it were every day he did so, he wiped it on the man's clothes, then offered it to me.

I hesitated.

"Take it," he said gruffly. "You did more than well. But you may have need of it again."

I reached out and took it, wondering if I'd be brave enough to use it again if we did bump into more danger. On the whole, I'd far rather be cut down by a warrior who mistook me for a man than have that warrior rape me.

"I'm sure you'll be safe enough," Drustans went on, with what sounded like false confidence, as he gathered his reins and prepared to remount. His horse spun around in an impatient circle, giving the dismembered head another kick that sent it spinning across the rough grass. "I think Cadwy will have kept all his men for the ambush. But listen out, just in case." He steadied his horse as he took one last look around, then swung himself up into the saddle. "And for God's sake, shut that baby and those women up. You don't want anyone hearing you coming, the way we heard *them*." And with that, he wheeled his horse and galloped away.

We were left alone in a clearing that no longer felt warm and sun-blessed. Blood had stained the grass and soaked into the bare earth in the track. Drustans' two friends must have felt the same because they didn't waste any time hanging about or complaining. They shoved Albina and Morgana into the back of the wagon, helped Ummidia into the driver's seat, and then dragged the bodies into the bushes and kicked dirt over the bloodstains as best they could. As soon as we'd all remounted, we set off along the track through the forest again.

In the wagon, Morgawse fed the baby, who soon fell asleep in her arms, and Cloelia managed to stop sobbing when we'd made her understand the threat of recapture by wandering foederati. While their mother drove, the girls sat in the rear near Morgawse, clutching each other, their faces haggard and red-eyed with crying. Morgana sat upright and hard-faced in one corner, refusing to look at anyone.

I brought my horse up beside the wagon, deliberately shutting what I'd just done out of my mind, and looked down at the sleeping baby. But my thoughts were by no means quiet, as I found myself wishing Cadwy had unleashed some of his bad temper on this child. How easy would life have become if Cadwy had done that job for me. With this battle of Bassas, another in the list that old monk Nennius had compiled, turning out to have been true, I was having a great deal of difficulty in not believing a lot of other elements of the legends. Medraut, and the part he was destined to play, being one of them.

The wagon could only move at about three or four miles an hour, and with over twenty to go, progress was painfully slow. Without the burden of the wagon, we could have been home in a few hours, but this was going to take us all day. I kept an ear out behind us, as I suspected our escort did as well, half expecting that at any moment we'd be overtaken by a host of fleeing men from Cadwy's army, or the victorious hordes of Arthur. But neither caught us up.

There was no food in the wagon, nor anything to drink, and I was very hungry. On top of that, I was pregnant. Not a condition in which it was a good idea to starve oneself. The only one having his needs met was Medraut, who had grown into a chubby, bonny baby with a head of very dark hair and an angry scream when he wanted something. Looking at him made me wonder what my own child was going to look like. Medraut had a distinct look of Llacheu, which you'd expect with cousins, I supposed. Although, with blond Theodoric as a father, I was surprised he wasn't fairer.

Raising my eyes from regarding Medraut, I found Morgana's eyes fixed on me with almost hypnotic intensity. I started, met her gaze for a moment and looked away, profoundly uncomfortable. My eyes returned unbidden to the dark-haired baby in her sister's arms.

This was the exact moment another aspect of the legends crept up on me. I'd known it before, but would have dismissed it as rubbish if I'd ever stopped to think about it. Yet now, with this little clone in the wagon sleeping in his mother's arms, it all came back to me. In some stories Medraut wasn't just Morgawse's child – he was Arthur's too, incestuously. The thought rested in my stomach like a rock, once thought, impossible to unthink.

I tried to push it out of my mind, back to the recesses from which it had come, clawing its way angrily to the surface. But I couldn't. The more I tried, the larger it loomed, until it seemed to fill my entire head with a mesh of whispering possibilities.

At last, I could bear it no longer. "D'you think he looks like his father?" I asked Morgawse, out of the blue. The feeling of her sister's cold dark eyes fixed on me wouldn't go away, but I was held now, desperate to delve further into this.

She looked across. We were on a level even though she was in the wagon and I was on my horse. "Not really." Her brows creased in a faint frown. "He's all Pendragon with very little Goth about him." She stroked his baby soft cheek. "We Pendragons have strong characteristics. Look at us all – dark hair, dark eyes, dark hearts."

I bristled in my husband's defense. "Arthur doesn't have a dark heart." Was that a smirk I saw out of the corner of my eye on Morgana's lovely face?

Morgawse gave a grimace that might have been a smile. "Perhaps, perhaps not. But a darker heart than you might think."

I didn't like the way this conversation was going. I remembered the brothel at Caer Luit Coyt where Theodoric had claimed Lucretia's blond baby as his. The blond baby. British mother plus Goth father had produced a baby as blond as a Goth, like Theodoric. So why wasn't his son by Morgawse as blond? Could this disturbing legend of the child's paternity, as well as the list of battles and the sword in the stone, also be based on truth?

Morgana's eyes bored into me and my son did a somersault in my stomach, pressing uncomfortably against my bladder for an instant. I wished I could take off the hot mail shirt, but Drustans had refused to allow it. Sweat ran down my back and my undershirt stuck hotly to my skin, which the flies seemed to like very much. "You'd think he'd have been blond like his father," I said, feeling irritable.

She shook her head. "Not coming from me. Look at Cadwy. His mother was a Saxon princess – his great-grandfather was Hengest himself – but he's as dark as all of us. Our father has passed a strong bloodline on to us all, and we stamp ourselves proudly on our children."

Maybe she was right. I tried again. "He looks a lot like Arthur."

There was that smirk again.

Morgawse looked proud. "Who better to resemble than a king?"

I wasn't going to find an answer to my questions in her responses. She sounded as though she was talking about Theodoric being Medraut's father, but she would, wouldn't she? Even if he were not. There was no way she'd tell me if someone else had fathered her child, especially not if it were her brother. I was back to square one, other than her assurance that Pendragon children were all born dark. Which made me think of my child again. I fell silent, my hand cradling my small taut belly, wondering where Arthur was now.

Chapter Twenty-Two

FULL DARKNESS HAD fallen by the time we reached Caswallan's villa. I felt faint for lack of food and from being overheated inside my mail shirt. I was also shaky from the aftermath of having killed a man. Trying not to think about what I'd done wasn't working. I kept seeing his ugly face and his eyes glazing over as he rolled off Ummidia with my sword jammed between his ribs. The grating of the sword on bone replayed itself endlessly inside my head, however hard I tried to distract myself.

When my horse halted in the farmyard, I was so exhausted, both mentally and physically, that I slumped forward onto its neck for a moment. It took a supreme effort to straighten up and pay attention to what was going on.

Alerted by his farmhands, Caswallan himself, a tall man with sparse white hair and a long face as ascetic as Abbot Jerome's, came hurrying out to meet us. With him came servants carrying bronze lanterns which cast circles of welcoming warm yellow light across the well-swept cobbles of the yard.

Caswallan's eyes widened with surprise as he saw the wagon load of extra women he'd not been expecting. He recognized Morgana immediately, stuttering, "M-milady," in tones of horror. When he saw she was bound, his eyes went even wider with shock and probably fear.

Morgawse spoke up. "My sister was in charge of taking us to witness the ambush my brother Cadwy planned." She handed the sleeping baby down to a servant. "Do not waste your sympathy on her. I've seen her true colors." She jumped from the wagon and took the baby back.

I slid down from the saddle and took off my helmet. Caswallan's gaze took me in. I didn't think he could look more shocked, but he did. "Is this...is this the *queen?*"

Morgawse heaved a sigh. "It is. And she's exhausted. We all are. We need food – straightaway." She was all imperious princess, and I had to admire her coolness in the face of adversity.

Caswallan remembered his manners. "Milady." I couldn't be sure which one of us he was talking to. At a wave of his arm, his farmhands took our horses, and one of them helped the other women down from the wagon. Ummidia looked as though she'd been the loser in a boxing match.

"Tell my wife to have a meal prepared," Caswallan ordered an elderly servant, who went running to do as he was bid. Then he turned back to us, his voice strained with anxiety. "Please, ladies, come this way and accept my humble hospitality."

We followed him through the gloomy cool of the inner courtyard and into the villa. Here, his wife and three serving women were already hastily organizing a meal, laying out platters of cold meat, bread, onions, and cheese, and jugs of wine and beer. I'd never been so glad to see a laden table as I was just then.

Morgawse must have been as hungry and exhausted as I was after a full day riding in that wagon in the heat, and having to feed her baby while she was doing so. Yet she seemed to have gained a second wind. She crisply told Caswallan's middle-aged wife, Melvina, that the other three women had been raped, the young girls very badly. Horrified, Melvina immediately took them under her wing and off for a bath and clean clothes. No such thing as preserving the forensic evidence in this day and age.

That left Morgawse and myself, and our two young escorts with their royal prisoner, to eat in the dining room with Caswallan. Starvation had made me giddy, and I took a long draught of wine that made me giddier still, but left a track of delicious fruitiness down my throat. Knowing that in my old time alcohol in pregnancy was frowned upon had no effect on me; it was drink wine or nothing where water could be such a germ carrier. And besides, after everything I'd gone through, I needed a drink, and the wine refortified me much more quickly than food would.

"What do you want me to do with the Lady Morgana?" Caswallan asked. He had a nervous look to him, as he might well have, considering he lived in her brother Cadwy's kingdom and must have known the powers she possessed. At his request, Morgana was untied and allowed to sit and eat with the rest of us, although she only deigned to nibble on a piece of bread and sip some wine.

The two young men who'd escorted us, deprived of Drustans' leadership, looked to be of a similar opinion to Caswallan. Morgana was a royal princess, sister of their own king, as well as Caswallan's, and they'd been glad to undo her ropes. Now, faced with a decision about her, they looked at each other in discomfort.

Morgawse was the one who spoke up. "She is my sister, and sister to the king. To both kings. She must be treated well, but kept under guard until Arthur returns. He will know what to do with her."

Morgana shot her younger sister a sharp look before schooling her face to equanimity. She must have known no one would dare touch her. It was written in her every haughty move. We ate in hungry and awkward silence.

Eventually, Melvina returned, but without Ummidia and her daughters. She told us she'd put them all together in a guest room after their bath and had food sent there. None of them had wanted to eat in company.

I would have liked a bath myself, but now, replete with food, I was far too tired, and all I wanted to do was sleep. Even thoughts of Arthur and the battle couldn't keep my eyes open a moment longer.

Perhaps, I thought, a little later as I drifted off in my bed, he'd be there beside me when I woke, and all of this would be a bad dream.

THE NEXT MORNING, on waking, the first thing I did was sleepily reach over expecting to feel him there by my side, only to find a cold void. This jolted me awake immediately, and without any hesitation, I pushed the covers off and got up. Yesterday's clothes lay strewn on the floor, redolent of body odor and horses, but I put most of them on anyway, leaving the stinky undershirt lying where I'd found it. It was cooler in just my tunic. Then I set off to find Caswallan and ask if he'd heard any news of the battle.

In the empty dining room the remains of breakfast still lay on the table, so I took a hunk of bread and some hard cheese. Eating them, I walked down into Caswallan's farmyard to find him organizing his work force for haymaking. Not even the urgency of battle could displace the cycle of farming.

Caswallan spotted me at the gate, where I'd halted, searching for any sign of a messenger from Arthur, but seeing none.

He hurried over, clad in only a tunic and sandals, as were his workmen, his long, rather sinewy legs burnt brown by the sun. "Milady." He performed an elaborate bow that looked most incongruous in the farmyard and gave me a good view of his bald spot. "This is no place for a queen. I trust you slept well? Are you rested?" His eyes alit on my hunks of half-eaten bread and cheese. "That's no breakfast for a queen. Let me take you back inside and find you something better."

I held up an imperious hand. "I like bread and cheese. And I also like farmyards. But I'm not here to look at your farm. I'm here to find out if you've heard anything from my husband's army."

His face fell, and he shook his head nervously. "Nothing, milady. Nothing at all as yet." He looked around at his men who were harnessing a pair of sturdy cobs to an empty hay cart. "I hope you'll excuse me getting my men out to fetch in the hay. It's been drying these five days and rain is coming. If I don't get it in today, it'll spoil."

I squinted up at the sky, but there wasn't a cloud in sight. I wished it would rain. It was far too hot to be wearing braccae and boots, but we'd left Din Cadan such a long time ago I'd not brought anything lighter with me.

Caswallan's face softened as though he were a mind-reader. "You're going to be too hot in those clothes, milady. Why don't you go and see my wife. She'll find something cooler for you. As soon as we hear anything, you'll be the first to know."

Thanking him, I abandoned the farmyard with reluctance, and walked back up to the house. His wife, Melvina, was in the garden picking roses. She looked up at me with a welcoming smile. "Milady."

Even after nearly eight months, I couldn't get used to receiving so much respect. "Please," I said quickly. "Call me Gwen."

Melvina looked surprised and pleased at the same time. She was of indeterminate middle-age, like her husband, with a soft, wrinkled face and blue eyes surrounded by laughter lines. I couldn't help but like her.

I went on. "I'm afraid I smell a bit. I'd very much like a bath and something to wear that's less likely to make me sweat. Your husband suggested I should ask you."

The villa possessed its own bath suite, which I used, and then put on a loose, sleeveless gown and sandals which Melvina found for me. Feeling a whole lot better, I decided it would be a good idea to go and find Ummidia and her daughters. I wasn't looking forward to facing them, but it needed to be done.

Timidly, I knocked on their door, with no firm idea of what I was going to say.

The shutters had been closed and the room was cool and gloomy. Only the shafts of piercing sunlight filtering through the gaps in the shutters lit it, and, when I entered, the light from the door. I left it open.

The two girls sat on one of the beds, not touching one another, knees drawn up to their chests and heads down, like a pair of beaten puppies. Gone were the ebullient teenagers I remembered. Ummidia sat alone on the cushioned bench in their room. I knew nothing about how to treat women who'd been raped, but surely locking yourself away in the dark couldn't be the answer.

I sat down next to Ummidia, instinct stopping me from reaching out and touching her, which was what I really wanted to do. She looked up. Her face was swollen and bruised from the beating the driver had given her, her lips thickened and split. I schooled my face not to look shocked.

She didn't beat about the bush. "This is your husband's fault," she spat, harsh bitterness in her voice. "If my Euddolen hadn't supported him in his bid for the throne of Dumnonia, none of this would have happened."

I recoiled in undisguisable surprise, but she ignored me and went on. "My husband would still be alive, and still be Seneschal to the king. My girls would be untouched by any man, happy playing together in the gardens of the Domus Alba."

I swallowed. Of all the reactions I'd imagined, it hadn't been this one. And the worst thing was, I agreed with her.

"I don't mind for myself," Ummidia continued. "I'm old and my life is nearing its end. But my girls –" She halted on a choking sob, turning to look at where they sat huddled on the bed. "They were untouched. On the brink of womanhood, preparing to one day soon become brides. Who will take them now? Broken and dirtied as they are. Filthy hands have touched them. Filthy, sweating, vile soldiers have slaked their lust on my girls. They'd be better off dead than left like this."

I sought for words of comfort. "It-it might seem unsurmountable now," I began, not feeling at all confident. "But, one day, maybe long in the future, it won't be so bad…I'm sure." I felt like an idiot and was conscious that my words made me sound like one.

"How can you know?" Ummidia spat back at me. "Have you ever been raped by a regiment of filthy Saxon soldiers?"

Words of futile apology sprang to my lips. "I-I can't possibly know what you're feeling. I'm just trying to offer you comfort."

She shook her head with violence. "There are no possible words of comfort. My daughters are ruined. My husband is dead. All his lands and property have been taken from him, and from us, on trumped-up charges of embezzlement. There's nothing left for us. Nothing left for my daughters."

I sat beside her in silence, unable to think of anything else to say. I'd had no training in rape counseling, or counseling of any sort, but common sense told me to shut up, to not tell her again that things would be all right in the end. That had been a crass thing to say and her reaction had proved it. But surely I was right, and with the passage of time, the memory would become less awful? Just as my own memory of my mother's death had faded. I struggled to imagine how they must be feeling, wishing there were something I could do.

On the bed, Albina began to bang the back of her head on the wall. Not hard, but rhythmically, like a caged animal under stress. It was painful to watch.

I couldn't do this. There'd been nothing in my life to prepare me for this sort of thing. Getting to my feet, I looked round at them all, tears running down my cheeks. Tears for all of them, and for my inability to help. "I-I'll come back in a while," I said to blank silence.

The girls, whom I remembered as so lively and charming, didn't even look at me.

"If you need me, send a servant and I'll come straight away." I paused. "I'll do anything – anything I can to help you. Remember that." And then I left, like the coward I was.

Morgawse found me sobbing in the garden, perched on the wall beside the small pool at the center. She didn't have the baby with her, so I guessed he must be sleeping somewhere. Sitting down, she put a hand on one of mine and squeezed it.

I wiped my nose on the back of my other hand and gave a big sniff which became more of an inelegant snort. She laughed, and I managed a damp laugh with her.

After a moment or two I looked up, warily. "Were you raped as well?"

She shook her head. "Of course not. I'm the king's sister."

That was some relief, anyway.

"What happened?" I asked. "When the soldiers came to Euddolen's villa? Do you feel able to tell me?"

She did.

The soldiers had come four days ago, unexpectedly marching up to the villa in the middle of the afternoon. As here, the farm workers were busy bringing in the hay crop from the meadows down by the river, and the soldiers managed to arrive with no warning. They were mostly Saxon foederati, but led by a British captain Morgawse vaguely knew, Donat. He stormed into the house and found Euddolen in his office where he served him with notice that he was being arrested for embezzlement. Of course, Euddolen denied it angrily, but the soldiers were taking no nonsense and dragged him, bloodied but still very much alive, through the garden toward the stable courtyard.

"One of them grabbed me, so I saw everything." Morgawse spoke with uncharacteristic coldness, as though recounting a chance meeting with a distant friend. "Ummidia and her daughters came running. They wanted to save Euddolen, I think, but the soldiers grabbed them, as well. Then Donat nodded to his soldiers – all of them Saxons – and –" She faltered. "They stripped the women naked and raped them all. Here, in the garden."

Of course, as Donat expected, Euddolen was unable to stand and watch this happen, and when he attacked the men raping his daughters, he was run through and lay dying on the flagstones while his daughters were deflowered before his eyes.

"I knew better than to resist," Morgawse said with a shiver. "I cowered with my baby in my arms, for once thankful for being Cadwy's sister. I was afraid lest any of the Saxons try to rape me as well."

When the men were finished, they loaded Euddolen's body into a wagon, threw in his terrified women, who were now clutching their torn gowns to cover their nakedness, and drove away with them. Some of the soldiers remained behind to make sure all the livestock were rounded up and everything of value looted. Morgawse was helped into the wagon with the other three women, and carried off to Viroconium.

"Once we arrived, they separated me from the others. At first I didn't know what had happened to them." Her face filled with disgust. "Then Cadwy himself told me what he'd done to the girls. He gave them to his foederati for their pleasures for a whole night. He was so pleased with himself...so triumphant. And he laughed when he told me they'd turned their noses up at Ummidia because she was too old."

Morgawse herself was housed in her old bedchamber, and although she wasn't allowed out of the inner courtyard, was afforded every other freedom. She took baby Medraut, for whose life she feared, to visit Karstyn, the woman who'd delivered him in the kitchen. And she sought out her sister Morgana.

"Morgana told me Medraut and I were in no danger." She sounded puzzled. "I couldn't think why. After all, Medraut is Theodoric's son – Arthur's ally. I was terrified lest they snatch him away from me – lest they decided to kill him, even though he's just a baby. But my sister told me he was a very special child, that at all costs he must be kept safe, and that she'd told our brother so. I was relieved, but I didn't understand."

Hearing this part of the story, my own heart gave a little skip of fear. Morgana possessed the Sight. Had she seen the future I half-suspected might lie before Medraut? Could she know he was destined to bring Arthur to his downfall in battle at fateful Camlann?

Morgawse had felt huge relief on hearing that her child was safe, a relief that lasted all of two days. Then Cei came to Viroconium, and Cadwy hatched his plot to trap Arthur at Din

Bassas.

"It was Morgana who said he must take the women, me included. I had no idea why until I heard the driver speaking to one of our guards. She wanted Euddolen's women, because after the ambush, which Cadwy was sure he'd win, he was going to execute them and leave their naked bodies tied to posts at the battleground. A warning to any who might think to cross him." She swallowed. "Morgana wanted me to see this. And most of all she wanted me to witness the death of Arthur."

This had understandably sown the seeds of doubt about her sister in Morgawse's mind.

Arthur. We still had no news of him or of how the battle had gone. A nasty knot of anxiety roiled in my stomach and my child did a frantic drumming on my insides, as if he knew his father was missing.

"I didn't know what to say to Ummidia and her daughters," Morgawse said, with deep sadness. "I wasn't raped. And yet they were. And I'd heard what was to happen to them after the ambush. They had too. There was nothing we could say to one another."

I nodded. "I feel the same. As far as I know, I've never known anyone who was raped. I couldn't think of anything remotely adequate."

Reflecting on our shortcomings, we sat in silence together without need of further words. Our lack of understanding, our feelings of impotence and rage, united us.

An hour later, Caswallan found us still in the garden. He hurried up the path toward us, his face suffused with excitement. "Outriders!" he shouted, waving his arms. "Outriders have arrived! News! The battle is won! Cadwy has retreated back to Viroconium. King Arthur marches this way!"

Morgawse and I leapt to our feet. Simultaneously, we turned to one another and embraced. I planted a kiss on her soft cheek. Arthur was coming back. He'd won, and Cadwy was in retreat. I should have had more faith in the history of the Dark Ages, the myths and the legends.

We ran past Caswallan down the path to the gates. Six warriors stood in the farmyard, their horses' heads hanging in exhaustion, a crust of white sweat matting their dark coats. The men had removed their helmets and were gathered around the water trough, taking turns to dunk their sweating heads under the water while their mounts drank, and standing up to let it run down their necks and over their roasting bodies.

"My husband?" I cried. "Is he well? Was he hurt?"

Their heads turned and I recognized Bedwyr, his short brown curls plastered to his head with water, his face covered in dirt and dried blood that might or might not have been his own. His eyes and teeth showed very white amidst the grime.

"Milady Guinevere," he started, with a weary bow. "King Arthur will be here shortly. He's not hurt, save for the battle bruises we all have. The day went well. Our losses were not great."

I ran past him to where the farm gates stood open. In the distance, a plume of dust hung in the air between the orchard trees, sparkling with the shimmering of sunlight on metal. Ignoring the stares of the farm workers, I ran down the track toward it.

Arthur rode at the head of the column of riders, his helmet and shield hanging from his saddle horn. Beside him rode Cei and Merlin. All three of them, their horses, and all the mounted warriors behind them, were covered in a fine layer of cloying dust that had stuck to their sweaty bodies.

Arthur saw me coming. A look of joy suffused his face as he swung himself down from his horse. As I ran into his arms, he swept me off my feet and into the air, planting a kiss on my lips before setting me back on the ground. A ragged cheer went up from the men behind him. I'd almost forgotten I was their lucky charm.

Taking a step back, I looked him up and down to reassure myself that Bedwyr had been telling the truth. He was filthy, covered in dust and blood from head to foot, but from the reception he'd given me, it couldn't be his own blood.

"Come on," he chided me with a wide grin, "we're all in dire need of food and drink and hopefully a bath."

I looked beyond him. Cei and Merlin both appeared intact, so my world was whole again. Cei gave me a nod and Merlin made a mock salute, smiles of success on their tired and dirty faces.

Arthur and I walked back to the villa hand-in-hand, leading his horse, me very content that he appeared to have forgiven me for stowing away amongst his soldiers, him just happy to be back. His hand, warm in mine, served as a remedy for all the sorrows I'd been feeling. Now that he was back, everything would surely be all right.

Inside the farmyard, the soldiers dismounted and began the routine of tending to their horses. A farm hand took Arthur's and Cei's, and another took Merlin's, and all four of us walked up to where Caswallan and Morgawse were waiting by the gate into the inner garden courtyard. Arthur clasped hands with his host before turning to his sister.

"Morgawse." With a smile of relief, Arthur took her in his arms and held her close, his face against her hair. "I thought we'd never see each other again."

Behind them, standing just inside the garden, Morgana fixed her dark gaze upon me, ignoring the look of longing Merlin was giving her.

The black cloud of jealousy and suspicion rose up in me again, unbidden. Was that hug from Arthur a fraction too long? Was she more pleased to see her brother than she should have been? If I was going to pay attention to some of the legends, it was impossible to disregard the ones I didn't like.

Morgawse kissed his dirty, stubbly cheek, and he released her.

I moved closer to him and slipped my fingers through his, with just a hint of proprietorial ownership.

Caswallan pushed the garden gate open wider, and I saw Morgana had gone. "You look like you need to visit our bath house, my Lord Arthur," he said.

We followed him through the garden, me hanging on tight to Arthur's hand, feeling the calluses against my own much softer skin. All around us, the scent of roses filled the air, butterflies fluttered in the bushes and heat shimmered over the clay roofs of the villa. I never wanted to let go of him again.

A single scream split the hot summer air.

All our heads turned. Melvina came running out of the bath house. Her dress was dripping with water and covered in blood. One hand covered her mouth as though she were afraid she would vomit.

The day stood still under the burning sun, as we halted, immobilized by shock. Cold fear clamped around my entrails and all the joy of Arthur's safe return was sucked away. Even the blackbird who'd been singing in the bushes fell silent.

Then the spell was broken.

We all ran toward her. She staggered to a halt under the shade of the colonnaded walkway, leaning her weight on one of the cool pillars, her breath coming in heaving gasps. Caswallan went to her, but she waved him away almost angrily when he tried to take her in his arms. With a wavering finger, she pointed at the gaping bath house door.

The men ran inside. I followed. Someone was lying on the tiles beside the plunge pool in an oddly unnatural position, legs akimbo, wet gown and hair spread red about her. I stepped closer, drawn inexorably to see who this was. Ummidia's eyes gazed sightlessly up at me, strands of wet hair plastered across her waxen cheeks. At first I didn't realize what I was looking at, and then it suddenly became clear. My stomach heaved. Unwillingly, my eyes slid toward the water.

In the plunge pool two bodies floated in a red sea, their hair spread about them like seaweed. Albina and Cloelia. On the side of the pool, a puddle of watery blood covered the tiles where Melvina had pulled Ummidia out. But it was too late, all three were dead.

I remembered what Ummidia had said to me about her defiled daughters. *They'd be better off dead.* And I knew without question that she'd brought her almost catatonic daughters here and slit their wrists for them. They'd probably gone without resistance. And now it was too late. Too late.

Chapter Twenty-Three

T HEY WERE ALL quite dead. Arthur and Merlin waded into the water and pulled the girls out, but every shred of life had left them. Their limbs hung loose, like broken marionettes, and their wet hair, that had haloed them in their watery grave, clung like clammy weed to their bloodless faces.

Morbid fascination held me in its thrall. How could people who had been warm and alive so short a time before, be so cold and dead so quickly? How could life be extinguished with only the flick of a sharp knife? Had those girls really wanted this? I'd said to Ummidia that eventually it wouldn't seem so bad, but she'd said they'd be better dead, and I'd walked away, unable to cope with their unfathomable grief. If I'd stayed, would this still have happened? Could I have stopped this if another day had passed? Or had she possessed the determination, whatever day it was?

My mind boiled with unanswerable questions. All I could think of was those girls as I'd first met them, half in love with my handsome husband, full of the joys of being teenagers in an age before that term ever existed, wondering if there were nice boys back in their home town of Caer Ligualid. And now – nothing lay ahead for them but the grave.

The news spread through the army like wildfire. Most of the men hardly knew Euddolen's family, but anger bubbled to the surface as the men gathered around their campfires in the orchards just outside the farmyard walls. All the joy of their victory had died, the deaths of the three women heavy on the conscience of every man. Particularly on Arthur's.

He walked away from us all. Still wearing his heavy mail shirt, his helmet discarded on the tessellated floor of the bath house, he shrugged off the hand I put on his arm and strode back down to join his men.

I went to follow him, but Merlin restrained me. "Leave him. Let him work through this alone."

I looked up at him. He was dripping wet, a pool of watery blood around his feet from where he'd waded into the pool with Arthur. His brown hair clung damply to his brow, and his eyes were deeply troubled.

Beside him, Cei gave a shrug of resignation. "People die every day," he said gruffly, in an effort to pretend this didn't matter. "Casualties of war." His blue eyes strayed down to the three bodies lying on the floor, limbs akimbo, blood-stained dresses clinging to them grotesquely.

"Not like this." I was too numb for tears. This world was too harsh for me. A world where women could be violated so badly they felt their only way out was death. A world where the monsters who'd done this would go unpunished, and they'd go on living while their victims lay cold and dead. What was I doing here? Why had I chosen this life when I could have been in my own world, safe and untroubled, living the quiet, secure life of a small-town librarian? And yet I knew atrocities like this existed in my own world, too, even though they were beyond my experience. Just because I wasn't a direct witness to the consequences as I was here, didn't mean these things didn't happen.

Caswallan spoke. "I'll have them prepared for burial." But there was hesitation in his voice.

"Where?" Cei asked. "What will you tell your priest?"

There was an awkward silence. I looked from man to man, puzzled.

"They're suicides." Merlin's tone was one of deep bitterness.

"Christian suicides. They can't be buried on consecrated ground."

I was horrified. "What d'you mean, they can't be buried on consecrated ground? Why not?"

"They killed themselves." Cei's voice was low, as though he didn't want to say the words. "It's a crime against the sixth commandment which says 'thou shalt not kill'. Those who take their own lives must be buried at a crossroads with a stake through their heart."

I couldn't believe what I was hearing. And then I could. Why was I so surprised by the primitive beliefs of the fifth century? I was a fool to have expected anything else.

"But we don't know they all killed themselves," I protested. "Ummidia said to me that they'd be better off dead. They may not all be suicides. We don't know that she didn't kill the girls herself. You didn't see them. The girls were in some kind of a trance. Their minds weren't working at all – they were shutting out the world. They couldn't have done this to themselves."

Caswallan raised his grizzled head, a new look of determination in his eyes. "You're right. Their mother couldn't stand the shame. She murdered her daughters while out of her mind with grief. The girls at least shall have a Christian burial."

I looked again at Ummidia, her battered face wiped clean of suffering, and knew she would be happy with that. Her girls were what had been important to her. She'd killed them for love, and for love, she'd be buried by a lonely crossroads with a stake through her broken heart. But I was certain she'd still be going to heaven, if that place existed, and she'd be with her daughters and her husband once again. The God I half-believed in wouldn't separate a loving mother from her daughters. Whatever was done to her body, it didn't change the way she'd felt for her children.

ARTHUR FINALLY CAME to our bedchamber long after dark.

I heard him come noisily through the door, bump into the bench seat and curse under his breath. Having only been sleeping lightly, I was wide awake in an instant.

"Arthur?"

"Sorry," he mumbled, and I realized with a jolt that he was very drunk.

Sitting up in bed, I pushed off the thin covers. Through the open shutters, moonlight spilled in across the room, illuminating him standing beside the bench, head down, shoulders hunched. He'd shed his mail shirt and tunic somewhere and was wearing just his braccae and undershirt, but he'd not been back to the bath house. No one had. It was going to take a lot of cleaning.

I slipped out of bed and approached him warily. I didn't have a lot of experience with drunk people, even after my years in university, and from the way he was swaying, he seemed to be very drunk indeed. He reeked of alcohol. A wine stain darkened his shirt front.

All my inbuilt motherly instinct rose. I put out my arms and he half fell into them, his head coming to rest on my shoulder, his body slumped heavily against mine.

"Come to bed," I said, into his ear. "You're exhausted and drunk, and you need to let me look after you."

His body stiffened against mine, and after a moment he pushed himself away from me. "And who was there to look after Euddolen's family?" His words were slurred. "I told him Cadwy had sworn not to touch them. I promised him his family was safe from harm. They didn't want to return to Rheged. Their home was here."

"You couldn't have known," I said. "No one could have known what Cadwy would do." I paused. "Nor let his men do…" My voice trailed away. Maybe we should have guessed. We all, me included, knew what Cadwy was capable of. That he'd left it till now to carry out his revenge was all the more surprising. Although I could guess that it was to provoke a reaction from Arthur that he'd killed Euddolen and taken his family prisoner.

I needed to distract him. "Tell me about the battle." With gentle force I guided him to our bed and pushed him down on it. He smelled of wine and dust and sweat.

I knelt in front of him and pulled his boots off. "Tell me what happened."

The story came in fits and starts at first, that I had to piece together. He was too drunk and maudlin to tell it properly, but as he spoke his story became clearer. He'd taken his thirty men to the island fort, across the narrow causeway that countless years ago long-forgotten men had made with stones and earth and wood.

"I was there first," he said, stretching his long legs. "Cadwy arrived not long after. We faced one another. I had my warriors ranged behind me. He had his. I didn't trust him and he didn't trust me."

I wasn't surprised.

Drustans had reached the main body of Arthur's army just in time, and under cover of the forest they moved around until their scouts picked out where Cadwy's men were waiting, managing to kill a few of his scouts as they did so.

"What happened next?" I wanted to put my arms around him and hold him close, but something told me not to. Not yet. He needed to get this story off his chest.

"Cadwy feigned giving up his prisoners to me. Said it was a 'clerical error', said he knew now they'd not been complicit in Euddolen's supposed guilt. He smiled his treachery at me." Arthur dropped his head into his hands. "As though the losing of a man's life was nothing to him. He swore he'd give back Euddolen's womenfolk. And I knew it was a lie. A monstrous lie, like everything else that comes out of his mouth."

I was reminded of Hamlet's lines about his murderous uncle, who could "smile and smile and be a villain." I doubted neither Arthur nor Cadwy had been fooled by the other.

"And then?" I prompted.

"We came to leave. He stood back to allow me to lead my

men off the island first. Of course, I suspected treachery, and expecting it made me wary. As we crossed, his army emerged from the treeline. But so did mine." He raised his head, staring out at nothing, perhaps seeing the battle in his mind's eye. "I led the charge off the causeway. Cadwy's men attacked us from behind, but we outran them. Battle was joined."

With the wetlands to their left and the forest to the right, the battle had been fought in a narrow strip of land that made cavalry charges nearly impossible. But Arthur's warriors, although outnumbered by Cadwy's home-bred soldiers and hired Saxon foederati, had the advantage of height and stirrups. Instead of having to dismount to fight, the new stirrups enabled them to lean left or right and bend low to attack their enemies, using their swords to far greater effect.

"It was difficult at first. With his foederati, Cadwy had more men than we did. But we have horses, and eventually we gained the upper hand." Arthur's voice was curiously calm. As though he were recounting the action in a film, not something he'd been part of.

"A battle seems to take forever and yet no time at all. Suddenly, Cadwy's men were in retreat. My men would have given chase, but the day was late, and they were exhausted. If we'd pursued them it would have become a siege. We aren't equipped for that. The battle was won. Drustans found me and I knew the women were safe. There'll come a time to mete out due punishment to Cadwy. It isn't now." He paused. "The battlefield was strewn with the dead – our men, his men, horses. Flies everywhere. Clouds of flies on everything."

In the humid warmth of the evening, they had tended to their wounded and made a pyre to burn the dead. The news that I should be safely at Caswallan's villa with the other women had brought relief to Arthur. So that night they made their camp at the forest edge, away from the charnel house that was the battlefield.

The next day they made their slow way back to us.

His voice died away, and he sat in front of me, silent and still.

"Lie down," I said, unable to think of anything else to say. "Lie down, and let me hold you."

I thought he'd refuse, but to my surprise, he complied, lying back on the bed, his arms by his side. I got up off the floor rather stiffly as I'd been kneeling there so long, and lying down next to him, put my arms around him and held him close. After a minute or two his body relaxed and he turned his head toward me, burying it in my shoulder. I held him close, and his arm reached over my body to hold me in return. It was a long time before either of us slept.

THE MORNING BROUGHT a different man. He was up before me, despite what must have been a killer of a hangover, and when I woke, the bedroom was devoid of any sign of his overnight presence. Wondering where he'd gone, I slipped out of bed, washed in the bowl of clean water someone had left for me, and dressed in the light gown Melvina had supplied.

I found Arthur with his men, his mood and theirs entirely changed. Much cleaning of weapons and horses was going on, as well as bathing in the nearby river, as I discovered when I walked down to it in the morning sunshine. Apparently one night was long enough to mourn the "casualties of war" as Cei had named them. Or at least, they'd shut away the thoughts of the battle dead and the women.

The men were splashing, naked and joyful, in the cold water of the river, seemingly recovered from the day before. Arthur and Merlin were with them, and none of them showed any embarrassment at my arrival. Naked men didn't bother me, so I sat on a rock waiting for Arthur to finish, and watching them wash away the aches and pains accrued in battle, and the sorrow for the needless deaths of those three women.

In only his braccae, feet bare, and wet hair slicked back from his face, Arthur walked me back up to the camp amongst the apple trees. Bedwyr had the wounded men all in one spot, where he was tending to their injuries. So leaving Arthur to find himself clean clothes, I went to help him.

The wounded were in a sorry state. Sword wounds abounded, but also crushing injuries from the axes wielded by the Saxon foederati. I washed and bandaged and comforted as best I could, but there were at least two men whom I didn't think would make it back to Din Cadan. With a heavy heart, I at last returned to the garden courtyard, tired and dirty from working so long in the warm sun.

I found Arthur there, fully dressed now, with Morgana and Morgawse. Caswallan stood a little back from the three siblings, fidgeting nervously. It was the first time I'd seen all three of them standing so close together, and I was struck anew by how similar they were. Arthur and Morgana were tall and slim, whereas Morgawse was petite and slight, but their bond of common blood was clear.

Morgana's dark eyes fixed on me as I walked up the path to join them, and I hesitated, that feeling of unease rising in me again, of her knowing what I was thinking. I forced myself to keep going, though, and came and stood beside Arthur, staring back at her in defiance.

"She has to go back to her brother," Caswallan said, as I touched my fingertips to Arthur's in support.

Arthur was glaring at her, exasperation on his face. She was his sister after all, but the fact that she was now his prisoner hadn't escaped any of them. And from what Morgawse had told me, she'd had quite a hand in plotting the fate of Euddolen's women at the ringfort of Bassas.

Morgana flicked her eyes from me to Arthur, a half-smile playing on her full lips. Someone, Melvina, I suspected, had provided her with a clean gown and she looked every inch the powerful princess. "He's right. You cannot keep me here," she said, her voice deep and resonant, almost caressing. Not the voice of someone who feared for her safety.

By now, Cadwy would know she'd been captured, and that Morgawse, too, was in our hands. The thought that we could kill Morgana here and now tumbled into my head, kill her and pretend she'd been slain in the chaos after the battle. After all, Ummidia and her girls were dead, whom she'd intended to have executed on the battlefield. Why not her?

"You're right," Arthur said. "We don't want to keep you." Had that same thought occurred to him?

Morgawse put her hand on Arthur's arm, her fingers small and pale. With a shock, the impulse came to me to knock her hand away. When I looked up, Morgana was watching me. Did she know I'd had that wicked thought?

"Send her back to our brother," Morgawse said. "She can take our message to him." She was the strong Morgawse again, not the scared mouse about to give birth in a kitchen during a skirmish. If that was what pregnancy did to you, I wasn't impressed.

"Yes, send her back," Caswallan said. Clearly, he didn't want to face the same fate Euddolen had, for sheltering us. "And leave. Once the women are buried, I want you to leave." He probably hadn't banked on us bringing back the king's sister – who could tell her brother exactly who'd given us help against him.

Arthur gave a curt nod. "You are my sister, and a woman. I cannot cause you harm. I will not harm women, as my brother does. Wars should not be fought against women and children. Not even Saxon women. You can take a message to my brother." He glanced down at me. "Tell him my wife is with child. That I have begun a dynasty of my own in Dumnonia. Tell him that if he crosses me again, including any move against Caswallan, who is innocent in this, I will take his kingdom from him. Not because I want it – I don't – but he won't understand that. I'll take it because I want him gone. And I always carry out my threats."

Morgana smiled at him, a knowing, sly smile. Her eyes flicked over my gently curved belly, hidden beneath the soft folds of my light gown, and her lip curled in contempt. She raised her dark brows at her brother in a silent mockery that made my skin crawl.

"You may take her, Caswallan," Arthur said, a pulse beating angrily in his neck. "Send your own men as her escort and assure my brother of your loyalty." Contempt edged his voice.

WE LEFT THE next morning, riding south through the foothills of the Welsh mountains, headed toward Caer Legeion gwar Uisc, modern Caerleon on the River Usk, where we could leave Morgawse with her husband, or, if he wasn't there, at least in his home.

From amongst the servants at Caswallan's villa we'd acquired a young girl to help Morgawse with the baby. Gitta was one of Melvina's housemaids, so needed very little training to take on the duties required of her, and Morgawse seemed pleased.

Our wounded were loaded into wagons to be sent directly to Din Cadan under guard, whilst we, and the majority of Arthur's somewhat reduced army, took the Caer Legeion road.

Along with Gitta, Morgawse was to ride in the single wagon that accompanied us. For once, I also found this a more comfortable way to travel. My belly was beginning to impinge a little on my riding, and I was exhausted by the events of the past days and weeks, so it was pleasant to ride on the piles of cushions and rugs in the back of the wagon with the two women and the little baby, and to sometimes doze away the afternoons. There were fewer flies to contend with as well.

Baby Medraut was charming, and despite my inbuilt distrust of him, I found myself liking his ready smiles and infectious giggles when Morgawse tickled him. He was like babies the world over – loveable, plump, impossible to get angry with. Although watching him as he sat happily on his mother's or Gitta's knees, I couldn't help but be forcibly reminded not only of what the future might have in store for him, but also that he looked so much like my husband.

Chapter Twenty-Four

W E TOOK OUR journey slowly. The wagon governed the speed at which the whole party could move, so it took quite a few long summer days before we eventually ground into Caer Legeion. The town lay about five or six miles inland from the Sabrina Sea by way of the twisting river Usk, less as the crow flies.

The long-abandoned legionary fortress still squatted in stony ruins beside the post-Roman fifth-century town that had grown up beside it, and warehouses clustered around the port. Visible just outside the fortress walls lay the crumbling remains of a large amphitheater. It had obviously once been both a thriving port and military center.

We rode into the town just as the bell in the tower of the small church began to chime, calling the people to worship. Down in the harbor, the masts of a dozen ships rose like a bare and spindly forest, so it looked as though we might be lucky and find Theodoric still in port. He met us in the street in front of his house, his big face flushed with joy to see his wife and son once more. With a cry of excitement, Morgawse handed the baby to me and jumped recklessly down from the back of the wagon to throw herself into his arms, clinging on like a limpet. He wrapped his strong arms around her, holding her close, his face buried in her dark hair. It was a touching moment. If I hadn't known of his predilection for sleeping around, I might have been moved by it.

By the time Arthur had helped me down from the wagon as well, they'd parted, her cheeks flushed and her hair slightly tousled after their vigorous embrace. She turned to me, eyes alight, and I willingly handed over the baby who was just waking up. The little dark-haired boy blinked up as Theodoric bent over him, his own blond hair shining in the sunlight. Not recognizing this gigantic stranger, the baby's face crumpled into a cry and his angry wail rose above the sounds of the town that surrounded us.

Theodoric scowled and Morgawse laughed. "He'll soon get used to you. It's been more than six months."

Had the baby reacted because Theodoric wasn't his father? Could a baby know such a thing? Or was it the normal fears of a baby for a huge man he didn't recognize suddenly looming over him? How would I ever find out without betraying my lack of trust in my husband?

We stayed two weeks at Caer Uisc with Theodoric in his spacious town house. Our men pitched their camp within the tumbledown walls of the old legionary fortress and set about relaxing after the stress of battle.

Merlin had a twinkle in his eye when I asked him how the men were amusing themselves. "If you were to take a walk into the town along the Street of the Coppersmiths you'd no longer find any coppersmiths, but several very good brothels. All of them regularly bulging with our warriors."

Knowing the men as I did now, I wasn't really surprised.

During those two weeks I did my best to emulate Arthur and push to the back of my mind all memories of the man I'd killed and what had happened to Euddolen's family. It wasn't easy.

But after two weeks our welcome was becoming a little strained as there were so many of us. The townspeople's patience had worn thin over the number of times drunken warriors disturbed their peace. So we marched east again, along the shores of the Sabrina Sea to the ferry which was to take Arthur, Merlin and me directly across into Dumnonia with half a dozen warriors as an escort. The rest of the army, under Cei, would take the longer land route up round Caer Gloui, modern Gloucester, to where a bridge crossed the river.

The ferry looked a ramshackle affair. A wooden sailing boat rested up against an ancient pier, with a gangplank I didn't much fancy risking. And that was before realizing our horses were also expected to negotiate this narrow plank. It hadn't occurred to me that our horses would need to travel with us, but of course, we'd require them on the other side.

Arthur and Merlin were already swinging down out of their saddles, their warriors following suit, so, with reluctance, I did the same. Alezan pricked her long ears as the first of the warriors led his horse up to the plank and began to cross it. Much to my amazement the horse followed her rider onto the small ship and down into the belly of the vessel. There was only just enough room in there for our nine horses, which seemed like a lot of weight for this little boat. A quick, and nervous, mental calculation brought me to the conclusion that horses and armed riders combined, we must have weighed almost five tons.

The owner of the ferry, a weatherworn little man whose brown clothes didn't quite manage to disguise their grubbiness, started waving his arms about irately. "If'n 'ee dursn't git they 'orses on board soon ye'll miss th'tide. 'Tis on th'turn." He wiped his dripping nose on the back of a grimy hand. "Ye'll 'ave ter wait twelve hours amore if'n yer dursnt git on me boat now."

Our remaining warriors swiftly led their horses on board. After Arthur had boarded his horse, Merlin stood back to allow me on next. I hesitated, uncertain. All the other horses had walked along that plank with no problem, but I was afraid, since Alezan, being so skittish, might be far less calm about it.

"She can do it." Merlin laid a hand on my arm, trying to be reassuring. But that didn't change the fact that beneath the plank a few feet of dark water glimmered, into which I had a clear picture of Alezan falling, taking me with her.

I bit my lip, and she curvetted sideways away from me just to illustrate what a handful she could be. If she did that on the plank, we'd be finished.

Arthur came and stood on the far side of the plank, looking exasperated.

The wizened little pilot possessed the air of someone who didn't care at all. "If'n we 'ave ter wait any longer then ye'll 'ave to unload 'er agin. I'm in no 'urry. Ye'll be payin' me whenever it be that I takes ye over."

"Hurry up." Arthur put his hands on his hips and looked irritated. He was eager to be home.

"Give her to me." Merlin shoved his own horse's reins into the hands of the wizened little man, and took Alezan. With no more ado, he led her across the plank as though she were a seaside donkey, and down to stand with the other horses. Watching her, I'd have thought she'd done this every day of her life.

After handing her to one of the warriors, Merlin came running lightly back to take his own horse, and I followed him on board, feeling absurdly grateful.

The crew, which consisted of a boy with a hare-lip and a distinct resemblance to his smelly superior, pushed the little ship off from the jetty with a weatherworn, silvered ash pole. Her sails unfurled and the wind took them. She wallowed in an alarming fashion under her heavy load, and I went to stand in the bows with Arthur and Merlin. The warriors remained chatting casually to one another in the belly of the ship with our horses, as though this was a normal occurrence for them. Where I stood with Arthur and Merlin was no more than a few feet above the cargo deck, but I felt much safer there than if I'd been down with the men.

Arthur must have sensed my trepidation because he took my hand and clasped it in a firm grip. "You don't much like water, do you?" he whispered into my ear.

I gave a brief shake of my head, and hung onto his hand, wondering what would happen if our boat were to capsize, or sink. In my present state, would I be able to swim to shore, or might the currents in the estuary of the Sabrina river be too strong to allow even that? My mind churned with possibilities, none of which included arriving in one piece on the other bank. I'd never been a particularly nervous person, but being pregnant had given me responsibilities, and as we negotiated that expanse of grey, white capped water, paranoia didn't feel far away.

Despite the warm day and the blue sky, the sea was choppy, and the little ship bobbed on the waves in a most unseaworthy fashion. On the cargo deck the horses shifted restlessly and the warriors whispered to them and scratched their ears to calm them.

If the boat sank, would I be able to grab hold of Alezan and get her to help me swim to shore? I'd never been fond of water from when, as a small girl, I'd fallen into a neighbor's pool and thrashed around at the deep end for what felt like an eternity before someone came to my rescue. Soon after that, I'd learned to swim with my twin brother Artie. However, whereas he'd been bold and fearless, I'd stayed the nervous wimp, swimming at the side of the pool, afraid to leave its safety. So taking a rickety ferry of indeterminate age and maintenance out into the mile-wide stretch of water that was the Sabrina estuary was not something I'd been keen to do. Doubly so now I bore the responsibility for another life within me.

The only good thing about being at sea was the breeze which ruffled my hair and cooled my sweaty brow, blowing away the clouds of flies that had pursued us down from Caer Legeion.

For an age we made no visible progress, before, at last, the salt flats on the Dumnonian side of the estuary drew near enough to see properly. Our skipper steered his boat toward a long wooden jetty which stuck out like a pointing finger into the river. He and his boy tied the boat up and shoved out their flimsy gangplank, in a hurry to get us unloaded before the tide turned their mooring spot into mud flats.

We led our horses off the ferry and down the jetty to the security of solid land, with me this time braving the gangplank with Alezan myself. Without a backward glance, the hare-lipped boy pushed off from the jetty and the boat set off back to the far shore.

I was more than glad to be on dry land, although in reality it was wet land as this was salt flats. Beyond the jetty a twisting causeway meandered inland between clumps of marsh grass, taking us to higher ground. The rank smell of the mudflats and the little meandering streams of brackish water filled my nostrils. The flies returned in force.

Night brought us to a tumbledown way station in a small town near the mouth of the River Afon. The town's Roman buildings, if ever it had possessed any, had long since crumbled away to be replaced by wattle and daub walls and thatched roofs, although a few tumbled pillars were visible poking out from beneath a steaming midden.

With only nine in our party, we weren't a huge burden to house, but nevertheless, we didn't linger, and the following day continued inland. As evening fell, we arrived at Caer Baddan and the house of its magistrate, Bassus. I felt a sense of relief when we discovered he and his boring wife were not in residence. Their steward informed us they'd retreated for the summer to their villa in the countryside to supervise the harvest and escape the hot weather stink of the city.

By then, I was so tired Arthur had to carry me to my bed-chamber and undress me, and the next morning he declared we were to spend a day recuperating in Caer Baddan before making the remaining journey back to Din Cadan.

I didn't stir before midday, and when I rose, I was more than happy to put on the light dress and sandals Melvina had given me. After breakfast, I wandered out to sit in the gardens in the shade of an overgrown arbor, dreaming of the baby I was soon to meet. My belly seemed to have grown a lot bigger in the last few weeks and I was conscious of feeling very pregnant.

A discreet cough disturbed me, and I looked up from con-templating my burgeoning baby bump to see a slight teenage girl standing before me holding a goblet – the same girl who'd waited on me here eight months ago.

She held out the goblet with a shy smile. "If it please ye, milady, I brung ye a cold drink. The 'ousekeeper did say as ye'd 'ave need of it, settin' in the sun as ye be."

I smiled at her. "Why, thank you very much." Taking the proffered goblet, I sipped the drink, surprised to find it wasn't alcoholic for once, but sweet and fruity. "It's lovely. What is it?"

She blushed. "'Tis a recipe my old ma did teach me. Made from the flower o' the elder bush, afore it do turn into they berries."

Elderflower cordial; who'd have thought it. But it must have been diluted with unsterile water so I hesitated before taking a second sip.

She saw my concern. "'Tis made with water from a pure spring in the 'ills." She gave me another shy smile. "We all do drink it and it 'ave done us no h'arm."

Reassured, I finished the drink and handed her back the goblet. "What's your name?"

She blushed even more hotly. "It be Bretta, milady."

I looked her up and down with more interest. "How long have you been a servant here then, Bretta?"

She shuffled her bare feet. "More'n five year, I do think. I begun 'ere when I were a slip of a girl. An' I'm a woman grown now."

I put my hand on my stomach, resting it there while I thought how to pose my next question without being too intrusive. "And your family? Do you have one? Parents? Brothers and sisters? Do they work here as well?"

She shook her head. "My mother did die when my youngest brother were born. My father, 'e did live a little longer, but 'e were in an accident in the quarry where 'e were workin', and 'e were all crushed. That were two year since. I do care for my brothers and sisters now. They be my family."

I'd seen her when, as a frightened visitor to the past, I'd first come here, and the fact that she might have had a story to tell had completely passed me by. Now, here I was, so enmeshed in this world, a past which had now become my present, that I at last had time to take an interest in the people who inhabited it. And here before me stood a girl without parents, little more than a child herself, who had the responsibility of caring for her younger siblings.

"Where do you all live?" I asked.

This time I sensed her blush hid more than self-consciousness. She looked down at her brown bare feet and shifted as though uncomfortable at my question. "I do 'ave a bed 'ere in the palace. My brothers and sisters, they 'ave to live in a room I do rent for 'em. My next brother, 'e do work down at the wharf, but 'e's not a big lad yet, so 'e can't carry much. 'E don't get a lot o' work, nor money."

"Oh." I patted the bench beside me. "Sit down, Bretta, and tell me about your brothers and sisters."

There were an astonishing six of them altogether. Every child born to her mother had by some miracle managed to survive, despite their poverty, with the older ones taking responsibility for the younger ones as each arrived.

She was proud of them all. "Even Pwyll, the youngest born, 'e be able to earn 'imself a crust fer sweepin' up fer the stall 'olders in th'market."

But from what she said, it appeared to be a hand-to-mouth existence, precarious in the extreme, with her earnings disappearing into the void that was the rental for their single tiny room.

I wormed the truth about the room out of her. "We 'ave but one room fer all on'us. It do b'long to my master. 'E do charge us top rate, I suspicion."

I wasn't so blind as not to know people still lived like this in the twenty-first century. Yet to hear how this motherless family lived, while my life was cushioned in the comparative luxury of the Imperial Palace, disturbed me, and reminded me of the vow I'd made on my first visit to Caer Baddan. As I'd ridden through the filthy freezing streets, I'd seen half-naked children grubbing through the rubbish piled in the gutters, searching for something to eat. Right then I'd decided that if I had to marry Arthur and become his queen, I'd make it my mission to try to help the poor, and in particular the defenseless children.

I'd made a start with the orphaned children of Caerwysg, and now the time had come to do the same for the ones closer to home.

When I broached the subject later with Arthur, his reply wasn't quite what I was after. "Caer Baddan comes under the jurisdiction of Melwas. He's overlord here, holding this city as subking to me."

I raised my brows in a silent question, suppressing the shiver that threatened to run down my back at the mention of that man's name.

"That means he rules this area," he explained. "Bassus is his man, as Melwas should be mine. That's the way things work."

"Then surely you can order Melwas to make provision for all the homeless children here? Get him to provide them with food and shelter?"

Arthur pulled a wry face. "You'd think so, but in practice it doesn't happen quite like that. Melwas is practically autonomous. He owes me taxes in kind, which he pays at harvest time, but it would be hard for me to force him to do something so bizarre as provide for his poor. He'd see it as untoward interference. And in a way, I'd agree with him. They're his people to do with as he likes."

"What's the point of him being your subking if you can't make him do what you want?" I was annoyed, thwarted by his arguments. I'd fondly imagined it would be an easy task to help these children. In fact, I'd thought I could get Arthur to make provision for their shelter and care himself. I'd never imagined it would depend on Melwas's goodwill.

Something glimmered in his eyes. "I suppose I could suggest this to him..." He spoke slowly, as though an idea had occurred to him. "I could make it difficult for him to refuse…" He stared over my head. "It's within my rights to increase the taxes he pays to me. I could threaten to do so if he doesn't sort out the problem within his city, and take action against him if he fails to obey me…" He seemed lost in his own thoughts, as though these remarks weren't directed at me at all.

"Can you do that? Force him to act before winter sets in?" In my head I could see a proper house for the orphans, people to take care of them, food on the table and clothes on their backs. Maybe apprenticeships for them too, like the children at Caer Pensa.

A slow smile spread across Arthur's face. "I could try." The smile became grim. "I could certainly try."

The man in charge of Caer Baddan during Bassus's absence in the countryside was one Kirwin, a solid, middle-aged and rather servile man with no pretensions to being Roman whatsoever. When Arthur explained what we wanted, he seemed inclined to agree that it would be beneficial to get the poor children off the streets. Listening to his practicalities, though, convinced me he had a different reason for wanting this. Quite simply the presence of poor child beggars in the city was bothersome and to be frowned upon.

"I want you to make sure Bassus gets this message," Arthur said, from where he sat in the ornate chair in Bassus's audience chamber. The room had been decorated in terracotta paint to waist level and above that with murals of a hunting scene. The huntsmen, hounds and fleeing herd of deer raced around the walls in perpetual motion. The chair was almost a throne. Merlin had told me it had been installed and used by the Emperor Constantine III, Arthur's great grandfather, soon after he'd had the palace built.

Arthur, in a dark tunic and braccae which gave no hint of his status, leaned back in the chair, long legs extended. Only the golden circlet in his hair told Kirwin he stood in the presence of a king – that, and Arthur's bearing and autocratic tone.

"Yes, milord." Kirwin almost scraped the ground with the top of his head, so low was his bow. "You're right that we need to clear the streets of these homeless children. I'm sorry the sight of them so upset the Queen." His too-close-together eyes slid sideways to look at me.

I was sitting beside Arthur on a somewhat less elaborate seat, the one perhaps that Kirwin himself might have occupied when Bassus held court. I narrowed my eyes at him, but didn't interrupt.

"Let me make it clear." Arthur steepled his fingers. "These children are the responsibility of your king. You must tell Bassus as soon as he returns, and make sure he informs Melwas. He must deal with this problem before the cold of winter sets in and the children suffer more. My wife has a kind disposition. She can't bear to see them cold and hungry. Do I have your word?"

Kirwin bowed again, giving us another good view of the flaky bald spot on the top of his head. "Yes indeed, milord." He was gabbling. "I'll make certain that your orders are carried out." His eyes swiveled toward me once more. "Milady the Queen need not worry herself any longer. And may God bless her own child thrice over."

I wasn't sure we should trust him. He didn't look a kind man to me, and I felt that was what was required here; a Samaritan, not a bean counter, which Kirwin undoubtedly was. When Kirwin had gone and we were back in our chambers, I mentioned this to Arthur.

"Don't worry." He pulled me onto his lap. "I'll send messengers to both Bassus and Melwas detailing our requirements, and include the threat of increased revenues when the harvest is over. I think…" Here he paused and that same far-away look came over his face again. "I think he'll find his wisest course of action is to comply."

I didn't know why, but a wave of cold unease washed over me as though someone had drenched me in iced water.

Chapter Twenty-Five

A STOMACH ACHE woke me. I lay for a few minutes wondering whether to get up and use the bucket in the corner of the bedchamber, dimly visible in the early morning light. The discomfort subsided though, and feeling better, I turned onto my side and snuggled as close to Arthur's warm body as my now swollen and nearly full-term belly would allow me, pressing myself against his naked back. There was a nip in the autumn air, and my nose was cold, so I pulled the covers right up and buried my head under them, breathing in Arthur's masculine smell.

Just as I was beginning to doze off again, a second pain wracked my body, drawing a gasp from my lips. That hadn't been nice. Maybe it was something I'd eaten. After a few moments, it passed like the first one, and I put my arm over Arthur's back, nestling closer still. He stirred in his sleep, but didn't waken, and I closed my eyes to try to get back to sleep as well.

The third time it happened, it brought me properly awake. Realization finally dawned. These were not ordinary stomach pains. This was labor. The thing I'd been half-dreading, half-looking forward to, for the last few months since we'd returned from Caer Baddan, the thing that might kill me if I were unlucky. I sat up and shook Arthur awake, anxious not to be going through this alone. "I think it's started."

By the faint light from the half-open shutters he went from sleep to wide awake in a fraction of a second, with the instincts of a warrior and a hunter. "Are you certain? What's happening? Are you in pain?"

"I think I'm getting contractions." I put my hand on my belly. "Not all that close together yet, so it's early stages. The midwife said first babies take a long time." My university friend Sian's certainly had. She'd given me every gory and unnecessary detail of her delivery, and it was thanks to her, and all the episodes of *Call the Midwife*, that I felt so nervous about what was about to happen to me. Ignorance can be bliss.

Arthur sat up in bed, giving me a full view of his lean torso and causing me a pang of jealousy that he was a man and not expected to do anything more than get a baby started. I wished very much that I could delegate this birth to someone else.

He licked his lips. "What can I do?" A certain nervousness edged his voice, even though he was already a father. "Shall I fetch the midwife?"

He'd had a midwife brought from Caer Pensa – Donella, a woman who'd been trained at Viroconium. There'd be no Mother Nara with her dirty hands tending me. Donella had already delivered four babies within the walls of Din Cadan, all of whom had lived, as had their mothers, so I was feeling a little more confident about the medical care available to me than I had been nine months ago.

I shook my head. "Not yet. It's only just starting. The sun's not even up, and she'll be in her bed." I rubbed my stomach as the pain began to tighten around my body like an iron girdle. "She's already given me lots of advice. I'd like it to be just you and me for as long as possible." I screwed up my face and stopped talking to concentrate on the pain.

"Lie down in the warm then." He patted my pillow. "See if you can get a bit more sleep."

Get a bit more sleep? Who was he kidding? He might already be a father, but he had no idea of what being in labor was like. The problem was, neither had I. Not really. I lay down on my side with my back to him, and he curled himself around me, holding me close.

That didn't work for long. I had no way of telling the time, of course, and had to estimate the passage of minutes. But I was sure these contractions were coming about ten minutes apart. Or maybe a bit less. Everything Sian said about how her labor had started had unhelpfully gone out of my head. My old life of working in the library and going for coffee at her house and admiring her chubby, blonde-haired baby seemed a distant memory.

But I did remember what Donella had told me. "The easiest births be them what 'appen to women what keep workin'. I've known women toilin' in the fields drop their babbies in minutes and get back to work straight after as though nowt 'ad 'appened."

I got out of bed, burying my bare feet in the thick fur rugs covering the flagstoned floor of our bedchamber. "Donella said to walk up and down, and that would bring the baby quicker and more easily. She said not to lie down for too long." Indeed, she was probably right, because during the only birth I'd actually witnessed, that of Medraut, Morgawse's little son, Morgawse had crouched on a stool to give birth rather than lain down.

Arthur got out of bed as well and pulled on his braccae, stifling a yawn. It was early still. I walked over to the door, turned around and walked back, feeling a little stupid. "Can we walk outside, do you think?"

He pulled his tunic over his head and yanked on his boots, then put mine on for me while I sat on the edge of the bed. Reaching my feet had become impossible lately. In fact, even seeing my feet had become difficult. He found me a loose, ankle-length over-tunic and helped me into it, this action punctuated by me having to stop and bend double while another contraction took control of my body.

Having draped a thick cloak around my shoulders, he took me out of the side door, through the little room where the records of the fortress were stored, and into the cool early morning air. In the east, the sky was gently pinkening, and the blue-black above our heads was rapidly growing lighter. Autumn mist draped the thatched houses of Din Cadan, and dew sparkled like jewels on a million autumnal cobwebs.

With Arthur supporting me, we walked between the quiet houses and barns until we reached the steps to the wall-walk which ran around the fortress perimeter. The morning guard shift stood at intervals along the walkway. As we reached the walk, the man nearest to us gave my husband a quick salute. "Milord."

Arthur nodded to him. "How goes it, Teithi?"

The man's ready smile told me he was pleased to have been recognized. "Quiet, as usual. No threats."

I bent over with another contraction and the man's face clouded with concern. "Is the queen all right?"

Arthur nodded. "It's her time. She's walking to ease the pain."

The man grinned. "'Twas the same with my woman. She were working in the vegetable patch until the moment she dropped our latest boy. 'Tis a good idea to walk. For a queen may not work in a vegetable patch!" He laughed at his own joke, and Arthur joined in. Ignoring them, I gritted my teeth and tried to keep my breathing steady.

We left Teithi and walked slowly along the wall-walk, stopping to speak with each guard we came to. By the time we'd done the entire circuit, a distance of a good three quarters of a mile, my contractions were coming closer together, and every warrior on the wall knew my labor had started. At every contraction, I had to stop and lean on the wall, but in between, the walking made me feel better.

The sky had grown much lighter now. The sun had risen above the eastern hills, and the fortress was stirring. A cockerel crowed on a rooftop, hens descended from their safe perches to scratch in the middens, and women emerged from their homes to start the milking. Mothers chased small boys out of their beds to go and feed the pigs in the pens which snuggled beside the houses, and fresh smoke began to curl upward from the dark thatch of the rooftops. People's heavy feet crushed the lacework of dew-laden cobwebs covering the ground. Suddenly aware of every little detail, I found the smells of the steaming middens and acrid smoke, the tang of cow pats and the smell of frying bacon, sharp and clear in my nostrils.

"Shall we fetch Donella now?" Arthur sounded cautious, as though, for once, he felt unsure of what he should do. After all, birthing was women's work, a mystery to men. How much might he have seen of Tangwyn's deliveries? Llacheu was a son to be proud of, but her other babies had all died. Had that been the fault of Mother Nara, or something else? Would my baby be at risk even after he was born? Probably.

I shook my head, unwilling to involve Donella too early. "Can we walk along the practice grounds?"

He helped me down the steps in the earthen bank that reinforced the walkway. At the bottom, another contraction had me doubled up, clutching his hand in an iron grip I never knew I possessed. His eyes widened in concern. "They're definitely closer together now. I think we should get Donella. And take you back to the hall."

"No." I was so determined to keep control, the word came out as a barked order. "I need to keep walking. It's helping me." Irritation sharpened my voice.

With a worried frown, as though it went against his better judgement, he took my arm and helped me walk the full length of the practice grounds. Our progress remained painfully slow, and by the time we reached the far end, the morning had advanced, and the fortress teemed with life.

At the rails of the horse pens, I rested, breathing carefully, and wishing for some of the painkillers Sian had told me about. When I glanced up from my last contraction, Llacheu was running down the slope toward us, his face suffused with excitement.

"Father!" He saw me. "Gwen!" He noticed my face. "Are you all right?" Not waiting for an answer, he looked back at his father. "Uncle Cei sent me to find you. A rider's come from Caer Baddan. He said you need to come and see her."

Arthur seemed torn. He looked at me, then at his son again. "Go and tell them we'll be there in a while. The Queen has reached her time. If the rider's come all the way from Caer Baddan, then whatever news she brings will wait a little longer." He paused, then said, as though noticing for the first time, "She? It's a woman?"

Llacheu nodded, his curls bouncing jauntily, reminding me vividly of his father – and of little Medraut in faraway Caer Legeion. But I refused to think of that now and pushed the unwelcome thought away.

I was curious myself to see what woman had been sent bearing a message for us. With Arthur's help, I struggled up the slope toward the hall, stopping half-way to breathe my way through yet another contraction.

"Go and fetch Donella," Arthur told his son, who was dawdling impatiently beside us in frustration. "Gwen needs her – now."

Llacheu ran off, apparently more eager to be sent on another errand than he was to find out what the messenger wanted.

I didn't protest, although I didn't think there was much for Donella to do as yet. She wasn't likely to have what I really needed – an epidural – tucked away in her skirts, or a canister of gas and air – anything to lessen the excruciating pain. I was even considering asking someone to whack me over the head with a blunt object. Nothing, not even Sian's grisly descriptions, had prepared me for the reality of labor.

We rounded the corner of the great hall at last and saw that the mysterious female messenger from Caer Baddan was Bretta, the girl who'd waited on me there. Her horse, more of a spindly pony, stood with its ugly head hanging between its knees, its scrawny sides heaving. With her ashen face and thin, blue-tinged lips betraying the fact that she was close to fainting, the girl was being supported by Cei and his wife, Coventina. Merlin stood by their side, his mouth a grim line. A group of warriors and women had clustered around the four of them to see what was going on.

I would have run to her, but my condition put a stop to that. It appeared we were both in need of medical aid.

"Arthur." Cei's big face glowed pink with the awkwardness of his situation.

At the mention of Arthur's name, Bretta's head came up, her face grey as dirty snow, and her eyes red-rimmed and wide with something worse than fear. Coventina had her arm about the girl's narrow waist, her kindly face furrowed with worry.

Another contraction swept through me, more forceful than the rest, and I staggered, digging my fingers into Arthur's arm. A low groan escaped my lips, and all heads turned to stare.

"The child is coming," Arthur said by way of explanation. "She's been walking to ease its passage." He glanced at Bretta and Cei. "Bring the girl inside the Hall, and she can give us her message there."

My contraction passed and taking my arm, Arthur escorted me through the open doors. Cei and Coventina almost had to carry Bretta, who seemed unable to walk unaided, her legs like wet spaghetti. Inside, the Hall was gloomy, the only light coming from the open doors and the glowing embers of the fire in the central pit. Coventina released her hold on Bretta and approached me, more worry etched into her face. Perhaps more so than me, she understood how dangerous childbirth could be.

Donella arrived, with Llacheu running at her heels. She paused on the threshold, taking in the wilting girl in Cei's arms and me, upright for the moment, my hands clasped round my belly.

I indicated the girl. "Take care of Bretta first. I'm only having contractions, and any fool can see she's ill."

Donella's gaze went to Arthur, who gave her a curt nod, and she approached the girl, whom Cei was lowering to a stool beside the fire. "Let's be havin' a look at ye."

Bretta waved her away. "No." Her voice scarcely rose above a whisper. "No. I 'ave to speak."

"What is it?" Cei asked. "Tell us what message you bring,

girl."

"The king." The words came on a hiss, as though she had no breath left in her body. "I 'ave to tell the king."

I sank onto another stool, Coventina hovering over me like a mother hen.

Arthur took a step away from me, and closer to Bretta. "Go on. What message do you bring?"

The gloom of the hall pressed in all around us, heavy and doom-laden, as though whatever this girl had to say was so momentous it would have a lasting effect on all those assembled there. Another contraction took me. Gripping the edge of the stool, I set my jaw to ride it out, but couldn't prevent myself from doubling over.

"You need to get to your bed," Coventina said, but I shook my head in determination.

Arthur stood over Bretta. "I am your king. Speak, girl."

She lifted her head and gazed up at him. Her bloodless face blanched further, if that were possible. "Ye ordered Magistrate Bassus, and through 'im our king, Melwas, to sort out the problem of the poor 'omeless and orphaned children of Caer Baddan..." Her words hung in the silent hall as everyone listened to her.

"I did," Arthur said. "What of it?"

She grimaced. "'E took ye at yer word. Melwas sent 'is men into the city and rounded up all what 'e called th'vagrant children into the forum." She took a long breath, her thin chest rising and falling quickly. "Then 'e marched 'em to Dinas Brent, 'is strong'old. Once there, 'e chose a few of the strongest boys and the prettiest girls to be 'is slaves. The rest..." She paused, and a sob wracked her exhausted body. "'E 'ad 'is soldiers cut their throats and throw 'em into the marshes. 'E said they'd please the old gods wi' their sacrifice."

A stunned silence hung over the hall. My contraction eased off and I straightened up, horror washing over me. Coventina's hand rested heavily on my shoulder. Perhaps she thought she needed to restrain me.

"How do you know all this?" Arthur wasn't disbelieving, he just wanted proof.

"They took me." Her voice sank further, but in the silence of the room it carried clearly. "Wi' all me brothers and sisters. I was 'ome visiting 'em, so they did take me, too, even though I'm near a woman grown. They marched all-on-us into the forum and sorted through us. My oldest brother and me, we was put in one group, the little ones in another. I tried to tell 'em I worked for th'magistrate, but they wouldn't listen. And then they marched us out o' the city."

"And no one did anything?" I was aghast. "No one raised a hand to stop them?"

Cei's honest face furrowed with anger. "How could they? Unarmed townsfolk, near as poor as the children, against armed warriors? They'd have been killed."

A hush fell over the hall. Outside, a cockerel crowed, and further off a dog barked, as though in another world.

"They took you as a slave?" Arthur's voice cut the silence. "How did you get away?"

She gulped. "O'ernight they locked all us slaves in a single 'ut. My brother and me did dig under th'wall and, bein' small, wriggled out. But no one else'd run with us. They said we'd be caught and killed." She paused. "They was right." Her head hung. "They saw my brother when 'e climbed o'er the palisade wall. 'E'd let me go first, 'anding me down into the ditch. They...they caught 'im and dragged 'im back. They didn't see me. I laid meself flat aginst the ground, like a right coward, listenin' as they killed my brother."

The enormity of what had befallen this child, for child she really was, hung over everyone in the hall. We lived in a time of danger and violence, but even the listening men, whose way of life was the sword, were shocked at what had happened to these children.

My next contraction interrupted her, this time even stronger than the last. Donella hurried to where I sat, feeling like a beached whale in a far too tight corset. Coventina squatted beside me, one hand on my tight belly, the other holding my hand as I panted in an effort to dispel the pain.

"The Queen." Donella's voice rose accusingly. "She needs to be in her bedchamber. This child's in a hurry."

"No!" I was determined to hear out Bretta's story. "This is my fault. If I hadn't tried to help them, they'd all be alive now." Guilt weighed more heavily on me than the pressing urge to be rid of this baby from my poor, pain-wracked body.

Arthur shook his head. "Not yours – mine. I should have guessed Melwas would have done something like this." Was there a hint of false contrition in his voice? Could he have been expecting Melwas to take this action? Or was this a figment of my imagination due to my present overwrought state?

Bretta put her face in her hands and slumped forward on the seat. "All me brothers and sisters be dead. All th'other little ones from Caer Baddan. The few what they did think old enough to be slaves be the only survivors." She paused, slowly raising her head, and looked straight at me. "There be no orphans left in Caer Baddan to offend yer eyes – *my lady.*" She spat the last two words out with contempt. Whatever Arthur said, Bretta blamed me, and rightly so.

Tears sprang into my eyes that were nothing to do with the pain of my contractions. "I'm so sorry, Bretta. I had no idea." What more could I say? I felt like a fool.

Donella helped me to my feet. "Into the bedchamber with you. Now. No more delaying. I'm in charge now." And with that, she and Coventina ushered me out of the great hall and into my room.

Chapter Twenty-Six

T HE HUM OF voices came to me over the wall that divided our bedchamber from the main body of the great hall. Voices raised in celebration. Arthur had become a father again, the kingdom had a legitimate heir, and the deaths of a few orphan children were being collectively swept under the rug. Much as the deaths of Ummidia and her daughters had been.

My whole body was tired and sore, but I was alive, which earlier in the day I would have disputed as a possibility. Nothing, not even Sian's overly explicit account, could have prepared me for the reality of childbirth. I remembered telling Donella and Coventina that I'd changed my mind, the baby couldn't be born today, and that I intended to curl up and go back to sleep instead. In fact, I'd also told them I never wanted to have sex again and risk getting into the same condition. Arthur could go back to Tangwyn for all I cared; he wasn't coming near me ever again. Donella had wisely shaken her head and, taking my hand, seen me through the next excruciating contraction.

From the wooden cradle beside the bed came a sleepy snuffling sound, like a puppy. My son. No, our son. Not so long ago, Arthur had taken him into the great hall, still wet from his birth, and held him up above his head for all the assembled warriors and their families to see. Arthur's voice rang out, full of pride, announcing our son's name. "Here is your prince, your little Bear Cub, born to be a great king. Amhar of Dumnonia." A cheer went up, and Arthur, smiling from ear to ear, brought the lustily crying Amhar back to me.

That had been two hours since, and darkness had now fallen outside the hall. Inside, torches had been lit and the clatter and smells of food being served came to me over the wall – a feast to honor their new prince. Joyful music wafted on the air as I slid gingerly out of bed and walked the two steps to Amhar's crib. Walking was harder than I'd expected, my legs a little wobbly and uncertain, my stomach feeling loose and devoid of muscle, like a deflated party balloon.

Amhar lay on his back, tightly swaddled in a linen shawl, his purple-pink face screwed up like that of a little old man. His mouth worked, but his eyes remained shut, and as I gazed down at him, amazed at the creature Arthur and I had made, he opened his rosebud mouth and began to cry, creakily like a rusty hinge. The door into the side room opened, and Donella came hurrying in.

"Back to bed, milady," she ordered, bending over the crib. "The little prince is hungry."

I climbed awkwardly back into bed, and she passed me the tiny bundle that was my son. His little mouth rooted for the nipple, and under Donella's guidance I managed to get him latched on and suckling. It was the oddest experience. If I'd ever imagined doing this, it had been with a baby bearing my old boyfriend Nathan's features. This little dark-haired scrap seemed so alien, and yet so natural. In so much as any baby resembles his father, this one seemed to tick all the boxes.

I was sleeping when Arthur came to bed, but his movements disturbed me, a mother's instincts having me instantly awake. The baby slept on, as Arthur tiptoed noisily toward the crib and stood looking down at his son.

"He's beautiful, isn't he?" I said with a sigh. It had taken me no time at all to decide this baby was the one thing I'd always wanted, and forget the strife I'd suffered to bring him into the world.

Arthur nodded, then bent over and ran his finger gently over the baby's soft cheek. "I'd forgotten how small they are." He straightened. "They grow so quickly. In no time he'll be as big as Llacheu and learning to be a warrior."

Over my dead body.

I kept quiet. No need to start an argument about that now, but it was immediately borne in upon me why the rift had arisen between Eigr and Uthyr, when his mother had seen Arthur's future in her scrying glass. Maybe I needed to ask her about Amhar's future; I'd never heard stories about the deeds of any sons of King Arthur.

After a few more moments of rapt gazing, Arthur sat down on the end of our bed and pulled off his boots. The rest of his clothes followed, and I snuggled down into bed while he washed himself and brushed his teeth. In a few minutes, he climbed in beside me and moved close enough to take me in his arms, my back to him, his body curled around mine.

"I don't think I've thanked you yet." He spoke into my hair, his breath warm on my scalp. "For the strong and handsome son you've given me."

I resisted the temptation to comment that this baby was as much mine as his, if not more so, considering the work I'd just done, and that no giving had been involved. But it would have been wasted on Arthur with his fifth-century mind set. He was my husband, and I loved him dearly, but he certainly had his failings.

Instead, I chose another moot point that had been preying on my mind and I'd not heard the end of, Donella having whisked me off before a conclusion had been reached. "Where's Bretta?"

Arthur's body stiffened. "She's been taken care of." His tone was one of dismissal. He didn't want to talk about this.

I twisted round to face him, my face inches from his. Despite the tooth brushing, he had a distinct smell of alcohol about him. "How?"

"Cottia has taken her." He put his hand up and smoothed my

hair from my face. That was normally a gesture of love, but here and now it was just a distraction tactic.

I persevered. "What about Melwas? What are you going to do about what she told us?"

He was silent. I guessed he was trying to think of something with which to fob me off.

I hammered my point home. "Melwas killed all those children." I could feel myself beginning to get worked up, the contented post-birth sensation wearing off. My gaze strayed to the crib, where little Amhar was making kittenish snuffling noises in his sleep. "How could anyone kill little children – like our son?"

"No babies were killed." Arthur was ever practical. "The orphans were older children capable of looking after themselves. Don't compare our son with them." In the dim light of the dying torches he sketched the sign against the evil eye in the air, as though my words could bring bad luck on our child.

I didn't believe in bad luck any more than I believed in prophecies. Or did I? "Melwas would kill him if he could." I wanted Arthur to put himself in the position of these children. But I was fighting a losing battle as it wasn't a skill he was good at.

"It's done." He had the distinct air of someone for whom this would be the final word. "There's nothing we can do to undo it. But I won't let this go unpunished." He kissed my forehead. "Go to sleep. You'll need some rest before Amhar wakes for a feed."

AMHAR WAS A week old when Arthur rode away from Din Cadan to wreak punishment on Melwas. I'd been up and about from the day following his birth, which neither Donella nor Coventina seemed to think was the done thing for a queen. Oddly, the midwife had no qualms about any of the other women going straight back to work with their baby in a sling across their bodies. But a queen? No, a queen was a different basket of wheat and had to stay in bed for at least a week.

I put my foot down. Hard. Apart from being a bit bruised and feeling as though I were walking bandy-legged, I was absolutely fine and knew that as long as I took it easy, it would be far better to be up and about than to lounge in bed.

The weather was good, with warm autumn days and chilly nights, even though the festival of Samhain, that would mark the start of winter, was fast approaching. A night, Maia, my maid, informed me, and Donella reiterated, when the spirits of the dead would walk abroad and all sensible people would be safe indoors in their beds. Coventina told me a little more – that on this night our ancestors would come to our hearth fires, and we would need to leave them food and drink.

With my logical twenty-first-century head on, I knew this was all a load of twaddle, but somehow, living as I was in the fifth century, a small part of me shivered at the thought of a night of ghosts coming so soon after my baby's birth. I found myself wondering if my father would be one of the ghosts coming to the hearth fire in the great hall, anxious to see his little grandson.

Arthur didn't tell me his intentions toward Melwas, and I didn't ask. Most of the time I was too taken up with my new baby. However, when I was alone and could think, I had to push away the thoughts of those blameless children lying dead in the marshes surrounding Dinas Brent, an image that mingled hauntingly with the dead faces of Ummidia and her daughters.

I glimpsed Bretta from time to time, wandering listlessly about the fortress in company with one or another of Cottia's daughters or granddaughters. She remained pale and lackluster, as though all the life had been drained out of her with the loss of her siblings, and I wished there were something I could do. After my failure with Ummidia, and its consequences, I feared this might drive Bretta to something similar.

My guilt over my part in their deaths, however unintentional, had left me with a feeling of disquiet over my son's safety, despite my determination not to believe bad luck could be brought in this way. It was as though I expected daily to have him taken from me in payment for the lives I'd had an unwitting hand in ending. But he thrived, daily growing stronger and noisier and hungrier. The more time I spent with him, the more I loved him, but I still couldn't shake off the thought that some terrible doom hung over him.

Arthur came to find me on the morning of his departure. I was sitting in bed feeding Amhar, cradling him in my arms and thinking of nothing more than how much I loved him. Arthur entered with a clatter, and through the open door I caught a glimpse of Cei and Bedwyr, waiting for him. At my breast, Amhar fed on hungrily, oblivious to his father's arrival.

Arthur approached the bed, his face solemn, and with reluctance I raised my eyes from gazing at my son to look up at him. He was dressed for battle. He carried his helmet tucked under his arm, and his curling hair, cut short in the spring to go off on campaign, was now long enough to tuck behind his ears. Setting his helmet on the clothes chest by the bed, he leaned over to kiss me. His stubble rasped my cheek as I surrendered my lips.

The sharp tang of horses hung about him, and his hair was damp from being out in the morning mist. "I've come to wish you goodbye. We're off to teach the lord of the Mount of Frogs a proper lesson. He escaped my retribution last winter. He'll not do it again. I'll have revenge on him for killing those children." He sounded as though he were listing reasons to justify what he was about to do, as though without them his intentions might be misconstrued.

He straightened, and my eyes slid over his mail shirt and the sword by his side. A distinct air of excitement hovered about him, as if he were about to do something he was going to enjoy, and not for the first time doubt assuaged me. Could he have deliberately maneuvered Melwas into this? The idea shocked me, but once lodged in my head it was difficult to shift. It was an awful thought. If true, then he'd knowingly used those children as pawns in his game of chess, guessing that Melwas would do something to them that he could use against him. I tried to remember what he'd said to Kirwin, Bassus the magistrate's deputy, but failed.

Arthur put out a hand to gently stroke Amhar's downy dark head, and I looked up into his eyes, searching for the truth.

But did I want to hear it?

He was still my handsome husband, still the man who could make my heart lurch with love, but there was something about him today that I didn't like. Something I mistrusted.

"What are you going to do?" That familiar knot of nerves tightened in my stomach.

He pushed his hair back from his eyes. "Show him that he can't betray his people. Mete out the justice of the King of Dumnonia."

Just as he'd been wanting to do since he got me back from Melwas all those months ago. And now he had the excuse.

That feeling of foreboding was strong. "Be careful. I have a bad feeling about today." Which wasn't like me at all. The fifth century must be rubbing off on me.

He retrieved his helmet from the clothes chest. "I make my own luck, Gwen. And so do you. Today is not the day of my death. I'll not be back for a few days, so don't worry yourself. Look after our son."

And he was gone.

I was left sitting with Amhar in my arms and a hollow feeling in my stomach I couldn't put a finger on. Unease. Distrust. Doubt. The hand of fate hovering.

The first day passed as normal. Amhar was a hungry baby and needed frequent feeds, and then rocking to sleep, so my time was taken up with him. Maia had proved a willing helper, having gained experience with all her younger siblings, and was always eager to give him a cuddle or have him fall asleep in her arms, which freed me to do what I wanted from time to time. And now it freed me to think.

That first day, when I knew Arthur would only be marching toward Dinas Brent, the feeling of foreboding loomed lightly.

It was the second day, when my mind imagined all sorts of scenarios on his arrival at Dinas Brent, that disquiet properly set in. Amhar somehow knew and spent the day crying incessantly, as though he, too, were worried for his absent father. I left him with Maia, whom he seemed to like as much as me, and went to stand on the fortress walls in the rising autumn wind, staring out toward the northwest where Dinas Brent lay.

On the third day, when I was standing wrapped in my long cloak on the walls once again, a fine drizzle falling from a leaden sky, Bretta came to me.

I didn't see her coming, so intent was I on the rain-washed plain and my thoughts.

She broke in upon the silence, making me start. "No matter 'ow 'e avenges my brothers and sisters, it won't bring 'em back."

I swung around to stare at her.

Someone had given her a warm cloak. Cottia, most likely. "I cared for 'em all since my mother died. Fed 'em, clothed 'em, tended their bumped knees and their colds. All for nothing. They was taken from me in a single moment." Her thin brows came together in a frown. "The king thinks what 'e does'll make a difference. It won't."

What could I say to this? I licked my lips uncertainly. "I'm sorry." The words sounded futile and inadequate. How could anyone apologize for the losses this girl had suffered?

"Yer words mean nothing – *my lady*." She spat out my title in contempt.

How does one comfort someone when comfort isn't what they want or can accept? It's an impossible task, and I wasn't up to it.

She looked out across the plain, where smoke curled up from the village and the scattered farms. "I was 'appy...once. My brothers and sisters 'ad a roof over their 'eads, no matter 'ow poor it were. We 'ad a fire most days in winter, and food more often than not. We managed." Her loose hair blew across her face and she had to push it out of her eyes. "I can never be 'appy again. It...it's like the reason for bein' me 'as gone out o' me life."

I wanted to say something, anything, to make her understand that despite her loss, this wasn't the end of the world. "One day you'll feel better." The words sounded crass as soon as they emerged. Just as when I'd spoken them to Ummidia.

She rounded on me, her pale grey eyes flashing in white hot anger. "Ye say that?" she spat. "'Ow would ye know? Marooned 'ere in your 'illtop palace? Ye'll never go 'ungry. Ye'll never wonder where the wood for a fire's comin' from when the frost bites 'ard. Ye'll never sleep in one bed with yer brothers and sisters 'uddled close fer warmth. Ye're a queen. Yer son's a prince." Her lip curled. "Ye thought ye'd interfere with my life. Ye thought ye'd make yerself feel noble by yer actions. Yet ye never thought to make certain yer orders was followed. It's yer fault this 'appened to my family." Madness burned in her eyes, madness and hatred. "I curse ye, Queen of Dumnonia, and I curse yer 'usband and yer son. Ye and yourn shall know the loss I feel."

Fear swept over me like a tidal wave, a base, primal fear. I was no longer a twenty-first-century woman marooned in the past, I was all fifth-century queen and Bretta's curse bit deep into my very soul. I turned from her, stumbling down the steps to the practice field, and ran, as fast as I could, back to the hall and Maia and my son, Bretta's words echoing in my head.

Chapter Twenty-Seven

T WO MORE INTERMINABLE days passed before tidings came of
Arthur. At last, late in the afternoon of the third day, three
outriders trotted up the cobbled road to the gates, to tell us he
was returning victorious from Dinas Brent. Merlin, who hadn't
ridden with him, brought the news to me where I was feeding
Amhar in our chamber. I'd not left my son alone since Bretta had
hurled her curse at me, too afraid that if I did, something would
happen to him, despite telling myself over and over that words
alone could have no power.

At the back of my mind lurked the constant nagging thought
that this was an age when magic still existed, however sparsely
scattered, and Bretta just might have invoked something with her
venom. I hadn't told Maia of my fears, but she must have noticed
how I'd suddenly become inseparable from Amhar when before
I'd been happy to leave the baby with her from time to time.

An hour after the outriders arrived, Arthur and his army rode
through the gates and into the fortress. And with them they
brought a prisoner. Melwas sat on a horse, hands bound in front
of him, forehead and hair crusted with dried blood.

I stood in front of the great hall with Amhar in my arms, my
anxious heart beating a rapid tattoo against my ribs as I waited to
welcome my husband. Over the heads of the gathered crowd,
Melwas's long cruel face stared across at me, his black eyes boring
into mine. The sight of Melwas within our walls brought back

vividly the days I'd spent as his prisoner. If I'd thought about his fate at all, I'd imagined Arthur killing him in battle, not bringing him back here as a prisoner. A shiver of cold unease ran through me.

In front of the stables, Arthur swung down from his mount with a stiffness that spoke of weariness and a possible wound. Passing his reins to one of the waiting servants, he walked up the slope to greet me, limping a little as he came. He took me in his arms, pressing me against his mail shirt. "The children are avenged." He planted a kiss on my lips. "And Melwas will stand trial for his misdeeds."

I stiffened at his words, my eyes drawn to the dark figure being dragged unceremoniously down from his horse by two of our warriors. Regaining his feet, Melwas shook off their hands and tossed his head with an arrogance that belied his situation.

One of the warriors gave him a hard shove, forcing him forward until he came to a halt, scarcely twenty yards away, ignoring Arthur and looking me insolently in the eye. His thin-lipped mouth curved into a mocking smile. "How lovely to see you again, Gwen." His voice cut across the murmur of the crowd that had gathered. "As beautiful as ever, and with a child, I see."

I turned to Maia who was hovering a couple of paces behind me, and held out the baby to her. "Take him to my chamber and stay with him." She took Amhar and hurried away obediently.

With a smirk Melwas went on, unashamed. "I hadn't thought to see you again so soon. We should get together to remember old times. I've missed your company." He threw a glance at Arthur. "I can't say I feel the same way about your husband."

A hiss of anger rose from those in the watching crowd who'd heard his words.

"Shut up!" Cei stepped forward and struck him with his huge fist on the side of his head, knocking him to the ground. Blood trickled from the corner of Melwas's mouth.

After a moment, he sat up, shaking his head as though to clear it, still staring at me. "I was sure your welcome would be much warmer than this. We have so many shared memories."

I bristled with indignation and would have taken an angry step toward him had not Arthur's arm restrained me. Instead I curled my own lips with as much scorn as I could muster. "There's nothing I want to share with you, and my only memories are of your callous ill-treatment."

Arthur's arm tightened around me, drawing me closer, and when I glanced up at him, half-fearfully, I saw how his face had darkened. He nodded to the two warriors who were standing over Melwas. "Take him away and throw him in the lock-up. I don't want to see him until his trial."

The two warriors dragged Melwas to his feet and marched him off, a shower of stones and rotting vegetables from the crowd sending him on his way. As he went, he turned his head and, unrepentant, called back to me. "I hope to see you again soon, Gwen."

I couldn't help myself. "And I hope you rot in hell."

A moment's awkward silence hung between us all before Merlin spoke. "Arthur, come inside. I want Gwen to look at your leg." He put an arm out that encompassed us both and ushered us into the Hall.

Once inside, Arthur discarded his sword belt on the table, then wriggled out of his mail shirt and padded tunic and threw them down on top of his weapons. Coventina brought a tray with a flagon of wine and horn beakers.

I bent to look at his leg.

He stretched it out, wincing a little. "I twisted it in battle. Bedwyr put a cooling dressing on it two days ago."

His knee was stiff and swollen even through his braccae. "I can't tell what damage you've done, but I think you'll need a support bandage." I gave his braccae a little tug. "You'll have to take these off for me to get a better look."

Without any further urging, Arthur obligingly dropped his braccae, and I knelt down in front of him. The knee was more puffy than I would have liked, and I hoped he hadn't damaged the cartilage. My brother Artie had done that playing rugby and had needed an operation to put him right. I ran my hands over Arthur's knee, feeling the heat of inflammation. My previous experience of bandaging legs had mainly been for horses, but the skill seemed to transfer well. What he really needed now was to rest it.

Coventina passed me a roll of bandage, and I bound his knee, conscious of not wanting to put it on so tight it would do more harm than good. An x-ray or scan would have been helpful, but he had zero chance of one of those.

"How did you come to capture Melwas alive?" Merlin asked, from his position sitting on the table where Arthur had piled his mail shirt and tunic.

I got to my feet again, worrying whether I'd done the right thing in putting a bandage on what might be a badly damaged knee. It was a long time since I'd done that first aid course back in my old world.

Arthur pulled up his braccae and gave his friend a triumphant grin. "We stormed the fortress. At dawn. He wasn't expecting us." He took a long draught of the wine Coventina had brought. "We stayed hidden in the forest until just before first light, then crossed the causeway in darkness and on foot. We were on the slopes of Dinas Brent before his guards saw us." He wiped his mouth with his sleeve. "We'd made scaling ladders in the forest, and had them up against the walls and were over as they sounded the alarm. It was a short fight but a sweet one." He grinned without mirth. "I told my men I wanted Melwas unharmed – well, not dead, at least. They all knew why we were there. They cornered him in his hall. It was surrender or nothing. He surrendered."

"And the child slaves?" I asked, thinking of Bretta. "Did you find them?"

He nodded. "There weren't many. We set them free, and I've had them sent back to Caer Baddan with orders to Bassus that they're to be housed and fed at his expense. Or he'll meet the same fate as his lord."

Surely Bretta would be happy with that? Although it was too late for her own family, saving the others must make a difference.

"What d'you intend to do with Melwas?" Merlin asked.

"Put him on trial." Arthur drained his horn beaker, his eyes meeting Merlin's in challenge over the rim. "Put him on trial and then execute him for his crimes."

A forgone conclusion – not a real trial at all, then. Did I think he deserved one?

I turned to Maia, who had slipped through the door from our chamber and was hovering nearby. "Go back to keep an eye on Amhar. I don't like him to be alone." She scurried off.

Arthur set down his empty beaker, and Cei, who'd just come in, poured one for himself then refilled Arthur's. "Melwas is safely stowed in our lock-up. He won't be getting out of there until we want him to." They both laughed, and I felt my stomach twist. Much as I hated Melwas, I feared what Arthur's justice in this case might entail. This was an era of the Biblical "eye for an eye, tooth for a tooth" and Melwas had taken many lives. Killing him in battle seemed a much more acceptable ending for him than cold blooded execution would.

A slight, bent figure darkened the doorway, pausing on the threshold, and we all turned our heads in curiosity. "Where is my son?" a voice quavered. Old Olwyn, Melwas's mother, stood there, her eyes and hair wild as she stared down the hall to where we'd gathered by the fire pit.

"Your son is in a safe place," Cei said, a look of distaste on his big face. He'd never taken to Olwyn the way I had, always steering clear of her as the mother of an enemy, and as such, untrustworthy.

She took a few uncertain steps into the hall, pausing by the first table to lean on it, her wrinkled face deathly pale. "He won't escape…will he?" Her crepey chins wobbled with emotion and her rheumy red-rimmed eyes glistened, moist with unshed tears.

I went to her and put my arms around her frail and somewhat

odorous body. "You've nothing to be afraid of. He can't get at you. He's imprisoned in the lock-up. He can't escape to hurt you. You're safe here."

The words seemed to have little effect on her. A tremor ran through her and she pulled herself free of my hold. "Ye don't know what he can do," she quavered. "Even from inside a cell, my son has power."

Bretta's hate-filled words echoed in my head. I wished with all my heart that Arthur had let his men kill Melwas when they'd cornered him, and not brought him back here to Din Cadan. His presence hung like a malevolent shadow over the fortress, and it felt as though we were collectively holding our breath, waiting for something awful to happen.

That night in our bed I asked Arthur why he'd done it.

"A quick death is too good for him," he said as I nestled close to his warm body. "I want him to suffer as those children did."

I shifted, restless suddenly, not wanting to think of the dead children, but there was no getting away from it. I had to ask the question at the forefront of my mind, the question that had been nagging away at me the entire time Arthur had been away. "When you gave Kirwin his orders to do something about the poor children and the orphans," I began, "did you ever think Melwas would do this?"

Arthur was silent for a long minute.

Then his chest rose in a deep sigh. "You think I could have condemned innocent children to death? You think me capable of that?" His voice rose in indignation, and I had to put a finger to his lips.

"Sshh, you'll waken Amhar."

He pushed my finger away, but his voice was lower when he spoke again. "Don't you know me yet? Do you think I'd sacrifice *children* to wreak my revenge on Melwas?"

The problem was, I did know him now. And a small part of me, the part that nearly a year ago had heard him suggest he'd poison his brother given the opportunity – that part thought he might indeed have done what I'd accused him of. I stayed silent.

"Well, I didn't." He was angry, not unreasonably, I supposed. Did I believe him, though?

"Did you think he'd obey you?" I asked, in my heart knowing the answer couldn't be a yes.

It was his turn to remain silent.

I pressed my point home. "What did you think he'd do?"

His whole body stiffened. I had him in a corner. "I thought he'd disobey me, for certain." His voice was hardly more than a whisper. "But I never thought he'd kill them."

I believed him. I had to, didn't I? He'd been looking for a reason to go after Melwas for a long time and had thought giving this order about the orphan children of Caer Baddan would give him the opportunity he desired. However, it had backfired badly. I thought about Bretta again, the venom in her eyes, the hatred. And the words of her curse rang loudly in my ears.

ARTHUR LET MELWAS rot in the lock-up for a full week before he had him brought out for judgement. I'd never been inside the lock up, of course, but from the outside it was obviously small, with no sanitary arrangements. By the end of a week confined in a space where he could hardly stand up, and with only the floor to lie down on – a floor he'd had to use as his toilet – Melwas should have emerged a broken man.

He didn't.

When the door was opened for the first time in a week, he stepped out and straightened up as though he'd spent a week in a London hotel. Yes, he stank, and he had the makings of a straggly grizzled beard coming, but he was unbowed by his sojourn in solitary confinement.

The guards, who'd come to let him out of the dark and noisome hole he'd been kept in, tied his hands behind him immediately, having been warned by both Arthur and Cei to watch out for his tricksy ways. Then they marched him up the hill toward the great hall where Arthur waited in front of the doors. His throne had been brought outside into the chill autumnal air so that everyone in the fortress could be present at the trial, and a crowd had gathered more than ten deep.

At the front of the press of people nearest to the throne I spotted Bretta, a savage expression on her haggard young face that rendered her old before her time. Not far from her stood the bent figure of Olwyn, no doubt come to see her wicked son face a punishment he'd deserved since he'd murdered his own brothers all those years ago.

I sat beside Arthur in my best gown, a golden circlet on my head. Wearing a crown gives one a certain air, but I'd fast realized why; in order not to lose my crown, I had to keep my chin haughtily in the air.

Melwas was deposited ten paces from us, his guards standing back, but not too far, drawn swords in their hands. There probably wasn't a soul here who trusted him, and they weren't taking any chances.

Cei, as Arthur's seneschal, a post I'd never realized he held, stepped forward to read out the charges against Melwas. The crowd fell silent.

Cei took a deep breath, cleared his throat and began, his loud voice ringing out above the heads of the watching people.

"Melwas, King of the Isle of Frogs, held by the grace of Arthur, King of Dumnonia, your overlord. You are brought here to face the judgement of your liege lord." He was reading from a lead tablet, the words scratched on it with a stylus. The literacy of the well-born had never been something I'd asked myself about before. I knew Arthur could read, and Merlin too, but somehow it had never occurred to me that Cei would be able to as well. Reading and writing and Dark Age Britain didn't seem to go together.

Melwas stood ramrod straight, an air of mild interest on his sallow face, as though an observer of the petty happenings of people who didn't matter to him, instead of being at their mercy. His coal black eyes roamed across his audience and came to rest on me. His lips curled again into that mirthless smile, implying, without a word, that something secret existed between us, binding us together in collaboration. I couldn't suppress the shiver that ran through me. Arthur turned his head and for a moment our eyes met. His were unreadable.

Cei went on. "You are charged with the offence of unlawful killing, in direct contravention of the Sixth Commandment given to the prophet Moses by our Lord God Almighty in days of old." Cei paused to let his words sink in on his audience. A rumble of approval passed through their ranks like the wind through barley. Cei continued. "You did not kill lawfully in battle, as is your right. Instead you took the lives of innocent children whom you should have protected. Not the children of your enemies, but the children of your own city. This is a crime punishable by death."

This time the buzz was angrier. These people had children of their own. Probably every one of them could empathize with his victims. Their hostile faces darkened with disgust.

The wind blew across the hilltop, bringing with it snatches of smoke and the stench of rotting middens, but they were nothing compared to the reek of Melwas. His once fine tunic and braccae were soiled and filthy, his face grimy. He looked what he was, a villain through and through. A soft vegetable of indeterminate origin sailed through the air and hit him squarely on the shoulder, spreading its rotting insides across his clothing and then falling with a thud to the ground.

Cei ignored the missile. "You are charged that instead of taking the orphaned children of Caer Baddan into your care, you did willfully order their deaths and enslavement. This is against the laws of the Council of Kings, and against the orders of your liege lord. For this you will stand trial here, on this day, before the people of Din Cadan and the warriors of King Arthur."

Another rotten vegetable missed Melwas, landing with a soft

splat at his feet, and a third hit him in the middle of the back. Several more flew through the air, encouraged, no doubt, by the success of the instigators.

Arthur held up his hand imperiously. "Enough. He is to stand trial. You must await my judgement."

The scorn on Melwas's face was written large and clear. He despised Arthur for his intervention, despised all of us, perhaps, for not having killed him when we could.

Cei lowered his tablet. "Melwas, sometime-king of the Isle of Frogs, do you admit the charges brought against you?" He paused. "Be advised; confession may make your punishment less severe."

Melwas, ignoring the fact that he was now festooned in rotting vegetable matter, spun slowly on the spot with a sneer on his face, as though he were the king and not our prisoner, to survey the watching crowd who were slavering for his demise. Finally, he returned his gaze to the front, not to Cei, his prosecutor, but to Arthur, and then to me. He flashed me a conspiratorial smile.

"I demand my right," his voice rang out across the crowd, "as laid down by the Council of Kings, to trial by combat."

The crowd erupted, everyone talking at once, excited and angry at the same time. No doubt, though, they relished the idea of the spectacle of Melwas fighting for his life in front of them.

Arthur got to his feet, his jaw set. He held up his left arm and waited until the crowd fell silent. Before him, Melwas stood, a smirk on his cold face, watching not Arthur, but me.

Arthur looked at Melwas, who took his eyes off me long enough to return his gaze. "You have a right, as you say, to trial by combat. You may choose a champion if you wish, to fight for your honor, or you may fight yourself if none will stand for you..." He looked over Melwas's head at the sea of hostile faces. Not a one would offer themselves to fight for such a man.

After a pause, Arthur went on. "And I will supply a champion to fight you. If you win, then you will go free, all of your crimes washed away. If you lose, then as a guilty man, proven in the eyes of God, you will die, if you are not already dead."

Melwas drew himself up a little taller. "I have no need of a champion." His voice dripped with scorn. "I will fight for my honor myself. And I demand that the man I fight is you, Arthur Pendragon, my accuser. I will fight no one but you."

A hiss of disapproval sibilated through the watching crowd. Arthur was their king. This man was their enemy. How dare a prisoner demand to fight their king? And yet, perhaps it felt right that their king should stand for all of them against this child killer. Their thoughts struck against me in a tidal wave of emotion.

I rose to my feet, putting my hand on Arthur's arm. I leaned close. "Don't do it." I kept my voice low. "It's too dangerous. Deny him trial by combat or choose a champion of your own. Don't fight him yourself."

"And if I win," Melwas said into the near silence, "then I'll take your queen with me when I leave. She seemed to like it at Dinas Brent."

Arthur shook my arm off. "Yes, I'll fight you." His face was suffused with anger. "And when you're dead I'll burn your stronghold down and drive your people out. I'll leave no trace of your existence on God's earth." He waved a hand at Cei. "Take him away and prepare him. We'll get this over and done with now."

Chapter Twenty-Eight

"WHAT DID YOU say you'd do that for?" Merlin shouted. It was the first time I'd ever heard him raise his voice in anger. We were inside the great hall and Cei was helping Arthur put his armor on. I stood alone beside the smoldering fire, but nothing could dispel the cold that was creeping over me as I watched my husband arm himself for a fight he didn't need to have.

Arthur glared at Merlin. "Because I want to have the pleasure of killing him myself. God will be on my side." He was calmer now, his voice more measured. I hoped he was thinking straight enough to avoid any stupid mistakes when he met Melwas outside in front of our people.

Merlin looked across at me. "Ask him not to do this." Exasperation had etched lines of worry across his face, leaching the youth from him and giving him the look of the much older man he really was. "He'll do it for you."

Would he?

Unconvinced, I moved away from the fire and put my hand on Arthur's arm, my fingers touching the cold chainmail above his elbow. "Please don't do this. Name your own champion. It's too dangerous. He goaded you into this – it's what he wants. He won't fight fair, I know he won't." I bit my bottom lip in consternation. "Think of your son. If you lose, and Melwas takes me for himself, he'll kill your heir." Llacheu's little face came into my head. "*All* your heirs."

Arthur shook my hand off. "Do you think I'll lose then?" He glared at me and then at Merlin. Cei wisely held his tongue and handed Arthur his helmet.

My heart felt as though it were beating in my throat. He was never going to listen to me. He was too much a man of his time to listen to a woman, no matter how much he loved her. No matter how much she loved him. And I knew now that I'd really loved him right from the start, from the first moment I'd met him, returning bloodied but victorious after defeating Saxon raiders. Loved him when he'd bested his brother and gained his kingdom. Loved him when he'd walked away from the sword Merlin had set in the stone in the forum at Viroconium without even trying to draw it. Loved him when he'd taken me back to Glastonbury Tor because he thought I wanted to return to my own world, despite the way he felt about me.

As time stood still about me, I looked at his angry eyes, his lowered brows, the set of his jaw, and saw the determination to have his revenge written clear on his face.

"He's a trickster," Merlin said, unconstrained by any fear of his lord's temper. "He'll use every trick up his sleeve to defeat you. And he doesn't intend just to win – he intends to kill you."

Arthur gave a shrug. "And I him."

I clasped my hands to stop them trembling, acutely aware he'd chosen to fight because of me. He couldn't have missed the looks Melwas had been giving me. That Melwas had done so on purpose to goad Arthur into single combat was obvious. Fear crawled along my spine as I remembered Melwas's daily sword practice when I was his prisoner – his vanquishing of any warrior that came against him. Arthur was an expert swordsman too, but was he as good as Melwas?

The thought that this was already written, something that was history in my time, rose in my mind then dropped away. It was not a story I'd ever heard. Had I somehow changed the course of history with my butterfly wings of doom? Was it possible Arthur could die, here and now, this very day, and never live to become the king of legend? And would it be my fault?

The thought that I might lose him lay not far from the surface, a cold fear snaking around my entrails. Never had I felt so unsure of the legends I knew, never doubted them so much. Surely the hand of fate that had brought me to Glastonbury Tor to be transported back to the Dark Ages couldn't take him from me so callously? The man I loved. A love so strong it had stretched its hand across time to bring me to him. I wanted to throw myself into his arms, implore him to change his mind, but I knew that would make no difference.

Maia came into the Hall carrying little Amhar in her arms, wrapped in a woven shawl. Inspiration seizing me, I caught her by the elbow and pulled her forward.

"Look," I said to Arthur, desperation driving me. "Look at your son's face. You don't need to put yourself in danger. Deny Melwas trial by combat. Execute him for his crimes. You've not recovered from your twisted knee. Please."

I should have known better than to suggest he might be weakened by his knee.

However, he paused and looked down at the baby's sleeping face, at the fluff of dark hair and the perfect little hand that had escaped the shawl to half cradle the baby's soft cheek as though he were deep in thought. Then Arthur's face hardened, and he turned away from us. "I'm ready," he said and marched toward the open doors.

We followed him outside into the harsh daylight. The sun had disappeared behind a rack of clouds as though it had turned its face away from the coming fight. Unwillingly, I moved toward my seat beside Arthur's empty throne.

Maia followed me outside and stood just behind the throne, gently jiggling the baby in her arms to keep him quiet. I sat down. I could do nothing else because my legs felt suddenly weak and unable to support me. My heart hammered in overtime in my aching chest.

Melwas, armed like Arthur in mail shirt and helmet, a sword at his side, a dagger in his belt, came striding up the hill from the lock up, looking as though he thought *he* were the lord of Din Cadan instead of Arthur. The crowd, which had swung apart to let him pass, now filled up the space like water into a hole in the ground. Behind Melwas marched his half-dozen guards, their swords drawn now their prisoner was armed.

The guards stopped on the far side of the circle delineated by the crowd, ranging themselves around Melwas, who stood, head held high, bristly chin jutting. He was a powerfully built man at the best of times, but now, in his armor, he looked formidable. I guessed he had a good two inches and thirty pounds on Arthur, who possessed the long slim build of a true horseman.

Arthur walked down into the circle, fastening the strap on his helmet. Only the very slightest remnant of his limp remained. He looked what he was – young, upright, noble, every inch a king.

I gripped the arms of my seat to still my shaking hands.

Someone had placed two blank white shields in the center. Arthur halted beside them. After a moment's dramatic pause, Melwas stepped up to the shields as well, and stood facing Arthur over them. Silence fell. The watching crowds seemed to be collectively holding their breath.

Cei, standing back half a dozen paces, gave the command. "Take up your shields."

They bent to pick them up. As Arthur straightened, Melwas thrust his own shield up hard, hitting Arthur on the chin and sending him spinning backward to the ground.

I let out an involuntary scream of terror and clapped my hand to my mouth to silence it.

Melwas's hand went to his sword as Arthur rolled away, still hanging onto his own shield. The sword came out with a swish and Melwas lunged at Arthur. The blade swung through the air, but Arthur had rolled again. He sprang to his feet, his shield between his body and Melwas, blood running from his chin. Melwas's sword thudded into the shield, and Arthur struck back, the blades clashing together before the two men sprang apart.

A gasp of relief hissed through the onlookers, and Cei hurried to get out of the way.

Ignoring Cei's dodging figure, the two warriors circled one another like a pair of wary dogs, their booted feet scuffing up the dirt.

"I'm going to enjoy your wife tonight," Melwas said. "Before I take her back to Dinas Brent."

I couldn't see Arthur's face, but I could guess his reaction. My hands gripped the carved arms of my seat, my knuckles whitened, as tension coursed through my body. For a terrible moment the world about me spun, the figures of the two angry men blurring out of focus, and I thought I might faint, something I'd never done before in my life. Just as quickly, everything sharpened again with startling clarity, and my attention was on my husband once more.

Arthur sprang at Melwas. Their swords clashed. Sparks flew in a flurry of blows. Then they sprang apart again, circling, both of them breathing hard. The audience, who'd staggered backward out of their way, surged forward a few feet again, diminishing the size of the arena, all eyes fixed on their king.

"After I've killed you, I'll stick your head on a spike at my gates," Arthur spat back, loud enough for all to hear.

Melwas laughed in contempt. "You can but dream of it."

They came together again, raining blows. The air filled with the sounds of metal on metal, rhythmic, like the frantic beat of a heart. My heart.

I forced myself to watch, although every instinct I had was to cover my eyes in fear.

They were well matched. Despite Melwas's advantages of height and weight, Arthur was a good fifteen years his junior, and pushing forty is old for a warrior. Added to that, Arthur's lighter bodyweight and youth made him faster on his feet. First, Arthur drove Melwas back against the crowd, who shrank away from their swords, and then it was Melwas who had the upper hand, using his superior body weight, and Arthur who faltered.

My eyes went unbidden to my husband's damaged knee, and every time he seemed to weaken, my heart was in my mouth. Surely his warriors wouldn't stand by and let Melwas kill him? But I couldn't be sure; chivalric code is a strange thing. Then, fear for myself reared its ugly head. Would Merlin let Melwas take me if Arthur fell? I looked sideways to where Merlin stood near Maia, just behind the empty throne, his hands gripping the top, knuckles as white as mine, his face drawn with concern.

The plain white shields were now crisscrossed with dark lines indented in the white paint. Each blow clearly marked the history of the fight. Time dragged on. Neither man, after that cheating start to the fight, seemed able to gain the advantage. They were too well matched. The weak autumn sun climbed behind the clouds and still they went on hammering at each other. Their breath came fast and hard. Sweat ran down their faces beneath their helmets. And as the time wore on, Arthur's limp became more and more pronounced.

In Maia's arms baby Amhar began to cry. I glanced over my shoulder, knowing he needed feeding but unable to drag myself away from the fight going on before my eyes. A horrible fascination held me transfixed. Maia gave him her little finger to suck to keep him quiet.

The fighting slowed. Their swords had to be getting heavier by the moment, their muscles aching with the effort. Age was not on Melwas's side. Now, when their swords clashed, the rhythm was slower, the beat of the heart less frantic. Their feet dragged in the dirt and their labored breathing sounded loud in the quiet of the day.

The crowd had fallen totally silent. Gone were the gasps of fear or triumph. Instead a dumb appreciation of the determination of the two men to best each other had taken their place. That neither of them would admit defeat was obvious. This fight was going to the bitter end.

For a moment, up against the crowd and separated by the

length of the battle arena, the two men paused, chests heaving, their notched swords sagging to the ground.

"Do you yield, Melwas of Dinas Brent?" Cei called out.

As if he would when yielding meant certain death. After a heavy pause, Melwas shook his head in defiance. Then the two men approached one another again. Arthur was now clearly dragging his leg. Melwas couldn't have missed it.

Before the throne, only yards away from me, they came together once more. Their swords, which must have felt leaden by now, clashed, bringing them face to face, so close that each inhaled the breath of the other, their shields locked. Melwas gasped for air. "I'll enjoy... your wife," he grunted in Arthur's face, only loud enough for those closest – Merlin and me, and perhaps Maia – to hear. His words came out in short staccato bursts. "Like I did...last winter...She's a slut...in bed...Just what...I like."

A flash of blind fury flared in Arthur's eyes. With an enormous effort, he shoved Melwas away, using his shield as leverage, and struck rather too wildly with his sword.

Watching their faces and hearing those words, my heart thudded with primal fear. I could see exactly what Melwas was doing. If he couldn't beat Arthur by swordsmanship, then he'd do it by goading him into an anger-fueled mistake.

Melwas's sword slid past Arthur's, slashing at his torso. The mail shirt deflected the blow. The sword flicked upwards, opening a gash in Arthur's sword arm just below the elbow. Arthur staggered backward as blood darkened the sleeve of his tunic.

My heart leapt into my throat. I couldn't swallow it down. My mouth was bone dry as for a moment, time stood still.

Then Melwas leapt in for the kill.

Arthur was fast. He dodged sideways, his shield up, and the blow went wide. The crowd was too close, and a woman fell backward clutching her stomach, blood fountaining. A cry of horror went up from her husband, a howl for revenge from the crowd and the audience seemed to surge forward as one.

Arthur held up his sword arm, blood dripping from his elbow. "Keep back! I promised him trial by combat, and that he'll have." His voice was harsh with effort, and his chest heaved.

Cei stepped forward. "Take that woman to be tended to immediately."

The crowd took a couple of steps back, but a lust for blood lingered in their eyes as they watched Melwas. If, heaven forbid, he should win, I didn't give a fig for his chances of getting out of Din Cadan alive.

Amhar began to cry again, unhappy with the finger he'd been given, but I waved Maia away with him when she approached me, unable to think of feeding him with my husband fighting for his life. I could think of nothing but Arthur, the fear for him eroding all else.

The two men circled one another once more, Arthur's right hand now slick with blood. It must have been making his grip on his sword hilt difficult.

They were both getting their breath back, Arthur noticeably more quickly. Warily, they edged around one another, feet shuffling in the dirt again in this deadly dance of death.

Their breath regained, they went at one another once more. Solid hit rained on solid hit in a clash of metal, like a blacksmith's hammer, ringing out time after time. But Melwas was flagging now, his age taking its toll. Arthur feinted a blow. Melwas went for it, and Arthur struck at Melwas's legs, slicing him across the back of the thigh. Melwas went down like a felled tree right in front of the throne, blood pouring from the wound and splattering across the dusty, scuffed-up ground, an expression of the utmost surprise on his face. Arthur limped back a step, watching, waiting. Melwas tried to get up, and failed. His leg wouldn't support him. The tendons must have been cut through.

Relief surged over me. I put a hand to my face to staunch the tremble that had started in my jaw. My teeth chattered together for a moment, then stilled.

"Do you yield?" Arthur asked, panting hard.

Melwas, half-kneeling on his good leg now, flashed him a look brim full of hatred, and shook his head. "Never." The word came on a gasp, as bright arterial blood pooled on the ground around him. "You'll have to kill me yourself." His voice was weak and thready, too low to be heard by any but Merlin and me.

"That won't be hard," Arthur snapped back, taking a step toward his fallen opponent. "Prepare yourself for the journey to Hell. There is a special place there for men who kill innocent children."

He knocked Melwas's sword easily from his hand. The damaged wooden shield slipped from the fallen man's hands onto the bloodied earth. His face was paling fast as the blood pumped out of him. He would be dead from loss of blood in a minute or two anyway.

Arthur threw down his own shield and stood over Melwas, looking down on him, his face a mask of anger and contempt. Two-handed, he raised his sword for the killing blow.

Melwas lifted his head with difficulty to glare up at him out of his coal-black eyes. His mouth opened and he spoke, his lips moving almost soundlessly. No one but Arthur could have heard what he said.

Arthur's eyes widened in shock. His face contorted as he hesitated for a moment. Then his sword swung through the air, biting into Melwas's neck beneath his helmet strap, slicing through flesh and bone and sinew.

The head went flying. For a second or two, the body, devoid of its head, remained upright on its knees, and then it toppled to the ground, blood oozing from the stump in feeble gouts as his heart beat its final rhythm.

For a long moment no one moved, the crowd mesmerized by the triumph of their king.

In slow motion, Arthur turned anguished eyes on me. Then his gaze slid sideways to the baby in Maia's arms. He let his sword fall to the ground. With one hand he unfastened his helmet strap and threw it down beside his sword, his hair plastered in damp curls to his head. Then he shrugged himself out of his mail shirt and let that fall beside his helmet and sword, as though with it he was shedding more than just his armor. His shoulders sagged.

A lone figure hurtled out from amongst the crowd. A small creature, bent-backed and frail. Olwyn, howling like an anguished wolf, ran toward her fallen son. She crashed into Arthur, and he staggered backward. Metal flashed, the red of blood blossomed, then Merlin pushed past the throne, throwing himself on top of Olwyn, pinning her right hand to the ground. In it glittered a dagger.

Arthur's expression held utter surprise. Blood seeped from between the fingers he'd clapped to his chest and the color drained from his cheeks. I leapt to my feet and ran to him.

"No!" I shouted, looking round for Merlin. He'd disarmed Olwyn and two warriors were dragging her to her feet. Between them she hung like a sack of dirty washing, deflated, harmless, ancient. Mad.

"My boy," she sobbed. "You killed my last boy." She struggled in the arms of the warriors. "He might have been a murderer, but he was my boy."

Arthur stretched out his free hand toward me, his eyes full of pain. "Tell me it's not true," he said, as I stared at him in horror. "Tell me he was lying."

Over his shoulder I saw Bretta, triumph in her face, staring at me.

Chapter Twenty-Nine

C EI AND MERLIN helped Arthur into the great hall and hauled off his tunic and undershirt. Where the blade had sliced along his ribs just under his armpit, the wound was bleeding freely.

By the fire, Maia stood clutching the angry baby whose howls rose to the rafters.

"For God's sake, feed him," Cei said, as he and Merlin pushed Arthur down onto a bench. Blood was running freely down his chest and forearm.

"I can't," I gasped, unable to take my eyes off my husband. "Can't someone else?"

Merlin rounded on me, angrier than I'd ever seen him. "Of course they can't. He's your baby. Feed him now and get him to stop that infernal wailing. He's your responsibility."

I sat down hurriedly on a bench, opposite Arthur, and Maia handed me a very red-faced Amhar, who took what felt like forever to get latched on. The action of his suckling began to calm me. I lifted my eyes to my husband.

He met my gaze across the table, eyes brimming with hostility. "I'm not dying. Look to your child."

My child. Not his. Not ours. Mine. I'd never heard him speak like this before. Why was he doing it? Tears formed, but I fought to hold them back. I didn't want any of them to see me cry. To know how much his words had hurt me. I had the sense to know that he was the most important thing now, and stopping his wounds bleeding took priority.

Bedwyr had come in behind Cei and Merlin, and now he expertly set to work on Arthur. He had Cei put pressure on the chest wound while he cleaned the cut on Arthur's arm with alcohol and stitched it. By the time he'd done that, the bleeding from the wound in Arthur's chest had all but stopped. He was lucky. The knife had sliced down his ribs, missing all the vital organs and arteries. His breathing returned to normal, and he wasn't coughing up blood. I heaved an inward sigh of relief, and, contented at my breast, little Amhar fed on, oblivious to the events around him.

Bedwyr produced a pad covered in healing honey – much cleaner than a pad would have been before my arrival – and bandaged it in place over the knife wound after he'd cleaned and stitched it.

I switched the hungry Amhar to the other breast, my eyes fixed on Arthur's still angry face, trying to read what was going on in his mind. What could Melwas have said to him that had affected him so badly? I struggled not to give credence to the thoughts tumbling through my head.

"You'd best get outside to show yourself to your people," Merlin advised. "They need to know you're not badly wounded."

Arthur shot me an unreadable glance, but said nothing, and got to his feet, waving Cei's helping hand away. With Merlin by his side, he walked to the doors and stepped outside. A great cheer went up as the waiting people welcomed the sight of him. But my heart was aching. A suspicion of what Melwas had whispered with his dying breath nagged at me. I'd seen Arthur's reaction, the cold fury in his eyes, the pain. But only he had heard those words, and only he knew for certain what poison Melwas had spewed before he died. But if it was what I suspected, how could Arthur believe it? Whatever it was, Arthur's whole attitude to me had changed in that moment.

And now Melwas was dead, and his words lived on, written

in fire on Arthur's heart.

MANHANDLED BY THE warriors, Olwyn was dragged off to the fortress lock-up and thrown unceremoniously into the cell her son had occupied so recently, a cell still reeking of his night soil. When they later came to retrieve her, they found her dead on the floor. Perhaps her poor miserable heart had given out at last, after all the years of suffering at Melwas's hands. Why she'd rushed to avenge his death we would never know.

From the accusing look in Arthur's eyes, it was apparent Melwas's words had done their damage. That he'd said something about me was abundantly clear. I nursed a horrible suspicion of what it was, but until I spoke to him by myself, I couldn't be sure. However, for the remainder of the day Arthur studiously avoided me, immersing himself in the promised retribution to be inflicted on Melwas's people.

As promised, he had Melwas's head impaled on a spike by the gates of the fortress, and his naked body thrown into a ditch outside Din Cadan, where foxes, or perhaps a brave wolf, might find and eat him. He dispatched a squad under Cei's command to Dinas Brent to evict what remained of its people and burn the fortress to the ground. "No one," I overheard Arthur say, "will set himself up as ruler of the Isle of Frogs again. From now on it's a part of Dumnonia."

That evening, with Amhar fed and sleeping in his cradle, I lay awake, waiting for Arthur to come to bed so I could finally talk to him alone. I had a long wait, but eventually, in the dark of the night, I heard the familiar scrape as he opened the door and came in.

The glow of the brazier showed me his grim face as he crossed the room to the chest of clothes where he kept his wash things. Was that all he'd come for?

I sat up in bed. "Arthur." I kept my voice low because of Amhar. I'd thought of asking Maia to take him so I could have it out with Arthur, but common sense and a feeling of unease had told me to keep him with me. The look on Bretta's face still danced before my eyes, and unless my son was with me, I couldn't be sure he was safe.

Arthur turned his head to look at me. With the light was behind him, I couldn't read his expression. He made no move to come closer. In the crib, Amhar made a puppyish snuffling noise, and Arthur's gaze strayed toward him.

"I'm not staying." His voice was strained. "Go back to sleep."

I was angry – angry he was shunning our bed, angry he hadn't told me why and given me a chance to refute whatever it was that had caused this. "Why?" I couldn't keep my feelings out of my voice, even though I knew I sounded both aggressive and defensive at the same time. "What have I done?"

Something about him told me his whole body had stiffened. He stood very still, his profile toward me as he looked at Amhar.

I had the distinct sensation of groping blindly in the dark. "What did Melwas say to you?" I thought I knew the answer, but I wanted to hear it from his lips.

His silence drove me on. I was gabbling, but I couldn't stop myself. "It was a lie." I tried to sound braver than I felt. "Whatever he said to you, it was a lie designed to hurt you. He knew he'd lost, so he hit back at you in the only way he had left." I paused, disturbed by his stillness and a terrible feeling of impending doom. "Don't let it come between us. Please."

The silence in the room lingered. Even Amhar was quiet. I couldn't read Arthur, didn't know what he was thinking. The differences between him and me had never been greater. I struggled to think of something else to say – anything, to break that heavy silence.

My thoughts ran overtime. At the same time the doubts I already had about Medraut groped their way to the surface from the depths where I'd locked them away these last few months. I didn't want to think about them. I didn't want to consider that my husband and his sister might have committed incest, but the thought was there, bubbling up like a festering sore. And as before, once thought, impossible to unthink.

He remained silent, his presence brooding, almost a threat, still gazing at Amhar.

I shivered involuntarily. "You have to ignore what Melwas said. He wanted to hurt you, and me, and Amhar, in the only way he had left."

I felt like a fool, my voice running on to fill the gaping silence, wishing he would speak to me. I'd spent the last few hours trying to put myself inside his head and guess what he was thinking, to no avail. He was a closed book.

"Everything was an act," I went on, wanting to convince him, and at the same time acutely aware I was sounding more and more desperate and giving veracity to whatever that evil man had said. "Everything he said and did was to goad you into fighting him and making a mistake that he could take advantage of."

Arthur turned his head to look at me again and licked his lips. "I know." He didn't sound convinced. His voice was oddly flat, as though the day had drained all the fight out of him. As though he could no longer be bothered.

I wanted to shout at him, to force a stronger reaction. I wanted him to challenge me so I could argue, to fight me as he'd fought Melwas, and I wanted to win. But he stayed glum and silent, oddly accepting of my words, and yet I could sense an undercurrent of disbelief running through him as prominent as the scales on a crocodile. An animal he would probably never have heard of.

"Sit down." I patted the bed. "Sit down, and let's talk about this. You have to tell me what he said to you."

He hesitated.

I patted the bed again and drew my feet up out of his way. "Please. We need to talk. We can't just ignore this."

Awkwardly, he eased himself down on the edge of the bed at

a distance from me, his wounds obviously paining him. What he needed was a dose of morphine and some antibiotics, but his chances of anything like that were zero. Honey was the most antiseptic thing available in the fifth century.

Slithering out of my bedcovers, I came and sat beside him, praying he wouldn't get up and leave. He stayed seated. The cold gap between us widened into a chasm. I had to bridge that gap, and I had to do it fast.

Reaching out, I took his hand in mine and felt a spasm as he stopped himself from jerking away from my touch. A great hollow was growing in my insides, a hollow where once had nestled the warm comfort of our love. "What is it? Tell me."

He kept his eyes down, looking at my hand in his, his lashes dark against his cheeks, the bruise on his chin already purpling, a bloody scab at its center. He swallowed, opened his mouth to speak and then closed it again. Was this the man I suspected might have committed incest? I pushed the thought away. Now was not the time to bring that up. It would only drive the wedge between us deeper.

"You can tell me." I kept my voice as gentle as I could, fighting to keep the anxiety and fear out of it. Instinct told me that if I showed fear, all would be lost.

He cleared his throat and raised his eyes. "He said Amhar was his." He was staring into my eyes. I saw his own fear, his hope that this wasn't true, his uncertainty that I was still truly his. I saw love dying.

What to say? I'd been held prisoner in Melwas's fortress for several days, and nine months later I'd produced a little dark-haired baby. The fact that both Arthur and Melwas were dark-haired was no help at all. A picture of Medraut leapt into my head, and it was on the tip of my tongue to leap into the attack and ask him if Medraut was his son. Luckily for me, common sense won.

"It's a lie." It was all I could think of to say. The bare truth. A part of me was screaming out my anger that he thought I could have deceived him this way.

I could see his face clearly now, the planes lit by the warm glow of the brazier, throwing shadows across his skin that gave him the look of a man sculpted in bronze. I'd have called that statue *Misery* if I'd been the sculptor.

I put my other hand on his as well. "I would never lie to you."

"I know." He was still staring into my eyes, perhaps watching for a sign that I was indeed lying, or searching for the truth. How hard would it be for him to believe me now Melwas had set that doubt in his head?

I tightened my grip on his hand. "I know you know," I said, trying to worm my way inside his head. "And I know you doubt. Why wouldn't you if he said that?" I paused. "He did it to get to you from beyond the grave." Words tumbled into my head. "He had no other way left to win. He hated you. He wanted to leave you with that doubt in your mind. He wanted to destroy us, bit by bit."

Tears sparkled in the corners of his eyes, and he dropped his gaze again as though he didn't want me to see his weakness.

I wanted to kiss away his sorrow, but instinct warned me not to. Slowly, he turned his hand over beneath mine and let our fingers entwine themselves; an intimate gesture that locked us together.

My heart began to rise from where it had been residing in my boots since Melwas's death.

He cleared his throat, but he didn't look up. "He never touched you? Not even once?" There was pleading in his voice. I could sense he wanted to believe me. He ached to believe me, but Melwas had planted that nagging seed of doubt and watered it well. And it didn't help that it was nine months after my kidnapping that Amhar had been born. I must have already been just pregnant when Melwas had me kidnapped. But how was Arthur to know that? It was my word against a dead man's. How could I ever win?

In answer, I shook my head. "I think he wanted to take me

for his own, but he was afraid." I remembered the moment I'd been brought before him, the awful moment I'd thought he'd force himself on me, when he declared that having seen me, he'd like to keep me for himself. Inspiration had come over me then, words of bravado had slipped from my lips. Could I find the same bravery now?

I put my hand under Arthur's chin to raise his head and felt him wince. Whether from the bruise or from the pain of my touch, I couldn't be sure.

Out of eyes full of hurt, he looked back at me.

"I told him I was from Ynys Afallon." The memories danced before my eyes, strengthening my resolve to tell him the whole truth. "I told him I'd been sent by Gwynn ap Nudd to help you defeat the Saxons. You and I may not believe in that prophecy, but Melwas did. I frightened him with my words. He thought I was a weak woman at his mercy, but words have power, even from the mouth of a woman. I used that power against him, and now he's turned the tables and done the same to us."

His fingers tightened on my hand. He opened his mouth as though to speak and then closed it again.

I waited.

"I want to believe you." His voice was low, choking back emotion that was perilously near the surface. "I know I should believe you. You're my wife. I love you." He paused and drew a long breath. "Melwas was an evil man who wanted the power he thought you might bring him." His eyes glistened in the dying firelight. "Cadwy set him on that path, but he would have taken it anyway at some point. You told me, and Olwyn did too, that he killed his brothers and father to get to the throne of Dinas Brent. My own father should have meted out justice for that. It went unpunished, and he grew more confident in his wickedness. It was only a matter of time before he wanted more."

Tears that had been brimming all day long, formed in my eyes. I blinked them away.

He went on. "Melwas was a truly wicked man. He snatched

you from me, thinking to please Cadwy. I was his lord, but Cadwy had convinced him that Dumnonia should have been his as well as Powys, no doubt with promises of great rewards. Cadwy was sure that by taking you, he would gain the power he craves. You were in a terrible position. Don't be afraid to tell me the truth."

I felt numb. Whatever he'd said, he still didn't believe me. I could hold my tears in no longer; they flowed down my cheeks unchecked. Telling me he knew Amhar was his didn't mean he didn't think I'd succumbed to Melwas's attentions. He knew I'd been alone and unprotected, a woman at the mercy of a merciless man.

I gave his hand an angry shake. "If Melwas had raped me, I would have told you." How to convince him? "When Abbot Jerome brought me back to you, I was angry – no, furious. I wanted you to go after him, to punish him for what he'd done. Not just to me but to poor old Olwyn too. Don't you think that if I'd been raped I'd have told you then and there, to force you to avenge me?" I'd seen rape victims now, seen their reaction. He'd seen them too and would have known if I'd been raped, surely?

I gazed into his eyes, searching for what, I didn't know. And he gazed back, searching, I guessed, for a truth he wasn't sure he'd find. I could see he wanted to believe me, but his inborn distrust was fighting back. Morgawse and Medraut leapt into my mind again and the impulse to voice my own distrust of him waxed large.

Instead, I scoured my brain for what I knew of rape survivors gleaned from the television and newspapers and having seen Ummidia and her daughters. I wiped my tears with the back of my hand, determination seizing me. "If I'd been raped, do you think I'd have gone happily to your bed the very night we returned? A woman who's been raped doesn't do that. It's an act of violence, of domination, not sex. If I'd been raped I'd have wanted no man near me. Not even you. Not for a very long while."

A long silence lingered between us. Tears kept oozing out of my eyes to run down my face as though I'd sprung a leak. I wanted to stop, but couldn't. My heart was breaking. For him, for me, for innocent Amhar. Nothing would ever be the same; the futility of fighting against fate was overwhelming.

Arthur's face softened; the tears that had been glistening unshed in his eyes ran down his cheeks at last, and he buried his face in my shoulder. I wrapped my arms around him and held him tight, refusing to think of Medraut. We'd get through this, of that I was determined, but at the back of my mind Bretta's curse kept echoing over and over again:

I curse you, Queen of Dumnonia, and I curse your husband and your son. You and yours shall know the loss I feel.

To be continued...

About the Author

After a varied life that's included working with horses where Downton Abbey is filmed, riding racehorses, running her own riding school, owning a sheep farm and running a holiday business in France, Fil now lives on a widebeam canal boat on the Kennet and Avon Canal in Southern England.

She has a long-suffering husband, a rescue dog from Romania called Bella, a cat she found as a kitten abandoned in a gorse bush, five children and six grandchildren.

She once saw a ghost in a churchyard, and when she lived in Wales there was a panther living near her farm that ate some of her sheep. In England there are no indigenous big cats.

She has Asperger's Syndrome and her obsessions include horses and King Arthur. Her historical romantic fiction and children's fantasy adventures centre around Arthurian legends, and her pony stories about her other love. She speaks fluent French after living there for ten years, and in her spare time looks after her allotment, makes clothes and dolls for her granddaughters, embroiders and knits. In between visiting the settings for her books.

Social Media links:
Website – filreid.com
Facebook – facebook.com/Fil-Reid-Author-101905545548054
Twitter – @FJReidauthor